"L

There was no fear in either Kassie's voice or her flashing eyes, only anger.

"Not until you explain yourself." Braden dragged her up against his powerful body.

"I think I made myself perfectly clear, *your grace*," she snapped back, still struggling. "But apparently you think I have no right to know who you've taken to your bed!"

"I wouldn't need to take anyone else to my bed, if you weren't so damned untouchable!" The words were pouring out before he could censor them, his rage making him reckless. "Damn you, Kassandra, I'm constantly aching, burning alive. And for whom? For you, my naïve little wife. For you."

"You have a very strange way of showing that you want me, Braden." She threw back her dark hair defiantly, her eyes twin jewels of fire.

"Want you?" he demanded in a rough, deep voice. "Do you want to see how much I want you?"

Before Kassie could speak, Braden had captured her mouth with his, devouring her with all the pent-up passion and none of the restraint of the past.

Uncontrollable hunger took over . . .

"Touching, sensitively written, intriguing suspense, a lovely, totally satisfying romance. Andrea Kane has a grand and glorious future in store for her."

—Elaine Barbieri, author of *Tattered Silk*

Books by Andrea Kane

My Heart's Desire
Dream Castle

Published by POCKET BOOKS

Dream Castle

Andrea Kane

POCKET BOOKS

New York   London   Toronto   Sydney   Tokyo   Singapore

An *Original* Publication of POCKET BOOKS

POCKET BOOKS, a division of Simon & Schuster Inc.
1230 Avenue of the Americas, New York, NY 10020

Copyright © 1992 by Andrea Kane

ISBN: 0-671-73585-3

First Pocket Books printing July 1992

10 9 8 7 6 5 4 3 2 1

With gratitude and love to those who made Dream Castle *possible:*

My family, my strength and my nucleus . . . Brad for building the castle, Wendi for naming it—and two talented, dedicated women who, to my great fortune, believe in me . . . my critique partner, Karen Plunkett-Powell, and my editor, Caroline Tolley.

Prologue

Her own scream awakened her.

Kassie bolted upright in bed, her heart pounding furiously, the night rail clinging to her sweat-drenched body. With tormented eyes she scanned the room, straining to latch onto the security of her surroundings, the simple, feminine oak furnishings that were so familiar, even in the shadows of night. She licked her dry lips, wrapping her arms around herself. But still the cold and the fear intensified. The expected shivering began. Her teeth chattered. *You're safe, Kassie. You're safe.* She recited it over and over, a litany in her mind, as she struggled to regain her sanity.

It was always like this. The same nightmare, for as long as she could remember. The heinous stalker, the engulfing abyss . . . the images were unchanging, the fear insurmountable.

She had to escape.

Kassie dressed in the dark, hurriedly donning the first gown she could find in her modest wardrobe. Seconds later she left her bedchamber, flew down the stairs, and went out the cottage door.

There was never a question of where she would go. For she had but one companion, one soothing balm for her pain and her loneliness.

Braden stood, unmoving, along the sandy Scarborough coastline, utterly oblivious to the brisk June winds of the North Sea as they whipped through his thick hair. The loathsome vision of Abigail in Grant's arms glared before him, and he squeezed his eyes shut, hoping to dissolve the memory. He strove for control, taking deep, cleansing breaths of the cool sea air. Rage, stronger than the currents, surged through his powerful body.

His anger was certainly not directed at Abigail, for she meant nothing to him and never had. Their betrothal had been a farce, a business transaction conceived by their parents when Braden was twelve years old and Abigail a mere babe. Both the Sheffields and the Devons had been enthused at the prospect of a future mating of their wealth and noble lineage. After all, it would be the perfect match.

It hadn't happened that way.

Braden had grown up independent and intense, devastatingly handsome yet indifferent to his striking good looks, and totally unimpressed by his own wealth and social position. He was a man of strong principles and even stronger loyalties, and he expected those loyalties to be returned.

Abigail had grown up spoiled and shallow, consumed with vanity and greed.

By the time Abigail had reached a marriageable age it was clear to Braden that he could never find happiness with her, much less love her.

With a muttered oath Braden picked up a stone and hurled it out to sea, watching the waters envelop it in their rough wake.

Having discovered the pleasures of the flesh when he was but fourteen, he had since explored all of passion's avenues with countless eager, vapid females. They had quickly fallen into two types: those who wanted to bed him for his virility and sexual allure, and those who wanted to marry him for his fortune. It was no secret into which category Abigail fell; she coveted the enviable position that accompanied marriage to the Duke of Sherburgh.

In truth, Braden felt nothing but contempt for Abigail Devon. But, being a realist and respecting his duty to provide Sherburgh with a proper heir, Braden had actually contemplated fulfilling his parents' wishes and marrying Abigail.

Until he had found her with Grant.

It was then Braden discovered that there were some things even he was unwilling to sacrifice. He could shrug away love and caring, cast tenderness to the winds, but integrity was something else. Something far more important.

Braden raked long fingers through his ebony hair, feeling the misty droplets that clung to each strand. He hadn't denied Abigail her flings. He knew she had been with men; quite a few men, actually. He was not such a hypocrite that he would begrudge her the same diversions he himself enjoyed. In his opinion, sex was one of the few pleasures afforded to the English nobility.

But his best friend. No, that was a betrayal even he, jaded though he was, could not accept.

Braden began to walk again, trying to come to terms with his anger. Friendship, it appeared, was as whimsical a reality as love. Both were mere illusions, existing only in poets' minds and dreamers' hearts.

He felt a chill inside him, encasing his soul in ice. Fleetingly he thought of his mother and father. They had felt no deep love for him while they had lived. Still, their very existence had given him a sense of identity, a knowledge of who he was, that had disintegrated once they were gone.

Braden was very much alone. In the end, he mused, all one really had was oneself. Nothing more; nothing less.

The sharp bark from behind him belied his thought, reminding him that he did, indeed, have a loyal companion. Braden turned and glanced down at the small brown and white ball of fur scampering determinedly to catch up.

"What is it, my little friend?" Braden inquired. The young beagle, as yet unnamed, was the offspring of Braden's sleek dog Hunter. Barely two months of age, the frisky puppy was enjoying his first evening romp. He had been busy trying to match Braden's stride, remaining so quiet that Braden had all but forgotten his presence. Until now. To Braden's amazement the wobbly little pup tensed, inclined his head at alert attention, then raced ahead, barking furiously at some unknown danger.

"Wait!" Braden hurried forward, concerned for the dog's safety.

The tinkling laughter was so unexpected that for one

moment Braden thought he had imagined it. Blinking, he stopped and glanced about the dark, deserted beach. Again the laughter sounded, light and musical, closer this time, and broken by another bark from Braden's beagle.

Braden moved toward the sound and all but tripped over the puppy and whoever was kneeling beside him.

"Who is there?" Braden demanded of the shadowy form at his feet.

There was a slight rustle of material, and the huddled figure rose to answer.

Braden caught his breath, for he found himself gazing into the expressive face of the most astonished and enchanting young woman he had ever seen. Her wildly blowing hair was as black as the darkest night, her skin a startling contrast of creamy white, her features fine-boned and delicate. Her huge, round eyes, illuminated by moonlight, were an exquisite and unusual color of aqua, as clear and fathomless as untouched waters, and heavily fringed with thick, black lashes. They stared up at him now, filled with a mixture of curiosity and apprehension. It was the curiosity that won out in the end.

"Hello," she ventured in a sweet, clear voice that danced through the chilly air, cloaking it in a blanket of warmth. The small dog, unwilling to relinquish the attention being bestowed upon him, tugged insistently at the hem of her gown.

"Hello," Braden replied with a smile.

"Who are you?" She answered his original question with her own, forthright and uncluttered by pretense.

"My name is Braden. And what, may I ask, is yours?"

She ignored the question. "Just Braden?" She cocked her head to one side. "That is quite unusual. Most adults have several names, and often several titles to go with them."

Braden's smile widened into a huge grin. "You're right. Very well, then, allow me to formally introduce myself." He stood up tall, his broad, powerful six-foot-one frame towering over her petite one. "I am Braden Matthew Sheffield, the Duke of Sherburgh. I have several other titles, as you suggested, but I will modestly refrain from mentioning them." He bowed deeply, delighted to hear her musical laugh again. "And to whom do I have the honor of speaking?" he asked, a twinkle in his charismatic hazel eyes.

Kassie could feel her heart rate accelerate, her senses come alive. Fascinated, she felt a curious swooping sensation in her stomach, a warm, lethargic feeling that claimed her limbs. She was both startled and intrigued by her intense reaction to Braden Sheffield's dark good looks and masculine charm. With awakening wonder she realized that she was physically responding to a man for the first time in her young life. It was a strange feeling, she reflected, but one that she rather liked.

Breathlessly she smiled back, revealing twin dimples in her flushed cheeks. She knew he had asked her a question, but she had all but forgotten what it was.

"And you are . . ." Braden prompted.

"You have the honor of speaking with Miss Kassandra Grey, Your Grace," she returned, willing the racing of her heart to slow. "I have no title to boast, and I live in the cottage that overlooks this beach." She turned and pointed to the top of the sloping land.

"The pleasure is mine, Miss Grey." Braden bent his head in a formal gesture and kissed her hand, scowling at the puppy, who yipped his jealous displeasure.

Kassandra's eyes widened, but not with the simpering awe that Braden was used to from the female sex. "How do you know that?" she asked bluntly.

"Know what?" Braden was confused.

"Know that the pleasure is yours. After all, we just met. I could be a frightful bore," she pointed out in a matter-of-fact tone.

Braden burst out laughing. The smooth words came so readily to his lips; it took someone who was little more than a child to point out their absurdity. "You are right again," he conceded, growing serious. "However, based upon our introductions, I sincerely doubt that is the case. In fact, I am beginning to wish that more of the ladies I am acquainted with were as charming as you."

Kassandra saw the disenchantment in his eyes and wondered at its cause. She considered his statement, bending to stroke the beagle's ears tenderly. "Perhaps I am different because the ladies of your acquaintance are better skilled at the proper things to say," she suggested at last.

"Perhaps," he echoed. "But," he added magnanimously, "I am not at all certain that is a compliment to them."

Kassandra shook her head emphatically, absently caressing the pup's silky fur. "Oh, I didn't mean it as a compliment, Your Grace. In my experience, most of the 'proper things to say' are, in fact, cleverly worded lies."

Braden was stunned. "How old are you?" he asked, studying her solemn face.

"Fifteen."

He didn't know which came as the greater surprise: her startling beauty and innate wisdom, so uncharacteristic of such a young girl, or the fact that she was out walking alone, unchaperoned, at night.

"Fifteen," he repeated reflectively.

"Yes. Today, actually," she added in a wistful voice.

"Today is your birthday?" Braden's dark brows went up. At her impassive nod he added, "You should be home celebrating with your family."

Kassie stood abruptly. "My mother is dead. My father is . . . busy."

Braden's eyes softened. "I'm sorry, Kassandra."

Kassie straightened her stance, lifting her chin a proud notch. "Don't be. I am quite accustomed to taking care of myself."

"I can see that you are."

In spite of her worn, faded gown and obvious lack of sophistication, Kassie radiated an inner grace and quiet dignity that were rare and special. Admiration and something more flowed through Braden, melting his earlier anger as he beheld the strong, proud, and neglected young woman before him. They were more alike than she knew, he thought.

Their gazes met, a rare and inexplicable current running between them.

Kassie spoke first, offering another part of herself to this enigmatic stranger who was somehow not a stranger at all.

"I love to stroll along this beach." Her legs felt weak as she melted beneath the caress of Braden's warm hazel eyes. She turned, staring at the turbulent wonder of the North Sea. "I've done so ever since I could walk."

Braden looked down at her delicate profile. "Have you? And why is that?"

Kassie grew quiet for a moment. "It soothes me," she explained at last. "And it keeps me company as well."

"What does?" He was lost again.

"Why, everything you see." She seemed amazed by his response. "The sea, the wind; by day the sun; by night the stars. They are always here for me. No matter what. And nothing can take them away." She paused. "Do you understand?"

He understood, possibly better than she, for he had lived thirteen years longer and knew far more of life's fickleness. He looked into her haunting eyes and abruptly changed his mind. Perhaps he did not know more. Perhaps he knew nothing at all.

"Yes, Kassandra," he answered softly, really looking about him for the first time. "Yes, I understand."

Tired of being ignored, the now bereft beagle plopped down upon the sand and began to whimper for attention, gazing soulfully at Kassie.

"Apparently you have made a friend," Braden commented, snapping his fingers in command, frowning when the dog refused to budge. "I am sorry if he is making a nuisance of himself."

Kassie shook her head. "He most definitely is not! He's precious." To Braden's surprise she leaned down and hugged the ecstatic canine. "Do not be angry with him; he is too young to understand authority."

"Evidently," Braden replied dryly. He made another, equally unsuccessful attempt to order the dog to his side. "He has taken a fancy to you."

"And I to him." The look in Kassie's eyes was tender, filled with longing. Braden felt another uncustomary tug at his heart.

"Why don't you keep him?" Seeing her astonished joy, he wondered if she had ever received a gift before now. "Consider him to be my birthday present to you."

"Really?"

"Really." He waved away her thanks. "Happy birthday, Kassandra."

Kassandra. It was a beautiful name, befitting the exquisite promise of beauty she contained. Not merely a beauty to behold, but a beauty to be savored and cherished; a beauty that was generated from within.

She looked at him quizzically, still clutching her new, squirming pet. "What are you thinking?"

"That Kassandra is a very beautiful name."

She nodded. "And I plan to use it in a year or two, when I am grown. But until then you may call me Kassie."

It suited her perfectly, a hint of the regal forename. "I would be delighted . . . Kassie." He gave her a charming smile. "However, you must then agree to call me Braden."

She considered the request. "Is that not deemed forward by the ladies of your acquaintance?"

"I thought we agreed that you were nothing like the ladies of my acquaintance," he reminded her.

She laughed, brushing rich strands of blowing black silk from her face. "So we did. All right, Braden." She tried it out. "I like it much better than Your Grace," she decided.

He could hardly remember his earlier somber mood. "So do I, Kassie," he agreed, thinking to himself what a delight she was, part woman, part child.

Kassie's thoughts were anything but childlike. The fluttering sensation in her stomach, until now unknown, was nonetheless understood. She also knew she should go back, but she was not yet ready to say good-bye to the magnificent man who towered above her, making her feel so alive.

Braden was equally reluctant to say good night. His gaze drifted across her small, fine-boned features. He felt utterly entranced by the soothing effect of Kassie's presence amid the natural splendor all around them. It had been years since he had taken the time to admire the beauty of the sea or the stars. Now he turned to view them through Kassie's innocent eyes.

The beach was smooth and undisturbed, though closer to the water the waves slapped up onto the sand, then receded, only to return again. On the far side of the beach towering cliffs rose high and jagged, dropping off sharply to the land below. There were few homes in this section of Yorkshire, and the land was vast and wildly beautiful. Although Sherburgh was not far inland, Braden had never noticed the house on the cliffs that Kassie had shown him to be hers. Now he looked up at it again, realizing that it was surrounded on three sides by the sea.

"Are there paths up there in the cliffs?" he asked.

Kassie nodded. "Yes."

"They must be lovely to stroll through. Do you walk there as well?"

"No."

He was surprised by the curtness of her tone. Troubled, he watched her wrap her arms about herself in a gesture of self-protection. He could actually feel her withdraw from him, caught in some turbulent emotion of her own.

The puppy barked, as if to remind them of the lateness of the hour.

"I must get back now, Braden," Kassie told him regretfully. Her tone was bleak, resigned, and Braden could almost swear that he heard a tremor of fear in her voice as she glanced toward home.

"I agree." He studied her expression carefully. "Why, I am certain that your father is crazed with worry by now!"

A veil of sadness settled over her flawless face, and suddenly Braden wanted nothing more than to see it lift.

"What would it take to make this birthday a special one for you?" he heard himself ask. "What one thing would you wish for?"

She gazed up at his strong, chiseled features, the thick black hair that the wind had blown off his tanned face, and the warm hazel eyes that glowed down at her.

There was only one thing she wanted, one unattainable dream to be fulfilled. Her answer was spoken in the softest of whispers, and Braden was still reeling from its impact long after Kassie had disappeared into the night, her new puppy gathered in her arms.

"I wish that you would wait for me to grow up."

Chapter 1

This betrothal was arranged twenty years ago, and I refuse to let you break it, Braden!" Abigail Devon was furious.

Braden was bored.

"Do you hear me?" she shouted. "I have given you ample time to reconsider your ludicrous decision of three years past. It is time to cease this nonsense and make me your wife!" Abigail's coldly beautiful features contorted with rage as she paced the full length of Sherburgh's impressive library. Her blue eyes flashed sizzling fire, and she whirled around to face Braden, tossing her pale blond curls over her shoulders and down the back of her lemon-yellow gown.

A muscle flexed dangerously in Braden's jaw as he stifled the urge to throttle Abigail and put an end to her outrageous demands. He leaned back against the intricately carved walnut bookcases that lined the pillared walls, struggling for control. "Yes, I hear you, Abigail," he said through clenched teeth. "In fact, the entire staff can hear you."

Two red spots appeared on her pale cheeks. "I don't give a damn about who hears me, Braden. Or about your servants. Or about—"

"Grant?" he added helpfully.

She exhaled sharply. Damn him for remembering. "Or about Grant."

He nodded. "Or about any of the other men you have since spread your lovely legs for?" he inquired in a deceptively silky voice.

Abigail looked stunned.

11

"Oh, did you think I knew nothing of them?"

Her mouth opened, but no words came out.

Braden pushed himself to his feet. "Let's end this deception, shall we?" He strode over to stand directly in front of her, every muscle of his powerful physique taut with suppressed anger. "The betrothal was a mockery from the start. Not only do I not love you, I do not even like you. I am aware of every man you have enjoyed. The reason I said nothing is that I never felt anything stronger than disinterest. Your life is your own, Abigail. But you will never be part of mine." He paused, his eyes flickering over her contemptuously. "The truth is you have absolutely nothing to offer a man but your beautiful, though somewhat soiled, body." He paused. "'Tis a pity you do not spend nearly as much time on your honor as you do on your back."

She gasped, then slapped him with all of her strength. "You are a bastard!" she spat out through clenched teeth.

He didn't even blink. "And you are a slut."

He walked around her, throwing open the library door. "We have nothing further to say to each other. Get out, Abigail."

Braden waited for the resounding slam of the entranceway door as confirmation of her departure, then poured himself a brandy. Abigail hadn't changed one iota. But then, he hadn't expected she would.

He could still remember her theatrics when he had ended their betrothal three years ago. It had been much the same as the scene she had enacted just now, only then she had protested her innocence, whereas today she had not. A wise decision, considering her continued wanton behavior.

Braden lifted the glass to his lips and swallowed deeply. Well, the whole damned *ton* was welcome to her. She was actually quite accomplished in bed, if one cared nothing about the consequences. As far as he was concerned, a paid courtesan was a far better choice. Braden was more than willing to part with his money, which was in abundant supply. But at least with a *fille de joie* he could retain his title, his name, and his self-respect.

The library door closed with a thud.

"What happened?"

12

Braden turned at the sound of his uncle's voice, facing Lord Cyril Sheffield with an expression carved in granite.

"I presume you are referring to my conversation with Abigail?"

The tall, middle-aged man nodded, displeasure evident in his rigid stance.

"I just saw her bolt out the entranceway door. She was quite distraught."

"Pity." Braden tossed down the remaining contents of his drink, then regarded the empty glass thoughtfully. "She came here today hoping that I had experienced a change of heart with regard to our severed betrothal." His lips quirked in amusement. "Or perhaps she hoped that I had suffered a selective memory loss and had forgotten all that had preceded our . . . er, parting."

Cyril sighed, smoothing the collar of his greatcoat as he broached the unpleasant subject of Braden's future with Abigail Devon. "Your father did make an agreement with William Devon when you were but a boy," he reminded his nephew.

Braden's magnetic hazel eyes darkened to a smoldering slate gray. "Let us not begin this argument again, Cyril. I have as little respect for my parents' wishes as they always showed for mine. What they may or may not have wanted me to do no longer matters to me."

"I am your uncle, Braden. What you do affects the Sheffield name. Think of that, if not your father."

Braden gave Cyril a contemptuous look. "'Tis a shame that Father could not have left his title to you when he died. You would have taken far better care of it than I do."

"Braden—"

Braden slammed his fist down so hard that the ornate wooden table shook from the impact. "That woman is a trollop at best. When I marry, it will be to someone I like and respect. Surely that is not too much to ask, even for a duke." The taunting words silenced his uncle. Braden's irreverent feelings about his title were no secret to Cyril Sheffield. There would be no winning this argument.

He took a deep breath and tried in a more understated tone.

"Braden, if you would just be reasonable—"

"Is it *unreasonable* that a man should demand some degree of respect from the woman he is *expected* to marry?"

Cyril grew silent at the implication of Braden's words. He was well aware of the fact that over the years Braden had shown not a shred of interest in the prospect of marrying Abigail. And her involvement with men hadn't helped.

Cyril shrugged. "I do not believe it is a question of respect, Braden. It is your duty to marry and provide Sherburgh with an heir."

Braden's lips tightened. "Of course it is. However, I am hardly ancient. I still have time to fulfill my familial obligations, Cyril, and I *will* choose a suitable wife. But," he bit out, his jaw clenched, "given the fact that I have a strange aversion to worrying over whether the heir to Sherburgh is indeed mine, my choice will not be Abigail Devon."

When Cyril opened his mouth to protest, Braden shook his head vehemently.

"The subject is closed. You are overstepping your bounds, Uncle." He lowered his empty glass to the table with a loud thud. "I am going out."

He needed some fresh air.

He needed some faith.

The air would be easier to acquire.

He slammed the door behind him, leaving the library and the house.

Outside, Braden strolled about the vast grounds of Sherburgh. He willed himself to relax, letting his mind wander where it would.

The words he had said to Cyril echoed in his head. A woman he liked and respected? A virtual impossibility.

Unbidden, an image appeared of an exquisite, ethereal creature with coal-black hair and eyes like flawless aquamarines. A young woman of strength and courage, of wisdom beyond her years. A breathtaking angel without guile or pretense who was on the very brink of womanhood.

Kassie. The earnest and lovely girl that had looked up at him so adoringly, asking that he wait for her to grow up, was by now a ravishing beauty of eighteen.

Braden had thought of her often these long years, feeling

strangely restless and vaguely unfulfilled at the memory. Countless times he had been tempted to seek her out for the sheer pleasure of her company but had resisted. She was young, *too* young, and she called upon emotions within him that he preferred to leave unexamined. He had, instead, contented himself with the hope that she was happy, that she would one day find someone worthy of her goodness. He was too old, too experienced, too jaded to be anything in her life . . . even merely a friend.

Braden turned in the direction of the beach, staring off into the darkened sky.

He could almost hear her call his name.

Dark. It was so dark. She couldn't see.

Cold. She could feel the cold. It gnawed through her body.

Oh God, she was so afraid, so alone. Oh please, someone come . . . someone help . . .

And still it grew colder, darker.

She began to run.

She cried out, but no sound emerged. She ran faster, faster still. She was falling . . . falling. She could feel the air rush by her, dragging her down, down. She couldn't breathe . . . couldn't breathe.

Suddenly it appeared. A huge black beast. It reared back on its hind legs, opening its cavernous mouth. It was going to devour her. And she couldn't stop it. She couldn't breathe. She couldn't run. She was frozen. Then falling . . . falling. Alone . . . alone . . .

The scream began deep inside her, rose up to her mouth, and pierced the silence of the room. An endless scream of inescapable terror.

Kassie was wide awake, trembling uncontrollably, struggling for air. She was assailed by a stark panic that would not be assuaged. Frantically she combated the fear, taking deep, deliberate breaths, purposefully wiping her mind free of the chilling images.

Moments passed. Slowly the insurmountable terror receded, diminished until it was a dull ache inside her. With a shuddering sigh Kassie eased herself back down onto the pillows, closed her eyes, and soothed herself in the same

manner that she had each night since her fifteenth birthday
. . . by conjuring up an image of Braden Sheffield.

Braden. Handsome, powerful, tender. Though they had
met for but an hour, it seemed she had known him for a
lifetime. He was compassionate and gentle, yet she could
feel his reluctance to display these qualities, his need to hide
them beneath a mask of self-protection that experience had
only served to reinforce. It had been three years, and still the
memory of their only meeting had not faded. If anything, it
had grown stronger, clearer. Kassie could remember every
detail of the way he looked, the things he said.

The things he didn't say.

His eyes had offered her his friendship, his strength . . .
and something more. There had been a magnetic pull
between them . . . or did she just will it to be so?

She knew what Braden's real world was like, for she read
about it every day in novels, in newspapers. The nobleman's
world, the world of the *ton;* vapid and without substance;
exciting and glittering, filled with carefree men and beautiful women. A world she could not understand and in which
she had no part.

Her dream of Braden disintegrated into sharp particles of
pain and loneliness.

It was but a fantasy, for he had, no doubt, long since
forgotten their encounter. In truth, Kassie would probably
never see him again.

Throwing back the covers, she jumped out of bed, reaching for the thin robe that lay upon it. She couldn't bear to be
alone. She just couldn't.

Seeing his mistress prepare to leave her room, the silky-
haired beagle jumped up from his warm spot by the fire and
hurried along behind Kassie on short, sturdy legs.

Kassie smiled down at her only friend, a warm, brown-
eyed reminder of that special meeting with Braden.

"Come, Percy," she whispered. "Let us go down to the
library and fetch a book of your namesake's poetry."

A light shining beneath the library door altered her plans.
Kassie spotted it as she descended the steps and felt a small
stab of fear. Her father was awake. She had no desire to see

16

him . . . or to have him see her. She knew what he was like when he was disturbed . . . and drunk. It was very ugly.

She turned to retrace her steps, gesturing to a bewildered Percy to follow her.

It was then that she heard the voices.

"You must try to understand . . . to be patient." Her father's speech was slurred, but his tone was clearly pleading.

"I have been more than patient, Grey," a second masculine voice snapped back.

"I will have your money very soon." Kassie winced at her father's idle promise.

"Really? And from where do you intend to get it, you sniveling fool?" the stranger demanded.

"That is my concern, not yours."

"I beg to differ with you, my dear Robert, but that is very much my concern. Now, I repeat, from what source do you intend to get such a large sum of money?"

There was a pause, during which time Robert was, no doubt, draining his glass of whiskey.

At last Kassie heard a barely audible reply. "My luck is changing. I can feel it."

A sardonic laugh. "And this is what you are pinning your hopes on? A change in your luck? I can hardly sleep easy, knowing that my debt will be repaid by your winnings. Judging from your luck thus far—"

"My luck"—Robert's voice broke—"has not been the same since Elena died." He moaned. "Oh, why was I such a fool? If only I could have controlled her, convinced her not to turn away from me . . . none of this would have happened. She wouldn't have had to die. But as it was, it was inevitable. She left me no choice but to do what I did . . . to her, to myself." A choked sob. "Don't you see that she left me no choice?"

The words echoed inside Kassie, setting off a warning bell as ugly memories threatened to claim her, to drag her down into their drowning darkness. From the moment the conversation had started her heart had begun to beat faster, reaching a frantic, erratic rhythm. Her palms were damp, her throat dry. The room began to close in on her. Escape was the only answer.

She backed away from the door, clapping her hands over her ears to block out the assaulting voices. She had to get away . . . now.

Desperately, with Percy at her heels, Kassie fled to the beach.

Chapter 2

A vague feeling of foreboding plagued Braden, together with a persistent restlessness that refused to be appeased.

He leaned back in his elegant traveling carriage, eager to begin the ride home from York. He had been more than pleased with the performance of his two-year-old filly, who had raced for the first time today. She was every bit as splendid as he and Charles had expected, and she promised to be a prime contender for the thousand guineas at Newmarket next spring.

Watching his horses race usually made Braden's blood pound with excitement and renewed energy. Much as lovers of ballet were moved by the grace and skill of the dancers, Braden never ceased to be awed by the tremendous speed and elegance of the glorious Thoroughbreds.

In contrast, today he had been unable to concentrate fully.

"Rather quiet, are you not, Braden?"

Braden started as a tall, agile man of middle years jumped into the carriage beside him. Thinning hair and slight facial lines could not diminish the vitality of Charles Graves's penetrating blue eyes or the warmth and strength of his very presence.

Braden forced the frown from his face.

"Were you displeased with the filly's performance?" Charles continued cautiously.

Braden shook his head. "No, she was spectacular. A true product of her unsurpassable parentage."

Charles heard the tension in Braden's voice, noted his

faraway look. Braden had been unusually moody for months now, and in poor humor since his confrontation with Lady Abigail Devon a fortnight ago. It puzzled Charles, for it was unlike Braden to allow anyone to incite his emotions. The damage had been done many years ago by Braden's parents, who had taken out their own frustration and resentment on their bewildered only child until Braden had withdrawn into himself. And now, as a grown man, Braden had erected towering, steellike protective walls around him that no one could penetrate.

"Then what is it?" Charles gently pressed.

"I don't know," Braden answered truthfully. He signaled to his coachmen to begin their journey home, then turned back to Charles as the gleaming carriage moved off slowly. "Perhaps Abigail's latest performance brought back memories I would choose to forget, and that served to remind me how predictably unpleasant the world really is."

"Not all things are unpleasant," Charles reminded him.

"No, only people." Braden gave an ironic shake of his head. "I do believe that you were luckier when you were a mere groom at our stables. During that time you had only horses to deal with, not cold-blooded human beings."

Charles chuckled. "True. But despite the fact that I can no longer keep to horses alone, training is much more of a challenge. Twenty years as a groom is enough."

Braden opened his mouth to reply but was cut off by a sudden loud commotion.

"Get out of 'ere, man!"

The resistant protestor was shoved unceremoniously out of the gates, where he teetered for a moment, then staggered toward the street.

"This is an outrage!" he muttered under his breath in a voice slurred from too much alcohol. "I am a guest . . . a spectator—"

"A drunken thief!" the ouster retorted. "Ye owe me the £100 ye wagered on that last race . . . and ye don't 'ave a blessed farthing with ye! Now get out of 'ere, and take yer bloody swindlin' elsewhere!"

Pushing limp strands of dark hair away from his face, the disoriented man stared around with unseeing bloodshot eyes, then stepped out into the road . . . directly into the path of Braden's moving carriage. The driver shouted a warning at the top of his lungs; the horses whinnied their rebellion at the sudden veering of their course. The drunk raised his head at the commotion about him, then froze in place, staring at the oncoming carriage. In mere seconds he would be beneath its wheels.

With a jolt the carriage stopped.

Braden reacted instantly, throwing open the carriage door. He had heard no sickening thud that would accompany an impact, and he prayed that the man had been miraculously spared. By the time he and Charles had alit the liveried coachmen were tugging the very much alive, disheveled drunk to his feet.

"Let go of me, I say!" he sputtered. "First you try to run me down, then you molest me! Unhand me at once!"

Braden made his way over. With a curt nod he dismissed his harried coachmen, then inspected the sputtering man. Braden's gaze was cold, brittle, clearly mirroring the disgust he was feeling. He noted that the man's clothing was rumpled and askew, but not inexpensive.

"Get up." Braden's tone left no room for argument.

The stranger blinked, then struggled awkwardly to his feet, dusting himself off with hands that shook.

"You are most fortunate that my driver is as quick as he is"—Braden's tone was filled with condemnation—"else you would be dead." He folded his arms across his broad chest. "How did you plan on getting home?" he demanded without preamble.

The man looked about with glazed eyes. "I'm not certain. I believe I hired a carriage. . . ."

"Well, as you can see, none is present," Braden said, cutting him off. Impatiently he gestured toward his own open carriage. "Get in. My driver will take you wherever it is you need to go."

The man stared at the elegant coach done in the Sheffield colors of crimson and black, the family crest embossed on its gleaming sides. He himself might be a mere member of the gentry, but he recognized the signs of nobility when he saw them.

"Is this your way of apologizing for your driver's carelessness?" he managed.

Braden motioned to Charles to help the man into the carriage.

"No. This is my way of being charitable to someone who is in dire straits. Worthy or not."

With that Braden strode back to the carriage and settled himself within the plush interior. Minutes passed, and Charles appeared, tossing the uncoordinated, still-muttering man into his seat, then climbing in beside him.

Braden leveled his cold stare at their passenger. "Where shall I instruct my driver to take you?"

A pause. "T'Scarborough, m'lord." Since he was unsure of his rescuer's exact title, "my lord" was a safe form of address. "I live in a cottage on the cliffs overlooking the North Sea. You can see it from the road, so it can't be missed."

Braden felt an odd constriction in his chest, and his earlier feeling of foreboding intensified. He called out instructions to his waiting driver, then sat back, silently admonishing himself for his irrational reaction. Surely there were many such cottages along the North Sea.

The carriage moved purposefully on its way.

"What is your name, sir?" Braden asked slowly, perusing the flushed cheeks and the unkempt clothing.

The man swallowed, feeling terribly uneasy and not quite sure as to why.

"Robert Grey, m'lord," he supplied.

Braden felt bile rush up to his throat, his worst fears confirmed. This miserable excuse for a human being was the father of that vibrant young woman who had so briefly but profoundly touched his life. Kassandra. Lovely, innocent Kassie. Braden's fists clenched in his lap. She deserved better than this.

Despite Robert's dazed condition, he was certain he had seen a tightening of his noble escort's jaw. Vaguely he wondered what chord his identity had struck in the younger man. Maybe Elena, he thought, anger rising inside him. But no, this man was too young . . . little more than thirty years of age, he would guess. And Elena had preferred her men older, more mature, and incomparably affluent.

Robert's fuzzy gaze turned to the other occupant of the carriage, and his stomach knotted. Whoever this man was, he would certainly suit Elena's tastes. The age was right, as were the rugged good looks. And while the younger man had reacted to the name of Grey with anger, this older man's face had drained of color.

Robert blinked. Could his befuddled mind be playing tricks on him? Perhaps . . . He shook his head to clear it, struggling to focus on the question the young nobleman had asked him.

"Pardon me, m'lord?" Robert managed.

Braden shifted impatiently. "I asked if you had a daughter named Kassandra."

Now Robert looked startled. "Why . . . yes, I do. How on earth do you know—"

"We met once, some years ago. She was an enchanting girl."

Robert massaged his temples. "Once? Then I am surprised you remember her . . . forgive me, m'lord. I don't seem t'be able t'recall our introduction. What is your name?"

Braden gave Robert a look of utter distaste and refrained from telling him that they had, quite fortunately, never met prior to now. "Braden Sheffield, the Duke of Sherburgh," Braden supplied. "And I beg to differ with you, Mr. Grey. Your daughter is not an easy person to forget."

Dull, dark eyes flickered over Braden thoughtfully, then moved on to Charles, who still remained silent.

"Your Grace," Robert acknowledged, addressing Braden, but staring at Charles. "And this is . . ."

"Charles Graves," Charles supplied in a cold, tight voice.

Braden glanced over at Charles, startled. He had never heard his friend sound so bitter. No . . . it was more than bitter; it was lethal. And Charles's hands were clenched tightly in his lap. Most odd.

"And what is your title?" Robert asked, feeling himself fade.

"I have no title, sir" was the clipped reply.

"No title," Robert repeated in wonder. "Now that is a surprise."

Braden had no chance to question him about the curious comment before Robert continued.

"I have no money t'offer you for your kindness," he drawled, leaning back against the satin seat covering.

"I assumed as much," Braden answered coldly. "Fortunately, I am not in need of your money, sir."

Robert nodded, his head lolling against the cushions. "I thought not," he muttered, his lids drooping. "Noblemen rarely need anything. And what they need, they take. Even if it belongs t'someone else." His words trailed off, and his chin dropped upon his chest.

"He's out cold," Charles said in disgust.

Braden nodded. "It is just as well. He sickens me." He glanced over at Charles, but the older man's earlier reaction had disappeared, and he was quite himself again.

"You are concerned for his daughter?" he asked Braden with his usual insight. He remembered Braden's recounting of the night he'd stumbled upon Kassandra and knew that Braden had never forgotten that meeting.

Again Braden nodded. "Yes, I am. And I will continue to be until I see for myself that she is well." He stared broodingly out the carriage window, wishing he had not chosen to stay away all this time, had not forced himself to resist the frequent urge to see Kassie. Pangs of guilt, of doubt, besieged him.

"What sort of life could she possibly have had with only that man for guidance?" he wondered aloud, remembering that Kassie had said her mother was dead. He threw a scathing look at Robert's crumpled figure, then returned his worried gaze to the passing scenery around them.

Charles's expression had hardened at Braden's words and was again set in grim lines of anger. Lost in his own thoughts, Braden did not notice. His only concern was for Kassie.

He reflected once again upon their first and only meeting. Certainly he had sensed her life was somewhat lonely and difficult, just as he had sensed that she, like him, possessed an innate resilience to combat her pain. But not until five minutes ago had Braden considered the possibility that Kassie was faced with a burden so great that its magnitude far exceeded the scope of her defenses. Something she was powerless to fight alone.

It was up to *him* to protect her from that parasitic excuse for a father.

The intensity of his own reaction startled Braden. He dismissed as absurd the fleeting thought that what he was feeling was far more complex than mere protectiveness. Kassie was, after all, little more than a child, while he was a grown man who had never really known childhood at all.

There were several hours of travel ahead along rutted roads. The trip was spent in silence, each man plagued by the afternoon's events.

It seemed an eternity before the carriage veered to the right, heading toward the Scarborough coastline. A short time later the road worsened, became rougher and more uneven. The carriage bounced unsteadily over the poorly paved surface, making its way to the Grey house. In the distance Braden saw the cottage and its grounds jutting out over the sea. He scanned the area, seeking out Kassandra. She was nowhere in sight. Not that much was visible over the tall and undisciplined lawns. Braden frowned. The grounds had been shamefully neglected and rose in uneven clusters of green and brown. Huge bunches of weeds towered over drooping flower beds.

Braden was struck by an inexplicable sense of dread. He swung out of the carriage almost before it had come to a complete stop.

Simultaneously the sound of joyful barking filled the air, and seconds later a floppy-eared beagle bounded into view. From his mouth dangled what appeared to be a lady's shawl.

"Percy!" a feminine voice called out. "Bring that back at once!"

Braden did not need to ask to whom the voice belonged. He would have recognized that musical sound anywhere.

Breathless with laughter, hair streaming down her back, Kassie tore across the grounds, her gown held high above her ankles so as not to impede her progress.

The beagle came to a grinding halt, turned, and wagged his tail at his panting mistress.

"Percy!" She reached where he stood and stopped. "I need my shawl! Give it to me!" She held out her hand, oblivious to her audience.

Percy perked up his ears and looked to the right and to the left, trying to decide which way to go in order to fetch whatever it was his beloved Kassie was so eager to have.

Kassie sighed with exasperation, placing her slender hands on her hips. "Percy," she said, striving for patience, "my shawl is not somewhere out there. It is the thing that you are holding in your mouth." She leaned over, tugging on the material that hung from the dog's clamped teeth. *"This* is my shawl."

Percy barked playfully in response, which immediately freed the damp, crumpled shawl. It fell to the ground in a ruined heap. Percy stared down in astonishment, as though realizing for the first time that the object his mistress had been pursuing was in his possession all along. He wagged his tail proudly at having been the one to find it.

Kassie shook her head, stooping to pick up the wet garment. "Oh, Percy, what am I to do with you?"

In reply the dog leapt up to lick Kassie's face with an enthusiastic pink tongue until Kassie dropped to her knees and hugged the silky-haired animal to her chest.

"I do love you," she whispered, "although you will never be the scholar that I had hoped you would be." She kissed his smooth fur. "But your heart is loyal and loving, and your friendship means the world to me."

Not prone to sentiment, Percy squirmed in her embrace, attempting to free himself. It was then that he spotted the unfamiliar carriage and its occupants.

A furor of barking exploded from the little dog as he sped off to defend his mistress. Kassie rose, the soft folds of her plain apple-green gown draping to her ankles. Her heart began pounding wildly in her chest at the sight of the tall, handsome man that stood forty feet away, watching her so intently. She took a hesitant step toward him. Surely he must be an apparition, the same wondrous daydream that she relived time and again in her mind. And that this time, just like all the others, she would open her eyes to find that it was no more than a fantasy.

Seeing her uncertainty, Braden walked toward her, taking in every detail of the miracle time and maturity had wrought. In place of the blooming young girl he'd met on the beach was a thoroughly intoxicating woman who, even in a drab, faded gown and with her disheveled hair tumbling wildly about her shoulders, could rival the most exquisite portrait ever captured on canvas.

He stopped inches before her and smiled down into her brilliant blue-green eyes.

"Braden?" It was both question and statement, spoken breathlessly through trembling lips.

"Hello, Kassie."

Chapter 3

Her elation died a rapid death when she saw why Braden was there.

Numbly Kassie watched her bedraggled father being hauled out of the splendid carriage. She barely heard Braden's gentle explanation of the circumstances surrounding his appearance at her door, for all her dreams were shattering around her. Unconsciously she began to walk toward the entranceway of her house . . . and away from Braden.

Shame. All that registered in Kassie's mind was the shame of having Braden see her life as it really was. It was not the worn state of her clothing nor even the deteriorated condition of the cottage that embarrassed her so. But her father, in his usual, dreadful drunken state, having to be delivered home in such a disgraceful, pathetic fashion . . . that was the true reason for her humiliation.

She swallowed the lump in her throat, refusing to give in to the urge to cry. The fact was that for a moment, just a fleeting moment, she had actually thought Braden had come to see her. That she had been in his thoughts, as he had dominated hers. Obviously she was wrong. Well, he would never know how much that realization hurt her. Never.

Kassie threw back her shoulders and looked straight ahead as she neared the cottage, showing neither her hurt nor her shame. Her protective mask was in place. Keeping her pain and fear locked up inside was, by now, second nature to her. She had done it all her life.

"Kassie." Braden's long strides brought him abreast of her. Percy ran along beside him, barking distrustfully and sniffing at Braden's heels. Braden ignored him. "Kassie," he said again, taking her arm and halting her progress.

She stopped in her tracks and raised her composed face to his. "Yes?"

Braden studied her expression, a mirror of one he had worn countless times and knew only too well, so he wasn't fooled by it now. "It's good to see you," he said softly.

Kassie gave him a careful smile. "I'm glad to see you, too," she answered. "It's been a very long time."

Her unasked question hung between them, but Braden heard it as clearly as if she had voiced it aloud.

"Kassie," he began, wondering how on earth he was going to explain his absence all these years. An absence that, to Kassie, would seem nothing short of abandonment. He cleared his throat roughly. "When we met you were a young girl. I thought it best not to . . ."

Percy found his opportunity, lunging at Braden's feet and sinking his teeth into the soft leather of his boot. Growling with rage, the beagle held on, eyes fierce with challenge as he waited to see what his adversary would do.

"Percy!" Kassie was horrified. "Stop that immediately!"

The little dog, unused to his mistress's strong display of emotion, let go of the boot and barked expectantly, awaiting further praise.

"I apologize for Percy's behavior," Kassie told Braden, her disapproving gaze still fixed on her panting dog. "He's not used to my receiving guests."

Braden chuckled, squatting to offer the suspicious dog his open hand. "He is *definitely* Hunter's son," he told her, coaxing the dog to accept his gesture of friendship. "He's loyal to you. That's as it should be."

"Loyal, yes," Kassie sighed, "and a warm, loving pet . . . but severely lacking in intelligence. I have tried and tried, but to no avail. Even his name hasn't helped."

"His name?" Braden, stood, perplexed, and desperately tried to control his amusement. Obviously Kassie took her pet's inadequacy quite seriously.

"I had hoped that by dubbing him with the forename of so great a poet I would inspire him to live up to Shelley's genius."

Braden's lips twitched in spite of his best intentions. "You named your dog after Percy Shelley?" he managed.

She nodded. "For all the good that it's done, yes."

"Oh, Kassie." He laughed, reaching for her instinctively. "You are such a treasure."

Just then James Gelding, the Greys' only remaining servant, scurried out of the house to the carriage and assisted Charles in half dragging, half carrying Robert toward the door.

The tender reunion between Kassie and Braden shattered into bits.

"I must go to him," Kassie murmured, tugging away from Braden and hurrying off, Percy at her heels.

Braden frowned after her, more than a little bothered by Kassie's reaction. It was as if she were responsible for Robert, rather than the other way around. Automatically Braden followed Kassie toward the house. He already knew that he would hate what he found there.

Kassie shooed Percy out from underfoot, then stepped into the barren hallway as her father was helped inside. "Oh, Father," she sighed. She said no more, but Braden arrived in time to see the utterly stricken, defeated look on her face. It made him wish that Robert Grey had been crushed beneath the carriage wheels.

"He's all right, Kassie," he assured her. "Only a bit out of sorts." They both knew it was a lie.

Braden stationed himself by Kassie's side, wanting to give her whatever support he could.

"Where would you like us to take him, Miss Grey?" Charles asked in his deep, precise voice, his sharp blue eyes fixed on Kassie's face.

Kassie blinked. "Oh, please . . . don't trouble yourselves anymore. I will see that he gets to bed."

"No." Braden stopped her with one word.

"He's my father, Braden," Kassie protested, raising her chin defiantly and meeting his gaze. "And my responsibility."

God, she was beautiful. Her skin was flawless, her features delicate and fine-boned. And those eyes . . . the most unusual shade of blue-green imaginable on this side of heaven, with flecks of gold scattered throughout, beneath the longest, thickest black lashes he had ever seen. Braden could feel something tug inside him, something he had felt only once before but remembered as if it were yesterday.

He took a deep breath, caught her small hand in his large, hard one, and gave it a brief squeeze. "Charles and your man can manage it, Kassie. Your father is too heavy for you to carry alone." He pressed on, anxious to spare her pride. "It is not unusual for a man to overindulge upon occasion."

She smiled, and the splendor of it left him breathless. "Thank you, Braden" was all she said.

Robert blinked and tried to clear his vision. "Kassandra?" he tried. His daughter . . . talking to the young nobleman who had brought him home . . . what had he said his name was? Braden Sheffield, that was it. The Duke of Sherburgh. Sheffield. Damn, why was that name so familiar?

"Yes, Father?"

Robert could swear that the duke was looking at Kassandra, not only with recognition, but with tenderness. No, that was impossible; they'd only met once. He lifted his head and looked up at the two men who were leading him purposefully to the staircase.

"Oh . . . James . . . all right . . . yes, I am very tired . . . think I'll go to bed." He glanced behind him in time to see Kassie's move to follow stopped by the duke's hand on her arm.

"Kassie . . . don't," Braden murmured, willing her to remain.

She hesitated, then nodded. "All right, Braden."

Braden. She knew his forename. Robert tucked the final coherent thought away. So their previous acquaintanceship was not his imagination. Nor was the look in their eyes when their gazes met. Damn. He would allow no complication to his plans. None at all.

Kassie stared bleakly after Robert's retreating figure until he and his two escorts had disappeared atop the second-floor landing. Then she turned back to Braden.

"I appreciate your kindness in bringing my father home." She moved her hands nervously, smoothing her rumpled gown. "But I'm not quite certain how to thank you."

Braden flashed her a teasing look, determined to restore both her spirits *and* her pride. "Well, you *could* offer me a drink and some pleasant conversation."

Kassie blinked. "Oh! Of course! Forgive me . . . I have totally forgotten my manners." She gave him an impish grin, the dimples in her cheeks making her look, for a scant second, like the young girl he had met on the beach. "But that should not surprise you, for, if you recall, we did agree that I was not a lady."

"No, as I recall we agreed that you were unlike any other lady of my acquaintance," Braden corrected. "In truth, that makes you the greatest lady of all."

Kassie's smile faded, and she automatically glanced toward the deserted staircase.

Braden followed her gaze. "Your value is not determined by your father, Kassie. It is determined by you alone."

She nodded, then turned and gestured for him to follow. "Come. We can use Father's library."

Braden followed her across the small hallway to the dim room. He couldn't help but notice the poor condition of the cottage. The paint was peeling, the floor was scratched, its wood lackluster, the furnishings sparse and drab. The library smelled dank and was permeated by the lingering stench of liquor. Braden's stomach lurched in protest.

Kassie lit some lamps and turned in time to see the repugnant expression on Braden's face.

"It has been a difficult year for us," she said defensively, "and all of the servants are gone except James. I do my best to keep the house tidy, but—"

"Don't you dare apologize to me." Braden didn't realize how severe his tone was until Kassie winced. But the true reasons for their "difficult year" enraged him. "I am not judging you on your affluence, or lack thereof," he continued, this time more gently. "I just had no idea. . . ." His words trailed off. There was no point in continuing this conversation, he decided, for anything he said would upset her or insult her. This new, very adult Kassie was a proud, fiery woman; the challenging spark in her eyes made that clear. He, of all people, knew the importance of respecting that pride.

"I believe you have become Kassandra, *ma petite,*" he murmured.

The drastic change in subject, his surprising words, and his melting smile startled her, and she gave him a questioning look.

Braden walked toward the dreary, dark sofa next to which Kassie stood.

"You told me that you would use your full name when you were grown," he reminded her. Without thinking he reached out and took a strand of her soft hair between his fingers, rubbing it slowly, carefully, studying the shimmering highlights that cascaded into a vibrant cloud of black silk down her back. Her sweet scent drifted up to him, and he inhaled its wonderful, familiar freshness. Of its own accord his gaze fell to her lips, which were softly parted and slightly moist. The total impact took his breath away.

Three years and countless women suddenly evaporated into nonexistence.

Troubled by his powerful response, Braden coughed and moved away. "I'll take that drink now," he said in an oddly strained voice.

Kassie nodded numbly, then walked over to fetch the decanter and pour Braden a brandy. Her legs were shaking so badly, she feared she might collapse. For a fleeting moment she had glimpsed the Braden that filled her dreams, her thoughts. She knew in her heart he had wanted to kiss her. Just as she had wanted him to . . . desperately.

The amber liquid sloshed against the sides of the glass as Kassie tried unsuccessfully to steady her trembling hand. Braden took the drink, watching the flush that stained Kassie's cheeks.

"Sit with me," he heard himself say.

She sat beside him on the sofa, her hands clenched tightly in her lap.

There was no point in idle chatter. The currents between

them were too potent, Braden's feelings too acute. Torn
between the desire to hold her in his arms and the equally
strong need to assure himself of her well-being, Braden
opted for the latter. It was safer. Carefully he placed his
untouched brandy on the low table beside him.

"Kassie, do you spend much time with your father?"

"No." She averted her gaze.

"When we first met you told me that your mother had
died."

Kassie swallowed, then nodded. "She died when I was
four."

All Braden could think of was his poor, precious Kassie
growing up alone, with only a selfish drunk of a father for
company. "I'm sorry," he murmured.

"Everyone says I look just like her," she continued,
wanting anything but his pity.

"Then she must have been beautiful."

A pained look crossed her face. "I don't remember very
much about her."

That was odd. Braden would have thought that Kassie's
steel-trap mind would have retained every detail of her
mother's character. But he wisely refrained from voicing his
thought aloud. Now was not the time.

Seeing the haunted sadness in her eyes, Braden felt a twist
of emotion he readily acknowledged . . . a deep sense of
protectiveness. He reached for her, drawing her gently to
him.

Kassie wondered if she might faint, her every nerve
tingling to life. She felt afraid, though not of the physical
awakening that consumed her. *That* she welcomed. But the
urgent need to depend upon Braden, to be enfolded in his
arms, to give in to his strength, to open up that part of her
soul that she shared with no one—*that* terrified her. She had
been alone for so long, had shouldered overwhelming bur-
dens with no help from anyone, had built a wall around her
fear and her loneliness. Why now did she suddenly want to
weaken, to break down, to let go? She gritted her teeth and
fought the impulse, attempting to move from Braden's
gentle hold.

Braden felt the motion and stayed it by tightening his

arms around her. "It's all right, Kassie," he murmured into her hair. "It takes courage and strength to lean on someone . . . even for a little while. Lean on me."

She sagged against him, unable to fight her inner yearning any longer. She buried her face in his crisp white shirt, digging her fingers into the edges of his wool riding coat. She didn't cry but just gave in to the need to be held and cared for, if only for a few moments.

Braden gathered her against him, stroking her back with slow, soothing caresses. They were both profoundly aware of the sensual contact. Neither of them moved, either to separate or to deepen the embrace. They just remained as they were, bodies touching, time indefinitely suspended.

Braden closed his eyes, rested his chin atop her head. Raw feeling surged through him. Never had there been anything more natural than holding this woman in his arms. He couldn't explain it; she just belonged there. It was the most damned unnerving sensation he'd ever experienced.

Kassie took a deep, shaky breath, exhaling it against Braden's solid warmth. "Thank you . . . again," she whispered. "It seems that you have become my hero on more than one occasion."

Slowly he eased her away so he could look into her beautiful, flushed face, giving her a devastating smile. "I don't believe I have ever been anyone's hero before." He caught her hand and brought it to his lips. "It would be my honor to be yours."

There was a light rap at the open library door.

"Pardon me, Braden." Charles Graves stood in the doorway. He was speaking to Braden, but his eyes were on Kassie.

"Yes, Charles?" Braden dropped Kassie's hand and turned to his friend. "Is Mr. Grey . . . resting?"

Charles nodded. "Yes. He is abed."

Kassie rose, striving to control the revealing blush she knew stained her cheeks and failing. She approached Charles. "We haven't been introduced, sir. I am Kassandra Grey, and I am very grateful for your assistance with my father."

He stared down at her with an unreadable expression that was gone as quickly as it had come.

"It was my pleasure, Miss Grey. My name is Charles Graves, and I work for His Grace."

At Kassie's surprised look Braden came to his feet and interjected, "As usual, Charles is being overly modest. He is one of the finest Thoroughbred trainers in England, sought after by owners of the most splendid horseflesh imaginable. Fortunately, he is also my friend; hence he remains at Sherburgh."

Kassie gave Charles a brilliant smile. "I have always wanted to ride, but my father always felt . . ." Her voice trailed off.

"Come to Sherburgh and you can ride as often as you like," Braden invited at once.

The look of joy on Kassie's face was instantly replaced by one of horror. "Oh, no, I couldn't. I mean . . . Father would never allow me . . . it isn't proper, you see, and I—"

"I would provide you with a chaperon," Braden interrupted her. "And I could send my carriage over to get you any day your father prefers—" He broke off at her frightened look and the wild shaking of her head. "Is there some other problem?" He was confused and bothered by her refusal, but more important, he was downright alarmed at the terror he saw in her eyes.

"You don't understand," she was saying, picturing her father's wrath if she even broached the subject of visiting with a gentleman, let alone traveling to his home. Robert's rage would be beyond her endurance. "It would be impossible . . . I just could not." She walked rapidly to the door before Braden could pursue the subject. "I don't want to detain either of you any longer. I thank you again for all your trouble. I will show you out."

Seconds later Braden and Charles stood at the open entranceway door, where Kassie politely waited for them to take their leave. Her face was carefully devoid of emotion, her exquisite eyes veiled.

Braden stared down at her. "Charles, please wait for me in the carriage," he instructed.

Charles paused, frowning as he gazed at Kassie. He looked as if he were going to say something, then abruptly changed his mind and, with a polite nod, went out to the waiting carriage.

Braden turned to Kassie. The first rays of moonlight caressed her delicate features, and again Braden was struck by her newly born beauty, a rare blend of innocence and wisdom. He would do anything to ensure that she retained that special, unspoiled quality that was Kassie.

She looked up at him, thinking that he was every bit as magnificent a hero as any woman could imagine. For one insane moment she contemplated flinging herself back into his arms, begging him to take her away with him, away from this hell. But she, better than anyone, knew that she could never escape. For the real hell came not from her father alone, but from the demons that raged somewhere inside her. Somewhere that even she could not reach.

"Good-bye, Braden," she said softly.

He shook his head. "No, Kassie, we both know that this is not good-bye." He brushed his thumb across her lips and felt the small shiver that went through her body at his touch. "I want to see you again . . . soon."

"No," she said at once. "I can't."

"But you want to."

"It doesn't matter what I want, Braden. I learned long ago that we often do not get what we want."

"I do." He lifted her chin with his forefinger and lowered his head, lightly brushing her lips with his. The poignant caress, though intentionally brief, sent wild tremors of sensation through them both. Braden looked down into her wide, startled eyes. "If you need me—ever, at any time—I will be here for you. Don't forget that."

She nodded, dazed, as he turned to go.

"And Kassie?" He paused. "I will be back. You can count on it."

And she knew he would be. Just as her soul had known it all these years. Only this time she was afraid.

Kassie turned and walked slowly back into the dismal house. *This* was her reality; there could be no other.

She closed her eyes. When her fantasies of Braden had been no more than an innocent dream, a young girl's infatuation, anything had been possible. But she was no longer a young girl, and what she was feeling now was hopelessly impossible . . . and *not* infatuation.

She was in love with Braden Sheffield.

Chapter 4

Robert Grey was responsible . . . of that Braden was certain. But how much damage had been done, and could it be undone?

There was something sinister about the man, a desperate sort of violence lurking beneath the surface. Grey was beaten, deep in his losses, deeper still in his cups. He had reached that lowest of points at which a man was capable of doing anything. And Kassie, alone and defenseless, was victim to his hostility. From a bright and spirited girl she had become a resigned and overburdened young woman, stripped of the inner light of joy and hope that had filled Braden's eyes and bathed his senses with pleasure.

What did he do to her? The heinous possibilities were unbidden . . . unendurable. Any one of the answers to that question made Braden feel ill. Kassie was alone, defenseless against any torment her father chose to inflict. Braden clenched his fists in his lap. He prayed that he was wrong, that his imagination was playing cruel tricks on him. Regardless of Robert's own personal failures, surely he wouldn't abuse the only gift life had bestowed upon him?

Braden had all but convinced himself, when he recalled Kassie's alarmed reaction at his suggestion that she go riding at Sherburgh. A moment earlier she had been warm and open in his arms, giving him her pain, taking his strength. But the mere thought of incurring her father's wrath had placed a dark veil of fear between the two of them. A muscle worked in Braden's jaw. No, something was definitely amiss, he thought; something he couldn't quite put his finger on.

But he intended to convince Kassie to confide in him. And then, if his suspicions proved true, he was going to find a way to get her out of that house.

"She is very beautiful."

Charles's words brought Braden back to the present. He blinked, surprised that the carriage had already passed through the formidable iron gates of Sherburgh and was now slowing down as it neared the front entranceway.

"Yes. She is." He turned to find Charles watching him intently. "And her father is beneath contempt."

At Braden's words something flashed in Charles's deep blue eyes, something unreadable but brutally intense. "He does not deserve such a daughter. And she does not deserve such a life." His voice was filled with anger.

Braden nodded. "No, she does not. And I cannot allow her to live it. Unprotected and alone." He slammed his fist down in frustration. "But what can I do? She refused my offer. Whether out of fear or pride, I don't know."

Charles inclined his head. "I have never known you to be deterred from anything you wanted in the past."

Braden gave him a tight smile. "Nor would I be now. If it were merely a matter of Kassie's pride, I would not hesitate to ignore it in order to keep her safe. It is not her pride but her fear that concerns me. She is quite obviously terrified of her father. I will not risk worsening the situation by forcing my visits upon her." He stared off into space. How magnanimous that speech made him appear! The fact was that Kassie elicited feelings and emotions in him that he did not understand, had never before experienced. All he knew was that he had to see her again, and not merely to assure himself of her well-being. He needed to hold her in his arms and immerse himself in the sweetness that had called out to him from the first time they had met. He wanted to taste her mouth, to bury his lips in the wild, fragrant masses of her tumbled dark hair. He wanted to explore the strange, inexplicable fascination that only Kassandra held for him.

"I can do it for you."

Once again Charles's words broke into Braden's thoughts. The carriage had come to a halt before a pillared stairway leading to the high arched front doors of Sherburgh.

"Pardon me?" Braden frowned, attempting to understand his friend's words.

Charles's expression was impassive, his gaze unreadable. "I can watch over Miss Grey for you," he repeated. He cleared his throat. "Your presence would be noticed at once, Braden. It is apparent that the young lady has very strong feelings toward you. Feelings of which her father would, apparently, disapprove. Whereas I could be more discreet, keep an eye on her without being observed." He gave a quick, mirthless smile, as if enjoying a private and ironic joke. "I am quite good at being both discreet *and* invisible. You are not."

Braden studied Charles's face. In truth, he wanted to dispute his friend's suggestion, for he needed an excuse to see Kassie again. But he could not disagree with what he knew to be true. And Kassie's safety took precedence over his wishes.

He nodded slowly. If, for the time being, he could not be with her himself, there was no one he trusted more than Charles to take his place. For one and thirty years Charles had been both parent and closest friend to Braden.

"Thank you, Charles." Braden smiled at him, feeling as if a great weight had been lifted from his heart. "If you see anything that makes you uneasy—*anything* at all—come to me at once. No one is going to harm Kassie."

He climbed out of the carriage, nodding to the footman that stood at attention beside its gleaming door, then strode up the stone steps of the house.

Charles's expression hardened again, his jaw tight with resolve. "No, Braden. No one will hurt her," he said quietly to the empty carriage. "No one at all."

"Braden? Is that you?" Cyril Sheffield peered around the corner of the library.

"Yes, Cyril, none other." Braden moved purposefully past the bustling servants and into the expansive marble hallway.

"I had to stop at the Grey cottage." Braden proceeded to give his uncle the sketchy details of Robert Grey's near-fatal accident.

Cyril frowned. "Grey? I remember your questioning me about a man named Grey some years back. Are we speaking of the same person?"

Braden nodded. "We are."

"Then he is the father of that young girl you met on the beach. . . ." Cyril paused, attempting to recall the details.

"Kassandra," Braden supplied.

"Yes, Kassandra," Cyril repeated, remembering. "And how is Kassandra faring?"

"She is unforgivably neglected."

Cyril shook his head sympathetically. "I have heard rumors from business associates of her father's behavior. 'Tis a pity for her sake that he is so pathetic."

"I want to kill him. Every time I think of it . . ." His voice trailed off, frustration etched on his handsome face. "I'd like to drop this subject, Cyril. It is something I need to work out for myself."

"Of course," Cyril agreed at once. He cleared his throat. "William Devon sent a messenger today with a contract outlining the specifics of your joint business venture."

Braden nodded absently. "Fine. I'll read it tomorrow."

"The messenger also brought a note from the Devon estate inviting us to their house party next month. I had hoped that you—"

"No."

Braden's abrupt refusal did not surprise Cyril. Still, he had to try to convince him.

"Braden, surely you would not begrudge him—"

"William is a knowledgeable business partner," Braden cut in. "We share many of the same views. But our opinion of William's daughter is not among them. I endure her presence when I must. However, I will not subject myself to an intolerable evening in her company." He shot Cyril a dark look. "I trust we understand one another?" The question was a mere formality, as Braden had already turned away and was striding toward his bedchamber. "If you will excuse me, Cyril, I believe I will go to bed."

Cyril sighed resignedly. "Of course. Good night, Braden."

"Good night." Braden had already dismissed the discussion of Abigail from his mind, his thoughts returning to Kassie.

And hours later, when exhaustion finally won its battle with Braden's turbulent emotions, he slept. But his dreams were uneasy, filled with visions of a black-haired enchantress who called out to him for help and penetrated his isolating walls, wrapping herself about his senses and burying herself inside his heart.

Sleep was not forthcoming.

That came as no great surprise to Kassie. The past few weeks had been terribly unsettling. Her nights were restless, filled with the usual dark dreams, broken by fervent longings and wistful fantasies of Braden. Her days were fraught with tension as her father's humor rapidly disintegrated from poor to black.

Today was no exception. After an unusually abusive tirade Robert Grey had slammed out of the house, leaving a relieved Kassie alone. At least this time he had not struck her. For that she was grateful. More and more often Robert's angry outbursts were accompanied by a harsh slap to Kassie's face and the threat of an even crueler beating. Thus far it had remained merely a threat. But his increased drinking and dwindling funds made Robert grow more hostile with each passing day. And Kassie feared that it was only a matter of time before he manifested his frustration in physical violence.

But tonight she was safe. Quietly Kassie padded down the stairs to the main floor, Percy at her heels. A good volume of poetry would help soothe her. It might be the very diversion she needed to ease her into slumber.

Abruptly she stopped. The library door was tightly closed, though a light shining from beneath it indicated that the room was indeed occupied. Kassie frowned. Had her father returned without her knowledge? She paused, uncertain as to what to do. To interrupt him if he was in the midst of one of his tirades would be foolhardy. No, the book could wait. Kassie had just turned to retreat to the safety of her room when she heard the muffled argument. Though indistinct, the other voice was the same as the one she had overheard talking with her father on the previous occasion.

"That is my offer, Grey. I assure you you will not receive a better one."

"Oh, cert'nly not," came Robert's slurred reply. "It is most generous indeed."

"You can consider your debts to me paid in full. Not to mention the additional seventy thousand pounds, which should do nicely toward restoring your . . . comfort," the self-assured first voice continued.

"Yes, it'll do that." Foxed but satisfied came Robert's reply.

"Fine. Then we have a deal?"

A pause, then the distant scrape of wooden chair legs upon the library floor as the men arose, presumably to shake hands.

"A deal . . . yes. We have a deal," Robert echoed. "And you will not be sorry. She is an enviable acquisition."

Acquisition? What on earth could her father have sold to this man? What did they own that was worth such an enormous sum? Their cottage was quite bare, devoid of valuable paintings or sculptures.

"Oh, I quite agree. She is a spirited beauty . . . I can tell."

A horse? Impossible. Their stables had been empty for years. Robert's gambling and liquor debts had necessitated the sale of all their animals save Percy.

"And not merely beautiful," Robert was adding. "She is biddable as well, if maintained with the necessary heavy hand."

A moment of silence. Then the stranger replied, "I will bear that in mind. But I am convinced that she will make an excellent wife."

Wife? The color drained from Kassie's face.

"Yes. And she is young, capable of bearing many healthy children."

"I agree. Your daughter will do quite nicely for my purposes."

Daughter . . . it took all of Kassie's self-control to restrain herself from crying out loud. They were discussing *her*, auctioning her off like a bit of prize horseflesh. Her own father had just sold her to a stranger for £70,000.

Overcome with shock and fury, she staggered to the steps and sank down upon the lowest one, burying her face in her trembling hands. She was half tempted to burst into the library and confront her father and her "buyer" face-to-face. But her drive for self-preservation was too strong. Her father would react uncontrollably and would vent his rage entirely upon her. She was too much of a coward to endure the ensuing abuse, and too proud to have her humiliation witnessed by the unknown visitor. The painful assaults she endured at her father's hands, both physical and emotional, were hers and hers alone to bear. The confrontation she now sought would have to wait.

Kassie raised her head, staring vacantly off into space. Surely not even her father could stoop so low as to sell her to a virtual stranger. And without a word of forewarning or preparation to her. It was unthinkable. She must have misunderstood. Please God, let her have misunderstood. She lowered her head back into her hands.

Percy's wet tongue on her cold face brought Kassie up with a start. There was no point in dreaming. Her small fists clenched in her lap, Kassie forced herself to face the cold facts as they existed, not as she willed them to be.

Her father had agreed to sell her to an unknown and obviously affluent gentleman. Once this marriage had taken place there would be nothing Kassie could do but accept it. She rose slowly to her feet, determined to act now, before it was a *fait accompli*. She would wait until Robert was alone. Then she would plead with him to change his mind, not to do this hateful thing to her. He would listen, she assured herself. He was a weak man, but not an evil one. And in his way, he loved her. She was certain of it. He would not enforce this blasphemous act once he knew how abhorrent it was to her.

She would present him with an alternative. Yes, that was it. She would offer to seek employment in order to recoup their financial losses. Surely she could find a position as a governess in a well-to-do home. True, it would not pay very much, but it was a start, a solution of sorts. It had to be.

Kassie turned and walked slowly back upstairs to her room. When her father came up to retire for the night she would explain everything and present him with her plan. Then he would release her from this mockery of an agreement.

Her forced bravado faltered when she heard Robert's first heavy, unsteady step moving in the direction of his bedchamber. Before she could reconsider Kassie threw open her bedroom door and stepped into the dimly lit hall.

"Father?" Her voice was soft, hesitant.

Robert stopped and turned around to face his daughter. His eyes were bloodshot, his once-handsome face ruddy, his mouth slack. He frowned, walking toward where Kassie stood.

"Kassandra? What're you doin' up at this hour?"

Kassie winced as the stench of liquor reached her nostrils. She called upon her failing courage and swallowed deeply.

"I need to speak with you."

His frown deepened. "About what?"

She licked her trembling, dry lips. "I was unable to sleep tonight."

Robert rubbed his arm across his forehead and stared down at her. "Another one of your nightmares?" he demanded, searching her face.

"No, Father," she denied quickly. Knowing how infuriated he became at the mention of her bad dreams, she rarely spoke of them, and on the nights when her screams awakened him she divulged only the sketchiest of details. "I had no particular reason; I was merely wide awake. I came down to get a book."

Robert's jaw tightened. "Oh, did you now?"

"Yes. I found the library door closed. I heard voices."

Robert shoved unruly locks of his limp hair out of his face. "And did you listen to the conversation?"

She took a deep breath. "Yes, Father."

To her amazement, he smiled. "Good. Then there is no need for me to tell you about it."

Kassie looked as if she'd been kicked. "How could you?" she blurted out without thinking. "How could you do such a thing to me?" Her voice shook.

Robert's expression grew dark. "And what does that mean?" he demanded.

"You sold me as if I were a common object."

"Indeed! And that is just what you are!" Robert bellowed, his fists curling with rage.

Kassie gasped, her hand going to her mouth. "How can you say that? I am your daughter!" She felt rage overcome her fear as all thoughts of compromise left her head.

"Yes, you are my daughter—I need no reminder of that!" All traces of drunkenness had vanished beneath a blazing anger such as Kassie had never seen. "And what does that entitle you to, Kassandra? Just what life did you think awaited you as *my* daughter? Did you ever dare to dream that you would marry an affluent man, a man with powerful connections? For that is what you are marrying, daughter. A man who has access to enough riches to provide for you *and* for me for all of our days. Does that not make you hold your tongue? A wealthy man's wife, Kassandra. That is what you will be. Now what do you say?"

"I don't care if he is royalty, Father, it doesn't change the way I feel!" Now Kassie was shouting as well.

"The way *you* feel!" Robert thundered, making the very walls shake. "I don't give a damn about the way you feel! Who did you think would marry you, Kassandra? Who would rescue you from this horrid life of yours?" He seized her shoulders. "Your beloved duke? Is that what this is all about? Did you actually believe that His *Grace,* the Duke of Sherburgh, would be the one to take you from all this misery?"

"Leave Braden out of this, Father." Kassie winced at the pressure he was placing on her shoulders.

"Braden, is it? Well, my dear, you are a bigger fool than I thought if you believe that *Braden* would ever think to marry you. I saw the way he looked at you. What's on his mind has nothing to do with marriage." He shook her hard. "Does it, Kassandra?"

Kassie felt a flash of fear shoot up her spine at the wild fury in her father's eyes. "I don't know what you mean, Father." She squirmed to free herself.

"No?" He stared down at her as if he were seeing someone

else. "I believe you know *exactly* what I mean. Tell me, have you lain with him already? Have you given to that bastard what I have promised to someone else?" He shook her violently. "Tell me, damn you. Tell me." With one hard push he sent her staggering until she was backed up against the wall.

Ignoring her sharp cry of pain, Robert seized her chin, glaring accusingly into her frightened eyes. "You have, haven't you?" he bellowed, relentless now in his frenzy. "Haven't you?"

"No, Father," Kassie managed, utterly terrified. "I haven't even seen Braden."

"Liar!" He flung her across the hall and watched her crumple to her knees. Then slowly, menacingly, he stalked her, dragging her to her feet. "You think I don't know what's going on right under my nose? Do you think you can continue to make a fool of me and never pay the price? Do you, Elena?" He drew back his hand and struck her, hard, across her face.

Kassie cried out, tasting the blood of her lip. "I'm not Elena, Father," she sobbed. "I'm Kassandra. Mother is—"

"Slut!" He struck her again, knocking her to the floor. He picked her up and stared into her tear-streaked, bruised face, seeing features identical to those that haunted his soul. "How many times will you betray me? How many times will I look away?" He wrapped the fingers of one big hand around Kassie's slender throat. "Not this time, Elena. No, not this time. This time you will pay. This time will be the last time."

Panic rose like bile in Kassie's throat. She felt Robert's grip tighten, squeeze, cut off her breath, her very life, until nothing mattered but survival. Calling upon her last surge of energy, Kassie brought her knee up hard, slamming with all her strength into his groin.

She heard his primal roar of pain as he released her, but she did not pause. Her body racked with hysterical tremors, she flew down the stairs, ignoring the sharp pain in her ribs, and raced out the door. Percy, who had been cringing in the hallway, bared his teeth and snarled at the disoriented man, then tore off after his mistress.

The night air was cool upon Kassie's wet face. The ache in her side worsened with every step, but she could not, would not slow her pace. She raced along the beach, but she didn't linger there, for tonight the beach held no solace for her agony. Shuddering sobs shook her small frame; her heart and her body were numb with pain and fear.

But her mind was clear. And she knew just where she had to go.

If you need me—ever, at any time—I will be here for you. Don't forget that. Braden's words repeated over and over, a litany in her mind. *I will be here for you. . . . I will be here for you. . . .*

Chapter 5

❧

"Thank you for a superb morning ride, Star. You have far more energy today than I." Braden stroked the sleek mahogany neck of the high-spirited Thoroughbred beside him.

"That is not surprising, considering how little sleep you got last night." Charles's dry retort came from the stable doors, where a young groom was inching forward hesitantly to cool down the temperamental horse. It was a well-known fact that only His Grace was a fine enough horseman to control Star's turbulent nature.

Braden watched Star being led off, noting with satisfaction that the spirited stallion was neither winded nor peaked from his brisk romp—a good sign for a healthy horse.

Charles walked toward Braden, taking in the dark circles beneath his eyes. "Did you go to bed at all? You look miserable," he informed him.

Braden grinned wryly. "Thank you. And yes, I did go to bed, but I did very little sleeping once I got there."

"You are still preoccupied with thoughts of Miss Grey." It was a statement rather than a question, and Charles watched Braden's face for a reaction.

He got one. Braden's jaw tightened, and his eyes grew stormy. "Yes, I am concerned about Kassie," he admitted in a flat tone. "I'm damned uneasy about her living alone with that . . . drunk."

"I've been by the Grey cottage several times this week. Twice I saw Miss Grey running about with her pup, but I saw

50

no evidence of her father on either occasion. Nothing appeared to be amiss," Charles replied.

"Appearances are often deceiving, as you well know," Braden responded coldly. He raked his fingers through his dark hair in frustration. "I know better than anyone what it is like to survive in the midst of hostility. I did it for many years."

Charles nodded. "I know you did," he said quietly. How well he remembered a young boy who never cried, yet never understood why he was resented by his mother and father. A mother who was too self-centered to care for anyone and a father who was too embittered to forgive the very person who had caused the unbreachable barrier in his marriage. "I know you did," Charles repeated, laying a gentle hand on Braden's shoulder.

Braden regarded Charles soberly, remembering all the times that he had sought solace in these stables from this kind and caring man who had filled such an important void in Braden's life. It was a debt that Braden could never repay.

"Why don't you try to get some rest?" Charles suggested, walking beside him toward the house. "It is barely past dawn."

Braden shook his head. "I'm too restless. I think I'll contact my shipping company to see when the new Arabian will be arriving. I'm eager to see if she is as splendid as I have been told."

Charles started to reply, but at that moment loud voices and sharp barking erupted from Sherburgh's entranceway. As the mansion came into view Braden could see Perkins, the elderly Sherburgh butler, adamantly refusing entrance to a small, disheveled waif. Beside them a brown and white flash of fur was leaping and barking frantically in between nips at the butler's heels.

"What the . . ." Braden sped up his pace, calling out as he neared the front stairs. "Perkins? What is the problem?"

Distress evident on his always-composed face, the uncharacteristically harried butler turned to Braden.

"Forgive the disturbance, Your Grace," Perkins began, mopping his forehead with a handkerchief, "but this . . . young lady"—he cast a disdainful look beside him—

"insists on speaking with you. I have repeatedly told her that the servants' entrance is around back, but she refuses to listen . . ."

Before he could finish his sentence the young lady in question turned in Braden's direction, limping painfully down the stone steps, the outraged beagle beside her. "Braden?"

Braden felt as if he had been punched in the stomach.

"Kassie?" He barely heard Charles's shocked gasp from just behind him. In ten long strides Braden was at the foot of the stairs, reaching out to help Kassie down to him. The bottom of her gown was shredded, her face was tight with pain, and her cheeks were tear-streaked. Ugly bruises marred her chin and neck, and her soft lower lip was swollen and covered with dried blood. "Oh, my God," he breathed, framing her face in his hands. "Kassie."

He drew her against him, cradling her protectively in his arms. He felt her flinch at the contact and mistook her discomfort for fear of his touch.

"Sh-h-h . . . relax. It's all right now. Everything is all right." Relief washed over Braden in waves as he felt the tension leave Kassie's small, slender body. Over her head he glared at the stunned butler.

"Could you not see that she is hurt?" he demanded in a furious tone.

"Well, actually, no, Your Grace, I could not," the horrified butler stammered. "What with all the commotion, and that animal"—he flashed a dark look at Percy, who had miraculously quieted down—"carrying on, I could not see . . . that is, I didn't know. . . ."

Braden bit down on his anger. After all, it was not Perkins he wanted to choke to death with his bare hands. "It's all right, Perkins. I understand. Now, I want you to go inside and send for Dr. Howell. Then, see that a room is prepared for Miss Grey. She will need hot water for a bath and some clothing as well. I don't care how you manage it, just do it. Is that clear?"

"Yes, Your Grace . . . perfectly." His dignity restored, the elderly man withdrew into the house.

Braden could feel Kassie trembling against him.

"Where are you hurt, sweetheart?" he murmured softly, afraid to carry her inside and inadvertently worsen any of her wounds.

She didn't answer, but her fingers dug into the front of Braden's shirt. He eased her back against his arm, touching her bruised face with a gentle hand.

She winced, looking up at him with tormented eyes. "I'm sorry," she whispered, "but I didn't know where else to go."

He shook his head emphatically, pressing his fingers to her lips to silence the unwanted apology. She flinched at the contact, and Braden's eyes went almost black with rage.

"Did your father do this to you?" he demanded.

Automatically she opened her mouth to defend Robert, then closed it again. She could no longer find excuses for her father's violent, irrational behavior. She nodded.

Braden cursed explicitly, feeling a murderous fury flow through his veins. He fought to control it. Losing his temper would do Kassie no good right now.

"Can you walk?" he asked her instead.

She nodded again. "I think so. It's just my side." She took a deep breath and shuddered. "The pain is so sharp."

"Her ribs." Charles ground out the words, his expression one of shocked outrage.

Braden nodded. Slowly, easily, he bent down and lifted Kassie in his arms. She let out a small whimper but leaned against him gratefully.

"It wasn't this bad . . . but I've been running for so long." She gave him a wan smile. "I had no idea Sherburgh was so far inland . . . at least by foot." She glanced down at Percy, who had begun barking again as soon as Braden had lifted Kassie from the ground. "Hush, Percy," she soothed. "We are among friends." The dog quieted but walked loyally beside his mistress while Braden carried her into the house. Charles followed close behind, should his assistance be needed.

Braden carried Kassie into the drawing room and placed her down upon the settee. Charles hurried over with several extra cushions to place beneath her head.

"Is that better?" Braden asked her softly, brushing strands of dark hair from her pale face.

Kassie nodded, struggling to hide her pain. "I'm fine," she assured him.

"Tell me what happened." It was a command.

Kassie swallowed hard, wishing to forget the details that had led to her unorthodox appearance on Braden's front steps. But she knew he had a right to know.

"I overheard my father and . . . another man talking," she began, lowering her eyes.

"What other man?" Braden demanded at once, tensing as he awaited Kassie's reply.

"I don't know," she whispered. "They were behind closed doors, and their voices were too muffled for me to hear distinctly." She raised her chin, looking directly into Braden's concerned, tender gaze. "But my father intended for me to marry him. In fact, he was in the process of selling me for the impressive sum of seventy thousand pounds."

Disbelief registered on Braden's handsome face. "Your father *sold* you to this man?"

Kassie nodded gingerly, wanting to sink into the sofa and die. "Yes. That was the agreement. And my father expected me to comply with it, no questions asked." Her lips quivered. "I know it is my duty as a daughter to obey him, but it just seemed so cold-blooded, so horrid. I couldn't bear the thought."

"And you told your father that?"

Kassie licked her dry, swollen lips. "Yes. When he was alone I told him. He flew into a rage, said some horrible things." She squeezed her lids shut, desperate to block out the memory. "Then he hit me. I tried to reason with him, but he was out of control by then. He had been drinking, and . . ." Her voice trailed off.

"Then what happened?" Braden asked.

"He became totally irrational, and more violent than I have ever seen him." She opened frightened, damp eyes and fought back the tears. "I was afraid . . . I think he would have killed me." Her voice was almost inaudible. "So I ran. I had nowhere else to go. You said that if I ever needed you—"

"And I meant it." Braden took both her small, cold hands

in his large, warm ones. "I promise you, Kassie, he will never hurt you again. Never. Do you believe me?"

"Yes," she whispered, staring up at his hard, furious expression. "What are you going to do?"

"The first thing I am going to do is have Dr. Howell examine your injuries. Then I will pay a visit to your father." At her frightened expression he shook his head. "Trust me, *ma petite*. All will be well."

Braden turned away from her, unable to hide the ferocity of his reaction. For a brief second his blazing eyes met Charles's hard blue stare. The older man looked more shaken than Braden had ever seen him. But that was understandable, for the idea of physical abuse would be abhorrent to Charles. And violence such as this, inflicted upon a beautiful, innocent young woman, was an abomination.

With a shudder of revulsion Charles looked away. "I will see if the doctor has been sent for," he said quietly, then he turned and left the room.

"Braden?" Kassie's soft voice pulled at Braden, forcing him to turn back to her, his brows raised in question. "I did not mean to be so much trouble." She struggled to sit up. "Coming here was not right. I should have . . ." She broke off as a spasm of pain shot through her. Shakily she lowered herself back down to the settee.

Braden was beside her in an instant. "What you just said is almost as ridiculous as your attempt to get up. Damn it, Kassie, you're hurt. No doubt your ribs are badly bruised, if not broken." He bent over her, his voice tender. "Let yourself lean on me just this once."

She gave him a weak smile. "I recall your saying those same words to me at my cottage. Leaning on you seems to be becoming a habit."

"Is that such a bad thing?" he questioned softly.

"I don't like being dependent upon anyone."

Braden nodded his understanding. She was a strong, self-reliant young woman. A rarity indeed. And still she had chosen to come to him when she was alone, to turn to him when she was frightened. A surge of pleasure coursed

Andrea Kane

through him, making his heart feel lighter than it had in weeks. He stared down into her beautiful, bruised face, her determined little chin lifted proudly. Kassie was a survivor. But Braden knew that she could not survive this alone. He would take care of her somehow. *After* he took care of her father.

"Braden? What in the name of heaven is going on here before the sun has even risen?"

Cyril Sheffield stood in the open doorway looking bleary-eyed and bewildered. He glanced into the drawing room, having been told by a flustered Perkins that an unknown woman was being tended to by His Grace. Stunned, he waited for an explanation from his nephew.

Braden turned, his broad shoulders blocking Kassie's prone figure from Cyril's view.

"We have a guest, Cyril," he replied, giving his uncle a warning look. "Unfortunately, she has been injured. Dr. Howell is on his way to see to her wounds."

Thoroughly at sea, Cyril sputtered, "Are you telling me that a perfect stranger is being tended to at Sherburgh?"

Kassie pushed herself onto her elbows, ignoring the stab of pain that accompanied the movement. "Forgive me, sir, but I am at fault." Fighting a wave of dizziness, she swung her legs over the side of the settee and attempted to stand. "I have disrupted your home, and I apologize. I will go—"

The rapid draining of color from her face was Braden's only sign. He lunged forward and caught her just before she collapsed at his feet.

"Nowhere," he finished for her, easing her back onto the sofa. "You will go nowhere, you stubborn chit." He shook his head in frustration. "This is not a stranger, Cyril," he clarified to his uncle, "but a friend." He smiled. "Kassie, may I present my uncle, Lord Cyril Sheffield. Cyril, this is Miss Kassandra Grey."

Cyril walked over, his dark eyes steadily fixed on the exquisite young woman before him. Even battered and dirty, she was breathtaking. For a long moment he was silent.

"Miss Grey," he said at last, bowing slightly. "I am

56

charmed. Please forgive me. I did, indeed, misunderstand the situation."

Kassie smiled. "You are very kind, my lord," she replied. "And I am very sorry to have barged into your home unannounced at the crack of dawn." She hesitated, knowing that some explanation was in order, reluctant to provide one. She had already humiliated herself before Braden, before Mr. Graves. She did not want to demean herself further in front of Braden's uncle.

Sensing her discomfort, Braden interjected, "I have ordered a bath and some clean clothes for Kassie. Once the doctor has seen to her wounds, I have a small errand to run that will take me from Sherburgh for several hours. I wonder if I could rely upon you to see to our guest's comfort during my absence, Cyril?"

"Excuse me?" Cyril looked dazed as he tore his eyes from Kassie's face. "Oh . . . of course, Braden; certainly. I would be delighted to provide company for Miss Grey until you return."

Braden nodded, then turned back to Kassie. "Unless you'd rather sleep?"

Kassie shook her head vehemently. "I don't think I could . . . not just yet."

"Fine. Then it is settled. However"—his glance flickered to Cyril—"I want Kassie to rest until the doctor arrives. Don't you agree?"

Cyril pressed his lips together, understanding Braden's implicit meaning quite clearly. Whatever questions Cyril had about Miss Grey's shocking appearance would have to remain unanswered. "Yes, Braden. I understand."

"Good. Then we will wait. After which"—Braden's jaw tightened—"I will see to my errand. Immediately."

Morning sunlight danced along the rutted road that led to the Grey cottage. During the solitary carriage ride Braden's anger had built and intensified until it was now a bright blaze of fevered fury. With the slightest bit of provocation he would be capable of splitting Robert Grey's head in two.

Thank God Kassie's injuries had not been severe. Alfred

Howell had declared several of her ribs to be badly bruised, but not broken. She was suffering from exhaustion and shock, and he had prescribed warm food, bed rest, and small doses of laudanum for the pain. In a few days, he had predicted, she would be as good as new.

But Braden knew better. No medicinal remedy could so quickly and completely restore Kassie's battered being. Her worst injuries, her deepest scars, were emotional, not physical, born from years of blatant neglect. Thus far her unfailing spirit and internal strength had kept her afloat. But even they could only last so long unassisted and unnourished.

The carriage came to a stop. Braden flung open the door, nearly knocking over the stunned footman. Braden never noticed. He strode up to the front door and pounded, the sound echoing in the silence of the morning.

After what seemed an eternity the servant Braden remembered as James opened the door, his eyes wide with surprise.

"Yes, m'lord . . . Yer Grace . . . what can I do for ye?"

"I want to see Robert Grey . . . now."

The butler shifted uncomfortably from one foot to the other. "Uh . . . I'm not certain if 'e's awake yet, Yer Grace."

"Then wake him. Or else I will." Braden walked right by the stammering servant and headed toward the stairs.

"Wait!" James called, and Braden stopped in his tracks.

"Yes?" He paused, one foot on the stairway.

Nervous eyes studied Braden's granite-set expression, then James said, "'e's not in 'is room."

Braden walked menacingly toward the butler. "Then where is he?" he demanded.

With a quick inclination of his head the frightened butler gestured toward the library. "Try in there, Yer Grace. 'e might be . . ."

But Braden was already on his way down the hall. With one violent motion he flung open the closed library door, slamming it behind him.

Robert Grey lifted his head from the littered desk, squinting as he attempted to focus on Braden.

"Who is it?"

Braden felt his rage further escalate as he surveyed the empty bottles of liquor strewn about the room. He swallowed deeply, knowing that if he allowed himself, he would lose all control and beat Kassie's father to death.

"It's Braden Sheffield, Grey. Now get up."

Robert blinked in surprise, both at Braden's unexpected arrival and at his icy tone.

"Kassandra is not here, Your Grace. She is . . . out."

Braden kicked a chair out of his way and leaned over the desk, lifting Robert up by his collar and dragging him forward until they were eye to eye. "She is alive and well, no thanks to you," Braden growled, nearly gagging at the stench of liquor that emanated from Robert.

Robert turned white. "I don't know what you mean . . . that is . . ."

"You know exactly what I mean, you filthy bastard." Braden flung Robert back into the chair as if his very existence was the worst of obscenities. "And I am here to tell you that you will never touch her again."

Robert licked his lips. "Now see here, Sheffield. I don't care who you are. I am Kassandra's father, and you have no right—"

"As of today I have every right, and you have none."

Robert stared. "And just what gives you that right?"

"This does." Braden reached into his pocket and took out a piece of paper, flinging it carelessly toward the desk. It fluttered slowly down in front of Robert.

"What . . . ?" Robert picked up the paper and gasped.

"It's a draft in the sum of one hundred thousand pounds," Braden told him. "As I recall, that is thirty thousand pounds *more* than you were going to receive from the gentleman who was to purchase Kassie. Correct?" He didn't wait for an answer but continued. "You can buy a great deal of pleasure with that amount of money, Grey. A great deal."

Robert's mouth opened and closed a few times before he managed to speak. "Are you saying that *you* wish to buy my daughter?" he said in disbelief.

"I'm saying that there is only one condition attached to that money. And that is that you sever any and all ties with Kassie. From this moment on your daughter will cease to be your responsibility."

"Will she become your mistress?"

"Do you care?" Braden shot back. At Grey's silence Braden gave a hollow laugh. "I thought not. You really don't care what happens to her, do you?"

"It's not that," Robert denied, still staring at the enormous sum of money. "But you can give Kassandra so many things that I cannot."

"We agree on that point, Grey," Braden replied. "Things such as safety, security, and tenderness. Things that she has done without all of her life, thanks to you."

Robert scowled. "The previous . . . er, party was offering marriage."

"The previous party was offering only seventy thousand pounds. Is your daughter's respectability worth thirty thousand pounds to you?"

Silence filled the room.

"I believe we have an agreement, then," Braden said at last, his tone deadly quiet. "Personally, I would prefer to kill you, but that would mean I would go to prison and Kassie would once again be without a protector. So, unfortunately, you must live." He stormed to the door, then turned. "Remember: As of this moment, you have no daughter. If you ever so much as look at Kassie again, I will show you what true violence is."

Chapter 6

It was done.

Braden had confronted Robert Grey and threatened his very life if he ever approached Kassie again. Now Kassie would be safe, for Grey was far too much of a coward to risk his neck for anyone. Besides, Braden thought in disgust, there was the added incentive of £100,000. That in itself would keep the bastard away.

Braden stretched his long legs in front of him and stared moodily out the carriage window. Something was still nagging at his mind. He pressed his fingers to his throbbing temples, closing his eyes to further analyze the plaguing feeling.

A picture of Kassie appeared before him; not the bright and beautiful girl who had danced through his dreams all these years, but the frightened, broken young woman who had clung to him for safety and comfort. All the joy, the spirit, the very light that sparkled from within her had been extinguished. And removing her from her father's destructive influence was only the beginning of restoring her rare and precious self. Now she needed time to heal, time to rebuild her shattered life, to recover from her humiliation, and to regain her pride and her self-worth.

Will she become your mistress? Robert Grey's question echoed in Braden's head.

With a start Braden sat up, the reality of the situation crashing down upon him. Grey was abusive, vile, despicable . . . and in this case, correct. What would become of Kassie now? Where would she go, and with whom would she stay? Braden frowned. As far as he knew, Kassie had no other living relatives. She had no money or worldly possessions. And she had but one friend. Him.

Braden's frown deepened. Kassie could not possibly live at Sherburgh unchaperoned, with only himself and Cyril. It didn't matter that there was a houseful of servants dwelling at Sherburgh as well. Within days of the new living arrangement the tongues of the *ton* would be wagging, and within weeks Kassie would be known as a fallen woman. Braden didn't give a damn what people said about him, but what they said about Kassie was something entirely different.

Pensively Braden contemplated his alternatives. He could impose upon any number of acquaintances, arrange to have Kassie live with a fine family and receive every conceivable benefit a young woman could desire.

He dismissed the idea as quickly as it had come. He could never desert Kassie like that, never send her away. No one else understood the hell she had been through, and Braden knew that her pride would not permit her to share it with strangers. No. She belonged with him. And there was only one acceptable way to keep her there, one respectable alternative to the dilemma.

Marriage.

The taut lines of Braden's mouth slowly began to relax as he contemplated the major step he was considering. For one and thirty years he had successfully avoided tying himself to one woman. The disaster with Abigail had freed him from his mockery of a betrothal, and he had given no further thought to matrimony. Until now.

For Kassie it would be the ideal solution. She would have the protection of his name, his title, his wealth, and all the luxuries she had been so unfairly denied in the past. As the Duchess of Sherburgh Kassie would receive instant acceptance by the most influential members of the *ton,* a wealth of invitations from all the right people, and more balls, dinners, and breakfasts than the days of the week could hold. Braden smiled. It would give him pleasure to cover Kassie in silks and satins, to shower her with jewels and other expensive gifts, to offer her a life that, prior to this, she would not have believed possible.

Without surprise or false pretense Braden recognized that the idea of marriage to Kassie was far from repugnant to him. She was intelligent, beautiful, honest, and caring, with an inner strength of character that Braden both admired and respected. And above all, she was, like him, a fighter, possessing a strong, indestructible spirit and fiery independence that would see her through any crisis and help her to survive.

That thought brought another to mind. The possibility existed that Kassie would refuse his offer. Braden understood Kassie well enough to know that she would turn him down flat if she suspected the offer was being made out of guilt or pity. The truth was, it was not. What Braden felt for Kassie was intense and complex . . . and had nothing whatever to do with either guilt or pity.

Braden smiled, remembering the description he had given of his someday wife to Cyril. A woman he both liked and respected. Well, Kassie was certainly that . . . and more. Much more. In fact, the more Braden thought about it, the more appealing the idea began to seem. After all, someday he would have to marry and produce an heir to Sherburgh.

An heir. An immediate image sprang to mind . . . of Kassie, in his bed and in his arms. She would be his wife, and he could at last indulge himself in the incredible fascination she held for him. He could imagine every detail of it. The picture was so clear, so strong, that he could almost feel her, taste her, hear her begging him to . . .

To what?

Braden forced the reality of the situation to the forefront of his mind. He could still recall the way Kassie had flinched when he had taken her into his arms. The only things she knew of touching were brutality and pain. She knew nothing of passion, of mutual desire and sensual pleasure. How could he expect her to eagerly anticipate an act she was bound to find frightening and invasive? Not to mention painful. For no matter how much time he took with her, no matter how thoroughly and tenderly he loved her, Braden knew that there had to be pain the first time. And how could he explain to her that it was her duty to succumb to his needs, to come to his bed and perform the role of his wife? Wouldn't she view that as physical domination, the very thing that she was desperate to escape?

Braden drew a deep, painful breath, once again facing his own feelings honestly. He had been drawn to her from the start, but since that day at her cottage it was more . . . much more.

He wanted her. In every way that a man wants a woman, he wanted her. Underneath him. Surrounding him. Naked and clinging. Calling out his name, coming apart in his arms. The mere image made him harden, made desire pour through him like a sea of fire. And that was only the thought of it.

With a groan Braden leaned back against the cushions of the carriage. Before he asked Kassie to be his wife he had to be quite certain that he could endure the consequences. Because as sure as he was that Kassie cared for him, he was equally certain that she was not yet ready for a real marriage, to be one in body as well as name. So if they were wed, Braden would have to steel himself to something he hadn't faced since his fourteenth birthday: prolonged celibacy. He could not risk hurting Kassie physically by taking her to his bed, nor would he hurt and humiliate her emotionally by seeking relief with other women. Oh, the latter choice was more than acceptable among the male members of the *ton*, but Braden knew without asking that it would be totally *un*acceptable to his principled Kassandra.

In truth, forgoing intimacy with other women presented no major problem to Braden. Of late, he spent every moment in their beds fantasizing about Kassie, imagining that it was she he was holding, loving. No, the real problem would be Kassie herself. Or, rather, controlling himself around her. Would he be able to endure the torture of living with her and yet not making her his?

In the end there was really no choice to be made. The need to protect her, to see her smiling and happy, was more powerful than any reservations Braden might have.

All at once he was quite eager to be home. He sat up straighter, pleased to see that the carriage was nearing the gates of Sherburgh. Knowing that Kassie was there, safe and waiting for him, gave him a sense of joy and a feeling of rightness.

Braden grinned. It seemed not to be his decision to make after all. Fate had determined his future one warm June night, three years past, on a deserted beach.

"Thank you so much, Mr. Graves." Kassie handed the empty water glass back to Charles with a smile.

In the hours since Braden had left she had managed to regain a modicum of self-control. The warm bath had helped, together with the soothing ministrations of a motherly chambermaid named Margaret. Perkins had done his job as well, magically producing a simple gray muslin gown and slippers for her to wear. He had apologized profusely for the gown's modest design, looking stunned when Kassie had thanked him with tears in her eyes.

The truth was, she was unused to so much kindness. Even now, refreshed and seated in Sherburgh's impressive drawing room, Kassie was amazed by the doting attention she was receiving from Charles Graves, who paced back and forth, pausing to stare at her with concern, and Lord Cyril Sheffield, who was seated beside her on the sofa, asking her time and again what she needed and would she prefer to lie down?

And soon Braden would return, making the dream castle complete.

"Are you certain I can't convince you to eat something more?" Charles asked her, placing the glass upon the table beside the settee.

Kassie laughed. "If I eat another morsel, I shall certainly explode," she returned. She did not add that she had never seen so much food in one sitting. Sherburgh's good-natured cook had prepared a huge breakfast, complete with both meat and fish dishes, piles of fluffy eggs, and the most mouth-watering strawberry tarts Kassie had ever tasted. She soon discovered that despite her earlier trauma she was quite famished, and she proceeded to devour an inordinate amount of food while enjoying the pleasurable company of Braden's uncle and Mr. Graves.

"You really should lie down, Miss Grey," Cyril said for the fifth time, studying Kassie's pale, bruised face.

She turned and gave him a warm smile. "I shall . . . in a bit. But I would prefer to wait. . . ." Her eyes went to the empty doorway.

"Braden will be returning soon," Cyril assured her. "But he will be very angry with me for allowing you to overtax yourself."

Kassie gave a merry laugh. "I have hardly overtaxed myself, my lord. In fact, I have done nothing but indulge myself in your kind hospitality."

He frowned, his gaze still fixed on her. "Nevertheless, you look quite peaked. Some sleep might refresh you."

"Goodness! Do I look that dreadful?" Kassie teased with mock offense.

Cyril was instantly contrite. "Of course not. You couldn't possibly look anything but lovely. But you have been through quite an ordeal."

Kassie's eyes dropped beneath his questioning stare. She was still not ready to discuss the events that had brought her to Sherburgh.

Cyril mistook her reaction for disbelief of his words. "Miss Grey," he said, "I assure you that your radiance is in no way marred by your . . . injuries. You have much the look of your mother, and as I recall, she was a rare and incomparable beauty."

Kassie looked up in surprise. "You knew my mother?"

Cyril nodded. "I knew both your parents, actually. Only casually, of course. We traveled in . . . different circles," he added diplomatically.

Kassie flushed. If Lord Cyril knew her father, then he must also know what he had deteriorated into.

"Of course, I haven't seen your father for some time now," Cyril continued, as if reading her mind. "From what I understand, he became rather reclusive once your mother died."

Kassie gave him a grateful look. "He loved my mother

very much," she said softly. "Her death came as quite a blow to him."

"I imagine it did," he sympathized.

Charles headed abruptly across the room and poured himself a drink. "We ought to change the subject," he suggested in a tight voice. "Miss Grey is upset enough as it is."

Cyril looked startled. "Of course, Charles, you are quite right." He stood, smiling. "Come, Miss Grey. Let me summon a maid to take you to your room. You can at least rest until Braden returns."

Just as Kassie opened her mouth to reply the sound of an approaching carriage interrupted her.

"Braden," she murmured eagerly, her gaze going to the door once more.

Moments later the object of her wait walked into the room. His eyes immediately sought Kassie out, and seeing that she was well, he visibly relaxed.

"Are you all right?" Kassie asked anxiously.

Braden blinked, then began to chuckle. "I believe you have things backwards. It is I who should be asking that question of you."

Kassie did not return his smile, for she knew where Braden had been. After a moment he nodded.

"All is well, as I promised you it would be." He glanced at Cyril and Charles. "Would you excuse us, please? I would like to speak with Kassie alone."

Both men looked somewhat surprised but quickly recovered and did as Braden requested, exiting the room.

Braden waited until they had gone before he spoke.

"I saw your father," he began without preamble.

"Yes," she replied in a half whisper, "I guessed as much."

He placed both hands on her narrow shoulders, looking down into her questioning aqua eyes. "You will never have to deal with him again." He shook his head at her panicked expression. "I did not touch him, although I was sorely tempted to kill him on the spot. I simply struck an . . . agreement with him."

"You paid him." She dropped her eyes to the floor, shame washing over her in great waves.

Braden flinched at her sad, humiliated little voice. He caught her chin in his hand and raised her face, forcing her to meet his gaze once more. "Listen to me, Kassie. I would do anything—*anything*—to get you away from that house. I merely negotiated a deal with your father, gave him something he wanted in return for something I want."

Kassie's eyes were bright with unshed tears. "What could he possibly have that you would want?"

"You."

She started at the firmly stated answer, met his unwavering gaze, and found nothing but truth in it.

"Me?" she echoed softly, explosions of pure pleasure erupting in her heart.

Braden nodded. "Yes, my beautiful Kassie, you. I want you to stay here, to make Sherburgh your home, to be with me and . . . what have I said?" He looked stunned as she turned away, her face strained with indecision.

"You want me to stay here . . . with you," she repeated. Swallowing, she knew the time had come to compromise her principles. She would have a home, security . . . and Braden, no matter for how brief a time. It was worth it.

She turned back to him, her head held high.

"I understand what you expect of me." She couldn't help flinching at the implication of her words.

Braden saw the flinch and was more convinced than ever that his earlier decision to leave the marriage unconsummated was the right one. It was obvious that the mere thought of being intimate with him made her cringe. He opened his mouth to reassure her but had no time to respond before Kassie continued.

"I have no experience at being a mistress, nor am I exactly certain what my duties would be," she told him in her usual forthright manner, "but I shall try not to disappoint you."

Braden burst out laughing. "I am delighted to hear that. However, I am not asking you to be my mistress, sweetheart, I am asking you to be my wife."

Kassie's mouth fell open. "Your wife?" she breathed, wondering if she had died and gone to heaven.

Braden smiled and took her hands in his. "If you will have me." He kissed her fingertips. "Miss Grey," he murmured, holding her stunned gaze with his tender one, "would you do me the supreme honor of becoming my wife?"

"Braden, you don't have to." She owed it to him to make one attempt to release him from his commitment.

"I want to."

"So do I."

He gave her a dazzling smile. "I take it that means yes?"

Kassie had no intention of giving fate another chance to change its course.

"Yes, Braden, that means yes."

Chapter 7

Kassie rubbed the soft lace folds between her fingers, staring, transfixed, at her reflection in the full-length mirror. Could that fairy-tale creature in yards of exquisite satin really be she?

Margaret stepped away from her with a proud smile. "There now, m'lady, you are as beautiful a bride as ever there could be," she declared.

In the whirlwind week that had preceded the wedding Margaret had taken Kassie under her wing and eased the bewildered girl into her soon-to-be role as the Duchess of Sherburgh. An instant rapport had sprung up between Kassie and the plump, motherly Margaret, and it was, therefore, an uncontested assumption that Margaret would continue as Kassie's lady's maid after the wedding.

Now the beaming maid pinned the fragrant wreath of blue and white wildflowers onto Kassie's hair, clucking her approval as the vibrant headdress stood out against the gleaming black tresses and enhanced the startlingly vivid color of Kassie's eyes.

"You will make His Grace very proud," Margaret said, squeezing Kassie's shoulders.

Kassie's eyes met Margaret's in the mirror. "Will I?" she asked in a small, hopeful voice, her gaze returning dreamily to her own image. She had to admit that she had never looked better. But then, who wouldn't look ravishing in a gown that had cost a small fortune to make?

She still wasn't quite sure how Braden had managed

everything so quickly. All she knew was that she had been measured, over and over, by countless simpering *modistes* who had displayed a breathtaking array of hues and fabrics for her to choose from. And since Braden had insisted the wedding take place in one week's time, a dozen seamstresses had been hired to complete the new wardrobe selected by the future Duchess of Sherburgh. Not to mention the five dance instructors who had been engaged to teach Kassie every fashionable step, from the quadrille and the Scotch reel to the minuet and, of course, the wonderfully intimate waltz.

The frenzied pace had left Kassie little time for sleep . . . and no room for nightmares.

"Of course! His Grace will be captivated by you!" Margaret answered definitively, brushing an imaginary speck off of the glittering silver and white creation that swirled about Kassie in shimmering layers of lace. The loyal older woman stepped back and nodded her certainty. "It is time," she announced, guiding Kassie toward the door.

Kassie dimpled. "That sounds so ominous," she teased.

"No, m'lady," Margaret pronounced, shaking her head. "The way His Grace looks at you, I have no doubt that you will be happy. Now come—the duke must be anxious."

The duke was as jumpy as a new colt.

"Charles, what the hell is keeping that damned clergyman?" he demanded, pacing inside the chapel's closed doors.

"He is not due here until ten o'clock, Braden." Charles kept his voice low so as not to be overheard by the guests. "It is still early."

With an exaggerated sigh Braden nodded, readjusting his perfectly tied white silk cravat.

Charles observed his friend's uncharacteristic nervousness with quiet concern. "I thought this wedding was what you wanted," he said at last.

Braden met his gaze. "It is. I want what is best for Kassie." *And that means keeping my own wants, my damned lust, in check,* he reminded himself. *Even if it kills me.*

"I see. Well, you are offering her the very best. Yourself."

Charles paused. "That is, of course, if you do intend to offer that to her."

Braden's eyes darkened. "What is that supposed to mean?"

"I think you know the answer to that question better than anyone." Charles felt Braden's growing anger and plunged on despite it. "That lovely young woman is in love with you."

Braden's jaw tightened. This was one topic he was determined to avoid. "What Kassie feels for me is gratitude and affection. Not love."

"You are so certain?" Charles prodded.

"It doesn't matter," Braden snapped, "what you choose to call it. It is infatuation at best. Kassie trusts me, and I have no intention of breaching that trust."

"Meaning?"

"Meaning that I shall never be the one to cause her pain, nor shall I take advantage of her innocence."

Charles's eyes widened in stunned disbelief at the implication of Braden's words. "Are you telling me that—"

"This marriage will be in name only," Braden said in a voice of quiet finality. Charles had no time to respond before the doors of the chapel opened, admitting a grim-faced Cyril Sheffield. "Ah, good morning, Cyril," Braden greeted his uncle. "Have you arrived for one final attempt to make me see the error of my ways?"

"Braden, it is nearly ten o'clock," Cyril began.

"Yes, I can see that the appointed hour is approaching."

Cyril ignored Braden's sarcastic tone. "There is still enough time to reconsider this decision."

"There is nothing to reconsider." Braden's jaw was set, his mouth drawn in a firm, stubborn line. "You have always wanted me to choose a wife, Cyril. Well, I have done just that."

Cyril scowled. "One who is far beneath your station and therefore unworthy of your name."

A furious light blazed in Braden's eyes. "I don't want to hear you refer to Kassie that way again. She is the worthiest human being I have ever known . . . far superior to one of the lying hypocrites you or my parents would have chosen for my wife."

"I am not questioning her character," Cyril replied in a milder tone. "However, caring for a mistreated young woman is one thing. Marrying her is something else. For heaven's sake, Braden, she has no title—"

"I will rectify that problem in"—Braden glanced down at his timepiece—"five minutes. Soon she will be a duchess and will therefore become instantly acceptable to the *beau monde.*"

"Braden—"

"Enough!" Braden spoke through clenched teeth, his voice vibrating with barely suppressed anger. "This is my decision to make, Cyril, not yours. And it has been made." At these words the doors opened, admitting the sober-faced vicar. Braden greeted him cordially, then rechecked his timepiece and frowned. "What could be keeping Kassandra?"

Cyril gave him a cold look. "I shall see what is keeping Miss Grey."

"Cyril." Braden's terse reminder stopped his uncle short. "I warn you. Say nothing to upset her."

Cyril turned back. "I have no intention of upsetting her, Braden. I have spoken my mind, told you that I feel this marriage is a mistake. It has nothing to do with Miss Grey personally; she is a sweet, charming young woman. I merely feel that—"

"Fine," Braden interrupted. "Then you may go ahead and see what is keeping my bride-to-be."

Cyril left, angry but resigned.

"Anxious, aren't you? Considering the fact that your feelings do not enter into this marriage?" Charles's inquiry was filled with poignant humor.

"Don't you start, Charles! I am warning you!" Braden growled. "I have had just about enough of today's inquisition!"

Charles watched thoughtfully as Braden stalked off. Braden's announcement that his marriage to Kassie would remain unconsummated had left Charles reeling. Instinct told him that Braden's feelings for Kassie went a lot deeper than he was willing to admit, even to himself. Perhaps there was hope of erasing the past after all.

Cyril recovered his composure just outside the huge Sherburgh chapel and began his search for Kassie. He didn't have far to go.

Coming toward him, a heart-stopping vision in white, was Kassandra, her face flushed with excitement, Margaret beside her. Cyril stopped, frankly staring as Kassie reached his side.

"Good morning, my lord," she murmured, looking up at him shyly. "Do you think that I will do?"

"I think that Braden is a most fortunate man to have such a lovely bride," he answered after a slight hesitation.

"I am quite nervous," she admitted with her usual honesty.

"You are wavering in your decision to marry my nephew?"

Kassie started at Cyril's sharp—or was it hopeful?—tone. No, it couldn't be; it was just her nerves playing tricks on her. "I am not wavering at all," she hastily assured him. "I just feel so unprepared for what will be expected of me." Her thoughts were on her duties as a hostess, not her duties in the marriage bed.

Cyril studied her face carefully, misinterpreting her meaning. "Braden's decision to marry was rather sudden. Nevertheless, he deserves a wife who is totally committed to him . . . on every level. If you feel unable to fulfill your role—"

"Oh, no!" Kassie burst in, eager to convince Cyril that he was wrong in his doubts. "I assure you that I am entirely devoted to Braden. I shall do everything in my power to be a good wife to him."

Cyril gave her a curt nod. "If you are certain . . ."

"I am."

"Then come." He offered her his arm. "They are awaiting your presence to begin the ceremony."

Her first glimpse of the spectacular chapel took Kassie's breath away. Exquisite stained glass windows and tall vaulted ceilings gave the room an aura of both solemn reverence and limitless power. It was fitting that it be so, for this room would forever mark Kassie's passage from her old life into her new one. Her life as Braden's wife.

She paused on the threshold, and the chapel grew still as all attention turned to the bride. Kassie was only minimally conscious of the guests' openly curious stares. On Cyril's stiff arm she began the ceremonial walk down the aisle, allowing her gaze to move to the front of the chapel, where Braden awaited her approach. He looked magnificent in his formal black dress coat and elegant white waistcoat, emanating the very magnetism and utter masculine strength that always made Kassie heady with awareness. Their gazes locked, and she gave him a brilliant smile, telling him how much this moment meant to her.

Braden saw nothing but Kassandra.

She seemed to fill the room with her presence, her incomparable beauty. Never had a woman looked more enchanting to him than she did at that moment, her face glowing with happiness, her brilliant eyes alive with the light of a thousand jewels. Everything she was, all her strength and her purity of soul, was reflected from within. Braden felt overwhelmed by humbleness and pride . . . and another, stronger, emotion, one that unfurled slowly, making his chest tighten and expand all at once. It was something he neither understood nor wanted to explore more closely, but it was there nonetheless.

Kassie reached his side, and he met her smile with his own. The moment belonged only to them—a moment during which a rare and special communication passed between them, one that required no words nor explanation.

Cyril stepped away, relinquishing Kassie to her future.

It was with a sense of peace that she and Braden turned to pledge themselves to each other. For they both knew that whatever the reasons, this was how it was destined to be.

Kassie watched with awe as Braden slid the symbolic ring onto her finger. The heavy gold band felt cool against her skin, and prisms of light sparkled from the sapphires and emeralds that circled the meticulously crafted ring.

"As rare as the blues and greens of your eyes," he murmured softly, lowering his head to kiss her.

Kassie's heart expanded with joy. With the exchange of a few words and the brush of Braden's lips against hers, she belonged to him. Now and forever. The reality was intoxicating.

And then there were congratulations to receive, followed by a traditional wedding breakfast, served in one of Sherburgh's cozier ballrooms, in order that the guests might mingle. Braden's chef outdid himself with mouth-watering salmon soufflé, succulent roast beef, glazed ham, and more kinds of fresh fruits and rich desserts than the tables could hold. The occasion marked Kassie's first opportunity to acquaint herself with her new social circle, for Braden had been very careful to keep her away from the prying eyes of the *ton* prior to the wedding.

It was an experience Kassie would never forget.

Braden had purposely arranged for the guest list to be small, in an attempt to lead Kassie gently and gradually into her new role. But to Kassie, who was unaccustomed to such elaborate gatherings, the pale green gilded room seemed to brim over with worldly, exquisitely clothed women and commanding, influential men.

"So you are Braden's new bride," said an elderly man whose distinguished appearance was belied by the hungry gleam in his eye.

Unsure of Braden's whereabouts, Kassie steeled herself for her first, and hopefully successful, performance as the Duchess of Sherburgh.

With a dazzling smile she replied, "Why, yes, I am. But you have me at a disadvantage, my lord, for we have not as yet been properly introduced."

The hot, ravenous eyes raked her slender figure, and Kassie could swear that the old goat licked his chops before he answered. "Forgive me, my dear," he said at last, lifting her hand to his jowls in a grand gesture. "I am George Marshall, the Earl of Lockersham." He brushed his wet lips across her hand, where they lingered for a scant moment. Kassie had to work hard to refrain from openly shuddering at the contact.

"A pleasure, Lord Lockersham," she replied, tugging her

hand away from him. Her smile never faltered. "And which lovely guest is Lady Lockersham?"

He scowled. "The countess is at home . . . ill."

Kassie's huge aqua eyes filled with genuine compassion. "How dreadful! Nothing serious, I hope?"

His scowl deepened. "Just another attack of the vapors." He looked around, then lowered his voice conspiratorially. "She is getting on in years, you know."

Kassie fought the laughter that bubbled in her chest. "Oh, I understand."

The earl brightened. "It does permit me a great deal of freedom, however." He took a step closer. "Freedom to indulge in . . . whatever I wish."

"Lord Lockersham, really!" Kassie never replied to the ludicrous, lecherous proposal she had just received, for just then an elderly woman with snow-white hair and a huge tiara scurried up to them. "Must you monopolize all of the young woman's time? We would all like to get to know her better." She smiled at Kassie, but the smile was frosty. In fact, with her sharp little teeth, her long, pointy nose, and her small beady eyes, she much resembled a lethal barracuda.

Kassie swallowed, ready to protect herself.

"I am Agatha Wurlington, the Dowager Duchess of Cromsmire," she announced, as if the title equalled that of King George himself.

"It is a pleasure, Your Grace," Kassie answered, wondering wildly where Braden had gone.

"Hm-m-m," was the reply as the dowager duchess sized up the new bride's appearance with undisguised censure. "It is easy to see what attracted Braden to you." It sounded more a criticism than a compliment, and Kassie closed her cold fingers around the solid weight of her wedding band, taking comfort in its presence.

"Many things attracted me to my wife . . . her incomparable beauty was just one of them." Magically Braden appeared and handed Kassie a glass of punch. "I am sorry, darling," he said smoothly, "to have been gone so long. I was waylaid on a business matter."

Kassie looked up at him gratefully. "And has it been resolved?" she asked sweetly, knowing that all eyes and ears were upon them.

Braden grinned, enjoying the performance. "No, but it will wait until later. For now"—he winked at her—"I want to be with my new bride." With that he turned to Agatha Wurlington. "Have the two of you been introduced?"

The elderly woman nodded. "Yes, your . . . duchess and I were just becoming acquainted."

Braden gave her a practiced smile. "I must ask that you continue your chat another time. There are so many people I want Kassie to meet. You understand." He didn't wait to see if the dowager understood or not but merely steered Kassie deeper into the room. He heard her sigh of relief and chuckled quietly. "That bad?"

"Worse," she admitted.

"You're doing beautifully. I'm half convinced that it was you and not I who was born to this world."

"Don't leave me," she whispered.

He looked down at her, his eyes growing soft and tender. "I won't, sweetheart. You can count on that."

Kassie's hand was kissed more times that morning than in all her eighteen years combined. But each moment that passed without mishap she relaxed a bit more. As did Braden. Just the same, he stayed by her side as much as possible, to ward off any unexpected comments or probing questions. And as if they sensed their host's unspoken warning, the guests were on their best behavior, the ladies flattering and friendly, the gentlemen charming and entertaining. In fact, so absorbed were the guests in their merriment that no one noticed the ruckus occurring just outside Sherburgh's front doors. No one but Charles Graves.

"Let me pass! That's m'daughter getting married in there!" Robert Grey staggered forward in an attempt to push by one of the equally stubborn footmen who guarded the entranceway.

"No, sir. I have my orders," the servant returned, blocking Grey's path.

"Orders? From whom?"

"From His Grace. No one is permitted inside the house without an invitation."

Robert frowned. "I must've misplaced mine."

The burly footman scowled at the disheveled man before him. "I'm sorry, sir, but His Grace was firm in his instructions."

"But I'm the bride's father!" Robert roared, shoving past. He took two unsteady steps into the room and collided with an immovable object. Blinking to clear his vision, he saw that the obstacle was, in fact, a man's chest. He backed off.

"I would suggest you leave at once, Mr. Grey," Charles said with quiet authority, "before Braden discovers your presence."

Robert shook his head, trying to focus. "Who're you? Do we know each other?"

A look of revulsion and contempt swept over Charles's face. Grey didn't even recognize him.

"We met at the race at York," he replied shortly.

Robert narrowed his eyes. "Oh, that's right! You're a friend of the duke's."

Charles nodded. "Yes, I'm a friend of Braden's. Now I must insist you leave Sherburgh. Immediately."

"I just want t'see m'daughter," Robert insisted.

Charles had had enough. He took a menacing step forward, his anger overcoming his good manners. "Get out, Grey. Now. Or I will throw you out myself."

Robert looked stunned. "But—"

"Now!"

For an instant Robert stared at Charles, as if deciding how serious he might be. The murderous look in Charles's eyes, along with his continued threatening advance, convinced Robert that to remain there would be foolhardy.

Slowly he backed away, his mouth set in angry defeat. "Very well. I'm going. For now."

He walked unsteadily toward the door, muttering a stream of obscenities under his breath. After three unsuccessful attempts he turned the door handle and staggered out.

Charles stared after him, watching until Robert's broken-down carriage had disappeared from view. There was no reason to alert Braden and to upset Kassie. For now, the parasite was gone.

Charles clenched his fists at his sides. In his heart he knew that it was far from over. Grey would be back. And that was all right, for he and Robert Grey still had much unfinished business to settle between them.

"Margaret, what time is it?"

Margaret grinned, smoothing back the silk sheets on Kassie's bed.

"It is near midnight, Your Grace."

Kassie sighed, chewing on her lip. "Where on earth could Braden be?" she wondered aloud.

Margaret chuckled. "I don't think you need to worry that His Grace will be missing his wedding night."

Kassie blushed. "I didn't mean that . . . not exactly, anyway. I just thought he'd be home by now. He's been gone since late this afternoon. How long could his business have taken?"

Margaret studied the beautiful, glowing young woman who was now the Duchess of Sherburgh. With her black hair flowing about her shoulders and the ivory satin nightgown clinging to her slender curves, she would have no trouble keeping His Grace home and quite happy at night. The thought made Margaret frown.

"Your Grace . . ." She wet her lips, glancing away from Kassie's questioning look.

"Yes, Margaret?"

"Do you know . . . are you aware of what to expect tonight?" the older woman managed.

Kassie gave her an assuring smile. "I have a good idea of what to expect."

It wasn't true. The only thing Kassie was certain of was that *it* involved sharing her bed with Braden, and that a baby could result from *it*. Neither prospect alarmed her. Having Braden's arms around her would be heavenly, and the thought of bearing his child was thrilling. So in whatever way the two things were accomplished, all would be well. Braden would never hurt her.

Margaret looked relieved. She had just opened her mouth to reply when the door connecting Braden's and Kassie's bedchambers swung open. Kassie turned in time to see her new husband enter the room clad in a black silk dressing gown. His surprised gaze went from Kassie to Margaret and back to Kassie again.

"I apologize, Kassie," he said after clearing his throat. "I thought you would already be abed."

With that, Margaret practically flew from the room, calling her good-nights over her plump shoulder.

Braden looked startled, and Kassie giggled, coming toward him.

"I think she needs some time to adjust to her new role . . . just as I do," Kassie told him.

Braden swallowed deeply, her words reminding him of his decision. He looked down at her, trying not to see how desirable she looked, trying to ignore the impact her luscious curves, so clearly evident through the thin silk of her gown, had on his starving body.

"Kassie," he began, keeping his arms firmly at his sides.

"I was beginning to worry about you," she said softly, seeing the tension in his face and wondering at its cause.

"I had business to see to." *And I didn't trust myself to be alone with you,* he admitted to himself. "I had thought you would be asleep by now. I didn't mean to disturb you."

Kassie frowned. "I wouldn't go to sleep without seeing you first," she responded, a trifle unsure. Disturb her? Whatever she had expected, it hadn't been this.

Braden nodded. "Are you all right? I know that it has been quite a day for you."

She ran her tongue unconsciously over her lower lip, and Braden's loins tightened so quickly and painfully that he nearly groaned aloud. Her scent, sweet and fresh, drifted up to tantalize his nostrils.

"I'm fine," Kassie was answering, oblivious to his torment. "Only a bit tired." She looked hopefully up at him.

Braden looked away, desperately trying to focus on anything but the lush beauty of the woman before him . . . a woman who was now his wife.

"Then I won't keep you awake any longer," he said at last. Turning, he walked toward the connecting door.

"Braden?"

He stopped. "What is it?" He hadn't meant to sound so sharp, but his body was at its breaking point. Slowly he turned back to face her.

Kassie was staring down at the brilliant ring now fitted snugly on her left hand. "I had thought you would stay. That is, I assumed you would want to . . . you would expect to . . ." Her voice trailed off in uncertain embarrassment.

"No."

Her head went up in shock. "No?" she echoed.

Braden shook his head adamantly. "No." He walked back to where she stood. "Kassie, that is not the reason I married you. I married you to make you feel safe . . . to make you feel protected. Not to satisfy my . . . not to hurt your . . . not for *that,*" he finished at last.

"Do you mean you won't . . . ." She still hadn't accepted what he was telling her.

Mistaking her surprise for relief, Braden gave her a weak smile. "No, sweetheart, I won't." He lifted her hand and kissed it. "I would never do anything to frighten or hurt you. Never."

He released her hand and turned away, convinced that he had done the right thing.

"Good night, Kassie." The door closed behind him.

It was a sleepless night.

Braden lay awake, his body burning with hunger, assuring himself again and again that he had done what was right, what would make Kassie happy.

Kassie lay awake, crying as if her heart would break.

Chapter 8

~✦~

The dining room was deserted when Kassie finally made her way downstairs the next morning. Her eyes burned from the tears she had shed and from lack of sleep. She felt bewildered and drained, and utterly incapable of handling even the simplest of conversations.

It was well past eleven o'clock, and Sherburgh reverberated with a quiet hum as the servants scurried about, seeing to their duties. Kassie watched them as they dusted and polished, performing the very chores she herself had been responsible for prior to her arrival at Sherburgh. And now she was mistress of this enormous house . . . a duchess. It was ironic, but she actually found herself envying the servants' sense of purpose. Her new title and position seemed overwhelming to her this morning. In truth, she lacked the energy even to begin tackling the challenge.

On the other hand, at least it would give her something to focus on, something to divert her from her confusion about Braden.

Idly Kassie strolled into the sun-drenched drawing room, lost in thought. She had never deluded herself into thinking that Braden loved her . . . not yet. But her every instinct had told her that he was drawn to her, not only spiritually, but as a man is drawn to a woman.

Last night had told her otherwise.

Sighing, she wrapped her arms about herself, stroking the soft silk of her apple-green garden dress. As was her way, she withdrew deep into herself, seeking answers that were beyond her reach. She had neither the experience nor the knowledge of men to make any sense of Braden's strange behavior. Why was he so reluctant to take what was rightfully his, what she would gladly give him?

She chewed her lip thoughtfully. There was a reason, of that she was certain; one that lay just beneath the surface, yet within territories that were unfamiliar to and untraveled by Kassie. Could she just ask Braden outright? No, that might be considered terribly bold and unladylike in a *ton* marriage. She had no way of knowing.

Remembering the few moments she and Braden had shared alone in her room last night—the terseness of his words, the taut set of his jaw—Kassie knew that something had to be done. Instead of feeling closer to Braden than ever before, she felt further apart from him than she had when they existed in two different homes, two separate worlds. Thus far, the only thing that marriage had succeeded in doing was to instill a new tension in the relationship, one that had never existed in the past.

"You look very far away."

Startled, Kassie spun around to find Cyril Sheffield leaning against the open doorway, regarding her with an unreadable expression. Automatically Kassie tensed, for she recalled Cyril's reproving manner at the wedding, and she knew that Braden's uncle still frowned upon her marriage to Braden.

"I'm sorry. I see that I've frightened you." Cyril strolled over, a practiced smile of questionable sincerity on his face.

"No . . . you didn't frighten me, my lord. I just did not hear you come in."

He took in her youthful beauty and defensive stance and gave a dry chuckle. "You have assumed your role quite nicely." He paused. "I am a bit uncertain as to how I should address you. Quite obviously, Miss Grey will no longer do. Is Your Grace more to your liking?"

Kassie flinched, stung by his sarcasm. Until yesterday Braden's uncle had treated her with cordial aloofness. Now he appeared almost hostile. Was she *that* unsuitable for her new role?

"My name is Kassandra, my lord. You are welcome to use

it." Kassie kept her head high, refusing to relinquish her pride before this man.

Cyril inclined his head slightly. "It is a lovely name. Very well, Kassandra. And please cease addressing me as 'my lord.' My given name is Cyril. As we are now family, it is quite proper for you to use it."

"Very well . . . Cyril," Kassie managed, with only the slightest of hesitations.

"I trust you slept well?" His gaze flickered over her, and Kassie had the feeling that she was being assessed.

"Very well, my l . . . Cyril."

"Braden was out riding early this morning."

Kassie turned away. "Really? And is that unusual for him?"

Cyril frowned at Kassie's back. "No, not under normal circumstances. But I had thought that today he would be spending the morning with his new bride."

Kassie felt hot color stain her cheeks. Was everyone going to be privy to her humiliation?

"I suppose he chose to let me rest," she responded without turning around.

"Evidently," Cyril agreed in a taut voice. "After all, it was quite an . . . eventful day for you."

Kassie nodded, too absorbed in her thoughts to hear the pointed tone of his question. "Yes, it was an eventful day," she agreed softly. She stared at the floor, a glimmer of hope dawning in her heart.

Could that be the reason behind Braden's odd behavior? Could it be something as simple as concern for her exhaustion that had prompted his curt withdrawal from her room and his decision to keep his distance, both last night and this morning?

Willing it to be so, she reasoned aloud, "Braden was no doubt being considerate of my feelings. Although I *would* have enjoyed riding with him."

Cyril swallowed. "I'm sure Braden felt you wouldn't be up to riding this morning."

The underlying meaning of Cyril's words was lost to Kassie. With great relief she turned back to face him. "Do you really think that could be it?" she asked eagerly. She didn't wait for a reply but continued with her thought, her brow furrowed in confusion. "But why wouldn't I be up to riding?"

Cyril blinked at the naïveté of the question and the innocent look on Kassie's beautiful face. He was speechless.

Oblivious to his shock, Kassie continued, "Yesterday's excitement didn't fatigue me *that* much! Maybe he thought I would be a hindrance because of my inexperience in the saddle."

Cyril continued to stare at her. Slowly the implication of her words sank in, and he shook his head in disbelief. Braden's new wife had *no* idea of what he meant. And *that* could only signify one thing.

The realization was staggering.

"You don't think that could be it?"

Kassie's question touched the periphery of Cyril's mind, breaking into his wildly careening thoughts.

"Pardon me?" He was totally at sea.

"You shook your head," Kassie pointed out. "Does that mean that you do not believe Braden would be troubled by my inexperience?"

"Your . . . inexperience?"

Kassie looked at him with utter exasperation. "Yes, my inexperience. After all, he knows that I have spent little time on horseback and therefore cannot ride."

"Oh . . . yes . . . riding." Cyril gathered his thoughts quickly, disgusted that he sounded like a blathering fool. "No, my dear, I am sure that Braden would not be deterred by your inexperience. In fact, I believe he finds you totally refreshing. As do I."

Kassie was startled by Cyril's sudden turnabout in attitude. "Why . . . thank you." She gave him an uncertain smile.

"You are most welcome. But no thanks are necessary, for I speak the truth. You *are* refreshing." He paused, studying her. He had to be sure. "It is difficult to believe you are very much a married woman. There is an innocence about you that contradicts that fact."

He waited. Not even the hint of a blush rose upon Kassie's ivory skin, and no spark of understanding flickered in her aqua eyes. Instead she laughed aloud, twin dimples showing in her cheeks.

"A ceremony does not alter a person so radically, my lord. Nor does a new name. I am as I have always been."

"Yes. I can see that you are." Cyril hid his vast relief with the greatest of difficulty. He was more than convinced. Nothing had happened. There was still time to rectify things, to undo a union that should never have occurred.

With that knowledge Cyril flashed Kassie a conciliatory smile and offered her his arm. "Come, Kassandra. I believe that I have been unforgivably rude to you this morning. I can only attribute it to a lack of fresh air. Let me make amends to you and improve my mood at the same time. We shall stroll through the gardens, and I'll show you the breathtaking grounds of Sherburgh. After all, this is your new home. And I promise that you won't be disappointed."

Kassie accepted both Cyril's apology and his arm with her customary grace and guileless charm. "I would be delighted to learn my way about and to see more of Sherburgh. Thank you, Cyril." This time she did not falter upon speaking his name.

Cyril beamed his approval and led Kassie out into the sunlit gardens.

Kassie's heart felt lighter than it had in days, alive with the hope that her new friendship with Cyril was a good sign for the future. Perhaps things would change . . . for the better.

The sun was directly overhead, signifying midafternoon, but the Grey house was cast in shadows. The drapes were tightly drawn to keep out the bright light, and a musty smell accosted Robert Grey's nose as he staggered into the hallway, slamming the entranceway door behind him.

"James!" he bellowed, blinking to accustom himself to the darkness. "James Gelding! Where the hell are you?"

Silence.

Muttering under his breath at the incompetence of hired help, Robert headed toward his library . . . and his brandy. He entered the semidark haven gratefully, kicking the door shut. It was just as well that James was not about. The only assistance Robert needed was awaiting him in a crystal decanter.

He poured the drink with hands that shook so badly, much of the potent liquid was lost upon the rug. Robert hardly noticed. Greedily he gulped down the brandy in three swallows, then poured another. This one he took with him to the large oak desk, for his head was spinning too badly for him to remain standing. He flung himself into the heavy chair and placed the full glass before him.

"You are by far the most wretched creature I have ever seen."

The clipped, angry voice brought Robert up with a start. "Who is it?" he demanded, blinking.

"Whom did you expect?" was the venomous response.

Robert swallowed, unnerved despite his inebriated state. "What d'you want?" He attempted unsuccessfully to rise.

The tall man came to his feet in one abrupt motion. "You know what I want, Grey."

Robert's watery eyes dilated slightly as he made out the form of the angry gentleman before him. "It's too late. She's already wed t'another."

His visitor's eyes flashed. "Do you think I don't know that, Grey?" His fists clenched. "We had an agreement, you son of a—"

"James!" Robert called frantically, pulling himself to his feet by holding onto the edge of the desk.

"I sent your man away. We are quite alone," came the taunting reply.

"You had no right—"

"*I* had no right?" The man leaned across the desk and grabbed Robert by the shirtfront. "*You* had no right, Grey. You reneged on our agreement, married your daughter off to another. What did he do, Grey? Offer you more than I did?"

"He *gave* me one hundred thousand pounds!" Robert burst out, his drunken bravado overcoming his fear and making his tongue loose. "And that's only the beginning! I intend t'be well compensated, not only today, but for the rest of my life!"

The enraged visitor hesitated. "Meaning?"

"Meaning that Braden Sheffield has more money than any other man I know, including you. Money that now belongs t'my beautiful Kassandra as well. And I plan t'enjoy my share of that wealth . . . beginning today!"

The other man swore and let go of Robert's shirt abruptly. "And you actually believe that Braden Sheffield will allow this?"

Robert sensed his advantage and smiled smugly. "He doesn't have t'allow it. He doesn't even have t'know about it. I will deal with Kassandra alone, away from her new husband. I couldn't get in t'see her yesterday at the wedding, but I'll do so today." He swayed slightly on his feet, then regained his balance. Reaching into his desk drawer, he withdrew a stack of bank notes and thrust them at his adversary. "So you can just take your money and get out, my affluent *friend,*" he said, sarcasm dripping from his words. "No matter what you do t'me, it cannot change what has happened."

Silently the other man grappled with his emotions, considering the best way to get what he wanted. At length he made a decision.

"This is not over between us, Grey," he vowed, his voice deadly calm. "You will pay for your betrayal. Not here, not today. But you will pay. *That* I promise you."

In a savage emphasis of his words he seized the glass from the desk and hurled it against the wall, where it shattered into hundreds of fragments, splattering brandy across the dingy, dark paneling. The echo of the crash was still reverberating through the room when the door slammed shut behind him.

Alone, Robert stared at the wall, watching droplets of dark liquid trickle down to the floor. He shuddered, sickened by the image it conveyed.

An image of blood.

Kassie leaned against the towering oak, smiling wistfully as Percy trotted by, looking adoringly up at his father beside him. Since their arrival at Sherburgh, when Percy was reunited with Hunter, Kassie had slowly reconciled herself to the fact that she was no longer the sole love of her dog's life. While his loyalty to her had not wavered, he was equally attached to the silky-haired, lean beagle that was his sire.

It was as it should be.

Kassie more than understood her pet's need to belong, to be loved and cared for by one of his own. It was a need she felt as well. Unfortunately, her need had yet to be satisfied.

She stared out over the vast acres of land that rolled endlessly before her. Sherburgh . . . a veritable castle that but a fortnight ago had existed only in her dreams.

Now . . . her new home.

For the remainder of the morning Cyril had been as charming as he had earlier been aloof. Together they had strolled through Sherburgh's exquisitely sculptured gardens and perfectly manicured lawns. He had pointed out the enormous stables where Braden's prize Thoroughbreds were kept, and Kassie had memorized every glorious detail she was shown.

Kassie welcomed Cyril's friendship with all the eagerness of a young and innocent child. To her, acceptance by Cyril made her that much more a part of Braden's life . . . of *her* life.

Kassie sighed. Her new life, her new home, her new title. All here.

Except her new husband.

Braden had remained conspicuously absent all day long. A few hours ago, when Kassie had forfeited her pride and inquired as to his whereabouts, she had been advised by Perkins that His Grace had gone to conduct business at the home of William Devon, the Duke of Lamsborough.

Kassie had no idea who the Duke of Lamsborough was, but judging from Perkins's respectful tone, he was someone of great importance.

Now dusk began to overtake day, extinguishing both the sun's light and the hope in Kassie's heart. Apparently Braden had no intention of coming home and no desire to be with her. The realization created a physical pain in Kassie's chest. Struggling to regain her earlier lightheartedness, she turned back toward the house.

"So here you are, daughter. I had hoped to find you about."

Kassie spun about in surprise, recoiling instinctively from the disheveled man before her. "Father? What are you doing here?"

He laughed, an unpleasant sound. "What is this? Do I need a reason to visit my own daughter?"

Kassie didn't reply but searched his face with experienced eyes, sizing up his degree of drunkenness. He appeared to be unusually sober.

Robert took a step toward her, and Kassie blanched with fear. Unfortunately, the grounds were deserted, and there was no assistance in sight. Quickly she glanced behind her, judging the distance between herself and the doors to Sherburgh. The great manor loomed several hundred feet away, close enough for her to attempt.

Seeing her intention, Robert hurriedly changed his tactics. "Please do not hurry off, Kassandra. I want only to apologize and to make amends."

Kassie paused. The second person today who wanted to make amends. But she was not so naïve as to believe in her father. She knew him too well.

"I do not want your apology, Father. Please just go." She took a hesitant step backward.

"I am still your father, Kassandra," Robert reminded her tersely.

"I have a husband now, Father." She continued to back away. "I do not need anything from you."

"Maybe *I* need something from *you.*"

Kassie halted in her tracks. "What could you possibly need from me?"

Robert gave her an exasperated look. "Come now, my dear. You have married a very wealthy man. I have seen to that."

Kassie ignored the blatant insinuation. "And I am quite certain you have been amply compensated for your trouble, Father."

Robert knew by her words that Kassie had no idea of the enormous sum Braden had paid him. All for the better.

"The duke did settle some of my debts," he said smoothly. "Unfortunately, there are many others as yet unsettled. I had hoped—"

"You are asking me for more money?" Kassie gasped.

"Merely a token sum."

"You must think me a total fool, Father." Kassie was on the verge of tears. "Whatever Braden paid you exceeded the seventy thousand pounds that my *other* suitor offered, else you would never have agreed to alter your arrangements." She brushed her hand across her eyes in a defiant gesture. She would *not* cry. "Now please leave Sherburgh at once, before my husband finds you here and removes you himself."

Robert's control snapped. "Why, you ungrateful little . . ."

He lunged for her, but not fast enough. Having expected just such an onslaught, Kassie was already in motion, racing toward the house with an unnatural speed born of her fear. She dared not look behind her but continued to run, her breath coming in hard gasps, until she reached the front doors. Wildly she flung them open and hurled herself inside, slamming them closed behind her.

For long moments she stood, her heart beating frantically, staring unseeing at the empty marble hallway. Sanity returned slowly as, with practiced control, Kassie took deep, calming breaths, repeating aloud the words that had accompanied this ritual for as many years as she could remember.

"You're safe, Kassie. You're safe."

Chapter 9

Y ou are quite safe, Braden."

Charles closed the stable door and shot Braden a knowing look. "It is close to midnight, and the house appears to be in total darkness. You have exhausted every imaginable excuse to stay away. Wouldn't you say it is time for you to go home?"

Braden scowled, wishing for once that his friend was not so astute. "I did not fabricate my business meeting with William Devon, Charles. It was scheduled long before I knew I was to be married this week. It was necessary that I attend."

Charles raised a disbelieving brow. "Really? And was it also necessary for you to personally supervise the evening procedure at the stables?"

"Star was limping a bit after our ride. I merely wanted to check on him."

"Was he? I hadn't noticed." Charles's eyes twinkled, although he kept his expression impassive. "Neither had your groom, Dobson, who cooled him down for me."

Braden's jaw was set stubbornly. "Apparently it wasn't serious. Still, I wanted to see for myself that he was well. He is often too much of a handful even for Dobson." The knowing look on Charles's face infuriated him. Turning on his heel, he strode off toward the house.

Charles fell into step beside him. "You will never be able to live this way, Braden," he said quietly, all traces of humor having vanished. "It is unnatural and unhealthy for you."

"For *me*, perhaps." Braden ceased to pretend that he did not understand Charles's words. "But what about Kassie?" He shook his head sharply. "No, Charles, I must stick to my resolve."

"And go mad in the process."

Braden came to a grinding halt. "What would you have me do? Frighten her? Hurt her?"

"No, of course not."

"Then what? Go to another woman? I could never do that to Kassie. She understands nothing of a man's . . . needs. It would hurt her terribly if she thought I had taken a mistress. Don't you see? I'm caught in an impossible situation from which there is no escape. Kassie is safe now, from her father's brutality and from the cruelty of her former life. The irony of it is that in giving Kassie her salvation I have created my own hell." He raked his fingers through his hair. "But if abstinence is the price of Kassie's happiness, it is a price I must pay." Frustrated and troubled, he resumed walking, taking long, angry strides toward his home, his room . . . and his empty bed.

"For how long?"

The softly spoken question brought Braden to another rapid halt. Charles had asked the very question that had plagued Braden day and night, one that he had been pushing from his mind. How long could he continue this way, wanting Kassie, painfully aware that she was his wife, but not joining his body to hers? Last night had been hell, knowing that legally, rightfully, she belonged to him; that he had only to go to her, to demand his rights, and he could appease the excruciating ache in his loins.

To be replaced by a sharper, more severe pain.

For if he hurt her he would never forgive himself. Never.

Braden inhaled sharply, meeting Charles's concerned gaze with his own tormented one.

"I have no answer for you, Charles," he answered truthfully. "I do not allow myself to ponder that question. I can only take each day as it comes."

Charles nodded sympathetically. "Time will show you the right path . . . for you and your wife."

"Perhaps." Braden glanced toward the house, his eyes

automatically going to the windows of Kassie's bedchamber. They were dark. Kassie was asleep.

With a mixture of relief and acute disappointment Braden walked up the front stairs, then turned, giving Charles a rueful smile. "Thank you for your advice . . . and your company. It is late. Go to bed."

Charles studied him with an unreadable expression. "Everything will be made right, Braden," he stated at last. Without elaborating he walked past Braden and into the house. "Good night."

"Good night, Charles." Like a condemned man Braden headed for his bedchamber.

Once there he dismissed his valet, Harding, and undressed in the dark, tossing his clothing carelessly to the floor. Naked, he slid beneath the bedcovers and folded his arms behind his head. With a will of its own his gaze moved to the closed doorway that led to Kassie's room. He could imagine her in bed with but a thin layer of silk to shield her from his eyes . . . his hands . . . his mouth.

Groaning, Braden felt his body react, tightening in unappeased hunger.

Another sleepless night stretched before him.

The nightmare returned.

In her bed and in her dream Kassie sobbed softly, looking for a place to hide. There was none.

The darkness converged upon her, suffocating her with its intensity. The cold seeped into her trembling limbs, causing her hands to grow numb and her teeth to chatter.

She had to get away.

Run. She had to run.

But he was behind her.

No matter how hard she tried she could not elude him. She ran faster and faster, opening her mouth to call out.

No sound emerged. Only the echo of her panting breaths, her racing feet. And the feeling of his presence behind her.

And then he was before her, and there was no escape. She heard the scream, yet it did not come from her, but from elsewhere. He loomed up, dark and forbidding. He was going to kill her.

She was falling now . . . endlessly hurtling toward her own death.

Oh, God, I don't want to die. Not now. Please. Help me. Someone . . . help me . . .

Braden was out of his bed and across the room before the scream subsided. He flung open the connecting doors and took Kassie's room in three strides. Reaching her bedside, he found her sitting upright, eyes wide with terror.

"Kassie!" He was beside her, pulling her to him. "What is it? Are you hurt?"

She didn't answer, merely continued to stare blankly out into space, little pained whimpers emerging from her throat. At his touch she started, then began to struggle, hysterically begging, "No, please . . . no," tears streaming down her cheeks.

"Kassie? It's me . . . Braden." Braden's voice trailed off as he realized that his wife could not hear him. She was asleep. "Kassie . . . Kassie!" He nudged her gently. His only response was another terrified sob and more frantic attempts to free herself.

Her lack of response to his presence made Braden's own fear escalate. Firmly he gripped her shoulders and shook her hard.

"Kassie . . . wake up, love, wake up! It's all right, I'm here. It's all right!"

A look of recognition replaced her faraway look of undisguised horror.

"Braden?" she whispered, her voice weak, her face wet with tears.

"Yes, sweetheart, it's me." Relieved, Braden drew her head gently to his shoulder. "Sh-h-h, don't be afraid. It was only a bad dream." Softly he stroked her disheveled hair, which tumbled around her shoulders like a shining black waterfall. He frowned, feeling her heart's violent pounding, the icy film of perspiration that covered her clammy skin. "Kassie?"

She clutched wildly at his arms when he started to move away. "Please, Braden, don't go," she pleaded. "Don't leave me. Please."

He felt the now-familiar fierce protectiveness swell inside him. "I won't. I'm not going anywhere, love. I'm right here." He kissed the top of her head tenderly, pressing her more firmly against the hard wall of his bare, hair-roughened chest, whispering calming words.

Gratefully she clung to him, willing the cold dread that always followed her nightmare to fade. She wanted to be absorbed into the haven of Braden's strong body, to forget everything else existed. If he let go of her, she would die.

As if sensing the urgency of her need, Braden remained silent, asking no questions. He closed his eyes, feeling the drumming of her heart begin to slow, the tremors that shook her delicate frame begin to subside. He continued to stroke her back, the damp silk of her night rail, murmuring over and over that he wouldn't leave her, that all would be well.

A timeless time elapsed.

At last Kassie took a deep breath and drew back. Much as she would like to, she could not bury herself in his strength forever.

"Thank you," she said, looking up into his worried face. "I'm fine now."

He brushed his thumb across her determined little chin. "Are you sure?"

She nodded. "Yes." She braced herself for the inevitable questions.

Braden studied her face. "This has happened before, hasn't it?"

Kassie was startled. She had expected his curiosity, but not his perception. Still, she should have known. This was Braden, after all.

"Yes." She couldn't—wouldn't—lie to him.

"Do you want to tell me about it?"

"Yes. But not now. Please." She knotted the sheet in tight fists of frustration. "I thought it was finally over. I haven't had the dream since I came to Sherburgh." She closed her eyes, her long lashes wet, silken fans upon her face.

Braden felt her pain. He was unsurprised by the events of the evening, for they verified his suspicions that Kassie's scars ran deeper than even he could guess.

He cupped her face and kissed her forehead gently.

"We'll talk about it later, when you're ready," he murmured.

"Thank you," she whispered. Her eyes opened, and she stared at his broad, tanned shoulder, now drenched with her tears. He was naked. She knew this even though she could not see all of him clearly in the darkness. Strangely, his nudity did not frighten her, only sent unfamiliar tingles through her body. Slowly, experimentally, she ran her fingers across his powerful biceps to his shoulder.

"I'm sorry; I've gotten you all wet."

The night's tension having heightened his senses, Braden's whole body leapt to life as her cool fingers trailed a path up and down the curve of his upper arm, his neck.

He swallowed deeply, reminding himself that she was too innocent to understand the effect she was having on him.

"I was happy to put my shoulder to such good use," he replied in a hoarse, shattered tone he had meant to be teasing.

"You were wonderful."

Did she *really* have *no* idea what she was doing to him? He felt her tentatively caress the nape of his neck, lightly graze the strands of hair that lay against it. Unconsciously he moved his head from side to side, seeking more of the sensual contact.

Kassie could feel something building between them, something she had sensed before, whenever they touched. It was a giddy, escalating sensation that began in her stomach and spread rapidly throughout her body, her very core. It was wondrous . . . and she wanted more.

Drawing back, Kassie looked up into his handsome face with expressive, searching eyes that reflected awe and awareness and a newly awakened sensuality that made Braden shudder with need.

"Better?" He forced back his rampant desire, brushing tendrils of damp hair off of her forehead. He ran his knuckles over her flushed face and high cheekbones.

"Yes." She shifted restlessly, her fingers still stroking his warm, smooth skin.

"Kassie . . ." Warning bells sounded in Braden's mind,

but he no longer heeded them. Lowering his head, he brushed her parted lips with his. He paused, savoring her warm breath against his mouth. Valiantly he struggled for control . . . and lost.

With a helpless groan he pulled her to him, pressing her against his chest, and covered her mouth with his.

He had dreamed of holding her, kissing her, but no dream had ever tasted this sweet.

Her lips were soft and warm and willing, and he felt her wrap her arms around his neck and return his kiss with an eagerness that made live flames erupt inside him. He indulged himself hungrily, desperately, molding her mouth and her body to his. The kiss deepened as naturally as twilight merges into night, and Kassie opened her mouth to Braden's seeking tongue.

Their first joining was a poignant mixture of tenderness and longing, emotion and desire coupling in an explosion of the senses that left them both gasping. Braden simply could not get his fill of her, drinking in her fragrance until he was immersed in her beauty, delving into the heaven of her mouth again and again, caressing her tongue, then drawing it into his mouth to mate with his own. His hands, unable to remain still, roamed restlessly over her back and shoulders, then along the bare skin of her arms.

Kassie was drowning in a welcome tide of pleasure. She knew not where they were headed, only that she wanted to go there, desperately, with Braden. She wanted to convey this new and wondrous feeling to her husband but had no idea how to do so. She settled for wrapping her arms fiercely about him, leaning into him, and returning his bone-melting kisses, one after the other.

Braden tangled his hands in her hair, feeling his tenuous control slipping away bit by bit. He lifted her off the bed until she was crushed against the hot, naked length of his body.

It was not enough.

Of their own will Braden's shaking hands slid around to cup her breasts. Wild jolts of sensation jarred him as he reveled in her warmth, her utterly feminine softness.

Kassie moaned aloud, crying out Braden's name.

The next minute she was alone on the bed.

"Braden?" Her voice was tiny, her eyes questioning her husband's sudden withdrawal.

Leaning against the bedpost, Braden took deep, calming breaths, trying to get his body under control. He stared down at his wife, and a wave of remorse swept over him. She looked so confused and innocent . . . so beautiful, so trusting, it made him ache.

What had he been thinking of? He had come in here to comfort her, to soothe her. Instead he had lost all sanity, nearly succumbing to his damned lust.

"Kassie . . . I'm sorry. I never meant for this to happen."

"Oh." Her voice was almost inaudible.

He sat back down upon the bed, draping the blanket across his lap to hide his nakedness, his blatant arousal.

He cupped her chin. "Look at me."

She raised her eyes.

"I would never hurt you. Ever. What happened tonight . . ."

"All you did was kiss me, Braden. You hardly have to apologize for that."

The abruptness of her tone startled him. He could only guess that she was angry. And she had reason to be. But damn it, he was only a man.

"Kassie," he began again, "I want you to understand—"

"I do understand." Somehow she managed to keep her voice steady, but her lower lip trembled despite her best intentions.

Braden smiled at the little-girl picture she made. "I wonder if you do," he said softly. He leaned over and kissed the tip of her nose. "You should get some rest."

He saw the fear return to her eyes. "Please don't leave me alone," she whispered. After what had just occurred between them, he knew how much that request cost her.

Braden glanced down at his naked body and knew that he would never be able to spend the night beside her.

"What if I leave the connecting door ajar?"

Kassie nodded, relief evident on her face. "Thank you. That would be a great comfort."

"Good." Braden eased her down against the pillows.

"Now go to sleep. I'll be right next door. If you need me, just call out."

Kassie gave him a weak smile and closed her eyes. "I will," she promised.

For a moment he just watched her, lost in thought. Then he stood, leaving the room as rapidly as he could.

Kassie opened her eyes and stared at the ceiling. Sleep was the farthest thing from her mind. Her body felt hot and tingly and strangely restless. The nightmare was forgotten. Her fear was forgotten. All she could remember was Braden, and the feeling of being in his arms.

And she wondered why he didn't want her.

Chapter 10

❧❧

Charles absently stroked the gleaming tan flanks of the bay foal, murmuring words of praise for a fine run.

Dobson had been unsurprised by Charles's early appearance at the stables that morning, for it was not unusual for the trainer to check on the Thoroughbreds at dawn. However, the young groom was quite startled by Charles's announcement that he himself intended to take Noble Birth for his morning exercise. Sensitive to the older man's sober mood, Dobson wisely asked no questions but merely nodded his compliance and moved on to the next stall, leaving Charles to his task . . . and his thoughts.

The new foal showed much promise. Both her parents were Thoroughbreds of extraordinary grace, speed, and endurance. So it followed that Noble Birth should be the same: rare in beauty and unsurpassable in quality.

Charles frowned. Unfortunately, this was not necessarily the case with human beings. Braden's new wife was a supreme example of the rarest of treasures sprung from the dregs of the earth.

But only partially so.

Charles's thought conjured up an image of a beautiful, laughing young woman with coal-black hair and Kassie's gemlike eyes. A woman who had everything to live for . . . until fate had cruelly crushed the life from her, leaving behind a husband who was no more than a parasite and an innocent, flawless child who would bear the scars of her isolation.

Noble Birth whinnied, protesting mildly at Charles's uncharacteristically heavy touch.

"I'm sorry, boy," Charles apologized quietly. "I suppose my mind is far away."

"Am I interrupting?"

Kassie's musical voice was soft, tentative, as was the questioning look in her expressive eyes. Her gown was of a pale blue muslin, and with the wind blowing gently about her she had the look of a fairy-tale princess.

Charles smiled, wondering at the coincidence of fate that had brought her here at this moment in time.

"Not at all, Your Grace." There was only the briefest of hesitations before the title emerged.

Kassie smiled back, making her way through the grass until she stood beside him.

"I was out walking, and I heard a voice. I was curious as to who was about." She paused, then corrected herself. "No, the truth is I was hoping to find you, Mr. Graves. I went to the stables, and Dobson said you had taken Noble Birth out." A slight hint of color tinged her cheeks. "I hope you don't mind. I did not mean to intrude."

Charles shook his head at once. "You are not intruding. If I look surprised, it is only because it is rather early for you to be up and about, is it not?"

"Is Braden still asleep?" she countered.

He met her questioning gaze with kindness and candor. "Braden left Sherburgh before dawn."

"A business meeting again, no doubt." Kassie lifted her small chin defiantly.

He winced at the pointed sarcasm in her voice. "Your Grace," he began, unsure of what he was going to say.

"Please stop calling me that, Mr. Graves." Kassie turned her face away, and the new angle allowed Charles to see the dark circles beneath her eyes. "Until last week I was Miss Grey, and now I am suddenly Your Grace," she continued, catching her lower lip between her teeth to stop its trembling. "It seems absurd that I should be regarded so differently when, ironically, I am so very unchanged." Turning back to Charles, she added, "I suppose I sound very ungrateful. I don't mean to. You have all been so kind to me. My life here at Sherburgh is more wonderful than anything I have ever imagined . . . a dream come true. I just wish . . ." Her voice trailed off.

Charles took a step forward, wanting to go to her, to comfort her . . . and unable to. He took a deep breath, understanding far more than she thought he did.

"What can I do to help?" he asked.

Kassie gave him a small smile. "You are a friend." It was a statement of fact. "I knew that from the moment we met."

He nodded. "Yes . . . I am your friend."

Her dimples deepened. "Very well. Then I have most certainly trapped you. Friends do not address one another formally—even those among the nobility—now do they?"

Charles chuckled. "I suppose not."

"Then you must call me Kassie, just as Braden does."

His blue eyes twinkled. "And you must call me Charles, just as Braden does," he retaliated.

She gave him an exaggerated curtsy. "Very well; I agree . . . Charles." That done, her curious gaze moved to the magnificent young horse that stood beside Charles. "He is splendid," she breathed in wonder, reaching out a tentative hand.

At her questioning look Charles motioned her forward. "Yes, he is," he agreed. "And he is quite gentle. He would not harm you."

"I'm not afraid." She stroked the Thoroughbred's silky neck. "'Tis a shame he will be unable to race," she said sadly, watching the horse toss his head exuberantly. "He has such spirit."

Charles looked startled. "Why do you think he will not race?"

It was Kassie's turn to look surprised. "Why, look at him! His legs are endless, totally out of proportion with the rest of his body. When he matures and gains weight his legs will never support him in a race!"

Charles's lips twitched, but he didn't laugh. "All Thoroughbreds have long, spindly legs when they are young, Kassandra. By two years old their bodies grow enough to catch up." He ran his hand down the white blaze on Noble Birth's forehead.

"Oh."

He took in Kassie's look of wonder, charmed by the fact that it did not occur to her to feel shame at her lack of knowledge, only joy at her discovery. She emanated all the grace of a beautiful, well-bred woman and all the enchantment of a candid child.

"Does Braden have many horses?" she asked, continuing to stroke Noble Birth's lean body.

"Yes, more than a dozen. He breeds and rears them, then races them." He grinned, adding, "And ofttimes wins."

Kassie turned glowing eyes to Charles. "With such a fine stable of horses, he himself must ride magnificently."

Charles nodded. "He does. Braden has been in the saddle since he learned to walk."

Kassie gave a bright laugh. "And I'm certain I can guess who his teacher was."

"It was my pleasure."

The warmth of Charles's words moved Kassie deeply. She had never known such love or loyalty in her life. And she wanted to be part of it.

"Charles? What was Braden like as a little boy?" She gazed up at Charles eagerly, brushing dark, wayward strands of hair out of her eyes.

"Much as he is now," he answered, with a soft expression that reflected cherished memories. "Proud, independent, intelligent, caring."

"What about his parents?"

Charles grew sober. They were approaching uncharted territory. "His parents?"

"He has never spoken of them to me. What were they like?"

Abruptly Charles stiffened, reaching for the bay's bridle. "I must take Noble Birth back to the stables to be fed. Would you like to walk with me?"

Kassie nodded, falling into step beside him. She knew it was no coincidence that her question had caused a new tension to fill the air, only she did not know why.

When Noble Birth had been restored to his stall for feeding Kassie made an attempt to find out.

"Charles, please." She laid a gentle hand upon his arm. "I want to understand Braden, to make him happy. But in order to do so I need to know him better. And I need your help. I am not asking that you betray him," she added softly, "only that you love him."

Staring down into her earnest face, Charles wondered if Braden had any idea how blessed he was to be married to this miraculous creature. Something tightened inside Charles's chest, something he could neither explain nor define.

She deserved the truth. Yet how much of it could he give her?

"Charles?" Kassie's voice was tentative, her eyes questioning. "Won't you please help me?"

The truth she sought now, at least, he could tell her.

Slowly they resumed walking toward the house.

"Braden's mother was barely sixteen when she married the late Duke of Sherburgh," he began. "His Grace was advanced in years and deeply enamored of his beautiful new wife. Perhaps she was too young to commit herself to the marriage, perhaps she never felt love for him in return, but most probably her values were too shallow and self-centered to include the loving of another human being. I do not know." As if to soften his words, he added, "In her defense, it was an arranged marriage, and from what I have heard, Lorraine Arlington begged her parents not to force her into it. She was a lively, spirited young noblewoman who, even after she was wed, looked forward to attending every ball and receiving attention from countless admirers. She wanted neither the responsibilities of her marriage nor the child that was created within it. In fact, she resented Braden from the moment he was born." *Even sooner,* he thought, remembering the days, so long ago, when the whole staff could overhear Lorraine Sheffield sobbing hysterically over the loss of her slender shape.

Kassie gasped. "Surely you are mistaken, Charles. How could any mother resent her child?"

"Does your father not resent you?" The words were out

before he could stop them. He could have kicked himself for uttering them as he saw a veil of sadness cloak her expression.

"That is different," she answered in a small voice. "He never resented me as a child. It is only since Mama died . . . and I look so much like her. . . ." She broke off, willing him to understand.

A pained look crossed Charles's face. "I never should have said that, Kassandra. I apologize. The truth is, the situations *are* entirely different. And to answer your question, I am definitely not mistaken. The duchess made no secret of her resentment. She pushed Braden away every chance she got. It did not take long before he realized that his mother felt no devotion toward him."

Kassie's face had gentled with compassion again. "And what of his father?"

Charles frowned. "Stephen Sheffield was an impenetrable, uncompromising man. His only vulnerability was his wife. He adored her, despised anything that kept her from him. Unfortunately, after Braden's birth Lorraine swore that she would never bear another child. She withdrew from her husband . . . completely."

"And he blamed Braden," Kassie finished, her voice choked with tears.

Charles nodded. "Yes. Despite the fact that it was totally irrational to blame an innocent child, Stephen gave Braden no quarter. He hardened his heart toward his son from that moment on, and nothing could soften it."

"No wonder Braden was—is—so independent," Kassie whispered, unaware of the tears that slid down her cheeks. "He has never had anyone to care for him, even as a little boy. At least I had Mama."

Charles made a rough sound in his throat and turned away.

Kassie blinked. "Oh, Charles, I am so sorry," she said at once, interpreting his reaction as one of hurt. "Of course Braden was not alone. He had you."

The look he gave her was unreadable. Then he nodded. "Yes. And he always will."

"Then he is a most fortunate man," Kassie declared,

blinking away her tears. "He has much to thank you for . . . and so do I."

"You?"

She nodded. "Yes, Charles, I. For without your love and friendship Braden would never have become the wonderful man he is today. And for that I thank you," she stated simply.

For a moment he did not reply. Then he said in a voice that was oddly husky, "You are wrong, Kassandra. If the fates have indeed smiled down upon Braden, then their most precious offering is standing right before me. For it is not I he needs to teach him of love and trust, but you."

At his words Kassie's thoughts returned instantly to the scene that had taken place last night in her room. All night she had tortured herself, wondering why Braden had pulled away from her when all she wanted was to be in his arms. The reason might lie in Charles's explanation. For based upon Braden's experiences in the past, he would not want to allow himself to care too deeply for her. And Kassie knew enough to understand that a physical union between them would strengthen the emotional one—something Braden would undoubtedly try desperately to avoid.

If she let him.

With a smile of radiant resolve Kassie reached out to take Charles's hand.

"Perhaps between the two of us we can provide Braden with the love he thinks he does not need," she offered, squeezing his callused palm.

Charles noted the determined lift of Kassie's chin, the spark in her eyes, and he grinned.

"I take it you have an idea?"

Her smile grew wider. "Oh, yes, I have an idea, Charles. Willingly or not, I intend to make Braden Sheffield fall in love with me."

Cyril Sheffield paced the length of the library, his thoughts brooding. He was more than a bit uneasy with the situation. While he was quite certain that Braden's marriage remained unconsummated, he was also aware of the fact that his nephew had strong feelings toward Kassandra. That complicated matters somewhat.

He stopped in his tracks, considering his options. He had to move slowly and carefully in order to arouse no suspicion. But for everyone's sake, the marriage had to be undone—now—before it was too late.

"Cyril?" Braden walked purposefully into the library. "I need to speak with you."

The older man started, wondering what this was all about. Braden looked tired and worried.

"Certainly," Cyril replied carefully, waiting.

Braden rubbed his eyes wearily, then crossed over to the windows. Silently he clasped his hands behind his back and stared out over the manicured lawns, seeing nothing but his own thoughts.

Last night had been hell, and the dawn had brought no relief or resolution for its torment.

His body and mind had been at war all night, the former hard and throbbing, needing only the blessed relief of Kassie's soft, feminine body; the latter refuting that need, then agonizing over the root of her terrifying nightmare.

Whatever had caused it, he was willing to bet his whole damned fortune that Robert Grey had something to do with it.

Abruptly he turned.

"How well do you know Robert Grey?"

Cyril blinked. Whatever he had expected, it hadn't been this.

Slowly he stroked his jaw. "Not very well. As you know, we do not share the same friends nor frequent the same places."

Braden gave a hard shake of his head. "Please spare me a lecture on the gentry's lack of distinction. Just proceed."

A look of annoyance crossed Cyril's face, but he nodded. "Very well. Years ago I entered into several business transactions with Robert Grey. Actually, we saw very little of each other; most of the work was done by our solicitors. But I do remember that Grey was a clever businessman, very shrewd with his investments."

"Was?"

For a moment Cyril hesitated, then he shrugged. "Yes . . . was. That was many years ago, before his wife died, and before he began to drink himself into oblivion. From what I hear now, he is quite unstable and of little use to anybody."

"So you are saying that he began to drink just after his wife died?"

"As I understand it, yes," Cyril replied.

Braden mulled this information over for a moment.

"What do you know of Kassie's mother?" he asked next.

A smile flitted across Cyril's face. "We met only two, possibly three times. Elena Grey was a lovely young woman. In many ways Kassandra favors her." His smile faded abruptly. "But Elena was far more withdrawn than Kassandra is."

"Withdrawn?"

"Yes," he said slowly. "It is difficult to explain. She always had a timid look in her eyes, as if she were frightened of something."

Or someone, Braden added to himself.

"Cyril, was Kassie's mother ill?" he asked instead.

Cyril raised his brows. "Ill? Not that I know of."

"Then how did she die?"

Cyril's mouth dropped open. "I thought you knew."

"Knew? Knew what?"

Cyril inhaled quickly, then let his breath out very slowly. He hoped that learning of the scandal would affect Braden's feelings for his new wife and thus tilt the scales in Cyril's favor.

He met Braden's gaze directly.

"Elena Grey committed suicide fourteen years ago."

All the color drained from Braden's face. "My God . . . I had no idea." He swallowed. "How?"

"I don't recall all the details," Cyril answered, studying Braden's reaction.

"Well, tell me whatever you *do* recall," Braden demanded.

"Apparently she threw herself from that hilly portion of their property that overlooks the sea. The fall killed her instantly."

Braden was shaking. Wildly he wondered how much of this story Kassie knew.

"Kassie," he murmured to himself.

Cyril heard him. "I doubt your wife knows the true story. I'm certain she was told only that Elena fell, else I'm sure Kassandra would have told you yourself," Cyril put in helpfully.

Braden uttered an angry curse and began to pace restlessly about the room. "And why could it not have been an accident?" he challenged, coming to a halt.

Cyril squinted, trying to recall an incident that had happened long ago. "I believe it had something to do with where on the ground she was discovered." He shook his head. "Truthfully, Braden, I do not remember anything more. It was a terrible tragedy. Obviously Kassandra's mother was not in her right mind."

Or she was driven out of it, Braden thought silently.

"Thank you, Cyril," he said aloud, striding toward the doorway. "You have been most enlightening."

"Where are you going?"

Braden paused. "To contact the authorities. I want to speak with anyone who can tell me more about Elena Grey's death."

Cyril leaned thoughtfully back against the bookshelves. "I would suggest, instead, talking with the man who discovered the body."

Cyril's words had their intended effect, and Braden spun about, a stunned expression on his face. "Do you know where I can find him?"

Cyril sighed. He had no desire to reopen old wounds, but some things just could not be helped. He gave Braden a compassionate look. "You can find him right here at Sherburgh, Braden. The man who found Elena Grey's body was Charles Graves."

111

Chapter 11

Charles started at the insistent pounding on his bedroom door. He barely had time to open it before Braden flung it wide and burst into the room.

"Why didn't you tell me?" he demanded.

Charles blinked in confusion. There was no possible way that Braden could know of the earlier conversation between himself and Kassandra. Then what could he be referring to?

"Tell you?" he asked. "Tell you what?"

Braden raked his fingers through his hair and bit off a curse.

"I was under the impression that we were friends . . . that there was honesty between us," he growled.

Charles flinched at the accusation in his friend's cold hazel eyes. Whatever Braden had learned, it was serious.

Charles's heart began to pound faster.

"We are friends, Braden," he said, his tone deceptively calm. "Now close the door and tell me what this is all about."

Braden violently kicked the door shut.

"How could you keep something like this from me?" he demanded again.

"What have I kept from you?" Charles ground out, his frustration mounting.

"Kassandra is my wife, Charles. My wife! Did you not think I had the right to know?"

Charles felt a chill begin deep inside him.

"What is it that you had the right to know?" he asked in a wooden voice.

Braden lunged forward and clutched Charles's shoulders, digging his fingers into the hard biceps and confronting him with a mixture of anger, pain, and confusion.

"Is it true that Elena Grey killed herself?"

Charles never looked away. "It's true."

"And that you discovered the body?" Braden persisted.

"Yes."

With a groan Braden released him and turned away. "Why?" was all he asked.

A great weariness descended upon Charles's soul. "You were in your teens when it happened, Braden, and away at Eton. By the time you came home the tragedy was over. You did not know the Greys, so there was no need to tell you. And in truth," he said in little more than a whisper, "I wanted to forget the image of that beautiful young woman lying on the beach . . . so still, so broken." He closed his eyes, knowing that he had never forgotten, knowing that he never would. "It will haunt me forever."

Braden was not ready to feel sympathy; he could feel only anger.

"And do you still think there is no need to tell me, Charles?" he got out, a muscle working furiously in his jaw. "Now that I am married to her daughter, is it still no concern of mine?"

"It happened over fourteen years ago," Charles protested.

"But when I first met Kassie and spoke of her to you, you said nothing. And when we dragged her bastard of a father to his cottage in a drunken stupor, *still* you said nothing. And when I told you that Kassie was to be my wife, *still* you said nothing. *Why not?*"

"Because I wanted no shadows present to mar your happiness," Charles replied quietly. "Kassandra is totally unaware of the true circumstances surrounding her mother's death. To tell her would only cause her senseless pain. And to tell you would only intensify the anger and hatred you already carry within you."

Braden met his gaze. "You believe she took her own life."

Charles's eyes were filled with sadness. "No fall could

have hurled her such a distance outward from the base of the jutting land. It had to have been intentional."

Braden slammed his fist against the wall. "Damn it, didn't she care that her daughter was little more than a baby? That she needed her? What kind of a woman would—"

"The kind that was beyond caring . . . beyond hope . . . overpowered by fear."

"Fear." Braden repeated the word slowly. That was the second suggestion that Elena was afraid of something. First Cyril had said it. And now Charles.

"Do you think that Grey drove her to suicide?" he asked Charles bluntly.

"We have both seen the harm he is capable of inflicting, Braden. What makes you believe that his wife was spared it?"

Braden felt sick. He crossed the room and sank down upon Charles's simple, neatly made bed, lowering his head into his hands.

"Did she look like Kassie?" he managed at last.

"Yes. Kassandra is the image of her mother."

Braden raised his head. "Charles . . . I'm sorry. I had no right to—"

Charles cut him off with a gentle shake of his head. "There is no need to apologize, Braden. I ask only that you understand my motives. I made the decision to keep this from you because it is in the past, and I felt that bringing it back would cause both you and your wife much pain. If I did the wrong thing, it is I who must apologize."

"I don't want Kassie hurt," Braden stated.

"Nor do I," Charles agreed. "She deserves to be happy— to be happy and loved."

Braden stood.

"Where are you going?" Charles asked curiously.

Braden reached for the door handle and paused. "To spend some time with my wife."

The door shut quietly behind him.

Charles stood alone in the room, a ray of hope penetrating his earlier resignation.

* * *

"Your Grace? Your Grace!"

Perkins hastened through the hallway, his pace as rapid as his dignity would allow. Relieved to have at last located the duke, the harried butler immediately noted His Grace's displeasure at being deterred from his destination. Having heard Perkins call out, Braden paused halfway up the staircase, impatiently awaiting the butler's approach, his dark brows drawn into a frown.

"Yes, Perkins, what is it?" Actually, Braden didn't care what it was. It would have to wait. Right now all he wanted was to find Kassie. He had already searched the entire main floor, and there was no sign of her.

"I have a message for you from the duchess."

That got Braden's attention. "From Kassie?"

Perkins nodded vigorously. "Yes. Her Grace asks that you join her at the stream on the far side of the estate as soon as possible."

Braden tensed. "The stream? Why? Is she all right? Her father hasn't tried—"

Perkins gave an emphatic shake of his head. "No, Your Grace, there has been no sign of Mr. Grey at Sherburgh. You would have been notified at once."

Braden relaxed slightly. "Did she tell you why she wanted me to meet her there?"

"No, she did not. She just said she was going for a walk and asked me to give you that message."

"How long ago was that?" Braden tried not to feel uneasy, but he hated the thought of Kassie being alone in so isolated a spot.

"Barely an hour ago."

Braden headed for the door.

"Star has been saddled and brought around front, Your Grace," Perkins called after him.

Braden turned and smiled. "As always, you anticipate my every need, Perkins. Thank you."

Braden mounted quickly, trying to shake his odd sensation of discomfort. The earlier events of the day could be the cause, he thought. Still, he wouldn't feel content until he saw Kassie safe and unharmed.

Kassie turned her face toward the sunshine, glorying in its wondrous warmth upon her skin. She had discovered this beautiful spot quite by accident during her morning's explorations and had fallen in love with it. It reminded her of her beloved beach, though they bore no physical resemblance to each other. Still, both places had a certain wildness, and at the same time a certain peace; an ability to soothe her senses and fill her soul. Yes. This was to be *her* spot. She had known it at once.

Contentedly, Kassie drew lazy circles in the clear waters of the stream with her bare feet. Her new haven was quite deserted, giving her the freedom to do what she would. She had taken immediate advantage of this, eagerly removing her slippers and stockings and hiking up her skirts so she could revel in the cool waters. It was perfect . . . utterly perfect.

Sighing with satisfaction, Kassie closed her eyes, wondering for the hundredth time when Braden would come. She knew he had returned to Sherburgh, for Margaret had whispered that detail to her while arranging her mistress's hair—the hair that now cascaded about in total disarray, Kassie noted with a grin. Well, that was what happened when one skipped about in a stream. She would rearrange the thick tresses before going back to the house, but for now she would enjoy the feeling of her wild, loose curls tumbling down her back in carefree abandon.

The breeze caught the wonderful aroma of the food beside her, and Kassie's stomach growled insistently, reminding her that her appetite was as impatient as she. But she had to wait, for the neatly laid place settings upon the blanket were for two. All that was missing was Braden. Until he arrived she would simply enjoy her solitude.

But Kassie was not alone.

The man stood behind the tree, totally obscured from view. Observing, yet unobserved. Intoxicated. Brooding.

She is waiting for someone, he thought; *that is obvious. Probably her husband.* He frowned. *I cannot allow myself to be misled by the air of innocence that still clings to her. I was fooled by that once before . . . but never again.* The faded image swam before his eyes. The most beautiful of women, she had seemed the purest of ladies on the surface, but in reality she was a conniving slut. Damn her.

He blinked. All that was over now. She was long since dead and gone. But she had left behind this perfect likeness of herself to taunt him.

Not this time, he told himself. *This time I will get what I want. She will provide me with everything that life has already taken away.*

His mind cloudy from the liquor, he took a purposeful step forward. *She will pay . . . oh, yes, she will pay.*

The sound of a horse's hooves brought him up short. Someone was approaching. He shook his head to clear it. The sound grew louder . . . closer.

With a sense of panic he drew back. *Am I mad?* he asked himself. *After all my careful planning will I now risk discovery? No. I have come too close to relinquish my claim. Wait. I must wait.* Silently, unseen, he retreated into the thick wall of trees, retracing his steps until he was gone.

Braden rode quickly, effortlessly, scanning the area and cursing himself for leaving Kassie alone. He was about to call out her name when he spied the bright colors of the blanket that lay upon the grass.

At that moment Kassie stood, her face registering delight at seeing her husband.

"Braden!" she smiled, waving at him.

Braden slowed, then dismounted, his curious gaze taking in everything at once: Kassie's adorable, disheveled appearance and the neatly set "table" beside her.

He turned to her with a tender smile, all his earlier anxiety fading. "And what is all this?"

"This," she replied, her dimples deepening, "is a picnic." She gestured toward the basket. "I had Cook pack everything I could think of. We have enough food and wine for four or five meals, I should say." Her candid blue-green eyes searched his. "Are you pleased?"

He took her hands. "I am both pleased and touched."

"I know how busy you are," she said hesitantly.

He smiled brilliantly. "I am never too busy for you, *ma petite."* Her hopeful look made him feel like a bastard. After all, it wasn't her fault that he could barely stand beside her without wanting to ravish her. In her mind he had simply been ignoring her.

She tugged at his hands. "Come and see our dining room! I have been most productive while awaiting your appearance."

He glanced down at the soggy hem of her gown, at the small, bare feet that peeked out from under it. "So I see. Have you been wading?"

Kassie followed his gaze and flushed. "I probably should not have been. But Braden, it is so beautiful here! The water is so refreshing, the grass so soft!" She broke off. "I suppose a duchess is not permitted such frivolities."

Braden burst out laughing. *"This* duchess is permitted anything that makes her happy," he assured her. "I rather like the way you look. It reminds me of the enchanting little girl I met three years past."

Kassie lifted her wet skirts in a mock curtsy, providing Braden with a melting view of her very bare, very lovely legs—a view that caused him to change his mind abruptly. There was nothing even remotely childlike about the effect she had on his starving body, which leapt to life with painful intensity. Stubbornly Braden fought his physical need for Kassie, which had been building for weeks. Once and for all he was determined to enjoy his wife's special company without focusing on how much he wanted her.

Kassie had already started laying out their meal.

"I brought everything I could carry," she informed him.

"I can see that." Braden was stunned by the quantity of food that was fast appearing on their makeshift table. Platters of cold chicken, roast beef and ham, bread and cheese, fresh fruit and a bottle of port completely covered the large blanket and the grass surrounding it.

Kassie looked up again and gave Braden a sunny smile. "There are pastries as well, but I think I shall unpack them later, if you don't mind. We seem to be rather short of space."

Braden lowered himself down beside her. "Are we expecting many guests—say, ten or twelve?" he teased, surveying the feast. "Or are you just trying to fatten me up?"

"Neither. 'Tis just the two of us, and"—her gaze moved shyly over his broad, muscular frame—"I like you just as you are."

She turned back to her task, but not before Braden had seen the flush that crept over her cheeks. He studied her, fascinated. Her innocence and her total honesty never ceased to amaze him. Such lovely traits in a child . . . such unheard-of qualities in a woman.

Braden watched Kassie finish arranging their luncheon, feeling something warm and tender unfurl inside him that had nothing to do with lust. When was the last time he had done something as simple and enjoyable as having a picnic? He was so jaded, he mused, so accustomed to his world, a world where nothing remained untainted. To be with Kassie, to soak up her purity and her goodness, offered more nourishment than any food. For what Kassie offered was sustenance of the soul.

"Oh, I've forgotten the utensils." Kassie suddenly groaned with dismay.

"It doesn't matter," Braden quickly reassured her.

"How can it not matter? There is no way for you to eat!"

Braden had to erase the look of desolation on her face.

"Did I never tell you?" he asked with feigned surprise. "Dukes must eat with their fingers . . . on picnics, of course."

Feeling more carefree than he had in ages, Braden reached forward and helped himself to a piece of chicken.

"Dukes do not eat with their fingers, even on a picnic," Kassie protested.

Braden gave her a dazzling smile. "This one does." He licked his fingers cheerfully, helping himself to a slice of ham.

Kassie looked doubtful. "Well, at least we have glasses for the wine."

With a wicked gleam in his hazel eyes Braden picked up the bottle and put it to his lips, swallowing deeply. "We don't need them."

"Braden!"

He lowered the bottle. "Oh, didn't I mention that fact

119

either? When on a picnic, dukes are further required to drink from the bottle rather than from their usual fine crystal."

Kassie raised her delicate brows, her vivid eyes dancing with mischief. "I see. Apparently I have more to learn about the nobility than I thought. You must instruct me further, Your Grace."

He considered her request. "Very well, if I must." He leaned conspiratorially forward. "The first and most important thing you must know is that dukes and duchesses are required to begin their meals with dessert."

Kassie nodded thoughtfully. "When on a picnic, of course," she stipulated in a helpful tone.

"Of course," Braden concurred.

Kassie gave an exaggerated sigh. "Well, we do what we must, I suppose."

So saying, she lifted six rich, creamy pastries and six plump apricot tarts from the bottom of the basket, placing them on the grassy spot between herself and Braden.

"There. Now we may behave like proper members of the aristocracy."

Braden eyed the confections hungrily. Baking mouthwatering French pastries was one of his cook's prime specialties. Eating them was one of Braden's prime weaknesses.

"Since we have no utensils," Kassie mused, chewing her lip thoughtfully, "how are we to manage these huge, fat pastries?"

Without replying Braden picked one up and held it to Kassie's mouth. "Bite," he commanded, his eyes twinkling.

Kassie stared at the flaky confection that was overflowing with cream. How on earth could she fit it in her mouth?

"Bite," Braden repeated.

Kassie was about to decline when she saw the challenge in Braden's eyes. That did it.

Opening her mouth as wide as possible, she sank her teeth into the pastry. A small portion went into her mouth. The remainder of it covered the lower half of her face.

She didn't need to ask how she looked. Braden's expression said it all. His shoulders began to shake, and he threw back his head with uncontrollable laughter.

"Now you are a true duchess," he managed, unsure of what sort of reaction he would receive. He was prepared for several: anger, tears, embarrassment. Braden was well acquainted with ladies' reactions to such things.

He had forgotten something Kassie had told him three years ago. She was unlike any other lady of his acquaintance.

Quick as a wink Kassie leaned forward and in one swift motion pushed Braden's pastry-filled hand back into his own face.

"And now you are a true duke," she announced as white cream decorated his chin and nose.

For one moment Braden looked totally stunned. Then he retaliated, lunging at her.

But Kassie was faster. She was already running, a trail of laughter drifting behind her, her bare feet giving her additional speed. Braden lost not a minute but leapt up and ran after her. His long legs gave him the advantage, and he gained on her steadily, catching up with her just as she reached the edge of the stream.

Kassie shook his hand off her arm and splashed into the water, turning to give him a challenging look.

"Well, Your Grace, I must admit that you have been uncharacteristically improper thus far. The question is, are you willing to cast all proprieties aside and come in after me? Or will you concede and admit defeat now?"

She never expected him to follow her, so by the time he was in the stream, knee-deep in water, it was too late. She turned to flee, but her wet gown was a hindrance, inhibiting her escape. She felt Braden's strong hands grab hold of her from behind, and she struggled against them, gasping with laughter.

"Let go of me!"

"If you insist, Your Grace," he replied nobly, releasing her all at once.

The next thing Kassie knew, she was on her knees in the stream, totally drenched. The water was icy cold, and it took Kassie a minute to recover.

Braden's laughter faded, and he frowned, seeing only Kassie's wet back and bent head.

"Kassie? Are you all right?"

When she didn't answer he felt a wave of fear.

"Sweetheart?" He leaned over her, trying to see her face, which was hidden by a wet curtain of dark hair. "Kassie? Did I hurt—"

He never finished the sentence. Kassie sat up, a determined grin on her face, grabbed Braden's arms, and pulled with all her strength.

It was enough. With a yell of surprise he went down in an awkward heap, making a huge splash in the rippling stream. For a moment he sat there staring up at Kassie, silently gauging the distance between them. Then he dived.

He caught her around the waist and lifted her, squealing, over his shoulder, carrying her to the grassy bank beside the water.

"That did it," he chuckled, lowering her to the ground. "Now my pride is at stake."

Kassie thrashed about, pummeling at his shoulders and giggling. "I merely wanted to wash the cream from your face, Your Grace."

"Well, you succeeded, Your Grace. Quite nicely, I should say." He watched her struggling to free herself, thinking that she looked like a beautiful mermaid.

Kassie felt his gaze upon her, and she ceased her struggle. "Not entirely," she murmured, reaching up to dab at the small spot of white cream that remained on Braden's chin and lower lip.

At her gentle touch Braden's heart began to slam against his ribs. He was suddenly very aware of her lying beneath him, her wet gown clinging to her body like a second skin. He could feel the warmth of the sun beating down on them, the softness of the grass beneath them, the heat of Kassie's skin burning through their layers of wet clothing. He closed his eyes, inhaling sharply. The action only served to fill his nostrils with the special floral fragrance that was Kassie.

He groaned as her slender fingers traced the curve of his lips. Reflexively he opened his mouth to bid them entry, letting his tongue graze the delicate tips of each finger until the taste of her was pulsing through every pore of his body. He heard her quiet gasp and opened his eyes, staring at the softly parted lips that beckoned him.

Drunk with a sensation that surpassed desire, Braden lowered his head, claiming her mouth with a hunger that he could neither contain nor deny. He shifted until he lay directly upon her, molding his hardened body to her pliant one and tangling his hands in her wet hair to keep her from ending the kiss.

Ending it was the furthest thing from Kassie's mind.

She accepted Braden's kiss, first with shy pleasure, then with tentative eagerness, and finally with uninhibited responsiveness. She succumbed to his unspoken demand, giving him her tongue and taking his in a wild, wondrous mating that surpassed her most vivid fantasy.

Braden's arms contracted around her, locking her against him in an intimacy that caused shudders of desire to rack his body. All he wanted, needed, was to possess her, to bury himself inside her until they both went up in flames. He tore his mouth from hers, pressing it to her soft neck, her graceful throat, her smooth shoulder. When he made contact with the wet barrier of her gown he tugged blindly at it, pulling it down from her shoulders and the upper slope of her chest to expose her bare skin to his greedy touch.

"Kassie . . ." He wasn't aware that he said her name. All he knew was sensation. He buried his face in the fragrant hollow between her breasts, knowing that no other woman had ever felt this good, knowing that he couldn't stop, not yet.

Kassie shifted restlessly, and Braden tugged again, bringing the gown down to her waist, trapping her arms against her sides.

He couldn't stop staring. Never in his life had he seen breasts this beautiful, a pure, untouched ivory with pale pink nipples that had known no man's gaze. A surge of possessiveness shot through him, and with a shaking hand he reached out to cup her sweet flesh.

They both moaned at the contact. Braden's reverent gaze lifted to Kassie's stunned one.

"Sweetheart," he murmured, lowering his mouth to hers, "I won't hurt you. Just let me touch you."

He didn't wait for an answer but took her lips in a scalding kiss just as his thumb moved ever so lightly across her hardening nipple.

Kassie whimpered, raw sensation exploding inside her. Never had she imagined anything so intimate, nor anything so wonderful. Her breasts ached for Braden's touch, and she clutched at his powerful arms, wanting to bring him closer, needing more of the heady sensations he was giving to her.

Braden lifted his head, his hot gaze returning to her swollen breasts, and he lowered his dark head to where his hands had been. Gently he drew her nipple into his mouth, tugging it lightly between his lips and soothing it with his tongue.

Kassie cried out and arched helplessly against him, offering him more of herself. Braden took her unspoken invitation, intensifying the pressure of his mouth until he was beyond rational thought, so caught up in her cries of pleasure that all his noble intentions were lost. He grazed her nipple with his teeth, then laved it with his tongue, only to move to the other breast to do the same. He was intoxicated, the sweet taste of her creating a bottomless craving inside him that only their joining could fill.

Control vanished. Reason vanished. There was nothing but the need that drove him, blazing through his body like a brush fire, igniting every part of his being.

Frantic for release, Braden slid his hand beneath the wet layers of Kassie's gown and petticoat, up the smooth skin of her thigh, until he reached the warm haven where he desperately wanted to be. Slowly, unerringly he found the opening in her pantalettes and slipped his fingers inside.

Kassie tensed, unintentionally crying out at the unfamiliar invasion of her body. Her growing pleasure receded beneath a fear of the unknown . . . and an innate need to protect herself from the helpless vulnerability that possessed her when she was in Braden's arms. She wanted him desperately, and yet she was frightened by the total self-relinquishing this untried act demanded.

She was already hopelessly in love with him. She could not sacrifice her very soul to him as well.

"Braden . . . don't . . ." At first it was a whisper, but when he made no move to comply she began to fight him, saying the words over and over, her whole body shaking with emotion.

Braden felt her resistance and lifted his head. His mind was cloudy with desire, his hand inches from where it needed to be. And yet something inside him commanded that he stop. Something he did not understand but needed to obey.

"Please," Kassie whispered, tears shimmering in her eyes. "Don't." She unconsciously used the very words that he dreaded. "I'm afraid."

Braden felt ill. He stared down at Kassie's beautiful, frightened face, and he was consumed with frustrated anger and self-loathing.

"Kassie," he murmured, lifting his hand to her face. Thank God she didn't flinch. He didn't know what he would have done if she had.

In tense silence Braden smoothed down her gown and tugged her bodice back up where it belonged. He stood then, reaching down to help her to her feet.

"Let's go back to the house," he said flatly.

"But our picnic . . ." She said the first coherent thing that entered her mind.

"Another time," he answered shortly. "The idea of a picnic no longer appeals to me."

With a sinking heart Kassie wondered if he was referring to much more than the picnic.

Chapter 12

 plashes of sunlight coaxed Kassie's unwilling eyelids to open. Soon Margaret would be in to help her dress for her riding lesson with Charles, an event that had become something of a ritual this past week. It was the only thing Kassie actually looked forward to lately . . . ever since that day at the stream . . . that last shattering moment in Braden's arms.

With each passing day the distance between them had grown wider, the strain more pronounced, the future prospects more dismal. Braden was seldom home. And when he was, he was barely cordial, closeting himself in his study or at the stables, seeing only his business associates, his Thoroughbreds, and Charles. Kassie could feel his anger whenever they happened by one another, whenever she caught him looking at her. There was accusation there, accusation and torment. And she was helpless to stop it.

In truth, Kassie, who had dealt with blatant conflict all her life, was incapable of combating this intangible, painful tension that was beyond her understanding. She only knew that something very complicated and irreversible had happened between them, and that because of it things had altered drastically.

The door flew open and a cheerful, bustling Margaret sailed into Kassie's bedchamber.

"Good morning, Your Grace," she greeted her mistress, scurrying over to the windows to pull back the drapes and allow more of the morning sunlight into the room.

"Hello, Margaret," Kassie replied, sitting up in bed and smiling faintly at her maid.

Margaret studied Kassie's pale face and frowned.

"Did you have another dream?" she asked, concern evident in her voice.

Kassie shook her head. "No, Margaret, no dreams. I just had a bit of a restless night."

Actually, she'd had a *very* restless night. The good thing was that since Kassie was only able to sleep for several hours at a time, she had been tormented but twice this week by the horrible recurring nightmare. On both occasions Braden had been away from Sherburgh, and it had been Margaret who came to soothe her, asking no questions, merely stroking Kassie's hair and crooning softly until the trembling stopped. Kassie adored Margaret and was thankful for her nurturing aid.

But she wanted Braden.

"Shall I have a tray brought up to you, Your Grace?" Margaret asked hopefully.

Kassie sighed. She knew that Margaret was worried over Kassie's lack of appetite and loss of sleep. The older woman was the closest thing to a mother that Kassie had known in fourteen years. A rush of gratitude swept over her, and she pushed back the bedcovers with a grin.

"That won't be necessary, Margaret. I believe that I will go downstairs for breakfast today."

It was worth it to see the broad smile that crossed Margaret's lined face.

"Wonderful! It will do you a world of good to be with people, to spend some time with your husband. . . ." Her voice trailed off as Kassie looked away. Margaret, more than anybody, knew how things stood between Braden and his wife. Although Kassie rarely spoke of them, her feelings for her husband were transparent as glass, and the fact that the duke never visited his wife in her bedchamber was no secret to Margaret. She was half tempted to give His Grace a piece of her mind for the shameful way he was treating his new wife. But wisely, she held her tongue, partly because she knew her place and partly because she sensed that there was more to this relationship than met the eye. Whatever was amiss between the duke and duchess, they would have to work it out themselves.

Thirty minutes later, washed and dressed, Kassie made her entrance into Sherburgh's huge dining room. She stood in the doorway, wondering if this particular room would ever cease to intimidate her. It was not just its immense size that made it overwhelming, but its elegant and intricate design. Rare and priceless statues stood everywhere between towering pillars that reached to a high, gilded ceiling and a dazzling crystal chandelier. Along the far wall of the room a fire was lit, its carefully stoked, boldly blazing flames as commanding as the white marble fireplace that housed them. Kassie's gaze went to the massive carved mahogany table and chairs, which bespoke wealth and quality. Several attentive footmen hovered about, serving hot platters of food to Lord Cyril Sheffield, who sat calmly eating his breakfast, and to His Grace, the Duke of Sherburgh, who was at the head of the table, buried behind the *Times*.

Upon seeing her enter Cyril stood, his dark brows raised in surprise.

"Good morning, Kassandra. What a pleasure to have you join us for our morning meal."

Kassie smiled. "Good morning, Cyril. I decided it was time to stop being so lazy and learn to rise at a reasonable hour."

Braden lowered the newspaper slowly to the table and rose to his feet.

"Good morning, Braden," Kassie said softly.

She could see it again, that confused, pained look that appeared briefly in his eyes, then vanished.

"Good morning, Kassie." He drank in her presence, damning himself for the feelings that refused to be quieted. Nothing had changed since that day by the stream—not his determination, not his ambivalence.

He saw the soft, questioning look she gave him as she sat down, and he felt an irrational burst of anger. What did she want of him? Damn it, she was no longer a child. Surely she must have *some* idea of what he was going through.

Until their picnic Braden had been willing to shoulder all the responsibility for curbing his desires, and all the blame when he could not. But everything had changed that day. Because just as he was sure that he had never known true passion before that moment, he was equally sure that Kassie had felt it, too. There had been neither fear nor revulsion in her response to his touch. She had asked him—no, begged him—to continue. Not with words, but with her body, which spoke to him in a language all its own. He had felt it, tasted it, reveled in it. Never had he wanted a woman that way, uncontrollably, irrationally, totally. He had been like an untried schoolboy, aware of nothing save the desperate need to join himself to her, to spend himself in her body, to give her pleasure.

And then she had pulled away. *Why?*

She was afraid, his conscience shot back. And he was a miserable blackguard to allow anger to mingle with his guilt and remorse.

He clenched his hands in his lap, watching her chat amiably with Cyril over her eggs.

She was so damned beautiful, so meltingly desirable. Her body was exquisite. Just the memory of it made Braden tremble like a callow youth. And he had bared only part of it to his hungry gaze, his seeking hands. The greatest treasure was left unknown and unexplored.

God, how he wanted her. It was becoming obsessive, his dreams filled with possessing her, his body no longer willing to heed the dictates of his mind. That angered him.

But he wanted her to want him as well, to welcome him into her arms, into her body, into her heart. That terrified him.

And all the while he kept asking himself which of Kassie's emotions would win out in the end, her fear or her desire.

"Braden, will you be leaving Sherburgh today?" Kassie asked, turning her haunting blue-green eyes to him.

Braden folded the newspaper and placed it beside his plate. "As a matter of fact, I need to speak with Charles and make some arrangements. He and I will be leaving for London in the morning."

"Why?" The moment it was asked Kassie wished she could recall the foolish question. She had heard enough from Charles to know that a big auction was to be held at Tattersall's that week.

Braden looked at Kassie's disappointed face and felt himself thaw. "Charles and I must attend the auction, and I must meet with some fellow Jockey Club members at the Subscription Room. We are discussing the possibility of buying additional land at Newmarket." He smiled in spite of himself. "It will only be for a few days, *ma petite*. I should be home by week's end."

Kassie nodded, appalled at her lack of control. She had all but begged him not to go! Composing herself, she replied, "Of course. I understand. I'll be just fine."

Cyril cleared his throat, trying to diffuse the obvious tension in the room.

"I shall take good care of Kassandra while you're away, Braden," he assured his nephew.

"I'm sure you will." Braden took a final sip of lukewarm tea and stood. "I had best be on my way."

"Will I see you before you leave?" This time Kassie managed to keep the eagerness out of her voice.

Braden nodded. "I'll see you this evening before you retire." He strode from the room.

Kassie flushed. Cyril would have to be blind and deaf not to infer from Braden's remark that they lived separately, not as husband and wife.

If he did, he kept it to himself, nonchalantly finishing his breakfast and continuing their chat.

"So, are you enjoying your riding lessons with Charles?"

Kassie looked surprised. "I didn't know you were aware that Charles was teaching me to ride."

He smiled, dabbing at his mouth with a linen napkin. "I saw the two of you yesterday. I was most impressed with your progress. Didn't you say that you couldn't ride?"

Kassie regarded him thoughtfully. "I did say that. Charles is helping me to learn. The horses at Sherburgh are magnificent."

"Yes, they are," he agreed. "And I'm sure it will please

Braden very much if you become an adept rider. His Thoroughbreds mean a great deal to him."

"I know." She smiled. "And I can understand why. They are loving and affectionate and gentle."

Cyril inclined his head to one side. "They can also be high-handed and skittish, especially with a new, inexperienced rider. Just be careful. I wouldn't want you to get hurt."

Kassie pushed back her seat and stood. "Thank you, Cyril," she told him warmly. "Thank you for your concern. I will not let my enthusiasm overshadow my caution, I promise."

He chuckled. "Good. Now run along and change clothes for your ride. You and I will have much time to talk over the next few days. After all, it is my job to look after you during Braden's absence."

He watched her go, pleased with the outcome of their chat. Actually, considering the way things were progressing between Braden and his new wife, Cyril expected that his job would not be difficult at all.

Kassie tossed in her bed, tears of frustration burning behind her eyes. How much longer could she go on without sleep? She was totally exhausted, her body craving rest, and yet her turbulent emotions refused to release her to the peace of slumber.

Through the closed door that connected their bedchambers she could hear the muffled sounds of Braden's deep, rich baritone giving last-minute packing instructions to Harding. The idea of Braden leaving Sherburgh made Kassie feel more alone and more frightened than she had since the day she ran from her father's home. It struck her that she had unknowingly become dependent upon her husband in a way that she had never permitted herself with another person. She needed him emotionally, physically. And *that* reality was what made her pull back.

Unbidden, the memory of their picnic came to mind. Being in Braden's arms, letting him touch her, *begging* him to touch her, with a helpless abandon that made her weak just to recall. With a lifetime of experience screaming its warning, how could she allow herself to be so vulnerable to another person?

Kassie closed her eyes. There was no turning back. She had to take the risk. She was in love with her husband, and come hell or high water, she was bound and determined to make him love her.

But tomorrow he is going away, Kassie thought, and she shivered with an internal chill.

The dream crept inside her.

It was night. She was alone . . . walking . . . pervaded by cold, chilled by apprehension. The sweet scent of lilacs hung in the air. An eerie silence prevailed. Then voices, harsh, pleading. Movement, rustling, heavy steps. The cold grew sharper. The apprehension swelled and exploded into raw fear. She began to run. Desperate to escape. Knowing she could not. A piercing scream split the night. The beast growled, reared back, and lunged. She was falling . . . down, down, into a bottomless well of blackness.

And the beast's laughter echoed wildly about her as she fell to her death.

Someone was calling to her, lifting her, dragging her back from the blackness. Kassie struggled wildly against the strong arms that gripped her, suddenly aware of her own sobs and gasping breaths.

"Kassie! Stop fighting me! I'm not going to hurt you! Sweetheart, it's me . . . Braden. Open your eyes now!"

Kassie heard the command and, with the greatest of effort, opened her eyes. Disoriented, she stared up at Braden's worried face.

"Braden?"

He nodded, tightening his grip about her. "Yes, love, it's me. I'm here."

"I was dreaming," she murmured. She voiced the obvious fact aloud, hoping to make the reality sink in that much faster. Slowly she became aware of her surroundings again. Braden was sitting on her bed, holding her against him and stroking damp strands of hair off of her forehead.

"Yes, you were," he replied soberly, searching her eyes for

any remaining traces of incoherence. There were none. "Kassie, how often do you have these . . . dreams?"

She sighed, laying her weary head against his shoulder. She noted that this time he was still fully dressed, probably because he had not yet been to bed.

"It varies," she answered softly. The aftermath of the dream was still very much with her, the cold and the fear making her tremble. "They vanished completely during my first week at Sherburgh," she murmured, half to herself. "But lately they've been relentless, more frequent than ever. Since the day my father was here—"

"Your father was here?" Every muscle in Braden's body tensed at Kassie's words.

She recognized the stupidity of her revelation at once but was too exhausted to deal with it. She merely nodded against Braden's taut shoulder. "The day after the wedding."

"Damn it, Kassie," he swore quietly into her soft cloud of hair, "why didn't you tell me?"

"There was no purpose to it, Braden. He did no harm to me. And he has not been back since."

Braden wanted to demand every detail of the meeting, to point out that Robert's brand of *harm* was not always manifested in physical abuse. But given Kassie's present state of mind, he refrained. At the same time Braden's logic told him it was no coincidence for Kassie's nightmare to have resurfaced on the very day she saw her father again. There had to be some connection.

Angry and frustrated, Braden tightened his arms about Kassie protectively, making a mental note to increase the number of servants that guarded the grounds and the gates of Sherburgh. He was beginning to feel very uneasy about being away for so many days.

"Sweetheart, about the dream," he probed gently.

Kassie shook her head against the sleeve of his shirt. She was not ready to discuss it.

Braden gave a frustrated sigh. "We cannot simply ignore this, Kassandra. We have to talk about it."

"Not tonight."

He frowned, hearing the plea in her voice. "Then when?"

She leaned back and stared up into his magnetic hazel eyes, now dark with concern. "When you get back. I promise. Only please . . . not now." She shuddered. "I can still feel it . . . see it . . . please don't make me relive it. I don't think I could bear it."

He cupped her trembling face in his hands. "All right, *ma petite,* all right. We don't have to talk about it now. But the minute I return—"

"Whatever you say," she agreed quickly.

He stared down at her tenderly. "What am I going to do with you?" he whispered, shaking his head.

"Hold me." She caught at his muscular forearms. "Please . . . just hold me."

He drew her against him, waves of feeling tightening his chest as her small, soft body curled trustingly against his enveloping strength. No matter how hard he tried, he couldn't shake free of the myriad emotions she aroused in him. He wanted to heal her every pain, to have her whole and free of the past, to see her light up the world with her smile.

He wanted to make love to her until neither of them could move.

And he had no idea what she wanted of him.

"You called me Kassandra."

Her husky observation, muttered against his shirt, broke into his thoughts and made him smile. "I suppose I did." He kissed the top of her head.

"I'll miss you," she whispered, so softly that it was barely audible.

But Braden heard it.

"I'll miss you, too, sweetheart."

She drew back, uncertainty in her eyes. "Will you? The way you've been acting lately, I thought . . ." Her voice trailed off.

"It seems we have a lot to discuss, you and I," he replied, easing her back against the pillows. He saw the shadows beneath her beautiful eyes and frowned. "But tonight is not the time. You are utterly exhausted, and I have yet to finish preparations for my trip. I want you to go to sleep. When I return we'll talk—about these nightmares of yours, about the visit from your father, about your behavior lately—"

"And yours," she added quickly.

He nodded, smiling faintly. "And mine."

He stood.

"Braden?" She leaned up on her elbow. "Would you just stay with me until I fall asleep . . . please?"

He sat back down beside her, thinking that when she looked up at him like that she could ask for the moon, and he would find a way to get it for her.

"I'll stay," he told her softly, "until you fall asleep."

She raised up and brushed his lips tenderly with her own. "Thank you." Then, like a contented child, she lay back and within minutes was fast asleep.

Braden watched her sleep, idly stroking the black cascade of hair that tumbled over her bare shoulders and down the back of her night rail. Her dark lashes, like ebony silk fans, swept the fine bones of her cheeks, making her creamy skin appear even paler in contrast. She was by far the most exquisite woman he had ever seen . . . and the most tantalizing embodiment of contradictions. He ran the pad of his thumb lightly over her soft, sensual mouth, feeling her deep, even breaths against his skin. He had to make some sense of these powerful feelings—and soon. Things could not continue this way; it was causing both of them too much pain.

Braden tucked the blankets tenderly beneath her chin and rose to his feet. He was so damned torn. He did not want to leave her alone, not even for a few days. But he had to go to London with Charles, for the meeting and for the auction. Besides, he reasoned, she wouldn't be alone. Cyril had promised to look after her, and there was a whole houseful of servants to assist him. And meanwhile Braden could use this time away to evaluate his relationship with his wife objectively.

The reasoning was sound.

The uneasiness persisted.

Chapter 13

❧❧❧

This is ridiculous," Kassie declared, leaning back on her elbows in the cool grass. "I did not see the man for three years, and I survived. Now here he is, gone for but four days, and I am doing naught but mooning about like a fool." Her bright eyes flashed as she regarded her silent companion. "It is not like me to behave this way. I am not at all certain that I care for the effect love has on me. I believe I was much better off when you were the only man in my life, Percy."

At the sound of his name Percy deduced that a response was in order. He gave an affirmative yip and licked Kassie's hand.

She stood, brushing blades of grass off of her rose-colored morning dress. "I'm glad you agree, my friend." She gave Percy a warm hug. "And I thank you for listening. Now I must take over for myself." She glanced off in the distance, possessed by a sudden, uneasy feeling that she was being watched. But the grounds about her were still. She frowned, a faint shiver running down her spine. It had to be her imagination.

A twig snapped, and Kassie started, gazing in the direction of the sound. She smiled, relieved, seeing a growing brown spot approaching them. "Besides, I believe that your sire has come in search of you," she informed Percy. "So you shan't miss me at all!"

Percy followed her gaze, then flew off in a fury of happy barking when he recognized his father. Kassie grinned, watching them trot off together, Percy gazing adoringly up at Hunter. Her pet was secure in his new life. Now it was her turn.

Thirty minutes later she appeared at the stables, determined and dressed in her riding clothes.

"Hello, Dobson," she greeted the surprised groom. With Charles away, the duchess had not been to the stables all week.

"Uh . . . good mornin', Yer Grace," he said respectfully. "Was there somethin' I could do for ye?"

Kassie nodded. "Yes, Dobson, there is. I would like you to saddle up Little Lady for me."

Dobson looked uncomfortable. "But Yer Grace," he began.

Kassie waved his protest away. "I know what you are going to say, Dobson. That Charles is away, and I shouldn't ride without his supervision. But I assure you that I can handle Little Lady quite well by myself. So please do as I ask."

Dobson shook his head slowly. "No, Yer Grace, what I was goin' to say is that Little Lady is favorin' her left side a bit." At Kassie's distressed look he added hastily, "It's nothin' serious. She stepped on a stone is all. She'll be good as new in a day or two."

Kassie looked relieved. "I see." She was thoughtful for a moment, then raised her chin purposefully once more. "Then I'll ride Star."

Dobson's mouth fell open. "Star?" he managed.

"Yes, Dobson, Star."

"Excuse me for sayin' this, Yer Grace, but ridin' Little Lady and ridin' Star are two different things."

"I'm aware of that Dobson," she answered, her tone pleasant but firm. "Now please get him."

"But he's not prepared for ridin'," he tried again.

"That's all right. I'll wait."

With a resigned shrug the groom disappeared into the stables.

Kassie felt very pleased and proud of herself. At last she was taking charge of her life. And she would do just fine. After all, how different could one horse be from another?

Charles was an excellent teacher and had taught her well. She was sure he would applaud both her decision and her initiative.

Thirty minutes later she was not nearly so certain.

Whenever Braden rode Star the stallion appeared to be so responsive, so . . . controllable. With Kassie on his back he was neither. From the moment Dobson helped her mount Kassie knew she was in trouble. The skittish horse was displeased by everything: the unfamiliar hand that guided him, the tentative quality of the commands, the amateurishness of the ride. Still, Kassie bravely started out, ashamed to back down beneath Dobson's knowing glance.

It was a mistake. Star went from annoyed to rebellious. And the more irritated the Thoroughbred became, the more unnerved Kassie grew. She knew she shouldn't show fear, but when she hesitantly urged Star into a slow trot and the spirited mount instead broke into a fast-paced canter, all thoughts of remaining calm were forgotten, along with everything that Charles had taught her during their riding lessons.

Utterly enjoying his mischief, Star picked up speed, galloping faster and faster, his long legs flying out from under him and carrying him along at a breakneck pace until Kassie was leaning over and clinging to the stallion's neck for dear life. What was it that made a horse stop? she thought frantically, trying to recall Charles's words. But no spark of memory came to mind. Frantically, without forethought, she reached down and tugged at the reins with all her might.

It was the wrong thing to do.

Star whinnied his disapproval, shaking his head against the reins and rearing back on his hind legs. Unceremoniously he tossed Kassie to the ground, then streaked off toward the stables without a backward glance.

Stunned, Kassie lay dizzy and unmoving for long minutes, trying to catch her breath and get her bearings. The ground was cold and hard, but fortunately thick with grass and free of stones in the spot where she had been thrown. Slowly she sat up, gingerly moving her arms and legs to assess her bodily damage. Aside from a splitting pain in her head and many assorted aches that would undoubtedly become dark bruises, she appeared to be unharmed.

The same, however, could not be said for her attire. The rich brown riding habit was torn and ruined beyond repair and hung in shreds from one shoulder, leaving her arm bare and covered with dirt and grass stains. Her hair was littered with blades of grass and clumps of dirt, and she was certain that her face looked the same. With a rueful smile she hobbled back toward the house, her pride in the same condition as her clothing.

The elegant carriage that stood before Sherburgh's grand entranceway was an unfamiliar one. Nevertheless Kassie felt weak with relief at its presence. Obviously Cyril was occupied with guests, which would enable Kassie to sneak quietly up to her bedchamber and repair the damage to her appearance without having to answer any questions or face further humiliation. After all, Cyril had warned her not to be overzealous in her riding—a warning she should have heeded but had not. Well, Cyril would know about it soon enough. She had no doubt that Dobson would fill the entire household in on the details of her stupidity. But by then she could at least salvage some of her dignity by appearing physically intact.

Sliding silently through the doorway, Kassie eased her way down the marble hallway and toward the stairs. Perkins was bound to be about somewhere, but Kassie knew that his fondness for her would ensure his discretion. She had only to reach the staircase and she would be safe.

The library door opened suddenly.

"I do wish Braden had been here, but I'm pleased that we were able to find you at home, Cyril." A distinguished-looking gentleman and a beautiful blond woman stepped into the hall a mere five feet from where Kassie stood frozen with embarrassment.

"I know that he'll be sorry he missed your visit, William," Cyril was replying as he, too, emerged from the library.

The three of them saw Kassie at the same moment.

"Kassandra?" Cyril's tone registered shock and disbelief. "What on earth happened to you?"

Kassie wished with all her heart that the floor could

swallow her up. "I took a small spill from my horse, Cyril," she replied, trying to keep her voice even. "I'm a little shaken but fine."

She saw Cyril's concern change to discomfort and finally censure. He cleared his throat roughly and gave a quick sideways glance at the gray-haired gentleman who stood beside him, his mouth hanging open in amazement.

"I see." Cyril's tone was wooden. "Well, then, I shall introduce you to our guests. This is William Devon, the Duke of Lamsborough, and his daughter, Lady Abigail Devon. His Grace is a business associate of Braden's. Our families have been close friends for years."

The name William Devon struck a familiar chord in Kassie's memory. He was an important business contact of Braden's. Evidently that importance was the cause of Cyril's blatant disapproval of her unseemly appearance and the obvious omission of her name from the introductions. Her pride returned in a rush, along with a surge of anger and hurt.

"Your Grace, it is a pleasure to meet you. Braden speaks of you often." Kassie raised her tousled head high and stepped forward, her hand extended. "I am Braden's wife, Kassandra."

The older man inclined his head slightly, studying the rumpled young woman before him. So this feisty little baggage was the reason for Braden's decision not to marry Abigail. He narrowed his eyes, carefully scrutinizing Kassie's dirt-streaked face. Having lived for fifty years, thirty-five of which had been spent in the arms of numerous desirable women, William was not fooled by Kassie's state of disarray. The young woman who met his gaze so candidly and directly with eyes the color of sparkling aquamarines and an innocent, natural sensuality of which she was totally unaware was a classic, unequivocal beauty.

He bowed, brushing her hand with his lips.

"My dear, the pleasure is mine."

Kassie barely heard William Devon's words. She was staring past him at the cold, majestic woman who was regarding her through haughty ice-blue eyes—eyes that were filled with hatred.

"So you are Braden's wife." She moved forward with the grace and arrogance of a queen, her blond curls sweeping the back of her rich blue silk gown.

"I am." Kassie kept her features carefully schooled, although she identified Abigail Devon as an enemy at once. The only question remaining was why.

A small mocking smile played about Abigail's lips. Her malicious gaze swept Kassie's disheveled figure with amusement and scorn. "A riding accident, you said"—she paused, frowning in apparent perplexity—"it is Kassandra, is it not?"

"Yes, it was, and yes, it is." Kassie could feel herself begin to tremble with anger.

Abigail nodded. "You are new to Sherburgh . . . and to your title, Kassandra. Surely you must be far too busy learning your proper role to spend much time at the stables."

"I find time for both, Lady Abigail."

"I see. Apparently, you are very resourceful, Kassandra." Kassie noted the purposeful absence of her new title in Abigail's address. Evidently the other woman resented her for marrying into the *ton* while being born only to the gentry. So be it.

Kassie took a deep breath. "I am delighted to meet both of you," she said calmly, addressing the duke as well as his condescending daughter. Holding her head high, she continued, smoothing her skirts as if they were not wrinkled and torn. "And I do apologize for my rather soiled appearance. Had I known that you were coming to Sherburgh, I would have postponed my riding disaster for a later date." She smiled, an enchanting smile that made a dimple appear in each cheek. "However, if you have only just arrived—"

"We were just leaving," Abigail shot back. "In fact, had I known that Braden was in London, I would never have made the trip out to Sherburgh."

"I am sorry to hear that," Kassie responded, feeling a knife twist in her stomach. Obviously this woman had been involved with Braden in ways that had nothing to do with either friendship or business. *Had been,* Kassie reminded herself silently. Now Braden belonged to her.

"Abigail, my dear," Cyril was saying in a soothing voice, "Braden made this trip quite suddenly." Kassie blinked at the blatant lie. "Had he known of his plans sooner, I am certain he would have contacted your family."

Abigail nodded, slightly appeased. "I suppose so." She brightened, speaking to her father and Cyril as if Kassie were not even in the room. "Then he will just have to reconsider and attend our dinner party in order to atone for his oversight." She pouted prettily. "I still haven't forgiven him for missing our house party last month. Although"—she cast a withering look in Kassie's direction—"I can well understand why it would be difficult for him to attend social functions. His life is . . . complicated right now."

What party? Kassie wanted to ask. Braden hadn't even mentioned a dinner party.

William gave an uncomfortable laugh and clapped Cyril on the back. "An excellent idea, Cyril. You must convince Braden to come out to Lamsborough—and to bring his lovely new wife, of course," he added hastily.

Cyril smiled. "I will certainly speak with him, William. Abigail is quite right, though. Braden has been caught up in pressing matters that have precluded him from accepting many invitations of late."

"Of course." William Devon seemed eager to take his leave and end the uncomfortable conversation that was taking place. "Come, Abigail. Our carriage awaits us." He turned to Kassie. "Again, it was a pleasure . . . Your Grace." Kassie wondered if he might choke on the words.

Abigail didn't even look back. "Good day, Kassandra. You might go and change your gown now. And I would suggest a bath as well." She sailed out of the house.

The door closed behind them.

A very unpleasant, never-before-uttered oath hovered on Kassie's lips.

Despite her brave front she was totally shaken and close to tears. Swallowing deeply, she turned to Cyril.

"Am I the pressing matter that is keeping Braden from fulfilling his social obligations?"

Cyril raised his brows. "Of course not, Kassandra. I meant *business* matters."

Kassie studied Cyril's surprised and innocent expression. "I am not a fool, Cyril. It is quite apparent that you are displeased with me. I assure you it was not my intent to be thrown from a horse, nor to be introduced to Braden's friends dressed like a waif."

Cyril nodded. "No, you are not a fool, Kassandra. And you are absolutely right. I was terribly embarrassed by the situation. William Devon is a highly influential man who was a dear friend of Braden's father and is currently involved in numerous business ventures with Braden. However, I do acknowledge that what occurred was not your fault, but rather an unfortunate set of circumstances. So forgive me if I seemed cold or unfeeling. My position was a difficult one."

Unprepared for Cyril's apology, Kassie blinked. "Oh. Very well, Cyril. I suppose I can understand the awkwardness of the situation. However . . ." She stopped herself. She had been about to boldly state her dislike and distrust of Abigail Devon, but common sense told her that it would be foolhardy to do so. If she hoped to retain Cyril's friendship, she had to refrain from criticizing his old and dear friends. No, she would simply ask Braden about Abigail when he returned.

"However?" Cyril prompted.

"However, I was surprised by Lady Abigail's mention of a dinner party. I knew of no such invitation," Kassie improvised.

Cyril gave her a shrewd look. "Most likely Braden did not mention it because he declined the invitation. Don't let Abigail upset you, my dear. She is a bit spoiled and outspoken, but I assure you she speaks only out of genuine affection for Braden. They have known each other for many years."

Genuine affection? Kassie thought not. But aware that Cyril was trying to spare her feelings, she said, "I'm sure you're right, Cyril. And now, if you'll excuse me, I shall take Lady Abigail's advice and see to a bath and a fresh gown."

"Of course. Are you certain you are uninjured?" The concern was back in his voice.

"Positive. I am stiff and sore and a bit bruised. By tomorrow I'll be good as new."

Cyril watched her go, thinking for the hundredth time how very lovely she was . . . and how ill-suited for his nephew. The thought of them appearing together at parties and balls, the reactions they would receive from the *ton* . . . Cyril drew himself up as an idea was born of his idle thought. *That might be the very thing to end this mockery of a marriage,* he mused. *Why didn't I think of it before now?*

He was suddenly most eager for Braden to return to Sherburgh.

"There, there, love, it's all right. Everything is just fine."

Margaret rocked Kassie gently against her own ample bosom, frowning at the violent trembling that assailed her mistress. The last few nights had been worse than ever before, Kassie awakening in a cold, frantic sweat twice each night from the dreadful dream.

Kassie took a deep gulp of air and nodded. "I know. I'm sorry, Margaret . . . so sorry."

The kindly maid gave Kassie a gentle shake. "Now don't be foolish, child. You have nothing to apologize for."

Kassie sat up, brushing the tears from her cheeks. "Because of me you haven't had a decent night's sleep in days."

"I've gotten all the sleep I need, Your Grace. Don't you worry." She tucked Kassie back into bed like a small child. "You're the one I'm worrying about. Why, you've got dark rings under those beautiful eyes."

Kassie managed a small smile. "I'll do something about them at once," she promised, settling herself against the pillows. "And you do the same. Really, Margaret, I'm fine now. Please go to bed."

Margaret chewed her lower lip. Regardless of what Her Grace said, she was definitely *not* fine. And once and for all, it was time the duke knew about it. Silently she promised herself that she would tell him everything when he returned from London.

"Very well, Your Grace, if you're sure."

"I am."

Margaret nodded. "Then good night."

"Good night, Margaret. And thank you," Kassie whispered. When she heard the door close behind her maid she sat up, wrapping her arms around her knees and staring off into the darkness. When would this torment end? she wondered desperately. Had her stressful meeting with Abigail Devon precipitated this onslaught of recurring nightmares, or was it the worry of Braden's imminent return and the impending conversation they would have about her father's visit to Sherburgh?

Kassie rested her forehead against her knees. She was worried, yes, but oh, how she missed her husband and longed for him to come home. They had so much to resolve, so much to talk over. She would make him share his feelings with her, make him understand why she had pulled away from him that day at the stream. And then everything would be as it should.

The memory of *Lady* Abigail Devon's proprietary air when she spoke of Braden flashed through Kassie's mind, and her confidence wavered. Next to Abigail's sophistication and obvious experience with men, Kassie felt childish and inept. Would Braden find her that way as well? The thought made her stomach tighten. What transpired in bed between a man and a woman remained a mystery to her, yet it was no secret to Abigail Devon. *That* was a certainty.

Renewed determination surged through Kassie's blood. No matter what her own past had demonstrated, she knew that Braden would never hurt her, never betray her love or her trust. She could no longer allow herself to hold anything back. Somehow she was going to overcome her own foolish resistance, because more than anything in the world she wanted to belong to Braden, to really be his wife—and not in name alone.

Chapter 14

Cyril headed toward his bedchamber, lost in thought. The idea was spectacular—just the thing Braden needed to open his besotted eyes to the truth and end this travesty of a marriage. Cyril frowned, weighing the fact that Kassandra would inevitably be hurt and humiliated by his plan. He shrugged the worry away. She would thank him someday, when she was able to perceive the impossibility of her having a happy future with Braden.

A door closed quietly at the far end of the hall. Cyril turned around in surprise, wondering who was about at this late hour. To his astonishment, Kassandra's lady's maid, Margaret, was scurrying down the hall toward the stairs.

"Margaret?" He made his presence known at once. Obviously Margaret had just come from her mistress's bedchamber. What on earth could Kassandra have required at two o'clock in the morning?

Hearing her name, Margaret started and looked about.

"Oh, m'lord, 'tis you," she said with great relief as Cyril retraced his steps to the second-floor landing.

"Did you just come from Her Grace's room?" he asked, his brows knit in concern.

Margaret nodded. "Yes, m'lord, I did."

Cyril's frown deepened. "Why?"

The brusque demand made Margaret distinctly uncomfortable. Lord Cyril had always been pleasant to her, and she had no reason to distrust him. Still, it was the duke's right to know of his wife's torment before anyone else did,

Margaret's instincts told her. Then he could determine how to handle it.

Her decision made, Margaret gave Cyril a partial truth.

"Her Grace has been having difficulty sleeping, m'lord," she said in a respectful tone. "I went in to check on her."

Cyril visibly relaxed. "She is looking more and more peaked these days," he agreed. "I only wish there was something I could do."

"You have been extremely kind to our new duchess, m'lord," Margaret replied at once. "And I know how much she appreciates your concern. I think she will improve greatly when His Grace returns to Sherburgh. She misses him very much."

Cyril's expression was bland. He remained silent, absorbing Margaret's words.

"Will that be all, m'lord?" she asked after a moment.

Cyril blinked. "Excuse me?"

"I said will that be all, m'lord?" Margaret repeated. "It is late, and if you have no further questions . . ."

"I'm sorry, Margaret, of course," Cyril said at once. "I didn't mean to detain you. By all means, get some rest. It will soon be day."

"Thank you, m'lord. Good night."

"Good night, Margaret."

Cyril stared down the hall at Kassie's closed door. Then, with a deep sigh, he turned and went to bed.

"God, but it's good to be back!" Braden stretched his legs and gazed out the carriage window, drinking in the familiar sights of Sherburgh.

Charles studied his friend silently. Never had Braden been so restless on a trip, and never had he so eagerly anticipated their return home. And all because of one beautiful young woman who had found her way into his heart.

Charles smiled. Oh, Braden had never admitted it, not even to himself. But having known Braden since boyhood, Charles recognized the signs of transformation. *And* their cause.

Braden Sheffield was in love.

"You're certainly pensive today," Braden commented, glancing curiously at Charles.

"I was thinking that you did not accomplish what you intended on this trip."

Braden's dark brows went up in surprise. "The meeting was most productive. And the mare we acquired at Tattersall's is a beauty."

"I wasn't referring to our business, Braden."

Dead silence.

"I was referring to your decisions with regard to your marriage."

More silence.

Charles leaned forward soberly. "Braden, you have successfully avoided mentioning Kassandra's name for five days now. The problem can be ignored no longer. What is it that you intend to do?"

"Because I have not spoken of Kassie does not mean I have not thought of her," Braden replied quietly. An understatement at best, he admitted to himself. He had thought of little else since leaving for London.

"And . . ."

Braden sighed. "And I am as confused as ever. I realize now that I was a fool to think I could squelch my desire for Kassandra. Quite simply, she is beautiful, she is my wife, and I want her." The words conjured up an image of Kassie lying half-naked in his arms by the stream. Braden gritted his teeth. "The question is, what does Kassie want? The answer, I'm afraid, is that she doesn't know *what* she wants. She is part grown woman, part frightened child. She is strong, yet so very fragile, and I am concerned about hurting her or reopening old wounds."

Charles nodded his agreement. "Then what course is open to you?"

"I must wait for her to come to me."

"I see. You are protecting Kassandra's feelings."

Charles didn't add that in his opinion, it was not only Kassie's feelings, Kassie's wounds that were at stake here, but Braden's as well. Charles was convinced that somewhere deep inside of him Braden was aware of his own powerful feelings for his wife—feelings he would prefer not to acknowledge nor to accept. He would fight this ultimate emotional commitment with every self-protective fiber of his being.

"Then there is the problem of Robert Grey," Braden continued, gazing out the window.

Charles's expression hardened. "Kassandra said that he hadn't returned since the day after the wedding."

Braden nodded. "I know. But my instincts tell me that we have not seen the last of that bastard. I am also convinced that he is in some way responsible for the recurring nightmare that torments Kassie."

"She has not told you any of the details of her dream?"

Braden shook his head. "Not yet. However, that is one problem that I plan to resolve immediately. Tonight my wife and I are going to have a long talk, after which I will know exactly what it is that terrorizes her. Then I can attempt to resolve it." His jaw tightened. "And God help Robert Grey if he is involved."

Charles put his hand on Braden's arm. "You don't know that Grey has any connection to Kassandra's dreams."

Braden turned blazing eyes to his friend. "Do you doubt that Grey is capable of any number of things when he is foxed?"

Charles paled. "No."

"Nor do I. And if he hurt Kassie in any way, I will kill him."

The carriage came to a stop. Two liveried footmen hastened to assist the duke from his coach. The front doors of the house were thrown open immediately, and an efficient Perkins appeared in the entranceway.

"Welcome home, Your Grace."

Braden nodded. "Thank you, Perkins. Where is my wife?"

Charles had to stifle a smile at the rapidly fired question.

Perkins blinked. "Why, I believe she went for a ri—walk in the gardens," he corrected himself. Her Grace had made it quite clear that she wanted her new knowledge of riding to be a surprise for her husband. She was doing remarkably well, Dobson had reported, despite her mishap with Star earlier in the week. And Perkins had no intention of doing anything to erase the sparkle from the duchess's eyes.

"Is she out walking alone, Perkins?"

"Why, yes, Your Grace. I believe she mentioned that she wanted some time to herself."

Braden turned, squinting, and scanned the gardens.

"I don't see her, Perkins."

"The gardens on the south side of the estate, Your Grace," Perkins quickly amended.

"There are no gardens on the south side of the estate, Perkins," Braden replied impatiently.

"Did I say the gardens? I meant the grounds."

"The grounds," Braden repeated. "Perkins, you said she wanted to be alone."

Perkins swallowed. "Why, she did, Your Grace."

Braden's body tensed. "The south side of the estate is where all my tenants' cottages are located, Perkins. That is hardly the place to go for privacy."

"Perhaps I misunderstood." Beads of perspiration broke out on the poor butler's forehead. "Perhaps it was the *north* side of the estate."

Fear clutched at Braden's heart. "Are you keeping something from me, Perkins?"

Pulling himself up to his full height, Perkins fairly bristled at the insult to his integrity. "Certainly not, Your Grace. I am merely trying to recall—"

"Where is she, Perkins?" Braden ground out, his control snapping.

"There she is, Braden," Charles broke in, pointing.

Both Braden and Perkins sagged with relief at the sight of Kassie strolling toward the house. Unaware that her husband had returned, she was lost in thought, still exhilarated by her ride on Little Lady, who was today as good as new.

Braden watched Kassie approach and felt a rush of warmth flow through him. Her elegant riding clothes fit her lush little body to perfection; her rich black hair was tied with a matching ribbon and hung in shining curls down her back. To his surprise, Braden felt a pang of sadness. Gone was the spontaneous young woman she had been. Before him, was a true duchess.

At that moment Kassie saw him.

"Braden!"

She screamed his name, instantly and indelicately lifted her skirts high above her ankles, and fairly flew to where her husband stood. She didn't hesitate but launched herself against him, flinging her arms about his neck and nearly catapulting them both to the ground with her enthusiastic welcome.

Five footmen and three gardeners gaped at the unheard-of display.

Characteristically, Charles grinned.

Uncharacteristically, so did Perkins.

Braden laughed out loud, wrapping his arms about his wife and steadying them both on their feet.

"Hello, sweetheart." He kissed the tip of her nose. "Does this mean that you're glad to see me?"

Kassie flushed, becoming aware of the number of eyes focused on her. "Braden," she began.

"I missed you, too," he told her gently, lowering her to the ground. And he had—more than he'd realized. He stared down into her beautiful face, frowning when he saw the dark circles beneath her eyes and the pale cast to her skin. "Are you all right?"

She nodded vigorously. "Just fine," she said, a little too quickly.

Braden studied her face a moment longer, seeing far more than she wished him to see. Then his gaze moved lower, and a perplexed look crossed his handsome features. "Were you at the stables?" he asked, noting her riding clothes for the first time.

"W-well," she stammered.

"Braden, Charles. Welcome home." Cyril stood on the front stairs, unknowingly rescuing Kassie from her dilemma. Not waiting for a response, he added thoughtfully, "It is good that you have returned."

"I agree." Braden gave Kassie one of his lazy grins that made her bones melt.

"Before you see to your unpacking," Cyril continued quickly, "I wonder if I might have a word with you."

Braden reacted to his uncle's serious tone and troubled

expression. "Of course." He watched Cyril's retreat thoughtfully, then, with mounting unease, turned back to his wife. "I won't be long."

"Braden?" She stayed him with her hand. "After you have spoken with Cyril, I wonder if you would do something for me."

He saw the sparkle of excitement in her eyes—another hint of the old Kassie—and he relaxed a bit. "Anything." His answer was emphatic.

"Change into your riding clothes and meet me at the stables."

His puzzled look returned. "Now? Why? Is there something—"

"Please," she interrupted. "For me. Just do it." She waited, her expression questioning.

Charles cleared his throat loudly. Kassie glanced over at him, and Braden had a brief glimpse of the dimples in Kassie's cheeks. Then they were gone, and she was serious again.

Braden shot Charles a suspicious look, but the older man was intently contemplating the leaves on the nearby oak trees.

"Kassandra, what are you up to?" Braden's tone was stern, but his hazel eyes twinkled. When she didn't respond he caught her chin in his hand, trying to read her expression. She kept it carefully blank. "Very well," he sighed at last. "I see the only way I shall find out what I want to know is to do as you ask. I'll meet you as soon as I can."

She stood on tiptoe and kissed his jaw. "Thank you." She stepped away. "Now hurry! I shall expect you shortly." She scurried off.

Charles headed for the house.

"You know something," Braden accused.

"I suspect something," Charles corrected. "And if what I suspect is true, you have a delightful surprise ahead of you." To avoid explaining further, Charles disappeared through the entranceway door.

Amused and curious, Braden strode into the house and headed toward the library. The sooner he had this discussion with Cyril, the sooner he would be privy to Kassie's little secret.

The dark look on Cyril's face made Braden's light humor disintegrate.

"What is the problem, Cyril?" He closed the door behind him.

Cyril rubbed his chin thoughtfully. "I'm not certain. But I have the distinct feeling that Kassandra is having a difficult time adjusting to her new life."

Braden frowned. "That is neither a problem nor a shock, Cyril. It's been less than a month since we married, and the change is a dramatic one for Kassie."

"She is unused to our ways and our priorities."

Braden wanted to point out that his priorities and Cyril's were vastly different and that he had no desire for Kassie to emulate the latter, but he held his tongue. "What exactly are you referring to?" he asked, sensing that Cyril had something specific on his mind.

"She has been having trouble sleeping," Cyril told him.

Braden started. "How do you know this?"

"I saw Margaret, Kassandra's lady's maid, coming from your wife's bedchamber in the middle of the night. I asked her if there was a problem, and she implied that Kassandra was unable to sleep."

The nightmares, Braden thought.

"Also," Cyril was continuing, "Kassandra had occasion to meet"—he hesitated—"some of our friends."

The pause was not lost to Braden. "Oh, really? Which *friends* in particular?"

Cyril swallowed, knowing what was coming. "William and Abigail stopped by to see you, and—"

"You allowed Kassie to be alone with that bitch!" Braden exploded.

"They were not alone," Cyril cut into the oncoming tirade. "I was present, as was William. Nothing inappropriate was said."

"Oh, I'm sure Abigail was her usual charming self." Braden's voice was laced with sarcasm, his heart sinking as he pictured the scene that must have occurred. Kassie's trusting gentleness was no match for Abigail's acid tongue.

"Kassandra did seem a bit unsettled after they left." Cyril saw no point in lying. Kassandra would only tell Braden the truth herself. And besides, the fact that Braden's wife had been unprepared for her earlier encounter would only work to Cyril's advantage.

"Unsettled?" Braden repeated slowly.

"Yes. Unsettled." Cyril walked over to where Braden stood. "She must learn to deal with women such as Abigail if she wants to survive in our world, Braden. As you know, Abigail is far from unique."

Braden gave a hollow laugh. "How true."

Cyril nodded. "I have a suggestion. Why don't you host a house party? Nothing too elaborate, just the most influential members of the *ton.*"

"That should limit it to a mere four or five hundred," Braden interjected dryly.

Cyril ignored the comment. "Kassandra is going to have to meet these people at some point, Braden. You cannot keep her locked up at Sherburgh, isolated, forever. This way she can meet them under *your* roof and with you at her side." He paused, trying to gauge Braden's reaction. "I believe that it would help to ease her way." Sensing victory, Cyril delivered what he knew would be his most convincing argument. "Besides, did it ever occur to you that your wife is lonely for the company of other women? Surely from a crowd of many there will be one or two ladies that will suit her needs. After all, she is surrounded by nothing but men here at Sherburgh, with only her lady's maid to provide her with companionship. Kassandra is a warm and caring young woman who has been shut off from the world her whole life. You must think of her happiness, Braden, and stop being so protective of her. Why, this could be the best, the most exciting thing that has ever happened to her—save marrying you, of course."

He took a deep breath and waited.

Braden stared at the floor. Although he was puzzled by Cyril's uncharacteristic concern, he could not deny that a great deal of what his uncle said was true. Maybe he *was* being unfair to Kassie. Maybe she *did* crave female companionship. And it was also true that she would have to appear by his side at social functions eventually. Why not begin now, when she was in familiar, and therefore less intimidating, surroundings?

Kassie inclined her head slightly, giving Star a measured look. "I suppose we must settle our differences and resume speaking to each other now that Braden is home," she informed the Thoroughbred, who pricked up his ears in response. "I recognize that some of it was my fault, brought on by my own inexperience and conceit. But you were to blame as well." Kassie punctuated her admonishment with an injured sniff. "So I propose that we forget the whole nasty incident."

Star snorted his agreement.

"Good." Kassie seemed unsurprised by Star's ready response. "Then that is settled."

Braden stared openmouthed at Charles. "I don't believe this."

"Kassandra has quite a way with horses," Charles replied, chuckling. "They seem to understand one another."

"So I see. And apparently I missed quite a spectacle while I was away."

Charles and Dobson said nothing, both giving Braden a blank stare.

Kassie's smile drenched her friends in sunlight. "Thank you. You are true gentlemen." She turned to Braden. "Shall we go?"

"Lead the way," he urged.

They rode for a time in silence, Braden thinking how natural his wife looked on horseback—as if she had been born to it. He knew she had done this for him, and he felt a warm glow unfurl inside his chest.

They both knew where they were headed. It was the one thing that had remained unchanged between them, the place in which they sought solace . . . the place where they had met.

Chapter 15

Braden dismounted first, reaching up to help Kassie to the ground. She placed her hands upon his shoulders, and he lowered her slowly, unable to resist prolonging the moments when her body was against his.

At last her feet touched the ground.

"Thank you, *ma petite.* It was a wonderful surprise." Braden's voice was deep and husky.

Kassie smiled. "I'm glad."

With his forefinger he traced the dark circles beneath her eyes. "You've been having the nightmares again."

She sighed. "You've been talking to Margaret."

"She's worried about you. So am I."

Kassie nodded. "I don't know why they've gotten so severe."

"Has he been back?"

Kassie knew Braden meant her father. "No. Not since that day." She raised her head to meet Braden's penetrating gaze. "I'm sorry I didn't tell you about it. I only wanted to block it from my mind. And I knew how angry you would be."

"What did he want? Money?"

"Yes."

"That miserable basta—"

"Braden, please," she whispered. "He's not worth it. I don't think he'll be back. I told him that I wouldn't give him any more money."

"Does he know about these dreams of yours?"

She nodded. "Yes. But he's always brushed them off as nonsense. He believes that my imagination is my real enemy."

Braden believed otherwise. "Tell me about the nightmare."

Kassie stepped away from him and wrapped her arms about herself, staring off into the sea.

"It's always the same," she murmured at last. "For as long as I can remember. It's dark. I'm alone, walking, and I'm frightened."

"Of what?"

"I don't know. Something."

Or someone, Braden thought to himself.

"And then a huge black beast begins to chase me." Her voice quivered, and she could feel herself grow cold. Braden came up behind her and drew her back against him, offering her his strength. But Kassie was hardly aware of his presence, so absorbed was she in her own words. "I try so hard to escape him, but I know that it's impossible. And then I am swallowed. . . ." She shuddered.

"By the beast?"

"No. By a huge, bottomless hole. I can feel myself dropping . . . falling . . . and I can hear the screams. But no one comes. No one saves me."

Braden turned her around, pressing her face to his chest and wrapping his arms around her. "I won't let anything or anyone hurt you," he vowed. "Not ever."

She looked up and gave him a tremulous smile. "I know." She stood on tiptoe and touched her lips to his, her eyes damp with emotion. "I missed you."

"Good," he responded with a lazy grin. "There's nothing sweeter than being missed by a beautiful woman."

Those were not the words Kassie wanted to hear.

She could feel the extraordinary mood shatter into a million fragments around her, all the insecurities of the past few days coming to the surface. Inadvertently she found herself wondering if another woman had kept Braden company during his absence.

"Why are you frowning?" Braden asked tenderly, unaware of the approaching storm.

"Exactly how many women preceded me?" Kassie blurted out.

Braden started. "Excuse me?"

Kassie flushed and stepped out of his grasp. "I said how many women were you involved with before you married me?"

"What kind of a question is that?" Braden demanded.

"A simple one. I want to know just how many women know my husband intimately . . . aside from *Lady* Abigail Devon, of course." Kassie couldn't keep the anger from her voice any longer. She had just revealed things about herself to Braden that she had never told another person, bared her soul and let her heart shine in her eyes. He had given her nothing in return except more fuel for her ever-growing doubt. And it hurt.

Braden raked his fingers through his hair. "Abigail. I should have known." He took Kassie's arms firmly and shook her. "Kassie, don't believe anything that woman says."

"Does that mean that you were not involved with her?"

Braden's jaw tightened. "It means that you have never come up against someone such as Abigail before. She is nothing like you—"

Kassie flung off his arms, tears sliding down her cheeks. "Obviously not."

"What the hell is that supposed to mean?" Now Braden was becoming angry.

Kassie ignored the question. "I notice that you didn't deny your involvement with her," she accused, her voice rising.

"Whether or not I was involved with Abigail Devon has nothing to do with you!" he shot back.

"Oh, really?" Kassie was furious. "I suppose that was my mistake. Here I thought I was your wife." She turned and ran down the beach.

"You are my wife, damn it, not my keeper!" Braden shouted after her. She didn't stop. Braden felt the combined emotions and frustrations of the last weeks converge, then explode inside him. "Kassie! Come back here *now!*"

She didn't even pause.

Braden tore off after her, feeling the blood pound in his head. He was going to catch up with her, and then he was going to wring her beautiful neck. The audacity of that blasted chit, asking him whose bed he had shared, when all these weeks she had been taunting him with that luscious, unattainable body of hers!

He grabbed her from behind and spun her around.

"Let go of me!" There was no fear in either Kassie's voice or her flashing eyes, only anger.

"Not until you explain yourself." Braden dragged her up against his powerful body.

"I think I made myself perfectly clear, *Your Grace,*" she snapped back, still struggling. "But apparently you think I have no right to know who you've taken to your bed!"

"I wouldn't need to take anyone else to my bed if you weren't so damned untouchable!" The words were pouring out before he could censor them, his rage making him reckless. "Damn you, Kassandra, I'm constantly aching, burning alive. And for whom? For you, my naïve little wife. For you."

"Is that why you left Sherburgh? You have a very strange way of showing that you want me, Braden." She threw back her dark hair defiantly, her eyes twin jewels of fire.

"Want you?" he demanded in a rough, deep voice. "Do you want to see how much I want you?" He dug his hands into her hair and anchored her head so she was unable to move.

Before Kassie could speak, Braden had captured her mouth with his, devouring her with all the pent-up passion and none of the restraint of the past. He crushed her lips beneath the heat of his kiss, moving his mouth back and forth roughly again and again against her soft, trembling lips. Kassie felt the insistent pressure of his mouth forcing hers open, and with a moan of protest she gave him what he wanted. His tongue swept inside to capture hers; his arms tightened around her like steel bands. Waves of dizziness seized Kassie, and as if in a trance she accepted Braden's brand of total possession. The kiss was violent, shattering

. . . and yet Kassie could feel a kind of sweet desperation within its whirling tempest. It was like Braden himself, she thought wildly: hard and impenetrable, yet possessing an inner softness that she alone could reach.

Responding to this unspoken core of gentleness, Kassie relented all in a rush, wrapping her arms about his neck and pressing herself unashamedly against her husband's powerful thighs.

The effect on Braden was electrifying.

Tremors shook his broad frame, and he ground out Kassie's name, lifting her off the ground and sliding one of his hands down her back to hold her against his hard, throbbing body. Half expecting Kassie to freeze with fear, Braden was stunned to feel her mold herself closer to him, sliding her fingers into his thick, dark hair and whispering his name with the same fierce longing that pounded through his famished body and into his loins.

Uncontrollable hunger took over.

The world existed only for them, between them, and no earthly force could have stopped the inevitability of that moment. Kassie felt the sand beneath her back, felt the sun on her face, felt Braden urgently unfastening her gown, tugging her clothes from her body. She helped him, as desperate as he to rid herself of the barriers that stood between them. She opened her eyes, and the dazzling light of the sun combined with the harsh, blinding passion that blazed in Braden's eyes, that was etched on every line of his handsome face.

The need inside Kassie was more than she could bear. Sitting up, she brought shaking hands to Braden's shirtfront, trying unsuccessfully to release the buttons and lessen the time until she could feel him against her. Braden rose to his knees and brushed her hands away, freeing the hindering buttons in mere seconds and tearing his shirt from his body. He tossed it carelessly onto the sand; then, seeing his own need reflected in her eyes, he lowered himself against her, melding their naked skin.

Kassie's eyes closed on a whimper. Never had anything felt so good. The soft abrasiveness of Braden's chest hair rubbed sensuously against her suddenly taut, straining nipples. Arching her back, she moved slowly back and forth, making the pleasure almost unbearable.

"Kassie . . . God . . ." Braden was being enveloped in flames, and he wondered for one intolerable second if he could control himself long enough to finish undressing her. He had never been so out of control. Nothing mattered in the world but having Kassie naked and under him . . . now.

Braden rose back to his knees, his chest heaving with the strain of waiting. Kassie opened her eyes and stared up at him, her gaze filled with wonder and unappeased hunger.

"Braden . . . please . . ."

Like a man possessed he tore off the rest of her clothes. As he pulled off his breeches and boots he stared down at her, knowing that no fantasy had ever come close to the perfection that was before him. He slid his arm beneath her back and lifted her, dragging his discarded shirt under her to protect her tender skin. Then he lowered himself beside her, stroking the length of her body, worshiping her with his gaze and his touch. Kassie felt his reverence, his whisper-soft caresses, and all her shyness and her doubts evaporated. This was Braden, her husband, and she belonged to him, totally and always.

"Kassie . . . you are so beautiful, so utterly, incomparably exquisite." He breathed the words against her throat, fighting the relentless urge to forgo words and caresses and drive himself deep into her flawless body. "Do you have any idea how much I want you?" he gasped. He kissed his way down to her shoulders, to her breasts, teasing the hardened peaks with light tugs of his lips and tongue. "I've never"—he drew her nipple deep into his mouth—"never"—he tugged again —"never felt like this in my life." Panting, he turned his attention to her other breast, drawing on it hungrily until Kassie cried out with pleasure.

"Braden . . ." Kassie arched upwards, offering more of herself to him. Her body was dissolving in liquid fire, a raging need like none she had ever imagined pooling between her thighs. Instinctively she opened her legs, not knowing what she needed, knowing only that Braden could ease the growing, pulsing ache inside her.

The innocent invitation was Braden's undoing.

His last shreds of control gone, he took Kassie's mouth in a scalding kiss and slid his fingers between her trembling thighs. Her wetness made his already painfully engorged manhood harden until waiting became an intolerable agony.

"Kassie . . . love . . . I'm sorry. . . ." Even as he spoke he was moving over her, settling himself in the cradle of her thighs. Their eyes met, and he saw no trace of fear, only passion, longing . . . and something even more beautiful than both. "Let me love you," he whispered, finding the heated entrance to her body with his. "Let me bury myself inside you . . . Kassie." He whispered her name again as he pressed himself into her wet, hot tightness. He held her gaze, bracing himself on his hands and, despite his urgency, pushing into her an inch at a time, letting her body accustom itself to his penetration. He watched her eyes widen, first with surprise, then with wonder, and finally with a flash of pain. But she never took her gaze from his, never attempted to pull away from his possession.

They both felt the delicate membrane tear.

Kassie's soft cry mingled with Braden's ecstatic, wondrous groan.

"Kassie . . . oh, Kassie . . . at last." He said nothing more, just lowered himself totally upon her tense body and wrapped his arms around her, sliding his hands down to her silky bottom. "Relax, love," he murmured in her ear. "Just let yourself feel me. I'm inside you, sweetheart. I'm where I belong. Ah, Kassie, yes, like that," he urged, feeling her relax, then lift her body experimentally up to his.

Kassie had entered a world she had never imagined existed. The initial pain of Braden's entry was already forgotten. She could actually feel him throbbing inside her, answering her own body's reflexive tightening with his own. He was huge and scalding, and hungry for a rhythm that she, too, sought, knowing instinctively that it would bring fulfillment to them both.

Braden taught her, helped her, whispering heated words in her ear while he increased his thrusts . . . harder, deeper into her softness. Kassie raised her legs to hug his hips, and he lost all control, lifting her up hard while he drove down into the very center of her being. She tightened her grip on his back, reveling in the wetness of his sweat-drenched skin and opening herself totally to his frenzied thrusts.

"Kassie!" Her name was a shout, a hoarse cry from deep within Braden's soul. He could feel his climax building to excruciating proportions, and he knew that there would soon be no holding back. But he needed more.

He raised up enough to slide his hand between their bodies, to touch her where she was aching and desperately needing to be touched. He continued to move, his strokes deep and powerful, and he felt her nails dig into his back, her body tighten around his. "That's it, sweetheart," he panted. "Let it happen. Let yourself go. Give yourself to me . . . all of yourself . . . now. I'll never hurt you. Never. Kassie!" Her name was a primal roar that exploded from his chest. "Now, love, now . . ."

Answering his frantic plea, Kassie's body spun away from her, erupting in a continuous spasm of ecstatic pleasure, carrying her to a world of pure sensation.

He heard her cry out, felt the clasping contractions of her body just as his own wild release claimed him. Their joy, their cries of fulfillment, their bodies' warm fluids joined in a pinnacle of sensation so stark, so intense that the pleasure was almost unendurable, leaving them totally drained and breathless.

For a long time neither one of them moved. Braden could feel Kassie's heart beating against his, her soft, damp skin pressed close to him, their bodies still intimately entwined. Slowly he became aware of the sea slapping against the shore, the warmth of the setting sun heating his bare back, the sound of their horses softly whinnying their impatience.

He smiled as contentment washed through him in great waves. Kassie stirred beneath him, and he lifted his head to look at her.

"Did I hurt you?"

In response to his soft question she reached up to touch his handsome, worried face, shaking her head, a dreamy look in her eyes. "No. And if you did, I've already forgotten."

Braden smiled, the slow, possessive smile of a man who had just made the most beautiful woman in the world his wife.

"Does this mean our argument is over?" he teased, rolling gently off of her.

She laughed, looking like an exquisite, naked, newly ravished sea nymph. "I suppose so."

"We'd better start home before Charles and Dobson come looking for us," he told her, standing. He laughed at the appalled expression on Kassie's face. "Don't worry, love," he assured her. "They would never know where to find us."

Kassie nodded, staring at him in wonder. "You are magnificent."

Her uninhibited honesty touched him as much as the compliment itself. Now that sanity had returned he had expected her to be embarrassed, maybe even mortified by their nakedness and the urgency of their first union. He had expected many things, but never this. "Thank you," he said simply, meeting her gaze. At her heated look he could feel himself harden, and he turned hastily away, unwilling to frighten her with the intensity of his desire. He actually wanted her again, he thought in amazement, donning his breeches and boots. After what they had just shared he thought he'd be insensate for a week. He should have known better. This was Kassie, after all.

He turned back and gathered Kassie's scattered clothes, then extended his hand to her. "Come, love," he said gently.

She gave him her hand and stood, pulling on her undergarments and gown in rapid succession.

Braden reached for his shirt and frowned at the small bloodstain that was the blatant reminder of what had just occurred. He felt Kassie's eyes upon him, and he raised his head. She blushed and lowered hers. He went to her.

"Are you all right?" he asked gently.

"Yes."

"You do know that you won't ever bleed again . . . only this first time?"

She nodded. "I know now."

He drew her against him and kissed the top of her head. Then, without a word, he strode over to the water's edge and dunked his shirt, holding it there until all traces of the bloodstain—and Kassie's childhood—were gone. He wrung out the wet shirt, then shrugged back into it.

Kassie finished buttoning her gown just as Braden returned to her side.

"Come, wife," he said softly, "let's go home."

Chapter 16

❧

I have never seen hair as lovely as yours, Your Grace—as rich and soft as black silk." Margaret drew the brush through the gleaming tresses that hung down the back of Kassie's night rail.

"Um-m-m," Kassie responded, totally oblivious to Margaret's compliment. She continued to stare at her reflection in the dressing table mirror, searching for the physical changes she was certain must be evident. The huge aqua eyes that stared back at her could find none. How could she look so very much the same when she was so totally transformed?

Kassie gave a blissful sigh. She was acutely aware of her body's soreness: the raw tenderness of her breasts, the twinges of discomfort between her thighs. She rejoiced in all the aching sensations, for they served as reminders of what had happened today on the beach . . . when Braden had made her his.

A small, self-satisfied smile curved her lips. She had not known what to expect, but nothing had prepared her for the consuming need and resulting euphoria she had found in Braden's arms. So this was what it meant to be a woman, to belong to a man. It was glorious!

"Your Grace?"

Kassie blinked, surprised to see Margaret watching her expectantly.

"I'm sorry . . . what did you say, Margaret?"

A knowing gaze took in the slight flush of Kassie's cheeks and the sparkle in her blue-green eyes.

"I asked if you would like something warm to drink to help you sleep." Margaret's lips twitched. "Although I must say you don't look at all tired."

Kassie dimpled, too elated to be embarrassed. "I'm not," she confessed softly. "In fact, sleep is the furthest thing from my mind." She turned in her seat and took Margaret's hand. "I'm so happy," she whispered.

Margaret squeezed Kassie's hand. "I can see that. Having His Grace home is obviously just what you needed."

"Oh, yes, it is!" Kassie agreed, rushing on breathlessly. "But it's not only having Braden home, it's that I finally feel . . ." She broke off as common sense asserted itself over her uninhibited need to share her joy with the loving woman who was becoming more a mother to her every day. How could she share such an intimate thing with anyone? But how could she keep it inside when she was bursting with her own awakening?

Margaret read the warring emotions on Kassie's face with understanding and tenderness. "I know, lovey," she said gently, her gaze conveying more than her words. "I know."

"Then you must also know that I couldn't even *think* of sleeping!"

"Fine," Margaret said, chuckling. "Your bed is turned down, and the novel you are so absorbed in is on your nightstand. Why don't you read until you become tired?"

Kassie nodded, rising from her seat. "I'll do that, Margaret. And you go off to bed . . . it is late."

Margaret stroked Kassie's glowing curls. "I'll just braid your hair, and then I'll be off."

"Leave it loose."

Braden's deep baritone made both women start. Neither had heard him come in, yet he leaned against the open doorway that connected his bedchamber to Kassie's. He was still fully clothed, but there was no mistaking the husky command in his voice nor the heated look in his eyes.

"Yes, of course, Your Grace," Margaret replied, recovering herself at once and beaming her approval in Braden's direction. "Then if there is nothing further the duchess needs, I'll say good night."

Kassie was staring at Braden. "Good night, Margaret," she murmured. Vaguely she heard the door close, signifying Margaret's departure.

Braden began to advance slowly toward Kassie, raking her lush, explicit curves with his hot gaze. In truth, he had come only to say good night, to hold her for a moment before they retired, to make certain that she was all right after their unexpected, fervent lovemaking. He had hurt her; undoubtedly she would be sore for days due to his total loss of control. Making love to her again was the furthest thing from his mind.

Until he saw the openly hungry look in her eyes.

"You are ready for bed," Braden heard himself say in a hoarse voice.

"I'm not tired."

His loins tightened at her hasty response. "Good." He stopped mere inches before her, reaching out to glide his fingers through her thick tresses. "I hope you didn't mind my request. It's just that it would be a sin to restrict such a silken treasure as this."

Kassie could hardly breathe. "I don't mind," she whispered.

Never taking his eyes from hers, Braden gathered a handful of her shining curls and buried his face in them. "I'm glad," he murmured, "because there are some things that are too rare, too exquisite to hide." He slid his other hand up her bare arm, feeling her tremble at his touch. "Your hair is one of those things." In one swift gesture he released her hair and seized both straps of her night rail, tugging them off her shoulders until the gown slid down her body into a satin pool at her feet. "So is your body," he breathed in a husky whisper that was filled with forbidden promise.

"Braden . . ." Kassie reached up to stroke his face, unashamedly breathtaking in her nudity.

Desire crashed through Braden's body in great, unrelenting waves, pounding through his veins and exploding into a tidal wave of need that nearly brought him to his knees. Without a word he swept Kassie up into his shaking arms and carried her through the doorway and into his room, lowering her upon the unmade bed. For reasons he refused to examine Braden needed to make love to Kassie here, in his domain, to possess her in the most fundamental way possible, to reestablish that she was totally and irrevocably his.

He stood, his chest heaving with each labored breath, and drank in every detail of Kassie's beauty. His gaze locked with hers, singeing her with the undisguised flames that burned in the hazel depths.

"God, how I want you," he rasped, beyond all reason or sanity.

Kassie opened her arms to him, holding nothing back. Wordlessly she offered him all of herself, everything she felt shining in her eyes.

Braden tore off his clothing, falling upon her like a man starved. "Kassandra." He whispered her name reverently, covering her mouth with his and taking all that she silently promised. He kissed her deeply, urgently, shuddering helplessly as she wound her arms around his neck, stroked her hands down his back. He was lost and he knew it, and a voice inside him cried out its warning. But it went unheeded, for nothing mattered now but Kassie and making her his again.

Already aroused beyond control, Braden fought the frantic need to pull Kassie beneath him and drive himself as deeply as possible inside her welcoming warmth. He craved her flesh as he had never craved anything in his life, and his body throbbed helplessly against hers, begging for admittance.

Braden refused to give in to his body's demand. For he felt another need, one far stronger than his need for release. He needed to bind Kassie to him, to make her so completely his that the memory of their joining would forever burn in her mind and in her heart.

He lifted his head. "I want you," he repeated in a raw voice.

"You have me, Braden," she whispered back. "You always have."

"All of you," he demanded.

"All of me" was the soft affirmation.

As if to challenge her words, Braden caught both her hands in his and lifted them over her head. He buried his lips against her neck, taking light, nipping tastes of her skin, reveling in the soft sounds of pleasure that came from deep in her throat and vibrated against his mouth. "Tell me what you want, Kassie . . . tell me where you ache for me." Braden's lips made a slow trail down to Kassie's breast. "Here, love? Do you need me here?"

Kassie's answer was a soft cry, her body arching helplessly up to his seeking mouth.

It was answer enough.

Braden took what she offered, drawing her nipple deeply into his mouth, grazing it with his teeth and circling with his tongue until Kassie whimpered, her hips undulating involuntarily in an age-old plea for more.

Braden gave it to her.

He moved to her other breast, tugging hard at the aroused nipple without preliminaries at the same time that his hand slid between Kassie's shaking thighs, claiming her warm, wet softness in a devastating caress that made her sob out his name and dig her fingers into his shoulders.

Openmouthed, Braden moved down her body, defining every inch with his lips and tongue, his fingers sensuously stroking the pulsing, yearning flesh between her legs. Kassie was writhing beneath him, unable to lie still and endure the nearly painful pleasure that coursed through her veins at each hungry caress.

"Braden . . . stop . . . I can't . . ." she begged.

This time he understood that her plea had nothing to do with fear.

"Yes," he whispered back. "You can." He circled her navel with his tongue at the same time that he slid his fingers deep inside her.

Kassie cried out, her inner muscles tightening reflexively around his fingers.

Braden felt his own body leap in response. "You're so tight," he rasped. He moved further down in the bed, pressing apart her legs and sliding his hands beneath her before she knew what he intended.

At the first stroke of his tongue her eyes flew open in shock. "Oh, Braden . . . don't . . . you can't . . ."

He was lost in her taste, her scent, the very essence of her. "Yes," he breathed, "I can."

Kassie never knew when her protests became pleas. All she knew was that she would die if he stopped, that a pleasure like none she had ever known was building inside her, coiling tighter and tighter with each stroke of Braden's tongue, each brush of his lips, until she was sobbing aloud for him to ease the unbearable longing inside her.

Again and again Braden took her to the very edge, refusing to relinquish her to the finality of her release, unwilling to give up the sheer ecstasy of this ultimate possession of his wife. At last, when Kassie's cries became frantic, when Braden's own need was so out of control that prolonging the moment became untenable, he tore his mouth from her dewy sweetness and moved his powerful frame up and over her soft, shaking body.

She opened to him without hesitation, wrapping her arms about him and gazing up at him with hunger, with adoration, with trust.

Braden ran his hands down her body, lifted her legs to hug his flanks. "I don't . . . want . . . to hurt you," he managed through clenched teeth, struggling for a control that had long since evaporated. With a will of their own his hips flexed forward, forcing his rigid, engorged manhood into the warm opening of Kassie's body. "Kassie," he groaned, closing his eyes and bracing himself as he fought to slow the penetration.

Kassie's inexperienced young body was desperate for release, a release that was a mere pulsebeat away and that she knew only Braden could give her. She sensed he was holding back for her sake, but she no longer gave a damn whether he hurt her or not. She was frantic.

Urgently she reached between their bodies, her fingers closing around his throbbing shaft, forcing him deeper into her wet, pliant body.

Braden's eyes flew open. "Kassandra . . ." He dragged her hand away and plunged into her with a driving thrust that made them both cry out.

There was no turning back, no slowing down. The floodgates of their passion burst open, and Braden took her with a wild desperation that he had never known he possessed. Again and again he buried himself inside her, helplessly surrendering to feelings that had everything and nothing to do with desire. He felt Kassie's nails score his back, felt her legs tighten about him mere seconds before she arched up to him on a broken cry. Braden crushed her to him, melding their bodies, swallowing her cry with his mouth. She shuddered beneath him, her inner muscles rhythmically contracting around him, caressing him in spasms of completion.

And then it was upon him. A climax that ignited inside him like a blazing inferno licked through his veins like live flames and erupted in scalding bursts of fire, flooding from Braden's body to Kassie's in an explosion of sensation that tore a hoarse shout from deep within his chest.

He called her name over and over, whispered it into her hair long after the highest peak had been reached and passed. Slowly he rolled to one side, cradling her in his strong arms, their bodies still joined.

Kassie couldn't stop shaking. She felt drained and renewed and more in love than she had ever dreamed possible. Closing her eyes, she buried her face against the warmth of Braden's powerful, hair-roughened chest, reveling in his tenderness, rejoicing in the passion and the pleasure she had brought him. *He loves me,* she thought with wonder, *I know he does.* No man could make love to a woman with such selfless intensity unless he felt something far greater than lust.

She sighed with pleasure, pressing herself closer to her husband's hard, damp body.

"Keep that up and I'm going to make love to you again." Braden's voice was a lazy caress, his lips buried in her hair.

Kassie leaned back in his arms and looked up at him with a dazzling smile. "Would that be so bad?"

Braden looked startled, then he chuckled, delighted by

her enthusiastic response to their passion. "No, my beautiful, honest wife, that would be magnificent." He rubbed his thumb thoughtfully across her kiss-swollen mouth. "I would never have waited so long to make you mine," he confessed huskily, "had I not been worried about hurting you . . . frightening you."

Kassie parted her lips, her warm breath teasing his thumb as she spoke. "I could never be afraid of you, Braden," she murmured reverently. "Never."

Braden watched the mesmerizing motion of her tongue, his body reacting instantly to her words, her mouth. "No," he said aloud. He eased gently from her clinging warmth but kept his arms locked tightly around her. "Your poor body has endured about all it can for one day."

Kassie looked puzzled. "Endured?" She slid her hands up his back to his shoulder blades. "But Braden," she whispered, still shivering a bit, "it was heaven."

Would he ever get used to the unique wonder of her astonishing, unspoiled innocence, her utterly guileless charm? Braden felt his chest tighten. "I'm glad I made you happy, sweetheart," he said softly, stroking her hot cheek with his knuckles. "But today was your first experience with lovemaking. I think you should rest."

Kassie flushed, reminded of how naïve she must seem to him. Braden had known so many women . . . had he shared these intimacies with them? The thought cast a small cloud on Kassie's euphoria, but she forced it away. Braden was hers . . . *hers*.

"It's been difficult for you, hasn't it, *ma petite?*"

Braden's words made Kassie tense. He couldn't know what she was thinking, could he?

"Difficult?" she repeated.

"Um-hum." He kissed her shoulder, wishing he hadn't promised himself not to make love to her again. Already he was on fire for her. With a resolute sigh he rolled onto his back and pressed her head against his chest. "You've been alone a great deal these past weeks."

Kassie looked up at him in surprise. "I'm used to that, Braden. I've been alone most of my life."

She said the words without bitterness or anger, but they

made Braden wince all the same. "I wanted more for you once you came to Sherburgh," he told her. "I want you to be happy."

She smiled, stretching like a contented kitten. "I am happy."

Braden's gaze fell to her full, naked breasts, feeling his body harden painfully in response. She was so incredibly beautiful . . . so totally uninhibited in his arms. Reflexively he bent his head and touched one nipple lightly with his tongue. "How would you feel about a house party?" he asked, knowing that in seconds he would lose his train of thought entirely.

Kassie's eyes were already becoming smoky with passion. "A house party?" she echoed, gliding her fingers down the taut planes of his abdomen.

Braden's breath came faster. "Yes. A party. Here. At Sherburgh," he managed, conscious only of her teasing fingers moving lower and lower on his body.

"It sounds wonderful," she murmured, hovering, watching his expression grow hard with passion, his eyes darken to a deep gray.

He caught her wrist. "I'll invite a minimal number of guests. But it is time for the world to meet my duchess." His burning gaze held hers.

"Yes, Braden," she said softly, tugging her hand free and snuggling closer. "I think it is a splendid idea."

He inhaled the scent of her skin, the musky smell of their lovemaking, and he felt his resolve deteriorate. "I'll go over the guest list with you," he rasped, licking his dry lips, "and answer all your questions so . . . you'll . . . feel . . . prepared. . . ." He broke off as Kassie's small hand found him and began to explore his hard, pulsing length. She caressed gently, reverently, enthralled by the velvety texture of his rigid flesh.

"I do have one question," she whispered, wriggling down in the bed.

"What?" Braden was aware of nothing but her touch.

"The way you loved me before . . . with your mouth. Would it give you pleasure if I loved you that way?"

Braden didn't answer. He didn't have to. Kassie got her

answer in the way Braden's hands clenched in her hair and drew her to him; in the wild leap his body gave when her lips closed around his throbbing shaft; in the broken, erotic words that poured uncontrollably from his mouth; and finally in the violent way he dragged her from him, crushed her beneath him, and buried himself within her wildly shuddering body.

"You're mine, Kassie," he gasped, pouring himself deep inside her. "Mine. Now. Always. You belong to me."

The words echoed inside Kassie's heart, lulling her to sleep in Braden's arms.

There were no nightmares that night.

Chapter 17

❧❧

"A re you *sure* the bodice isn't too low?"

Kassie turned anxious eyes to Margaret, who shook her head firmly from side to side.

"The gown is perfect on you, Your Grace! Why, it is the very height of fashion! Stop fretting so. The duke will be speechless with admiration!" Her eyes twinkled.

Kassie raised a skeptical brow. "I doubt that, Margaret. I have yet to see Braden speechless." She cast another anxious glance at her reflection in the huge oval mirror. "Do you really think I will do?"

Margaret beamed. The rich sapphire gown swirled in delicate folds of silk about Kassie's ankles. The deeply cut bodice and long, tapered sleeves were trimmed with velvet, and the hemline was embellished with fine layers of lace. Kassie's cheeks were flushed with excitement, the brilliant color of her eyes more vivid due to the gown's vibrant blue shade. Her carefully arranged ebony curls provided a startling contrast to the creamy expanse of skin revealed above her bodice. Around her neck sparkled Braden's latest gift, a magnificent strand of emeralds and sapphires identical to the ones that shimmered on Kassie's wedding band.

"Will you do?" Margaret repeated, shaking her head in disbelief. "Why, not another woman in the room will compare to you in beauty or grace!"

Kassie chewed her lower lip, still plagued by insecurity. "They are all accomplished noblewomen," she reminded her maid.

"You are a duchess," Margaret countered.

"A duchess in name alone," Kassie replied sadly. "No amount of finery in the world can make me what I am not."

"Nobility of the blood pales beside nobility of the heart" was the wise reply.

Kassie gave Margaret a tender look. "'Tis a shame it is not my heart that will be on display tonight."

"But it is your heart that has captured His Grace's."

Kassie's face lit up with hope. Margaret had given voice to Kassie's most fervent wish, one that seemed more plausible with each passing day . . . and night. Could Braden be falling in love with her?

Suddenly all her doubts seemed foolish, her reservations inane. She might be going into the lion's den, but she was going on her husband's arm. And *that* made all the difference in the world.

With a determined nod at her reflection Kassie made note of the time and headed toward the door. She had agreed to meet Braden at the foot of the stairway in five minutes, and she had no intention of being late.

"Thank you again, Margaret," she said with a smile. "And wish me good luck—I shall need it!"

She made her way down the stairs leading to the ballroom Braden had designated for tonight's festivities. Already the musicians were playing, the sound of soft music drifting out into the hallway mingled with laughter and conversation. In the ballroom's open doorway Kassie could see Braden chatting with a group of gentlemen and patiently waiting for her to appear. The sight was both reassuring and oddly touching. Obviously her husband had not forgotten his promise to stand by her side and ease her way through the numerous introductions that would accompany her debut.

Head held high, Kassie glided toward Braden and the onset of the evening.

"Well, hello."

A deep masculine voice from behind her made Kassie jump.

"I am terribly sorry. I did not mean to frighten you."

Kassie studied the tall, lean man before her. He was very

handsome, with dark brown hair and a ready smile. He was elegantly attired in formal evening clothes, a warm, interested look in his light brown eyes.

"I wasn't frightened, only startled," she denied. "I had no idea anyone was out here."

He smiled. "Nor did I. But I must say that I am delighted that I was wrong." His admiring gaze drank in her radiant beauty.

Kassie inclined her head, giving him a curious look. "Have you just arrived?" she asked in her customarily straightforward manner.

He looked surprised, then pleased. All the women he knew would have dropped their eyes and feigned a blush at his openly hungry appraisal, while this luscious beauty was doing neither, but staring back at him with candid interest. Perhaps tonight would not be so unpleasant as he had originally anticipated.

"Yes, it would seem I arrived at precisely the right moment," he answered in a voice as smooth as honey. "And forgive my poor display of manners; we have not been introduced." He took her hand, caressing it lightly with his thumb. "I am Grant Chandling, Viscount Chisdale. Our host and I are old friends."

Kassie broke into a dazzling smile, ashamed that she had for a moment misread his intentions. If he and Braden were boyhood friends, she had obviously mistaken sincere friendliness for blatant flirtation. "I am delighted to meet you, my lord," she said with genuine enthusiasm. "And I apologize for not knowing you. But in truth, I do not recall Braden ever mentioning your name."

"And with good reason."

While Braden's stance was relaxed as he strolled over to them, the hard set of his jaw displayed a barely controlled rage. Kassie gave him a puzzled look.

Grant released Kassie's hand, his brows arched in surprise. "Now why would you say such a thing to this lovely lady?"

"Because," Braden replied, placing a possessive hand on Kassie's arm, "this lovely lady happens to be my wife."

Grant looked startled, reading Braden's unspoken message very clearly. *"This* is your wife?" His gaze returned to Kassie, and he shook his head. "I had no idea . . . but then, I should have. You always did have the most exquisite taste in women, Braden."

Kassie felt Braden stiffen beside her as once again the viscount took her hand, this time brushing it in a brief, chaste kiss.

"Your Grace, I am enchanted," he murmured.

Kassie had no idea why Braden was so angry at their guest. She could sense an undercurrent between them—a friendly spat, perhaps? Whatever it was, it did not concern her, nor would she let it affect her role as a proper hostess.

"Thank you, Lord Chisdale," she returned. "And please, my given name is Kassandra, not 'Your Grace.'"

Grant acknowledged this liberty with a slow nod. "Kassandra, then. And you must call me Grant."

She smiled. "Certainly."

"Braden, you never told me that your wife was so breathtaking . . . or so charming."

Braden's grip tightened on Kassie's arm. "We haven't seen each other in some time, Grant," he returned. "Besides, I rather suspected you would notice Kassie on your own." He didn't wait for a reply but turned to his wife. "Come. I want you to meet the rest of our guests."

Kassie tried unsuccessfully to read Braden's closed expression. "Of course, Braden."

"We'll be in the ballroom, Grant." Braden's words were a dismissal.

"And so will I." He paused. "I hope your bride will do me the honor of a dance."

"You may hope so." Braden strode off, taking Kassie with him. He knew his anger was irrational, but the memory of Grant's betrayal three years past was still too vivid in his mind. Had the choice been Braden's, Grant would not be here tonight. But Cyril had convinced him that omitting Grant from the guest list would only reawaken tongues that had long since ceased to wag. It wasn't worth providing gossip for the scandal-hungry *ton.* He would simply have to ignore Grant's presence. But not without the knowledge that this man he had called friend possessed no scruples whatsoever.

Braden felt Kassie hesitate when they reached the entranceway. His wife's eyes were wide with apprehension as she surveyed the elegant ballroom, which was crammed with people, alive with activity. He followed her gaze, surprised by her reaction. To Braden it appeared to be just another house party.

Kassie, on the other hand, felt waves of insecurity sweep over her. This gathering bore no resemblance to the intimate assemblage of guests at her wedding reception. Tonight barely an inch of the plush oriental carpet was visible, so lost was it beneath countless moving feet; and the priceless paintings that lined the gilded walls were no more than blurs of color hidden behind swirling gowns and scurrying footmen. The room's only treasure that remained unconcealed was the splendid crystal chandelier that hung proudly, casting its light about the room and making it look even more formidable. Empty, a room this size would be intimidating. Filled, it was staggering.

Kassie's nervous gaze was drawn to a corner of the ballroom where a group of elaborately dressed, simpering noblewomen stood together, whispering and staring in Kassie's direction with coldly appraising eyes.

A small house party was definitely a misnomer. This would more appropriately be called a massacre.

Braden saw Kassie's stricken look and felt his heart melt. "Have I told you how dazzling you look tonight, *ma petite?*" he murmured softly.

She looked up at him, her eyes bright with apprehension, and shook her head. "No, you haven't."

He grinned. "Then allow me to rectify that." He drank in her flawless beauty with a hotly intimate look that made her forget everything but her husband. "You take my breath away," he told her in a husky whisper.

And she did. What he saw filled him with a combination of pride, desire, and possessiveness. She was utter perfection, far superior to any other woman in the room. And she was his.

Kassie gave him a shaky smile. "Thank you."

"You're welcome." He took her hand and squeezed it. "Keep in mind your very low opinion of the ladies of my acquaintance," he teased gently, drawing her into the room. From the corner of his eye Braden could see the men looking their way, practically salivating at their first glimpse of Kassie. Scowling, he hoped that his wife's opinion of noblemen would be as low as her opinion of their female equivalents. But somehow he doubted it.

Kassie tried to keep her head up and her gaze from faltering. But everywhere she stepped a new pair of curious eyes was studying her, evaluating her suitability or lack thereof. Quietly, with his deep, commanding voice, Braden made the introductions until Kassie was dizzy from trying to remember all the names. From midroom old Lord Lockersham watched her hungrily, but he did not return her warm smile. It took Kassie mere moments to figure out why. Beside the earl stood a statuesque woman with gray hair and a huge bosom that threatened to erupt from the confines of her gown. From her proprietary stance Kassie deduced that she was none other than Lady Lockersham, the countess who had been "ailing" on Kassie's wedding day. Kassie shot Lord Lockersham an understanding look, her heart sinking. The fact that she had actually been regarding the old lecher as an ally was an obvious indication of her frenzied state of mind.

Silently Kassie counted the hours until bedtime.

"May I persuade your lovely bride to share a dance with me?"

The voice was familiar.

"That is up to Kassie, William," Braden responded. He looked from William Devon's cordial expression to Kassie's anxious one. "Kassie?"

It was time to jump in with both feet.

"I would be delighted, Your Grace," she said, smiling. Leaving the security of Braden's side, she moved onto the dance floor with the duke.

"You look enchanting, my dear," he praised, a smile fixed on his face.

"Thank you, Your Grace. I hope it is an improvement over the state of my attire when last we met."

A flicker of humor danced in his eyes. "Do not underestimate the power of your beauty. It was apparent despite your rather rumpled condition. After all, Braden did marry you."

Kassie bristled. "I assure you, Your Grace," she heard herself say, "that my beauty is but a small part of why Braden and I are wed."

William started but recovered himself quickly. "Apparently you have other redeeming qualities as well."

Realizing how her remark had been interpreted, Kassie felt her face redden. She was about to make a sharp retort when it suddenly occurred to her that if William Devon was present, it was highly likely that Abigail would be, too. Quickly she scanned the room, trying to see past the swarms of guests.

"Are you looking for anyone in particular, my dear?"

Kassie's eyes flew back to William's face, but his expression was merely curious.

"I was wondering if your family had come to Sherburgh with you." Oh, why was she always so damned honest?

He cleared his throat. "If you mean Abigail, no. She is . . . not here this evening." He sounded as if he had wished to say more but thought better of it.

"Oh. I see." Kassie wondered if Braden had anything to do with Abigail's absence. After all, Kassie had made her dislike of the other woman no secret; perhaps it was out of consideration for these feelings that Braden had omitted Abigail from the guest list. The possibility made Kassie giddy with pleasure.

"May I borrow my wife back, William?" The very object of Kassie's thoughts appeared at her side, dark and devastatingly handsome. His request was a mere formality, for he was already pulling Kassie into his arms and moving to the soft strains of a waltz.

"I didn't want to leave you for too long," Braden murmured, stroking the palm of her hand with his thumb.

Kassie felt waves of heat radiate through her body. She loved the way he was holding her . . . just a tad too close . . . and the possessive gleam in his eye as he looked down at her. She loved his strength, his overwhelming masculinity . . . she loved him.

"Later," he said in a husky whisper.

Kassie started. "Later . . . what?"

He caressed her with his eyes. "Later . . . what you're asking me."

"I haven't said a word."

"You don't have to. Your eyes talk to me in a language all their own. They always have."

Kassie could feel herself blush. "I'll have to make sure that my eyes are far less outspoken, then."

Braden chuckled. "That is something you have no control over, my lovely wife. Your feelings, your thoughts, your entire soul is reflected in those beautiful aqua depths. And I wouldn't have it any other way."

Kassie's heart began to pound. "Braden . . ."

"Come now, Braden, don't be so stingy. It is time to share your bride with the rest of us!" Winston Black, the Marquis of Somerset, tapped Braden on the shoulder. "I believe this dance was promised to me!"

None too graciously Braden released Kassie and allowed his friend to lead her into a frolicking reel. Kassie looked as reluctant as her husband for the waltz to end. But the whole purpose of this party, Braden reminded himself, was for Kassie to meet people and thus to become more comfortable in her new world. Everything was going as planned. Nevertheless, the sight of her in another man's arms bothered him . . . a lot.

Rather than dancing with a nauseatingly simpering substitute, Braden helped himself to another drink. He was just finishing it when Grant strolled over.

"Hasn't it been long enough, Braden?" he asked quietly.

Braden regarded him impassively and shrugged. "This is one of those things that time cannot heal, Grant."

Grant shook his head, perplexed. "Abigail Devon was hardly worth our friendship. She's an insatiable little slut, and we both know it. You never even gave a damn for her! In a way I did you a service by saving you from an unwanted marriage."

Braden put his empty glass down. "You still don't understand, do you? Anger had nothing to do with this; Abigail had nothing to do with this. This was, and still is, about our trust and our friendship, both of which you betrayed."

"She's just a woman, for heaven's sake!" Grant looked positively bewildered.

Braden sighed at the hopelessness of the situation. "If it makes any difference to you, my feelings about your actions have changed since then. Three years ago I felt nothing but rage. Now I feel only pity. I'm very sorry for you, Grant." He gazed around the room. "In fact, I'm sorry for the whole blasted lot of you." He walked off, suddenly needing only his wife's presence.

Needing. The depth of his own emotional involvement slapped Braden in the face like a cold dousing of water. When had that happened? When had tender caring and intense physical need become more? When had he become so damned vulnerable to his own wife?

Shaken, he bypassed the bowls of Regent's punch and helped himself to a glass of straight brandy, feeling it burn its way to his stomach. He poured another, then scanned the room for Kassandra.

She was dancing a quadrille with Horace Blackbery, the Earl of Welbourne, both of them laughing and having a wonderful time. Kassie had the most amazing effect on everyone. She was like a breath of spring, infusing the world with her sunshine.

Noting the besotted look on Welbourne's face, Braden was assailed by an unexpected surge of jealousy. The fact was, it galled him to see the men flocking around his wife. He knew he was being totally illogical, that his jealousy was unjustified, but it rankled him nonetheless. Until now she had belonged exclusively to him; had done so since she was fifteen. There had been no suitors, no contenders for her hand. She had come to Braden not only a virgin, but a complete and total innocent. The virginity she had given to him, but the innocence was a fundamental part of her. Braden willed it to stay that way. He didn't want Kassie amid his ugly world of shallow relationships and casual liaisons. He wanted to protect her from it, to keep her as untouched as she was. For her own sake.

Who was he kidding? Magnanimity had nothing to do with this. The truth was, he wanted to keep her his. Period.

Braden went to get another brandy.

"Braden?" Kassie touched his arm gently.

He looked down at her with glazed eyes. "Oh, hello, wife." He raised his glass in salute.

Kassie flinched. She, better than anyone, recognized the signs of drunkenness, and they made her sick and afraid. "I think you've had quite enough to drink, don't you?"

Had he been sober, Braden would have read the unease in Kassie's voice and understood it. But being utterly foxed, he knew only that the object of his raw and conflicting emotions was adding fuel to his ever-growing fire. "Enough to drink? To the contrary, my lovely wife, I have but begun my evening's pleasure." He gave her a measured look. "Are you enjoying yourself?" He was half hoping her answer would be no.

Kassie did not understand Braden's odd, brooding behavior. But whatever its cause, there was no excuse for his inebriated state. Anger overcame concern.

"How can I enjoy myself when my husband is so deep in his cups that he is barely coherent?" she demanded.

He heard only the anger and none of the pain, and it was like pouring salt on the open wound of his newly discovered vulnerability. He narrowed his eyes, his internal walls instantly re-erected. "You're overstepping your bounds, Kassandra. What I do is none of your concern."

Kassie's eyes widened, hurt and disbelief merging. After their closeness of the past week, how could he put her in her place so cruelly? She opened her mouth to tell him just that when a commotion from the entranceway interrupted her.

"You see, Cyril, I was right. We are dreadfully late!"

Kassie saw Braden's eyes dart toward the sound of the voice, then darken with some undefinable emotion. She turned in time to see Lord Cyril stroll into the crowded ballroom, smiling a reply to the captivating woman on his arm.

It was Abigail Devon.

Braden murmured something indistinguishable, then headed in Abigail's direction without a backward look at his wife. With a sinking heart Kassie watched him greet his uncle, then bring Abigail's gloved hand to his lips. The possessive look on Abigail's face only confirmed what Kassie had long suspected. This haughty and beautiful noblewoman dressed in yards of rich red velvet intended to stake her claim on Braden. Tonight.

Kassie's insecurities returned in full force.

She turned away, fighting back the tears. Her youth and inexperience were no match for Abigail's sophisticated charm and sexual allure. Ill-equipped for the oncoming battle, Kassie was armed only with her love for Braden. Would that be enough?

"Well, hello, Kassandra; we meet again." The hated voice crooned a welcome to Kassie's back.

Straightening her shoulders, Kassie turned. "Good evening . . . Abigail." She applauded herself on the omission of "lady." "I didn't know you would be here this evening. Neither, for that matter, did your father."

Abigail tossed the pale blond curls from her shoulder in a haughty gesture. "It was a last-minute decision. Cyril was so kind in asking me to attend as his guest that I couldn't refuse."

Cyril. Kassie wanted to strangle him.

"How lovely of him," she replied instead. "And how fortunate for all of us."

Abigail's cold eyes were already moving restlessly about the room. "Ah," she said with a brittle smile, "I do believe my presence is required. If you will excuse me . . ." And she dismissed Kassie with a grand sweep of her gown.

"There is no excuse for you," Kassie muttered under her breath.

"Kassandra? Are you speaking with someone?"

Kassie glanced up at Cyril with a definite lack of enthusiasm. "Yes. Myself."

He inclined his head to one side. "Is something wrong, my dear?"

"Why did you bring her here?" she blurted out.

He looked surprised. "Abigail? She has always attended our parties. Why? Is there a problem?"

Kassie counted slowly to ten, willing herself under control. "No, no problem," she said at last. "At least nothing I cannot deal with, I assure you."

Cyril nodded, studying her silently for a moment, then extended his hand. "May I have the honor?"

Kassie placed her hand in his. "Of course."

Cyril was a pleasant and frequent partner, as were the next three men who requested Kassie's hand for a dance. But for Kassie the magic was gone. And it seemed that every time she looked up Abigail Devon was dancing in Braden's arms, laughing up into his face. Snatches of their conversation reached Kassie's ears, making her blood run cold.

"You always were a superb dancer, Braden," Abigail was telling him in a husky whisper.

"Really?" he replied in his deep baritone. "Funny, I don't remember us spending that much time on the dance floor."

"Well," she teased coyly, in an intimate tone that made Kassie's insides twist with pain, *"that* is because you are even more accomplished at other, more pleasurable pastimes."

"Kassandra? Are you all right?" Grant's concerned voice broke into Kassie's turmoil. She blinked and looked up at him.

"No . . . actually, Grant, I do feel a bit lightheaded. Would you mind terribly if we went out for some air?"

He took in her pale face, then followed the direction of her stare. "Of course not." He led her out the French doors onto the balcony. Kassie stood for long moments, taking deep breaths and trying to calm her careening emotions.

"Better?" he asked.

She nodded. "Thank you."

"Why don't we take a stroll around the grounds?"

Kassie looked dubious. "At night? Alone?"

Grant gave her a charming smile. "I've been coming to Sherburgh since I was a boy. I assure you that I know my way around most thoroughly. There is no chance of us becoming lost." His eyes twinkled.

That was not precisely what Kassie had meant, but the memory of Braden's and Abigail's conversation burned away any doubt she might have had.

"I'd love to take a walk with you, Grant."

His look of surprise was quickly replaced with one of total pleasure. "Wonderful!" He offered his arm, and they moved off into the night.

Cyril watched their retreating backs thoughtfully. The evening was proceeding even better than he had originally planned.

"Cyril? Have you seen Kassie?"

Braden was deep in his cups and sinking fast. Cyril frowned.

"The last I saw your wife she was on the balcony with your friend Lord Chisdale," he supplied helpfully, seeing his nephew's jaw tighten with anger. "After that . . . I have no idea."

Braden cursed, striding onto the balcony and staring off into the night. "Where the hell are they?" he barked loudly.

Cyril hurried to his side. "I don't know, Braden. But keep your voice down. The entire *ton* doesn't need to know that your new bride is alone with another man."

Braden gave him a murderous look. "Make my excuses to our guests," he got out between clenched teeth.

"Where the deuce are you going?" Cyril demanded.

"Out," he shot back. "Somehow I am no longer in the mood for a party." Without another word he left the room.

"Cyril?" Abigail Devon appeared by his side.

Cyril smiled. "You are just in time, my dear. I believe Braden is in bad need of some comfort. Comfort that only *you* can provide."

She smiled. "Say no more. I am on my way." She made her way gracefully through the ballroom.

Cyril rejoined the party, convinced that the proper seeds had been sown. Kassandra could never have survived this world, he concluded. She was far too innocent.

At that very moment innocent Kassandra was slapping Grant Chandling soundly across the face. "How dare you!" she gasped, totally outraged by his unwanted advances.

Grant rubbed his cheek ruefully. "It was only a kiss, Kassandra."

"Only a kiss? Need I remind you that I am married to your friend?"

"I wasn't asking you to run off with me, for God's sake!"

"Oh, really? Then what were you asking me to do? Or need I ask at all?" She was actually trembling as she spoke. "You are all alike, every last member of your *noble* class— immoral, self-centered, and corrupt!" She lifted her skirts and moved past him, wishing she could run away from the world. "I will see myself back. Good-bye, *Lord* Chisdale. You are no longer welcome at Sherburgh."

She went in through the rear of the house, making her way to her bedchamber without being seen by any of their guests. She would face them all tomorrow, but for tonight, she had withstood all she could. She slammed her door closed and paced the length of the room.

How dare these unprincipled people call themselves *noble*men? *Nothing* was sacred to them, not even the sanctity of marriage!

Kassie sank down on the bed, her face buried in her hands. The sanctity of marriage . . . it was all that Kassie knew, for she had witnessed the epitome of marital commitment firsthand. For if ever there was a man who worshiped his wife, placed her on a pedestal, it was Robert Grey.

Unbidden, distant memories from her childhood floated through Kassie's mind. Her mother, dressed in silk, applying her sweet-scented lilac fragrance while Robert stood indulgently by, gazing down at Elena with a passion and possessiveness that even a young child could sense. In Robert's eyes Elena had been nothing short of a saint, and for him no other woman had existed. When she was taken from him he had crumpled.

Memories. Her father, just after her mother's death . . . a broken man, consumed with pain and guilt and disbelief. *Elena . . . don't leave me . . . don't do this to me. . . .*

He had gone on for hours, crying openly, begging Elena not to desert him, then cursing her for doing so. He had never forgiven her for leaving him, nor himself for being unable to save her.

Kassie shuddered, remembering the night she had run to Braden, her own final night at the cottage. Robert's violent assault had, even then, been accompanied by unintelligible babbling about Elena's betrayal. There was no doubt; when Elena died, everything good in Robert had died with her.

But infidelity? Robert would have considered even looking at another woman blasphemous.

Kassie lifted her tear-streaked face, forcing her way back to the present. In truth, she believed that Braden was too principled to make a mockery of their marriage vows by actually taking a mistress. He might not love Kassie as she did him, but the trust between them was simply too strong.

Still, his behavior tonight had been inexcusable. Didn't he realize how much he had humiliated her by his actions? Flirting with that witch right in front of her?

Kassie stood, her decision made. Blatant dalliance might be acceptable by the twisted standards of the *ton*, but not by her standards. And it was time Braden knew it. She yanked open the connecting doors between their rooms, determined to wait up for him, no matter how late he returned to his bed. They had to talk—tonight.

"Braden? I'm glad you're back." The soft female voice drifted lazily from Braden's bed.

Kassie froze. In the dim light cast by the lamp she watched numbly as the naked woman, clad only in a thin sheet, sat up and met Kassie's stunned gaze. "Oh, Kassandra, how dreadfully embarrassing," she purred, her mouth curving into a triumphant smile.

It was Abigail Devon.

Chapter 18

❧

The color drained from Kassie's face as the full implication of the situation hit her. Her husband and Abigail Devon either had just been intimate or were about to be so. Either way, she had interrupted their little tryst.

Kassie could actually feel her entire world crumble around her. She had survived both physical and emotional abuse, but nothing compared to the devastation of this moment. She wanted to die.

She was turning to flee from the loathsome evidence of Braden's betrayal when she saw the cruel smile on Abigail's face, the expectant, victorious look in her eyes. Kassie's deep-rooted internal strength rallied fiercely, refusing to let her back down and creep off in utter humiliation. If nothing else, she would salvage her pride.

Head held high, she marched over to the rumpled bed.

"Get out of my house." Was that really her voice, so filled with authority?

Apparently it was, for Abigail's smile vanished, replaced by a look of shock, then fury.

"How dare you?" she spat out.

"How dare *I?*" Kassie shot back, tearing the sheet from Abigail's naked body. "How dare *you* use my home for your disgusting, immoral carryings-on!"

Abigail swung her legs over the side of the bed, searching Kassie's expression to see how much she knew. "This is Braden's home, Kassandra, not yours," she taunted, gauging

Kassie's reaction. "Just as this is *his* room and *his* bed. And just as I am here by *his* invitation."

A rage that Kassie never knew she possessed exploded inside her. She scooped up Abigail's clothing, wildly flinging the discarded gown and underthings at her. "I am the Duchess of Sherburgh, Abigail—*and* Braden's wife! This house is therefore mine, and I want you out—*now!* Else I will summon a servant to *throw* you out . . . in whatever state of undress you happen to be in!" She stood panting, her eyes blazing in challenge.

Abigail rose, shaking with anger. She made no move to dress. "Did you really believe that a mere child like you would be enough to satisfy a man like Braden in bed?" she taunted. "You're a fool, Kassandra, an innocent, ill-bred little fool. What Braden needs is a woman. A woman who can fulfill his needs. A woman worthy of his passion and his title." She tossed her blond hair back defiantly. "I was foolish enough to turn him away once. I won't make that mistake again. You might have his title, you stupid chit, but I have his body."

Without thinking Kassie drew back her hand and slapped Abigail across the face with every ounce of strength she possessed.

For an instant they both froze, each of them shocked beyond belief by Kassie's action. Abigail's trembling fingers hovered just above the spot where the stinging slap had been delivered, her wrath a tangible, escalating entity. Numbly Kassie stared at the white imprint her hand had made on Abigail's cheek, one glaring flaw on the utter perfection of alabaster skin. And Kassie had put it there.

Then Abigail's outraged scream echoed through the halls of Sherburgh.

Braden took the stairs two at a time. He had just arrived home, a trifle unsteady from the number of drinks he had consumed at a local pub, when he heard the scream. He burst into his bedchamber in time to see a totally naked Abigail lunging at a disheveled, defiant Kassie. He was instantly sober.

"What the hell is going on here?" he thundered.

Hearing Braden's voice, Kassie turned to him, trembling with the force of her reaction.

"It seems I arrived a trifle unexpectedly, husband." The Kassandra who addressed him with hatred glittering in her eyes was a stranger. "But I shan't keep you from your *mistress* any longer." She walked around him, avoiding any physical contact, as if his touch sickened her. She turned in the entranceway, and Braden had a glimpse of the pain beneath the hatred as Kassie's control began to evaporate. Her lips trembled, and unshed tears glistened on her long, dark lashes. But her head was held high, and her gaze never faltered. "In the future you and *Lady* Abigail"—she spat out the word—"will have to find some other meeting place. If Abigail Devon ever sets foot in this house again, I shall have her bodily removed from the estate. Good night, Braden."

The door slammed behind her.

Braden stared at the closed door, disbelief mixing with pride and admiration. His innocent little wife was a breathtaking, magnificent woman. A woman who was jealous as hell.

"Braden?" Abigail's husky voice broke through Braden's dazed state. His head snapped around in her direction, and he watched her walk toward him, making no move to conceal her nakedness. She paused, looking up at him with coaxing eyes. "I've been waiting for you for hours."

"Have you?" His tone was dispassionate.

Encouraged, she continued, sliding her hands possessively up his shirtfront. "Cyril said you might need me. And I can see now that he was right."

He didn't move a muscle.

She stroked the nape of his neck. "You and I both know how good we were together, Braden. None of that has to change. Anything you want of me"—she looked down at herself suggestively—"is yours."

Braden's gaze flicked impassively over her body. "Get dressed, Abigail." He walked away.

"What?" She was stunned.

"I'm telling you what I want of you. I want you to get dressed and get out."

She stared at him in disbelief. "But Cyril said—"

"I don't give a damn what Cyril said," he interrupted. "You heard what *I* said." A smile tugged at his lips. "Or, more importantly, you heard what my wife said. And I would suggest you take Kassie's warning to heart and not return to Sherburgh. My wife does not make idle threats."

He slammed out of the room.

Cyril stood concealed by darkness as Kassandra tore through the empty hallway and out the front door. He winced as the door reverberated behind her, thinking how fortunate it was that the guest wing was far removed from the remainder of the house. It would never do for such a violent commotion to be overheard—first Abigail's scream, and now Kassandra's noisy departure. The gossips would be in their glory; their tongues wagging as they relayed the juicy scandal to one another.

Cyril waited until he was certain that silence prevailed. Then he turned and went back to the solitude of the library, a satisfied smile upon his face. It appeared that his plan had worked splendidly. Kassandra had found Abigail in the arranged compromising position, and as Cyril had suspected, Kassie's strict moral code prevented her from accepting Braden's infidelity, despite the fact that she and Braden were husband and wife in name alone.

Lowering himself to the settee, Cyril leaned his head back against the cushions. With a small amount of luck, Abigail was now sealing their fate. Between her blatant gift at seduction and Braden's starved body, things should reach their natural culmination quite nicely and quite soon. He glanced at his timepiece. At this very moment, as a matter of fact. Abigail might be a practiced little piece, but she was better suited for the life of a duchess than Kassandra was. As far as Kassandra . . .

The door exploded open, fairly flying off its hinges. Cyril barely had time to come to his feet before Braden stormed into the room, his eyes ablaze with anger.

"What the hell were you thinking of?" he demanded.

Cyril blinked. "I beg your pardon?"

Braden kicked the door closed behind him, his fists clenched at his sides. "Don't even pretend not to know what I mean, Cyril. I'm warning you, my patience is at its limit."

"I presume you are referring to Abigail's late appearance at the party?"

"I am referring to Abigail's naked appearance in my bed." He waved away Cyril's denial. "She told me you sent her to my chamber. Now I want to know why."

Cyril sighed, bracing himself for the unavoidable confrontation. "I did it with your best interests at heart, Braden."

Braden shot him an incredulous look. "My best interests? You know I loathe the woman and have no interest in renewing our relationship—in bed or out. You must also recall that I am married . . . or did that minor detail escape your memory?"

"I am well aware of your marital status. Possibly more aware than you think I am." Cyril fixed Braden with a steely stare, his tone equally hard. "Have the marriage annulled, Braden. Now. Before it is too late."

"Annulled? Why?" Braden shot back, his control fragmenting into shards of rage. "Because Kassie is not highly bred, like the genteel crowd that now fills our guest rooms? Those principled, *noble* people that change bed partners as frequently as they change their breeches?"

"And are you so certain Kassandra is different?" Cyril tried. "As I recall, your innocent little wife spent an inordinate amount of time alone with your friend Lord Chisdale."

Braden's eyes narrowed threateningly. "I am more than certain. Grant might be an unscrupulous blackguard, but Kassie is nothing like any member of the *ton*. She is incapable of their falseness and deceit. You know it as well as I do."

"Yes, I *do* know it," Cyril said in bitter exasperation. "And that is my point. The fact is, the *ton* is our world, Braden. And Kassandra will *never* fit in. Never. She is just not the right woman for you."

"That is *my* decision to make, not yours!"

"Except that you are blind when it comes to Kassandra!"

Cyril's control was fast deteriorating. "I know you feel compassion for the girl, and God knows I can understand it, but pity is no basis for a marriage!"

"And what is a basis for a marriage, Cyril? Distrust and dislike?"

"Common backgrounds. Producing a suitable heir for Sherburgh."

"Is that what is worrying you, Cyril? That I provide an heir for my estate?" Braden's eyes blazed. "Well, rest easy, uncle. I assure you that I will fulfill that obligation . . . *and* be certain of the child's paternity."

"And just how do you plan to produce a child when you and your wife have not even shared a bed?"

The words echoed through the room as Braden regarded his uncle with stunned fury. But Cyril plunged on, past the point of discretion.

"Do you think I don't know that Kassandra is as untouched as the day she came to Sherburgh? Do you think I am blind? How can a child be conceived by a woman who is a wife in name alone?"

Braden's expression turned murderous, his tone ominously quiet. "Kassandra is my wife in every way."

He saw his uncle's horrified reaction and continued, violent currents underlying his every word. "Obviously, Cyril, you are under a gross misconception. The truth is, Kassandra is my duchess *and* my wife. She shares not only my name, but also my bed. She will bear my children, the future heirs to Sherburgh. Those are the *unalterable* facts, Cyril, and I suggest you accept them." He strode off, gripping the door handle so hard his knuckles turned white. "Further, if you continue to interfere with my life, I will be forced to retaliate. We would both regret the consequences." He threw open the door. "I am going to consider this subject closed. I shan't upset my wife further by telling her of your involvement in tonight's disaster. But Cyril"—he turned—"I never want to see Abigail Devon in my house again. Never."

Cyril watched him go, a curious sense of unreality permeating his mind. *Kassandra is my wife in every way.* Braden's adamant statement replayed itself in Cyril's shocked mind. *In every way . . . in every way . . .*

He closed his eyes tightly, trying to block out the finality of the words. When had it happened? How could he not have known?

But it had happened. He had seen the truth on Braden's face. And now all his plans for the future were altered forever. It was too late . . . too late . . .

Rage exploded inside him, transforming Cyril's handsome features into twisted fury. His eyes glinted with emotion, defeat tasting bitter on his tongue. His hand brushed against the walnut end table; his dazed eyes followed the action. And then, slowly and deliberately, he lifted the table and heaved it against the wall, watching it splinter into a hundred pieces.

"No!" The primal roar resounded throughout the room on the heels of the shattering crash.

The guests slept on. No one but Cyril was aware of the irrevocable damage that had been done.

Chapter 19

Breathless and chilled, Kassie paused, resting her throbbing head against the closest oak tree within reach. Percy limped to a stop beside her, panting and hopeful that his mistress had at long last reached her destination. Even *he* was physically depleted.

The stables were just ahead . . . Kassie's sanctuary. She had already walked the grounds of Sherburgh for hours, blindly trying to escape her anguish. She was bodily spent and emotionally numb. She had to regain her strength. Then she would decide what to do. On quivering legs she hobbled the rest of the distance to the stable doors. Quietly she slipped past a sleeping Dobson and made her way into Star's stall, the most spacious in the stable. Murmuring softly to the surprised but accommodating stallion, she dropped wearily to the ground and curled up, Percy in her arms.

Despite Kassie's exhaustion, sleep did not come at once.

The painful events of the night replayed themselves again and again in her mind, ending with the gruesome realization that tonight, for the first time in her life, anger had driven her to *want* to hurt another person. In all of her eighteen years she had never raised a hand to anyone nor contemplated doing so. Not even her father's cruelty had been enough to evoke her retaliation, except to save herself that last night. Yet five minutes alone with Abigail Devon had enraged Kassie to the point of violent aggression. And what was worse, she could not bring herself to feel remorse for what she had done. Given the circumstances, she would do it again.

Kassie recalled Abigail's gloating expression, the triumph in her ice-blue eyes. She had implied not only that she and Braden were currently lovers, but that they had been deeply involved in the past—an involvement that Abigail, and not Braden, had ended. Could that be true? Could Braden have been in love with that cold-blooded witch? Did he still have feelings for her? As far as sexual intimacy, Kassie had no doubt that her husband and Abigail Devon had slept together many times. And why not? Abigail was lovely, both dressed and undressed, Kassie recalled dryly. And she obviously knew how to please a man in bed. Her vast experience was evident, blatant sexuality oozing from every traitorous pore of her body.

Kassie's insides knotted in doubt. Was she really as naïve as Abigail had said? Was the bond between herself and Braden not the deep and lasting commitment that she prayed for, but merely dutiful affection and no more?

Afraid to contemplate the answers, Kassie was certain of one thing. She could not sleep at Sherburgh after the scene with Abigail . . . after seeing her in Braden's bed. Cowardly as it was, Kassie needed to hold tonight's qualms and revelations at bay. Tomorrow. She would deal with it all tomorrow.

Unable to stay awake any longer, Kassie tucked her gown around her and buried her face in Percy's fur. Her last thought before falling into a deep, troubled sleep was that Braden probably hadn't even noticed her absence.

He had to find Kassie.

Braden paused, his back against the closed library door, and took several calming breaths. Cyril was lucky he hadn't struck him for the damage that had been done. Kassie had been hurt . . . and all in the name of some hypocritical class distinction.

Braden headed for the second floor and Kassie's room, intent on nipping her erroneous thoughts in the bud. He took the steps two at a time, praying he would find her there. But even if he didn't, he would speak to Margaret. If anyone knew Kassie's true state of mind, it would be her loyal and trusted lady's maid.

As he had feared, Kassie was not in her bedchamber. But sure enough, Margaret was there, pacing the floor and wringing her hands with worry.

"Margaret," Braden began.

She whirled around, surprised at his appearance.

"Have you seen Kassie?" he demanded. "There was . . . a misunderstanding, and I've looked everywhere, but there is no sign of her. I was hoping that you could help me."

Margaret gave him an incredulous look. "Help you?"

Braden might just as well have asked her to commit murder, from the tone of her voice. "Yes, Margaret, help me. You saw Kassie tonight. Did she seem herself to you?"

She frowned. *"Earlier,* she was excited about the ball and determined to please you, Your Grace." The accusation in her tone made Braden wince.

"What about *after* the ball?" he pressed.

Margaret raised her chin, making it quite clear that the only reason she was answering his questions was that she was required to. "She was very distraught and wanted to be alone, Your Grace. But I could hear her crying . . . crying as if her heart would break. She looked as if her whole world had fallen apart."

Braden felt his stomach muscles clench. "Did she say why, Margaret?"

She shook her head. "No, Your Grace. As I said, the duchess wanted to be alone, so I had no choice but to leave her. When I came in to check on her moments later, she was gone. I haven't seen her since." Her lips trembled. "She was so happy these past weeks . . . I don't know what happened to hurt her so deeply."

Braden felt Margaret's censure and met her gaze. "I'll find her, Margaret," he vowed in an anguished voice. "You have my word; I *will* find her and make things right." He turned and left the room.

He searched the entire second level, then the first, his worry increasing by the minute. It was approaching two o'clock in the morning. From far off Braden heard the muffled laughter that signified a few final guests retiring for the night. Whoever they were, they were probably too deep in their cups to have overheard any of tonight's mayhem, Braden thought in disgust. He didn't pause to find out, striding down the main hallway.

Where could Kassie be? he asked himself frantically, pausing inside the green salon. And what must she be thinking?

He could recall with perfect clarity the expression on his wife's face when he had burst into the room to find her arguing with Abigail—a look of betrayal, withdrawal, agony. Plainly, she thought he was sleeping with his ex-mistress. Which was absurd.

With a wave of self-contempt Braden recalled the amount of time he had spent at the ball appeasing that spoiled, vindictive little bitch. Part of it was to keep her as far away from Kassie as possible, for he knew that Kassie was no match for Abigail's biting tongue. But, Braden thought to himself with brutal honesty, there was more to it than that. The reality was that with Abigail he was safe. She aroused nothing in him but his scorn, called upon no emotions that begged to remain untouched. Perhaps that was why he had once considered marrying her. With Abigail there was no risk of hurt, and Braden could belong entirely to himself. Once that would have been reason enough. Not anymore.

Not since Kassie.

Braden frowned, struck by an alarming thought.

What if Robert Grey had somehow managed to gain entrance to Sherburgh and had harmed Kassie? Or taken her away?

Propelled by the loathsome possibility, Braden raced toward the front door, needing reassurance that this could not be. It was an impossibility, he reasoned with himself. The number of servants he had guarding the borders of the estate was simply too great to bypass. Still . . .

Perkins reached the marble hallway at precisely that moment, and Braden seized the butler's arm.

"Perkins, have you seen the duchess?" he demanded.

"No, Your Grace." Perkins took in Braden's haunted look, the deep circles beneath his eyes, without batting an eyelash. "But I have been discreetly questioning most of the servants for the past hour. No one has seen any sign of the duchess since she left the ballroom earlier this evening."

Braden's brows went up. "I don't recall mentioning my wife's disappearance to you before now. How is it that you know of it?"

Perkins gave a haughty sniff. "If you will forgive me, Your Grace, little happens at Sherburgh that escapes my notice." Ignoring Braden's stunned expression, Perkins continued, "However, something dreadful must have happened to make Her Grace vanish like this." He gazed pointedly at Braden. "Someone must have upset that extraordinary girl a great deal, or she would never have—"

"You made your point, Perkins." Braden scowled in the butler's direction. First Margaret, now Perkins. The last thing Braden intended to endure was his servants' censure. "You may resume your duties," he directed the butler, his tone formidable.

Perkins's expression remained impassive. "I shall continue to search," he announced, and with another dignified sniff he went off.

Braden was too consumed with worry to argue further. With mounting fear he considered his options. If no one could locate Kassie, then she must have left the house. If so, where would she go?

The beach.

Braden hastened to the stables, which were dark and quiet. By the door Dobson shifted in his sleep, unaware of Braden's presence. Braden did not stop to awaken him but went inside. A quick count told him that all the horses were in their stalls. He double-checked Little Lady to be certain. She was there, settled in for the night.

Panic exploded inside his head. If Kassie *was* outside, she was on foot . . . and vulnerable. He *had* to find her.

The beach was ruled out. For her to have ventured there by foot would have taken all night; it was simply too far. She would have needed a mount.

He stared blankly across the darkened grounds, his mind groping, tortured. Where else would Kassie go if she sought peace?

As if in answer, the memory of Kassie's happy face, her

laughing voice drifted into his head. *But Braden, it is so beautiful here! The water is so refreshing, the grass so soft. . . .*

The stream. She *must* be at the stream!

He didn't stop to have a horse saddled. He wanted to go by foot, to be able to search even the most minute hiding place within the thick cluster of trees that cloaked his property. He took off at a run.

"Braden?" Charles's voice halted him in his tracks. Eagerly Braden turned to his friend, hoping to find the answer on his face. But Charles's words dashed his hopes. "Perkins told me you were looking for Kassandra, that she is missing."

"She is. I don't know where she's gone, Charles, but I know that she is upset." A muscle worked in his jaw. "Very upset. We have to find her."

Charles asked no further questions. "I'll search the immediate grounds, you go to the far sections of the estate." He paused, his blue eyes penetrating, his mouth set in a grim line. "Do you have reason to believe that Grey—"

"I don't know!" Braden snapped back. He didn't want to think about Charles's implication. He was sick with worry and guilt. "I'm going to find her, Charles. I don't care if it takes all night."

"We'll find her, Braden" was the solemn reply. "I promise you we'll find her."

Despite the cool night air, Braden was sweating by the time he reached the stream. It was deserted. The moonglow reflected off the languid water, and silence ruled the world.

He lowered his head in despair, fear streaking through him in sharp waves. If Kassie wasn't here, he had no idea where else to look. Particularly since it was becoming obvious she didn't want to be found. And how could he blame her, especially after that escapade with Abigail? He couldn't, nor could he expect her to believe in his innocence.

For what had he done to convince her of it? Nothing. As if his supposed love affair hadn't been enough, he had been utterly foxed, his mind so clouded with liquor that he hadn't had time to react.

Clouded with liquor. Braden clenched his fists at his sides.

How could he have been so stupid, resorting to the very vice that Kassie feared the most? Braden cursed himself for twenty times the fool. He remembered Kassie's white face when she had witnessed him becoming more and more intoxicated at the party. She had obviously been afraid. Only he had been too damned caught up in his own emotions, too stunned and resistant to his newly discovered feelings for his wife to notice. Not to mention his jealousy, Braden reminded himself. He despised seeing her with Grant—seeing her with *any* man—when she belonged to him. *Him.*

The intensity of his reaction struck Braden like a blow to his gut, reducing him to a state of imbalance that he had not allowed himself since childhood. But since Kassandra had come into his life everything was changed. *He* was changed. He had known from the first that Kassie needed him, and he had grown accustomed to the fierce protectiveness and equally fierce passion she aroused within him.

What he hadn't counted on was needing her in return.

The moon disappeared behind a cloud, and Braden stared off into the dark, desolate night. Kassie was out there somewhere, and he had absolutely no idea where she had gone. He closed his eyes in frustration and despair. God, where was she?

"Kassandra!" Braden's primal shout echoed eerily through the trees and drifted back . . . unanswered.

Chapter 20

꧁꧂

Kassie stirred, feeling something dry and abrasive scratch against her cheek. She frowned, brushing it away, only to encounter handfuls of the same coarse substance. Resettling herself, she sought a comfortable spot so she could sink back into slumber.

From just beside her a soft whinny urged her to reconsider and arise. Slowly she opened her eyes to a layer of straw and a dark stall. She sat up and blinked, feeling cramped and disoriented. Where was she?

It was near dawn. Kassie could tell by the weak rays of sunlight that were trickling into the dark, silent stables—the same stables that had served as her haven last night. A determined bark claimed her attention, and she turned to gaze into a pair of soulful brown eyes and to feel a warm, wet tongue lap at her face.

"Percy," she murmured, automatically reaching for her pet and the comfort that holding him brought. He snuggled willingly into her arms, nuzzling her throat and licking her chin. Loyal little Percy, she thought, giving him a warm hug. *He* would never turn away from her.

A flood of memories assailed her. Last night. The ball. Braden dancing with Abigail. Abigail lying naked in Braden's bed.

Feeling sick, Kassie wanted nothing more than to remain in the stable forever.

A whinny sounded, interrupting her thoughts, louder than the first and accompanied by an attention-getting stomp.

Kassie looked up at the stall's other occupant, the sleek Thoroughbred who had allotted a portion of his sleeping quarters to her last night.

"Good morning, Star," she said with a tired smile. "And thank you for sharing your bedchamber with me." She looked away, tears filling her eyes. "Under the circumstances, it was my only tolerable choice."

Star snorted his agreement, and Kassie rose stiffly, setting Percy upon the ground. Her legs felt wobbly and her head ached dreadfully, both from crying and from lack of sleep. Pieces of straw clung to her hair and her gown . . . the beautiful gown that just hours earlier she had proudly worn to her first Sherburgh ball, and now it hung in disheveled ruin.

Kassie brushed off the dirt as best she could, fully aware that she was in desperate need of a bath. But she was not yet ready to face a houseful of curious guests, well-meaning servants . . . and Braden. Especially not Braden.

Kassie felt ill.

"Who's there?"

She jumped at the sound of Dobson's booming voice. "It is just I, Dobson," she called back quickly.

Seconds later the young groom stood wide-eyed and openmouthed before Star's stall. "Yer Grace? Oh, m'God!" He rushed in, his face a mask of fury. "What 'as 'e done t'ye?" He looked her over anxiously. "Where are ye 'urt?"

Kassie was appalled. Was the whole staff privy to her dishonor? And what did they think had transpired? Yes, Braden had hurt her . . . terribly. But certainly not physically; never that.

"I'm not hurt, Dobson, truly," she began, an embarrassed flush staining her cheeks. "He would never harm me."

Dobson cast a scathing look at the glistening horse at Kassie's side. "'e must 'ave done something, Yer Grace, t'mess up yer gown like that! I told ye never t'try and 'andle 'im without me or 'is Grace 'ere."

Realization struck. "Star?" Kassie stroked a hand instinctively down the horse's neck. "You thought that Star had hurt me?"

"Well, who else, Yer Grace?" Dobson looked puzzled.

Kassie shook her head. "Star would never harm me, would you, boy?" She reached up to stroke the Thoroughbred's sleek mane and was rewarded with an adoring whinny and a warm nuzzle.

Dobson's mouth fell open. "Well, I'll be . . ."

Kassie didn't understand his shock, but she had enough on her mind this morning without worrying about Dobson's imaginary fears. "I'll be back for a visit later today, my friend," she murmured, giving Star one last loving pat. "All right?"

Dobson could swear that the normally wild, unmanageable stallion nodded his assent.

"I'll be out of your way now, Dobson, so you can get on with your day. Come, Percy."

Kassie strolled through the dewy grass, thinking how beautiful and peaceful Sherburgh was at this time of day. Pale lemon-colored sunlight drifted from the heavens. Dawn in the country . . . nature in all its gentle splendor.

Gentle. Instantly a picture sprang to mind . . . a picture of Braden's face when he made love to her . . . the tenderness in his eyes . . . the heated words he breathed against her skin . . . the reverence of his touch. No. She had not imagined it. *Lady* Abigail was wrong. It was there, and it was something far more intense than mere affection. And yet, if that was so, a little voice inside her cried out, why did he need Abigail Devon?

A low growl from Percy made Kassie start.

"What is it, boy?" Kassie asked nervously. The friendliest of dogs, Percy rarely growled at anything or anyone. And he *never* bared his teeth so. . . . She was on the verge of assuring him that no one was about when she was struck by the sudden sensation that she was being watched. Her head flew up, and she searched the acres of grass through uneasy eyes. The estate seemed deserted.

"There is no one here, Percy," she declared aloud, more for her own sake than for his. Abruptly Percy stiffened, letting out a loud warning bark. Kassie felt the hair on the back of her neck stand up, and her heart began to pound faster. "What do you see, boy?" she asked fearfully, wishing they were closer to the house.

Percy barked again, louder this time.

"Who's there?" Kassie called out, trying to keep her voice from trembling.

Silence was her only answer.

"Who is it?" she demanded again, fear constricting her chest.

Again, nothing.

An undefinable wave of panic swept over Kassie. Someone was out there; she could feel it. And whoever it was wanted to remain unseen. And he was watching her.

"Come on, Percy," she urged, already beginning to run. "Let's go back to the house." Blindly she raced off, praying that she could outrun whoever was out there. Her feet flew out from under her, her breath coming in short pants. She felt the scratches inflicted by passing branches, but an innate sense of self-protection spurred her on and refused to let her rest. Percy just behind her, she fled the danger that awaited. She was but several hundred feet from her goal when a strong hand caught her arm.

"Let me go!" she screamed, struggling to free herself.

"Kassandra? What is it? What's happened?"

At the sound of Charles's voice huge waves of relief swept over Kassie. She sagged against him, grateful for the strength of his arms as they held her up.

"Have you been hurt?" he asked anxiously. When she didn't respond Charles shook her gently.

"No," she whispered, glancing behind her. "Not hurt, just frightened."

"Why are you frightened?" he demanded. "And where have you been? The entire household has been frantic looking for you!"

Kassie blinked. "They have? Why?"

"Why?" He raked his fingers through his thinning hair in exasperation. "You were gone from Sherburgh all night! Braden was crazed with worry!"

Kassie's jaw tightened. "Oh, was he? I didn't think my presence would be missed . . . under the circumstances."

Charles looked puzzled. "Circumstances? What circumstances?"

Suddenly the whole experience was more than Kassie could bear. Mortified, she felt helpless tears fill her eyes and spill down her cheeks. She turned away, unused to allowing anyone to witness her weakness or share her pain.

Charles placed gentle, work-worn hands on her shoulders. "It's no sin to confide in a friend," he told her softly.

Kassie fought for control. "I thought someone was following me," she whispered. "I was so afraid."

Charles stared off, taking in the peaceful grounds beyond, then shook his head. "There's no one about, Kassandra. And no need to be afraid. Braden has assigned countless servants to watch Sherburgh at all times ever since you came to live here."

Neither of them mentioned Robert, but his name was there nonetheless.

Kassie nodded. "I know. Thank you."

Charles turned her to face him. "That doesn't explain the state you're in, both mental and physical. What's happened?"

"Didn't Braden tell you?" she asked in a small, defiant voice, drying her tears with the back of her hand.

Charles shook his head. "Braden was in no condition for conversation last night. He was searching Sherburgh room by room to discover your whereabouts."

Kassie paled. "So all the guests know?"

"No," Charles reassured her quickly. "Only the family and a few servants know you are missing. Braden wanted to protect you from unnecessary gossip."

Kassie gave a harsh laugh. "Me? Or Abigail?"

"Abigail?" Charles's brow furrowed. "Abigail Devon? What has she got to do with—" He broke off as Kassie dropped her eyes. "Ah, I begin to see the light. Something happened at last night's party to upset you." His astute gaze took in Kassie's telltale flush. "Tell me," he urged.

Kassie's inner strength crumbled. Without a second thought she poured out the whole horrid incident. Charles did not interrupt until she had finished. Then he sighed.

"Come, Kassandra. Let's take a stroll, you and I. It is time you learned something more about your husband . . . and about *Lady* Abigail Devon."

Intrigued, Kassie fell into step beside him, a now docile Percy following in their wake.

"Braden's parents and Abigail's parents decided that their children should wed." Charles began without preliminaries.

"Wed?" Kassie echoed weakly.

"It was an arranged marriage, one that was applauded by Abigail and rejected by Braden," he added quickly.

"But they were betrothed."

"In a manner of speaking, yes." He paused, taking Kassie's chin in his hand. "You claim to be in love with Braden. You told me once that you wanted to understand him. Are you still willing to do that?"

Kassie swallowed. "Yes."

Charles gave her a warm smile. "Good. I've told you of Braden's parents, Kassandra. They were neither warm nor sensitive people. Braden is both. So he learned to bury these qualities inside himself at a very young age, to demonstrate them on few occasions and with fewer people."

Kassie nodded. "Such as you."

"Yes. As well as a few chosen friends. Especially one—Grant Chandling. The two of them were inseparable from their youth, more brothers than friends. They went to school together, grew from boyhood to manhood together. Between them there was mutual respect and trust, the two most important ingredients in a real friendship."

Kassie felt a surge of renewed anger as she recalled Grant's unwarranted advances during the ball. "I met the viscount last night. He was less than a gentleman with me," she replied candidly. Her mind jumped to Braden's curious reaction to Grant's appearance at Sherburgh, and a puzzled frown clouded her lovely face. "It seemed to me that there was a great deal of tension between Lord Chisdale and Braden."

"There is," Charles concurred. "And with good reason." He stared off into space, his words slow and purposeful. "Braden is a man of strong principles, Kassandra. While he has little faith in love and tenderness, he demands both integrity and honesty from everyone he deals with, especially his friends. Betrayal is not something he will tolerate."

Kassie's eyes filled with new tears. "Then how could he—"

He met her gaze. "He couldn't. And wouldn't."

"But I saw for myself."

"What you saw was a scheming, conniving woman determined to get back into Braden's life. An ambition, I might add, that is doomed to failure. And no one knows that better than Abigail."

Kassie's eyes widened. "Why?" she managed.

"Because during their supposed betrothal Abigail was busy sampling the charms of every other man she fancied. She made her way through the ranks of the *ton* until her reputation was in complete tatters, yet she felt neither embarrassment nor remorse."

Kassie gasped. "How could she?"

"Easily. Abigail is a spoiled, shallow young woman who is accustomed to getting everything she wants in life without regret or repercussion. If she craved variety, then variety it was."

Kassie swallowed past the lump in her throat. "And eventually Braden found out?"

"Yes."

"So he ended their betrothal."

"No."

Kassie started. "No?"

"No," Charles repeated. "By then Braden didn't give a damn what Abigail did or with whom she did it. He never actually committed himself to making wedding plans, but since there was no other woman in his life, he let the betrothal stand."

"So as far as the world knew, they were to marry," Kassie said quietly. She took a deep breath. "Then what happened?"

"Abigail took her indiscretions one step too far," Charles replied soberly. "Three years ago Braden discovered her in a compromising situation with an unforgivable partner."

"Who?" Kassie asked, but, God help her, she already knew.

"Grant Chandling."

"Oh . . . Charles." She closed her eyes, picturing the pain and the hurt Braden must have felt, not from the detestable woman he was expected to marry, but from his best friend. "How horrible for him."

"It was the luckiest day of Braden's life."

Kassie's eyes flew open, and she stared at Charles in amazement. It was not like him to be so uncompassionate. "I agree that it is best Braden found out about Grant's faithlessness. But to call it the luckiest day of his life—"

"It was," Charles insisted quietly. "For on that night Braden sought solace on a deserted stretch of beach along the sea. And there he met the most enchanting, loving young woman life has to offer. A woman who, in the months and years to come, will bring out everything his heart already knows but his mind cannot accept. A woman who, through her own wondrous gift of love, will teach him how to love in return."

Kassie's eyes filled with tears. "I love him so much, Charles," she whispered in a small, shaken voice.

"I know you do," he replied solemnly. "Now go home and show Braden."

Kassie took both his hands, stood on tiptoe, and kissed his weathered cheek. "I will, Charles. I promise you, I will."

Charles watched her go, knowing in his heart that the man she went to was already totally, hopelessly in love with his wife, needing only her gentle strength to show him how much.

Blinking back his own tears, Charles raised his eyes to the heavens. He was certain that somewhere, in a place far above them, another extraordinarily beautiful woman, a woman who was the image of Kassandra, was looking down upon them . . . and smiling.

Chapter 21

P erkins! Has there been any sign of her?"

Perkins had just returned to his post and now stood stiffly in the front hallway, his lips pursed, giving the disheveled, haggard-looking duke a cold, accusing look. "No, Your Grace," he advised him. "None."

"Dammit!" Braden slammed his fist against the wall in frustration. Since he had returned from the stream he had searched everywhere imaginable, and short of ransacking the guests' quarters, he had left no stone unturned. Where on earth was that impulsive, independent wife of his, and where in heaven had she spent the night?

Braden stared at his butler's tense, worried face, feeling the knot of fear inside him tighten as the nagging possibility that had plagued him for hours returned to haunt him.

What if Robert Grey had taken Kassie?

At this point Braden was prepared to ride to the Grey estate himself. And if Robert had Kassie, Braden would kill him.

"Have Star brought around, Perkins."

"Excuse me, Your Grace," Perkins replied, mortified, "but this is hardly the time for recreation. I shall not rest until the duchess is home safe." With that Perkins turned and stalked off.

Braden stared after him in amazement. After countless years of faithful service his staid and proper butler had just refused to obey an order and, without words, had told Braden that he was as low as the serpent in the Garden of Eden.

215

And all because Perkins believed it was Braden who had hurt Kassie.

For the hundredth time since last night, guilt stabbed at Braden's heart. Perkins was right.

He was heading out of the house to saddle Star himself when he collided with an overwrought Dobson.

"Yer Grace! Yer Grace!"

"Yes, Dobson, what is it?" Braden's voice was taut with impatience. At that moment he cared about nothing but Kassie—not even his Thoroughbreds.

"It's 'er Grace! I 'ear that ye're lookin' for 'er!"

Braden's heart began to pound faster. "Have you seen her, Dobson?" Unconsciously he clutched the younger man's shoulders in a vise grip.

"Yes, Yer Grace, I 'ave." Dobson nodded emphatically.

"Well, where is she?" Braden demanded.

"I don't know where she is right now, but an hour ago she was at th' stables."

"The stables." Braden felt a surge of relief so great that it nearly brought him to his knees.

"Yes, Yer Grace." Dobson extricated himself, his brows knit in concern. "And if ye ask me, she seemed awful upset about something."

Relief exploded into irrational anger. "I didn't ask you!" Braden bellowed. Stalking out the front door, he left the stunned groom standing alone, dazed. Braden was too furious to notice. He had endured just about enough of his staff's blind loyalty to Kassie. Thinking of the hellish night he had just endured, Braden was livid, all his earlier tenderness and self-censure gone.

Now that he knew Kassandra was all right, he was going to kill her.

"She slipped inside a few minutes ago and is up in her bedchamber, Braden." Charles stopped him just outside the entranceway door. "She is tired and disoriented, but unharmed. I believe Margaret is with her." He darted a quick glance toward the second-floor landing. "Why don't you calm down a bit before you go to her?"

Braden faced his friend with barely leashed anger. "Fine,

Charles," he replied in an ominous tone. "I'll calm down a bit." He turned abruptly and headed for the stairway, counting to ten under his breath to retain control. "And then I am going to find my wife and wring her beautiful neck!" He took the steps impatiently, then strode down the hall, a determined Charles at his heels.

"Fine, Braden." Charles hurried ahead and planted himself firmly between Braden and the closed door of Kassie's bedchamber. "But I think you should wash and change your clothes first. Perkins and Harding have already arranged for a bath to be brought to your chambers at once . . . to soothe you," he added pointedly, gauging Braden's reaction.

Braden stared, eyes blazing. Harding, too? Now even his damned valet had fallen under his wife's spell!

Fighting the desire to go *through* Charles in order to get to Kassie, Braden hesitated, realizing that his friend was correct. He glanced past Charles at the closed door, then nodded tersely.

"All right, Charles. You win. I will take that bath and change of clothing." His jaw clenched. "But after that *nothing* is going to keep me from talking to my wife. Is that understood?"

"Perfectly, Braden," Charles responded, stifling a smile. He generally made it a policy never to interfere in Braden's personal life. Yet when it came to Kassandra . . . well, some rules had to be bent, if not completely broken. Charles moved away from the door and headed toward the stairs. "Once you are yourself again I'm certain that Kassandra will be eager to talk with you."

"I doubt that, Charles," Braden responded in a derisive tone. "Truly, I doubt that."

Precisely thirty minutes later Braden stepped from his bath and waved away Harding's offer to assist him. "Leave me, Harding. I am perfectly capable of dressing myself. And I would like to be alone."

Harding knew that tone and was more than happy to comply. With a quick "Yes, Your Grace" he was gone.

Braden briskly toweled himself dry. The warm bath had done wonders toward soothing his weary body but had done little to calm his rampaging emotions. In the last twelve hours he had experienced a myriad of feelings more intense than he had ever known. First possessiveness and vulnerability, followed by acute worry, self-accusation, bone-melting relief, and explosive rage. He was confused and drained, his nerves taut to the breaking point, furious with Kassie for doing this to him, more furious with himself for allowing it.

Behind him the door closed quietly.

"I said that I wished to be alone, Harding." Braden tossed his towel onto a chair without turning around. "I meant it."

"I'm certain that you did," Kassie replied softly. "But I need to see you nonetheless."

Braden turned abruptly at the sound of his wife's voice. Droplets of water still clung to his broad chest and shoulders, glistened in his damp, dark hair. Kassie met his gaze, keenly aware of the sheer magnetism that emanated from her husband's burning stare, the corded muscles that defined every inch of his totally bare, utterly masculine physique. He was magnificent in his nakedness, but what she sought penetrated far deeper than Braden's powerful body, was buried deep within his soul.

She started forward, her gaze never leaving his, the silk of her pale peach dressing gown swirling about her ankles.

"Where the hell were you?" Braden's cold, accusatory tone cut through her like a knife. Kassie flinched, but she didn't slow her step.

"In the stables."

"All night?" he demanded in a raw voice.

"All night."

She stopped inches before him, watching a muscle work in his jaw, a multitude of conflicting emotions registering in his eyes.

"Do you have any idea"—he swallowed—"how worried I was?"

"Yes," she murmured. "Do you have any idea how humiliated I was?"

He stared down at her, remembering what he had subjected her to the previous night. All the anger and resentment drained away, to be replaced by a wave of longing so acute, he couldn't speak. He fought it, closing his eyes to block out the beauty that made every rational thought flee from his mind.

It didn't work. He could still feel her presence beside him, smell the sweetness of her skin, ache to take her in his arms, to lie with her. How could one woman hold so much power over him, he wondered wildly. Worse, how could he *permit* it? With his last filaments of self-protection he battled to retain control of his mind, of his heart.

Kassie watched the struggle on Braden's face, his tortured expression telling her everything she needed to know. There was much left to resolve between them. But that would come later. For now, Braden needed her. And it was up to her to show him how much.

"I didn't mean to worry you, Braden." With the tip of her index finger Kassie traced a drop of water from his shoulder down to his clenched fist. "I just didn't know how to cope with my anger and my hurt." She lightly stroked his closed fingers, his wrist, the hair-roughened skin of his forearm, then slid her hand back up his powerful biceps to his neck. She could feel his muscles contract, feel the inadvertent shudder of his body. And she could feel him fighting it, fighting her. She ached to tell him that only by losing would he win.

Standing on tiptoe, Kassie pressed her lips into the damp hollow at the base of Braden's throat, sliding her fingers into the thick, wet strands of hair at his nape.

Braden stiffened, instantly and painfully aroused. He could not, would not give in to this feeling that was so much more than physical desire. "Stop it, Kassie," he commanded hoarsely, even as his body throbbed its command for her to continue, burned to be joined with her.

"No." The word was a breathy whisper against the sensitized skin of his neck, and Braden could feel himself drowning, dissolving into a million fragments of helpless need.

"Dammit, Kassie," he got out between clenched teeth, "I don't want—"

"Yes, you do," she breathed, pressing herself lightly against his straining, engorged manhood, the evidence of his craving for her.

Braden threw back his head and groaned, unconsciously gliding his fingers through the loose dark waves of her hair. He opened his eyes, caught her face in his hands, and lifted it to meet his smoldering gaze. "My body wants you, Kassie. Is that what you want from me?"

Kassie stroked her fingers across his lips. "That . . . and more."

"I have nothing else to give you."

She smiled dreamily. "You're so wrong, husband. Even you don't know how much you have to give. But I do. I *know* you. I've always known you . . . from the moment we met. You've given me everything . . . everything. And I don't mean my jewels and my wardrobe. You've given me a home, security, a place where I can belong." She paused, letting everything she was feeling shine in her eyes. "And you've given me *you*. Your protection, your name, your loyalty. You've taught me what it means to be a woman, to be wanted by a man. But most of all, you've given me something I've never had. Someone I can rely upon, someone who will always be here for me." She pressed her fingers to his lips when he tried to reply. "You've told me on several occasions that I should lean on you. Did you mean it?"

He was watching her intently. "You know I did," he murmured against her fingertips.

Kassie nodded. "Yes, I know you did. And I believed you then, just as I believe you now." She slid her hands down his arms, catching his fingers and entwining them with hers. "Do you remember when we first met?"

A small smile played about his lips. "You were the most precocious fifteen-year-old I'd ever encountered."

"And the loneliest," she added. "Do you recall what I told you about my love for strolling along the beach?"

The memory was as clear in Braden's mind as if it had happened yesterday. "You said that the beach soothed you; that the sea, the wind, the sun, and the stars were always there for you."

Kassie nodded again, bringing his fingers to her open

mouth. "And they are. But so are you. I never dreamed there would be someone in my life I could count on the way I count on you."

"You're grateful to me," he qualified, in a tone filled with raw hope.

"I'm in love with you." She said the words without hesitation or shame, willing him to believe her. For his belief would be the first step toward their future.

For a fleeting second joy and relief flashed in Braden's eyes. Both were quickly replaced by a skepticism that refused to be quieted. "What you're feeling," he began, "it's . . ."

". . . love," Kassie finished definitely for him. She twined her arms around his neck, pressed her face against his chest. "I love you, Braden," she whispered, a tremor in her voice. "I always have. I always will."

"Kassie . . ." His voice broke as he absorbed her words.

But Kassie gave him no time to think. "Take me to bed," she breathed against his damp skin. "Please, Braden, make love to me."

It was all he needed to push him over the edge.

With a groan of total capitulation Braden dragged Kassie to him, crushing her soft lips beneath his urgent mouth. Scooping her up in his arms, he carried her to the bed, dropping down heavily with her, never breaking the kiss. She wrapped her arms about his neck, murmuring some unintelligible endearment, but Braden barely heard her. He was wild with a bottomless hunger that gnawed inside him, eating its way into a part of his soul that had never before been touched. He stopped fighting the feeling, and his whole body pulsed with its demand, exploding into a primal need to totally possess the beautiful, giving woman in his arms. *His* woman. His wife.

"God, I was so afraid," he panted between kisses, tangling his hands in her hair and anchoring her head to receive his plundering mouth. "So afraid. I thought you were lost . . . or hurt . . . or worse." He crushed her to him, feeling the cool silk of her dressing gown caress his feverish skin. "Don't ever do that to me again. Ever."

"I won't," Kassie promised breathlessly, closing her eyes

and surrendering herself totally to her husband's stormy passion. "I won't. . . . Oh, Braden . . ."

His hot kisses trailed down her neck to the swell of her breasts. At the same time he seized the hem of her gown and dragged it upwards, running his greedy hands up her bare legs to the softness of her thighs. "The gown," he managed in a hoarse rasp.

Kassie's eyes flew open, and she stared at Braden with a dazed, dreamy expression, totally lost to the sensations that were claiming her body. "The . . . gown?" she repeated blankly.

Waiting was fast becoming unendurable agony for Braden. Impatiently he raised up on one elbow and solved the problem on his own, tearing the interfering garment in two and flinging the fragments of material to the floor. Kassie gasped as cold air shivered across her bare skin.

"You're so damned beautiful."

At Braden's husky words the cold vanished instantly, to be replaced by a liquid heat that flowed through her. Kassie's heart began to pound wildly as she lay unmoving and watched her husband's openly carnal gaze explore every inch of her nakedness.

Braden's smoldering eyes returned to her face, and Kassie began to tremble from the undisguised longing that blazed within them. "Come here," he commanded in a deep, sensual voice that was rich with promise. "Come to me now."

She moved toward him, but he had already caught her arms, dragging her to him, molding her soft, pliant body to his hard, muscled one. Every inch of her was claimed by his power, and Kassie relinquished herself to Braden's urgency, letting it dominate their lovemaking, knowing that it expressed feelings that her husband was not yet willing to admit.

Braden was beyond coherent thought. Over the past weeks he had come to accept his consistent loss of control when he was in Kassie's arms. But until now there had always been a small, protective portion of his mind that was aware of Kassie's youth, her inexperience; an inner voice that demanded he take care not to alarm her with his lust or shock her with his actions.

This time that voice remained silent.

Braden's mouth and hands were everywhere, touching, stroking, arousing Kassie beyond endurance. He barely heard her cries of pleasure, so lost was he in her scent, her taste, the sensation of her satiny skin against his face, his hands. Drunk with desire, he slid his open mouth down the hollow between her breasts, turning his head from side to side to allow him access to each tight, hardened nipple. Lifting her from the bed, he anchored his arm beneath her back so that he could deepen the contact, drawing her aroused flesh into his mouth with a suction that made Kassie arch against him, sobbing his name.

Braden raised his head, his eyes glazed with passion. "That's it, sweetheart, tell me how much you need me." He buried his face in the curve of her neck, shuddering as her small hands stroked the corded muscles of his back. "Tell me, Kassie," he muttered thickly against her ear, drawing the soft lobe into his mouth. "Because, Lord help me, I need you." He took her mouth in another scalding kiss, groaning aloud when he felt her tongue tease his lips, then mate with his own.

He couldn't stay still. Tearing his mouth from hers, Braden continued his frenzied possession of his wife, moving down her quivering body, shaking his head and pushing her hands away when she reached for him. "No," he whispered hoarsely, "not this time. This time it has to be me." He pressed his face against her soft abdomen, licking a slow circle inside her navel, repeating the gesture when he heard her whimper aloud. "Tell me, my beautiful wife," he urged softly, gliding his hands over her gently rounded hips. "Tell me you need me."

"I need you . . . oh, Braden, I need you," she sobbed, meaning so much more than the words implied.

"Kassandra . . ." He breathed her name like a prayer, sliding further down in the bed. He parted her thighs with his hands and began to make slow, devastating love to her with his mouth.

Kassie cried out, begging him to end the torture, to come to her, but Braden ignored her pleas, burying himself more deeply in her sweetness. He lifted her legs over his shoulders, leaving her helplessly open to his warm lips, his seeking tongue.

Kassie was drowning. She tossed her head from side to side, pleasure coiling inside her until she wanted to scream with it, to die from it. There was nothing but Braden's mouth and the desperate need for release that her body sought. She tugged at his hair, wanting him inside her . . . now.

Braden needed something else. While his own body craved the same release as Kassie's, he couldn't stop loving her like this, in the most possessive and intimate way a man could love a woman. He had to feel, to taste her pleasure. Only then would his own pleasure be complete.

"No, love, not yet," he gasped, pushing her hands away.

Kassie clutched his hands, frightened by the intensity of sensation that was flooding her. "Braden . . . I can't . . . I'm going to . . ."

"Let it happen," he demanded, wrapping his fingers tightly around hers. "God, Kassandra, let it happen." He intentionally deepened the caress.

"Braden!" She cried out his name as unimaginable pleasure exploded inside her, coursing through her body in wild, wondrous waves of completion. Submerged in their wake, she could do no more than call her husband's name over and over, shuddering helplessly in his arms.

Braden could wait no longer. Before Kassie's body had stilled he raised up and thrust himself deep into her softness, crying out hoarsely as he felt her contractions pulling at him, drawing him deeper into her hot, pulsating center. "Kassie . . ." He answered her body's plea, driving himself into her again and again, keeping pace with each involuntary spasm of her inner muscles as they closed around him.

"Oh . . . yes . . ." she whispered in a shattered voice, wrapping her limbs around her husband, dizzy with the pleasure that continued, escalating with each drive of Braden's hips. "Oh . . . Braden . . . I love you . . ."

"Say it again," he ordered, taut with the strain of holding back.

"I love you," she cried out, feeling his thrusts grow faster, harder, with her words.

"Again." Beads of perspiration broke out on his brow, her words robbing him of his last shred of control.

"I love you," she whispered, floating back down to earth. "I love you, Braden. I love you."

Braden lunged forward, erupting in a release of such intensity that it robbed him of thought, of breath. It was like plummeting from a height so great that it was both terrifying and exhilarating at once. He had no choice but to surrender to its magnitude, to give himself up to its incomparable force. And he did so. Gladly.

Because Kassie was in love with him.

Chapter 22

❧

"You were very angry at me." Kassie murmured her straightforward observation into the damp warmth of Braden's chest.

Braden was silent. Long moments had passed since their bodies had been joined, yet he was still awash in sensation. Physically he was blissfully at peace, but the stirrings of his soul, until now ignored, refused to be silenced. He felt emotionally raw, stripped of his defenses, exposed and vulnerable. And afraid. Afraid of his newly discovered need for the woman in his arms. Afraid to let himself believe what his heart knew to be the truth.

"Braden?" Kassie shifted slightly, gazing up at him with a question in her eyes.

"What?" His voice sounded shattered to his own ears.

"I said that you were very angry at me. Are you still?"

The innocent irony of her question sliced through his emotional turmoil. "No, sweetheart, I'm not angry." He wrapped his arms more tightly about her back and drew the bedcovers up over them for warmth.

Kassie rested her chin on his chest, a small pucker forming between her finely arched brows. "But you *were*. Why?"

Braden shook his head in astonishment. "Your staying out all night is not reason enough for me to be angry?"

"I meant earlier. At the ball, long before you left the party. Did I behave improperly or do anything to embarrass you?"

Recall hit Braden like a wave of icy water, along with a

226

fresh surge of self-accusation. He remembered vividly the disgraceful way he had treated Kassie. He also remembered why. And he couldn't allow his softhearted wife to blame herself.

"You did nothing," he replied, rubbing his knuckles gently against her flushed cheek. "You were every bit as magnificent as I knew you would be. It was me. I suppose I am unused to the . . . attention you are receiving from other men."

"You were upset because I danced with your friends?" Kassie was still trying to understand.

"I was jealous as hell."

Kassie stared at him, stunned. "Jealous? Oh, Braden, how could you possibly be jealous?"

Braden smiled inwardly at the naïveté of the question. "Sweetheart, you may not know it, but you have grown to be a very beautiful woman," he began. "So it is only natural—"

"I'm well aware of my physical attributes, Braden," she interrupted in a matter-of-fact tone.

Braden blinked, taken aback. "Oh . . . but you asked me—"

"I understand *what* you were jealous of," she qualified, reminding Braden of the refreshing young girl of three summers ago. "What I *don't* understand is *why*." She searched his eyes. "I was only being kind to your friends because that is my role as your wife." She reached up to touch his face, willing him not only to hear, but to see. "I don't want any other man but you," she whispered.

He kissed her hand, covering it with his own. "My beautiful, innocent Kassie. Did it ever occur to you that many other men might want you?"

She shrugged her slim shoulders. "That changes nothing."

"But some might try . . ."

"They already have."

Braden's mouth snapped shut, and he felt rage begin to boil inside him. "Who?" he demanded through clenched teeth.

"Does it matter?"

"Yes. It matters." He paused, a muscle working in his jaw. "Was it Grant?"

"He's not worth your ire, Braden."

Braden's fingers closed over her wrist. "Did that bastard touch you?"

Kassie winced. "You're hurting me," she said softly, and instantly he released her. "He kissed me," she answered, determined not to lie to her husband. "Or rather, he *tried* to kiss me."

Braden's whole body went taut, and Kassie could feel the long-repressed fury and betrayal of the past converge with the explosive rage of the present.

"I'll kill him."

"Braden." Kassie moved up until she was lying over him, staring directly down into his blazing hazel eyes. "He's not worth it," she told him softly, stroking his chin, soothing his anger with her touch. "Besides," she added, her aqua eyes beginning to twinkle, "I don't think he found my response to his advances quite to his liking."

"Meaning?"

"I ordered him away from Sherburgh . . . *after* I slapped him."

Despite his outrage Braden felt his lips twitch at the thought of his gentle little wife striking Grant across his stunned, traitorous face.

"I don't believe in infidelity, Braden." Kassie raised her chin a notch, her expression having grown serious. "Not for either of us," she added pointedly. "I was on my way to your bedchamber to tell you that when . . ."

". . . when you found Abigail in my bed," he finished.

"When I found Abigail *undressed* and in your bed," she qualified.

"I see." He enjoyed watching the possessiveness on Kassie's face.

"She didn't find my response to her advances quite to her liking either," she informed him, a mutinous look in her eyes.

"Meaning?"

"I slapped her, too."

Braden wanted to laugh out loud—with amusement, with

pleasure—but Kassie was gazing at him with a serious, expectant look on her face.

He cupped her cheeks, forcing her to see the truth in his eyes. "I did not invite her to my bed," he promised quietly. "I would never humiliate you like that." He paused, then continued, giving her what she needed, what they both needed. "I have not been with another woman since the day you and I were wed. Nor do I plan to be. Further, Abigail Devon has been banned from this house forever."

"Thank you," Kassie said with dignified simplicity.

Braden stroked his fingers through the silky, tousled waves of her hair. "You're welcome," he replied solemnly, silently knowing that he had relinquished nothing that had not already been relinquished. The fact was that no woman but Kassandra could satisfy him—not the cravings of his body nor those of his soul. It was an absolute knowledge that Braden accepted, yet one that he could not yet express . . . at least not in words.

Feeling his chest tighten with emotion, Braden rolled Kassie to her back, reveling in the rosy afterglow on her face and the joy he saw reflected in her eyes. She looked well loved and, at last, blissfully happy. Could it really be because of him? he wondered. The possibility filled Braden with an intoxicating sense of elation. He drank in his wife's beauty, wanting always to be the one to bring her pleasure, wanting to protect her from the world and all of its ills.

His train of thought led him to a sudden unresolved question. "You were furious when you left last night." He stated the obvious, looking into Kassie's eyes for his answer.

"Yes," she agreed with a contented smile. "I was."

"What made you decide to come back?"

"The fact that I love you . . . and some wonderful insight given to me at just the right time," she replied softly.

Braden smiled quizzically. "Insight?" he repeated in a puzzled tone. "Into what? By whom?"

She eluded the second question and answered the first.

"For one thing," she hedged, "into the fact that you might be worried about me. That hadn't occurred to me until this morning."

He frowned, her answer reminding him of all he had

feared over the past hours. "Don't ever stay out all night again," he said quietly. "I was frantic."

"Um-m-m." She nibbled on his chin. "I noticed."

"Kassie, I mean it."

There was pain in his voice, and Kassie heard it. She nodded. "I won't."

"I'm not trying to frighten you," he said more gently, lowering himself beside her so that he could enjoy the feel of her body against his, "but it isn't safe for you to roam the endless deserted grounds of Sherburgh alone at night."

A flash of fear crossed Kassie's face. "I thought you said there were guards."

"There are." He was unaware of her changed expression as he threaded his fingers through her hair, marveling at how the sunlight illuminated each silky tendril. "But that doesn't make it impossible for someone to steal in somehow." He felt her stiffen, and his gaze snapped back to her ashen face. "Sweetheart, I'm not telling you this to worry you needlessly, but—"

"Someone was watching me today."

"What?"

"This morning. Before I came back to the house. Someone was out there. I know it." She squeezed her eyes shut, remembering the terrifying awareness that she was being stalked, Percy's inexplicable barking, running away from the sense of danger, finding Charles . . .

Braden stared down at her, tension knotting his stomach. Seeing the fear on her face, he had no doubt that Kassie was telling the truth. "Did you see anyone?"

She shook her head, her eyes tightly closed. "No. I called out to whoever it was to show himself, but he never did. But he *was* out there, Braden. I know it. Percy knew it, too. He just kept growling and barking, and you know he doesn't do that unless—"

"Sh-h-h." He drew her against him, resting his chin atop Kassie's bright head, trying not to let her see how worried he really was. "It's all right, love. Just start from the beginning and tell me what happened." His words were gentle, but his expression was hard.

Her voice trembling, Kassie recounted everything she could recall of her early morning scare. With each word Braden could feel himself becoming more and more furious. When she had finished he remained silent for a moment, willing himself to control.

"Kassie," he said at last, still stroking her back with gentle, soothing motions, "it's all right. No one is going to hurt you."

"You don't believe me." There was resignation in her voice.

"I believe you." His correction was immediate. "And I plan to remedy the situation at once."

"What are you going to do?"

He weighed his answer carefully. "I am going to take Hunter and search every inch of the section of grounds you mentioned. I shall, of course, question all the guards who are watching Sherburgh, and—"

"And then what are you going to do?" she interrupted softly.

Braden sighed. His wife was making it impossible to protect her from the truth.

"Braden," she persisted. *"Then* what are you going to do?" She leaned back in his arms, her gaze locked with his.

"Then I am going to do something I should have done weeks ago," he replied, thinking what a fool he was to have imagined he could hide it from her.

"You are going to see my father."

"Yes, love, I am going to see your father." He watched Kassie carefully for a reaction. Her expression didn't alter, but Braden could feel the imperceptible tensing of her body, see the slight trembling of her lips.

"Please be careful," she whispered.

"I'll be fine." He pressed his lips to her forehead. "Now I want you to sleep. You are exhausted."

"And you?"

He pressed her back against the pillows and slid out of the bed. "I'll rest later . . . after I'm convinced that our intruder was not your father." He smiled tenderly down at the worry on her face. "All will be well, sweetheart. I promise you."

The problem, he thought to himself later as his carriage approached the Grey estate, was that every instinct told him that it *was* Robert Grey who had been stalking Kassandra. Braden's search of the grounds and subsequent questioning of his guards had yielded no further information. The only people they had seen about this early in the morning were the gardeners, several ambitious guests on horseback, Dobson, and Charles Graves. No one else. Yet Braden knew in his heart that the danger Kassie sensed was real. And that it had to come from her father.

But why? Grey could gain nothing from frightening his daughter; certainly not money, which Kassie had already denied him. If it were money he wanted, it would be Braden he would seek out, Braden he would appeal to. And I would probably give it to him, Braden thought to himself in disgust. *Anything* to protect Kassie from the likes of that bastard.

But in his heart Braden knew it wasn't money. It was something more. And whatever it was, he was going to find it out.

Robert's head lolled on the pillow, his hand clutching a bottle beside him. *Elena* . . . He could still see her face, just as he continued to do day after day, night after night. *My beautiful Elena* . . . He had almost been with her again, almost chased that frightened look from her eyes . . . until *he* had come into her life. Damn him. Nothing would be the same until he was gone from their lives. Nothing.

The door slammed open, bouncing off the chipped wall. Robert started, then struggled to a sitting position. "What . . ."

Braden stormed across the room, tearing open the heavy drapes and letting the morning sun pour into the clammy, odorous room. The bedchamber was filthy, clothes strewn all over, bottles tossed carelessly about, the stench of liquor so heavy that Braden could barely breathe. He flung open the windows to allow the air to clear his head.

Robert whimpered like a small child, covering his eyes with his arm and gagging at the intrusion of light and sound.

Braden kept himself under control with the greatest of effort. "All right, Grey, get up. You were at my home. I presume you were looking for me. Well, I'm here. Now tell me what you want, and then give me one good reason why I shouldn't kill you right here in your own excrement."

Robert blinked at him, desperately trying to focus. "What . . . I don't know what you mean. . . ."

"Why were you at Sherburgh?" Braden demanded. "You were told to stay the hell away from my wife."

"I wasn't at Sher—"

"You're lying," Braden cut him off. "Kassie told me she saw you." He took two strides to the bed and grabbed Robert by the arms, hauling him out of bed and watching impassively as he dropped to a crumpled heap on the floor. "Now tell me why, you miserable scum."

"For money, damn you, for money," Robert whined, pushing himself to his feet and holding on to the nightstand for balance.

"I gave you one hundred thousand pounds."

"It's gone."

Braden gave him a look of utter revulsion. "And I don't need to ask what you spent it on, now do I?"

"I needed it."

"And you don't care how you got it," Braden accused, his eyes spitting fire at Kassie's father. "Even if it meant hurting your own daughter."

"I didn't hurt her!"

"Didn't you?" Braden took a menacing step closer. "Why did you come back again, even after Kassie refused to give you any money?"

"I didn't—"

Braden was upon him in an instant, grabbing him by his throat. "Don't lie to me! I know you returned to Sherburgh. What I want to know is why."

Robert shook his head, reality and fantasy converging, unable to discern between the two. "I wanted to see her . . . I had to see her again."

"Why?"

"Because I love her, dammit! Because I've always loved

her." He closed his bloodshot eyes, seeing the memories once again. "I'll always love her," he whispered aloud, "Elena . . ."

Braden felt ill. "Kassandra is your daughter, Grey, not your wife," he said quietly but distinctly.

Grey opened his eyes slowly. "Kassandra?" He gave a harsh laugh. "Yes, Sheffield, I *know* that she is my daughter. She is the image of her mother." At that moment he sounded totally coherent.

Braden took advantage of the opportunity. "When was the last time you came to Sherburgh?"

Grey gave him a sardonic smile. "I haven't been at your palatial home, Your Grace."

Braden's eyes narrowed with anger at the blatant lie. "What do you know of Kassie's nightmares?"

For an instant terror dilated Robert's pupils, then disappeared. "I don't know what you're talking about."

The hell you don't, Braden thought, fury tightening his chest. "Kassie's nightmares. The horrible dreams she keeps having. What do you know of them?"

Robert shook himself free, straightening his clothing with shaking hands. "I don't recall Kassandra's mentioning any nightmares, Sheffield. Could it be that marriage to you does not agree with her after all?"

With a will of its own Braden's fist connected with Robert's jaw. The crack resounded throughout the room, and Robert jerked backwards, then sank slowly to the floor. All the bravado was gone from his eyes now, replaced by pain and a fresh surge of fear.

"Stay the hell away from her, Grey." Braden's tone was lethal. "The next time will be the last."

Braden was in a foul mood when he arrived back at Sherburgh. His head was throbbing from the combined stress of the sleepless night spent searching for Kassie and the ugly confrontation he had just had with her father.

Robert was lying.

That much was certain in his mind. What he was unsure of was to what degree, and for what purpose? About the nightmares Braden knew Robert lied, for Kassie herself had told him that whenever she spoke of her bad dreams to her father he had dismissed them as the result of an overly vivid imagination. Not to mention the stark terror Braden had seen in Robert's eyes just before he had denied knowledge of Kassie's dreams. No, he was lying . . . lying and afraid.

Braden made his way up the stairs, feeling no closer to the truth than when he had left. What was Grey afraid of? And how did Kassie fit into those fears? Had he done something that he thought Kassie might know about? A chill went up Braden's spine. And if so, what did Grey plan to do about it? Was he coming to Sherburgh just to keep an eye on his daughter, or did he plan something more? No, Braden denied to himself. If Robert planned to harm Kassie, why hadn't he done it while she lived unprotected in his home? Because, Braden's mind argued back, Robert had been able to observe Kassie every minute then. She had been alone, with no one to talk to, no one to make sense of her fears. Until now.

Braden's uneasiness mounted. Grey was irrational, barely coherent most of the time. That made him unstable—and dangerous. And, if he had found a way to steal into Sherburgh unseen . . .

Racing down the hall, Braden flung open Kassie's bed-chamber, surveying the empty bed with haunted eyes and a pounding heart. Where was she? He had left her sleeping, had been advised by Margaret that she was still abed, but there was no sign of Kassie anywhere.

His room. The answer clamored its way into his frantic mind. He had left her sleeping in *his* bed.

He strode through her deserted bedchamber to the connecting door and threw it open.

The sight of Kassie blissfully asleep in his bed made Braden sag against the wall with relief. She looked like an angel upon his pillow, her long, dark lashes lying like silken fans upon her cheeks, her still-tousled hair spread out like a black satin cloak over her bare shoulders and back. Braden walked quietly to the bedside, drinking in her innocent beauty, filling his senses with Kassie until there was no room inside him for the ugliness of the past hours.

Slowly he shrugged out of his clothes, wanting nothing

more than to lie down beside her, hold her in his arms, and sleep. Naked, he slid into the bed, careful not to awaken her with his movements.

But Kassie felt his presence and stirred.

She opened her eyes and blinked groggily. Then awareness spread across her face like rays of sunshine. "Braden." Her voice was husky with sleep, and Braden felt a wave of tenderness engulf his heart.

"I'm here." He drew her against him, feeling her curl trustingly into his arms and knowing a sense of protectiveness so fierce that it hurt.

"Did you see him?"

"Yes . . . sh-h-h, not now," he murmured softly, more for his own sake than for hers. He didn't want Robert's presence to intrude into the perfect peace he felt right then, with Kassie in his arms.

Kassie drew back, searched his eyes, then nodded. "All right," she whispered back, her innate understanding of Braden advising her to comply.

Braden gazed down at her, seeing the unconditional acceptance in her eyes, and all thoughts of rest vanished in a rush of need. Unexpected, renewed desire exploded through his body and, though he could explain it no more than he could control it, the need to be inside her was suddenly more than the need to breathe.

"Kassie . . ." He was hardly aware that he spoke her name as he covered her body with his, capturing her mouth in a deep, drugging kiss of wordless possession. He felt her soft breasts beneath the hard wall of his chest, felt her arms go about his back and knew that this time there could be no waiting. They simply had to be one.

"Love," he rasped, moving against her, "let me in . . . now." He was stunned by his own urgency.

Kassie was not. She understood better than Braden what he needed, and she gave it to him in the only way he could accept it, opening herself to his demand.

He entered her with a savage groan, taking her with a wildness that made them both cry out. Again and again their bodies merged until, with a hoarse shout, Braden let go, giving himself to his wife, pouring himself into her and losing himself inside her love.

Kassie felt the surge of wet warmth flow through her, and she closed her eyes, clinging to her husband's powerful body as her own release came in hard, sharp spasms of pleasure. She heard Braden call her name, felt him lift her to him, heightening the sensations and drawing them out. And then she felt the utter bliss of his sated body heavily pressing hers deeper into the soft bed.

"Did I hurt you?" His voice was raw, shaken.

"No," she whispered, touching her lips to his wet shoulder. "I love you. And you didn't hurt me."

Braden closed his eyes, his fists clenched in the pillow beside her head. *And no one else will hurt you either,* he promised her silently, breathing in the scent of their union. *No one.*

Chapter 23

Hours later it was Kassie's strangled cry that brought Braden out of a deep, troubled sleep. He was instantly awake, reaching for his shuddering wife, who was still in the throes of her nightmare.

"Kassie." He shook her firmly, familiar now with the symptoms. "Wake up, sweetheart." No response. "Kassie!" Braden's guts knotted with fear. "Come back to me, *ma petite*. Wake up!"

Come back to me. Please. Come back to me.

The plea echoed again and again through Kassie's head, a harsh masculine urging that was both litany and prayer, a wisp of memory extinguished by a stronger force of self-preservation.

Was that Braden calling to her?

Kassie fought her way out of the emotional abyss, her heart hammering against her ribs, sweat trickling down her back. She clung to the sound of Braden's voice, reaching toward it as a flower does to the sunlight that offers it the promise of life.

He knew the moment she came awake, felt the rigidity leave her damp body. Slowly he drew her against him, whispering words of comfort into her hair and stroking her back in gentle circling motions. "I'm here, love. I'm right here," he assured her softly.

"I thought the dream had gone . . . that it was over," she whispered.

Braden knew better. But all he said was "I know, sweet-

238

heart. It's probably just the result of the past days' turmoil."
He hesitated. "Is it unchanged?"

"Yes."

"You. The beast. The fall. Nothing else?"

She groped for a memory that was gone. "Nothing else."

He was quiet for a moment, staring off into the late afternoon shadows, reflecting on the coincidence of the nightmare's reoccurrence and Robert's reappearance in Kassie's life—a coincidence that Braden was certain was no coincidence at all.

"Braden?"

Her small, frightened voice brought him back. "Yes, love?"

"Do you think that I'm insane?"

He started, drawing back to stare down at her. "What kind of a question is that?"

"A perfectly logical one. I continue to have inexplicable, bizarre nightmares, despite the fact that I have never been happier in my life. What other explanation could there be?"

"You are not insane," he denied hotly, cupping her face between his hands. "And I never want to hear you say that again. Is that understood?"

Relief flowed through her, and Kassie gave her husband a small, shaky smile. "Yes, Braden, I understand."

Unconvinced, Braden continued to search her eyes, his jaw clenched. "I mean it, Kassandra. Don't ever refer to yourself as insane again. I won't have it."

Determined to regain her composure, Kassie stroked her husband's angry face with trembling fingertips. "This is the second order you've issued to me today," she reminded him with forced lightness. "I am discovering that you really are quite overbearing, Your Grace."

Braden understood Kassie's attempt to diffuse her fear and he relaxed, only too happy to oblige. He gave her a lazy grin, anxious to take her mind off her dream. "Overbearing. Am I really?"

She nodded. "Oh, yes, you are. Why, it's no wonder your servants are becoming disgruntled with you."

His forefinger stroked the bridge of her slender nose. "To

the contrary, my lovely wife," he replied, growing serious. "My servants are not becoming disgruntled with me. They are becoming enchanted with their new duchess." His voice became husky. "As am I."

Kassie felt her heart soar. Enchanted. He was becoming enchanted with her. It was the closest Braden had ever come to admitting that he loved her. Perhaps enchantment was not quite love, but it sounded perfectly glorious just the same.

Kassie thought back to all Charles had said about Braden, to what he had implied. *Soon, my husband,* she promised silently. *Soon you'll be able to say the words.*

"Would you like to go back to sleep now?" he asked tenderly, unaware of her thoughts.

Kassie tensed. "No. I would much rather get up. Please, Braden."

He kissed her forehead gently. "Fine. Besides, it is way past our mealtime. My stomach is beginning to protest."

Kassie scrambled gratefully to her feet, frowning as she gathered up the fragments of her ruined dressing gown. Braden chuckled at her attempts to piece it together. "I'll buy you another. Several others, in fact. One can never tell when I might become . . . impatient again." He rose from the bed, all sleek muscle and towering height. "I'll send Margaret to your room to help you dress. In the meantime I shall charm Cook into preparing us a very late light luncheon. How does that sound?"

Kassie gave him a dazzling smile. "It sounds wonderful. Thank you." She made one last futile attempt to wrap the satin gown around her and then gave up gracefully, providing Braden with a melting view of her luscious body as she left the chamber through its connecting door. Enchanted, he thought to himself. Yes, he certainly was that. And worried as well. He had to get to the heart of these nightmares. Soon. Before Kassie got hurt.

"I don't like the dark circles beneath your eyes, Your Grace." Margaret stood behind Kassie, shaking her head as she regarded her mistress's pale countenance.

"I'm really fine, Margaret," Kassie assured the older

woman, smoothing her chemise along the contours of her body.

The motion only served to draw Margaret's attention to the duchess's too-slender curves, causing her own frown to deepen. "And you're far too thin. Why, before long you're going to disappear into nothing at all!"

"That's why I'm going to join Braden for luncheon," Kassie replied brightly, hoping to ease her beloved maid's worry.

Margaret made a clucking sound and folded her arms across her chest. "One meal won't make a difference, Your Grace. As it is, many of your gowns have grown too large for you."

Kassie turned, her brows knit. "Did you have the chance to alter any of them, Margaret?" she asked anxiously. "If not, I must do one immediately. Else I have nothing suitable to wear."

"Of course I have, love." Margaret hurried to the door. "Not to worry; I've fixed four or five of them. I'll bring them in at once."

Kassie sagged with relief. "Thank you, Margaret. What would I ever do without you?" Alone in the room, she allowed her thoughts to return to her unfinished conversation with Braden. The one that involved his encounter with her father. She had been sidetracked, first by Braden's urgent passion, then by the horror of her nightmare, and last by the wonder of Braden's near declaration of love. But now she realized that they had never spoken of Robert and what had transpired today at the cottage.

She sank down on her bed, idly fingering the lacy edges of her chemise. What could have happened? Was her father the person who had been watching her this morning? And if so, had he told Braden the truth? She squeezed her eyes shut, the fear closing in on her again. Was there no end to this feeling of foreboding? At a time when she should be overflowing with happiness, when she was so close to finally reaching Braden's heart, why must a veil of darkness overshadow the splendor of her joy?

The door to her bedchamber opened and Kassie struggled to bring herself under control. She wouldn't allow Margaret to see her worry; the poor woman was already beside herself. With this thought Kassie swallowed deeply, fixed a bright smile upon her face, and opened her eyes.

A startled Cyril Sheffield met her gaze.

Kassie jumped to her feet in astonishment, instinctively covering herself with her arms. "Cyril? What on earth are you doing in here?"

He stared intently at her, silently taking in her state of undress, then cleared his throat roughly. "I came to see if you were well. I knocked . . . there was no reply. I had no idea . . ." He broke off, his dark gaze still fixed on her near nakedness.

Kassie felt herself grow warm, her cheeks stained with color. Here she was, clad in nothing more than a flimsy undergarment, alone in her bedchamber with Braden's uncle. "I am fine," she managed in as normal a tone as she could muster given the circumstances.

He nodded absently. "We were all concerned about you last night, and when you weren't present at luncheon—"

"I am fine, Cyril," she reiterated, wishing desperately that Braden had not destroyed her dressing gown. "But as you can see, I am not prepared to entertain guests."

The pointed remark seemed to snap him out of his reverie. "Oh . . . of course. Forgive me, Kassandra. I didn't expect that you would be awake yet." He dropped his eyes politely. "I trust you are suffering no ill effects from last night. Now, if you will excuse me . . ." He shut the door quietly behind him.

Kassie had no time to ponder Cyril's strange behavior, for an instant later Margaret burst back into the room carrying five elegant garments over her capable arm.

"Here you are, love," she said cheerfully, lifting a pale green silk gown for Kassie's inspection. "This is the one you'll be wanting to wear. Now let's hurry and get you ready for His Grace."

Kassie grinned at Margaret's enthusiasm, dutifully slipping into the lovely gown. But her grin faded as she remembered her earlier thought, and she lifted her chin a determined notch. This evening, regardless of any possible interruptions, she would speak to Braden of his encounter with her father.

She wasted no time, beginning along with Cook's mouth-watering oyster soup.

"What did my father say?"

Braden came up with a start. It wasn't as if he hadn't known what was on Kassie's mind. In fact, he had anticipated her question, for he had been brooding over the situation himself. But as usual, her forthrightness managed to catch him off guard. He recovered himself quickly, leaning back and studying Kassie's beautiful, earnest face. She was flawlessly lovely, and yet so pale, so drawn, the delicate bones in her cheeks so damned prominent. Braden frowned.

"What did he say, Braden?" Kassie had no intention of allowing her question to go unanswered.

Braden gave her a measured look. "Actually, he said very little."

Kassie placed her spoon emphatically upon the table. "Please, Braden, don't dodge my meaning in order to protect me," she said with quiet dignity. "He is *my* father, and I need to know. Was he or was he not the person I sensed watching me this morning?"

Braden reached over and took her hand. "I honestly do not know, sweetheart. He, of course, denied that he was here. But his word is hardly reliable."

Kassie lowered her eyes, then raised them to meet Braden's, bleakness clouding their aqua brilliance. "Was he sober?"

Much as it pained him, Braden owed her his honesty. "No. He was barely coherent."

A look of remembered pain flashed across Kassie's face, but she merely nodded. "I see."

Braden brought her fingers to his lips. "I won't let him hurt you."

Kassie swallowed. "Do you believe he would?"

"He has in the past. Under certain circumstances, yes, I believe he would again."

Kassie didn't flinch. "You're probably right," she whispered. She regarded Braden from beneath thick, damp lashes. "Did you strike him?"

Braden wished he had killed him. "Yes. But not nearly as hard nor as often as he struck you." Taking a deep breath, he plunged onward, trying to ignore Kassie's agonized expression. "The man is an animal, Kassie. An animal, a drunk, and a liar. He not only denied coming to Sherburgh since you've been here, but he denied all knowledge of your nightmares."

Kassie's fingers grew cold in his. "You confronted him with my dreams?" she gasped.

"Of course I did. And according to him, you've never mentioned them at all."

"If he was drunk—" she began.

But Braden interrupted her with a disgusted shake of his head. "No. I won't accept that excuse any longer. And neither should you. He was lying, Kassie, *lying.*"

"But why?" Her voice was barely audible, her face white.

Braden's heart ached for her, but he had to go on. "Did it ever occur to you that your nightmare returns every time you must deal with your father? Couldn't there be some connection between the two?"

"No!" She was on her feet, trembling violently, her eyes wide with terror. "Please . . . no," she whispered, her voice, her gaze far away. Braden caught her just before she crumpled to the floor in a dead faint.

"I'm really all right, Braden. Honestly." Kassie gave him a weak smile from where she lay upon the sofa.

He sat down beside her, pressing the cool compress to her forehead. "I'm relieved to hear that, sweetheart." His casual tone reflected none of the worry or guilt that he was feeling. "However, you'll just have to humor me until I feel more convinced."

Before Kassie could reply, Charles strode into the drawing room, his riding clothes dusty from a day's work, his face tight with worry. "Perkins tells me that Kassandra fainted."

Braden nodded, rising to face his friend. "She did."

Charles's gaze went right past Braden to where Kassie was struggling to a sitting position. "Being out all night was too much for you. I should have realized that. You looked so peaked—"

"I'm fine, Charles. Really." Kassie sat up, taking the cloth from her forehead. "Braden and I were just discussing my father, and I got a bit upset."

Charles looked at Braden as if he had lost his mind. "After all that Kassandra has endured, what would prompt you to discuss Grey now?" It was not a question, but an accusation.

Kassie answered for him. "Braden seems to feel that seeing my father triggers the recurrence of my nightmares— that there is some connection between the two." Her voice shook, and she swallowed quickly to keep back the fresh surge of hysteria that threatened to erupt. "Maybe he's right," she said in a barely audible whisper, closing her eyes.

Charles's expression hardened instantly, and he took Braden's arm, leading him to the far corner of the room. "You've pushed her enough, Braden," he said quietly for Braden's ears alone. "To continue would be cruel."

Braden saw the steel in Charles's gaze, heard the warning in his tone. And it stunned him. "I am trying to help my wife," he countered firmly.

"You are treading where you have no knowledge."

"No one knows Kassie better than I," Braden shot back, his eyes ablaze.

"I agree" was the solemn reply. "Therefore you, of all people, should see that she has reached her absolute limit, that she simply cannot take any more."

Charles's words struck home. Braden reeled with their impact, with their truth. Slowly he nodded, instinct telling him that he could not combat this enemy alone. "You are quite right, Charles," he conceded. "Kassie is deteriorating, and I don't seem to be able to do a thing to stop it." He paused. "Perhaps it is time that I sent for someone who can."

Some of the anger left Charles's face. "Who?"

"Dr. Howell. He can give Kassie a thorough examination and make some sense out of this madness." For a moment some of the anguish Braden was feeling registered on his face. "I cannot bear to see her like this any more than you can, Charles. Maybe Alfred can rid her of the pain that torments her." A muscle flexed in his jaw. "Because no one can convince me that Grey is not somehow involved."

"Would the two of you kindly stop discussing me as if I weren't present?" Kassie demanded from the sofa. "If I am the subject of your heated conversation, then please permit me to take part in it as well."

Braden walked back to her side. "I am going to send for Dr. Howell. I want him to examine you."

Kassie's eyes widened. "Do you believe that I am ill?"

"I want to rule it out." He caressed her pale cheek. "You are too thin, you rarely sleep, and you just fainted. I would feel better if a doctor examined you."

"As would I." Perkins's bold announcement came from the doorway, where he stood with a fresh cloth in his hands. All stunned eyes on him, he scurried across the room and tenderly laid the wet compress on Kassie's head. "There you are, Your Grace," he crooned, ignoring the room's other occupants. "That should help." He removed the used cloth from her hands and smiled encouragingly. "Dr. Howell is the gentleman who tended to your injuries upon your arrival at Sherburgh some months back. He is a fine physician who has cared for His Grace for many years. I have already sent for him." He stood stiffly, efficiently, and turned his gaze to Braden. "Will there be anything else, Your Grace?"

Wrestling with the instinct to remind Perkins who worked for whom, Braden decided to forgive the butler his impertinence, knowing that it was caused by his worry for Kassie. "No, Perkins," he said dryly. "You seem to have taken care of everything quite well."

Perkins nodded. "Yes, Your Grace. I shall let you know the moment the doctor arrives."

Kassie watched the butler go, then glanced anxiously at Braden, attempting to judge the intensity of his reaction. "Please don't be angry with him, Braden. He has the highest regard for you. It's just that he and I have become rather fond of each other."

Braden quirked a brow in his wife's direction. "What you're saying is that he *respects* me, but he *likes* you."

Kassie nodded eagerly, relieved at Braden's unruffled

response. "Exactly." Then, struck by the unflattering implication of her answer, she bit her lip. "What I meant was—"

Braden felt a rush of tenderness flood through him. His Kassie was loving and honest and good, and he only wished that the rest of the world were as sane as she. He pulled her off the sofa and into his arms, burying his face in her hair. "I know what you meant, sweetheart," he murmured, meeting Charles's sober gaze over Kassie's bright head. "We will conquer this thing, Kassie," he whispered fervently to Charles, to himself. "I promise you we will."

"Tell me more about Kassandra's dreams." Alfred Howell sipped thoughtfully on his brandy, watching Braden pace the length of the study.

Braden stopped short. "What did Kassie tell you?"

Dr. Howell shrugged. "Very little, actually. She was silent through most of my examination, speaking only when I asked her a direct question. She seemed very nervous."

"That should come as no shock to you, Alfred," Braden replied bitterly. "You recall the condition she was in when she first came here, as well as the reason for that condition. This examination—*any* examination—is very difficult for her."

The stout, elderly man shuddered with distaste, raking his fingers through his thick white hair. He recalled only too well the extent and the cause of the duchess's injuries when he had first tended to her. His disgust and rage had intensified by the moment as he bandaged her bruised ribs and cleansed the numerous cuts and scrapes that marred her perfect beauty. What manner of human being could have inflicted wounds such as these on his own daughter? Howell had wondered, sickened by the thought. He remembered feeling grateful that Grey's damage had been stopped before it was too late.

Apparently he had been wrong.

Howell's long silence unnerved Braden. "You're quite sure that she's well—that there is no physical cause for her to faint?" he demanded.

The doctor sighed. "I've assured you again and again that

your wife is not ill, Braden. There is no medical reason for her depleted state."

"No *medical* reason," Braden repeated.

"That's what I said."

"Kassie believes that she is insane." Braden watched Alfred's expression carefully.

The doctor inclined his head slightly. "In my experience, those people who fear that they are insane rarely are. It is those who manifest bizarre behavior and *insist* that they are quite well who are the more likely candidates for insanity."

Braden drained his own glass, staring intently, silently, at the oriental rug. Finally he seemed to arrive at some decision, lifting his head purposefully to meet Dr. Howell's curious gaze. "Alfred, we've known each other for quite some time," he began, weighing his words.

"Since you were a boy," the doctor agreed, waiting.

Braden nodded. "You know that I am by nature a realist, not given to fanciful thought or intangible explanation. However, I truly believe that Kassie's depleted state is the direct result of her recurring nightmares. And that the nightmares are the direct result of some horrible event that her mind cannot forget but, at the same time, refuses to remember."

Dr. Howell received Braden's words without visible reaction, finishing his brandy and then placing the empty glass carefully upon the edge of Braden's desk. "Kassandra's problem is not her inability to remember, but her inability to recall," he corrected at last. "Remembrance is the spontaneous retention of past experiences. Recollection is the active search to recover these past experiences. Therein her problem lies."

Having been prepared for Alfred's skepticism, Braden started. "Did you originate that philosophy?"

The doctor smiled. "Hardly. The credit for that goes to Aristotle, over two thousand years ago. But I do subscribe to it wholeheartedly."

"Then you believe that my explanation is possible?"

"Not only possible, Braden, but probable." He leaned forward in his chair, his own words giving credence to

Braden's. "From what you have implied, I would venture to guess that someone or something in Kassandra's past left such a profound impression on her memory that it resurfaces as disjointed images in her dreams. The images themselves, though I am most anxious to hear of them, might not be accurate, but their persistence tells me that they are significant. And they are indeed depleting her energy and her strength. So, in answer to your question, is your wife in good health . . . yes and no. I believe in treating a patient's whole self—not only the physical being, but the soul as well."

"Then will you consider staying on at Sherburgh to help Kassie?" Braden wasted no words, feeling the first rays of hope emerge inside him.

Alfred formed a steeple with his fingers, resting his chin thoughtfully atop it. "This is most unorthodox. You know that, Braden."

"I know."

The doctor regarded Braden silently for a moment, then nodded. "Very well. Let me speak to Kassandra again, alone. Then, if she is agreeable, I'll stay."

Braden leaned forward, extending his hand to the older man. "Thank you, Alfred," he said with solemn gratitude. "I am forever in your debt."

"That remains to be seen." Alfred shook Braden's hand warmly and stood. "Now I'd like to return to Kassandra's bedchamber so that we might talk."

Kassie sat by the window, gazing out at nothing in particular. She felt frightened, confused, out of control. She knew that her reaction to Braden's innocent questions had been extreme, and yet even the memory of the conversation left her feeling cold and desperately afraid.

Sighing, she lowered her face into her hands, wondering for the hundredth time if she really was going mad. What other explanation could there be for her inexplicable panic?

The soft knock broke into her thoughts, and she looked up in time to see Braden walk into the room. He came to her side, then squatted down beside her, taking her small, cold hand in his strong, large one.

"How are you feeling?"

"I'm sure Dr. Howell told you that I am fine." She had trouble keeping the tremor out of her voice.

"Dr. Howell said that he'd like the chance to talk with you again. He is prepared to stay on and help us, Kassie," Braden told her gently. "But only if it is what you want."

Kassie searched his face, a myriad of emotions flashing across her own. "I'm afraid," she whispered.

"I know you are, sweetheart." He brought her fingers to his warm mouth. "But we have to find out what is tormenting you like this. And then, no matter what it is, we'll face it . . . together."

Kassie drank in his strength, then nodded, white-faced. "All right," she said in a determined voice. "I'll speak to him."

Braden had never been as proud of her as he was at that moment. He cupped her face and looked deeply into her eyes. "You're not alone, love. I'm here for you. And I will be for the rest of your life." He kissed her gently and stood, crossing the room and opening the door. "Come in, Alfred. Kassie is ready to speak with you now."

Kassie watched, trancelike, as Braden admitted the stout, white-haired doctor and quietly left the room.

"I'm glad you agreed to see me again, Kassandra," Alfred began, lowering himself into the chair that was closest to where Kassie sat. "I think it's important for us to talk."

Kassie regarded him bleakly. "I'll ask you the same question I asked Braden, doctor. Do you think that I am insane?"

Alfred met her gaze directly. "What I think is that it is a crime for such a beautiful and sensitive woman, who is obviously very much in love with her new husband, to suffer from the sort of pain that you are obviously suffering from, Kassandra," he replied. "But insane? No, my dear, quite the contrary. I think you are brave, unspoiled, and utterly charming. And I knew from the first that you were the best thing ever to happen to Braden. Now, have I answered your question satisfactorily?"

Kassie blinked in surprise. "But we hardly know each other!"

"Ah, but I *do* know Braden. And he believes in you. So the decision is yours. Do we accept defeat, give in to whatever it is that ails your soul, or do we fight it and prove ourselves worthy of Braden's faith? The choice, my dear, belongs to you and you alone."

A small smile tugged at Kassie's lips. "You would make a superb politician, doctor." She raised her chin and gave him a definitive nod. "Very well. I place myself in your capable hands in the hope that together we can unlock the past and nurse my soul back to good health."

Chapter 24

Cyril swallowed the last bite of his omelet and turned his attention to today's *Times,* lying unopened beside the empty place setting at the head of the table. He had just settled back in his chair to read when the dining room door swung open and Braden entered. Head bent, brow furrowed, Braden approached the table, totally oblivious to Cyril's presence, thinking only of Kassie.

At this very moment she was speaking with Alfred in the drawing room, where they had been closeted since dawn. Braden knew precisely when they had begun, for he had forfeited his morning ride, opting instead to pace the floor outside the firmly closed doors, waiting anxiously for the outcome of the talk. He would be there still but for Perkins's pointed suggestion that some breakfast would be in order, for without food His Grace could not live, much less continue his vigil. Braden had taken the less-than-subtle hint and had reluctantly come to the dining room for a minimal amount of sustenance, intending to bolt his breakfast and return to his post.

"Good morning, Braden." Cyril refolded the newspaper and greeted his nephew cautiously. After their verbal encounter of two nights past he was unsure of the status of their relationship. When Braden did not respond, Cyril cleared his throat roughly, trying again. "I presume you did not go for your usual ride?"

Braden glanced up at Cyril blankly. "Pardon me?" He signaled for his coffee, and three footmen sprang to life,

252

filling his cup and simultaneously arriving with steaming plates of eggs, bacon, and toast with raspberry jelly. "Just toast," Braden instructed, glancing at his timepiece as he sat. "What was it you were saying, Cyril?"

"You apparently didn't ride Star before breakfast," Cyril repeated, gesturing toward Braden's morning coat, indicating the lack of his customary riding attire.

"No, I didn't."

Cyril frowned, trying to decipher his nephew's odd behavior. He seemed not chilly and aloof, as Cyril would have expected, but preoccupied. "Our guests departed over an hour ago," he commented, a pointed reminder of the house party that Braden had conspicuously abandoned. Despite the conciliatory expression on Cyril's face, there was more than a touch of exasperation in his tone.

Braden ignored the censure and nodded, taking a deep swallow of coffee. "Fine. It's just as well that they have taken their leave. Truthfully, I'd forgotten their presence entirely."

"So they noticed" was the dry retort.

Braden concentrated on finishing his piece of toast. Even his outrage and resentment toward Cyril was secondary at the moment. "I wouldn't worry, Cyril," he countered smoothly. "I'm certain our guests had a splendid time without Kassie's or my presence. And just think—now they have something to gossip about until the next gathering."

"You really don't give a damn, do you?" Cyril demanded incredulously, all attempts at placating Braden forgotten.

"Honestly? No." Recalling the unpleasant details of the ill-fated house party, Braden shot his uncle a dark look. "Did Abigail leave?"

"Less than five minutes after you threw her out, yes. And I don't expect that she or William will be back."

Braden gulped down the remainder of his coffee and shoved away his plate. "For her sake, I hope not. As for William, fear not, Uncle. The moment he remembers that his wealth takes precedence over his pride, he'll be back. Our investments have made him a great deal of money. He won't be eager to sever our business ties." Braden pushed back his chair and rose. "Oh, and since we are discussing our amended list of those still welcome at Sherburgh, you can strike Grant Chandling as well. My duchess ordered him away the night before last immediately following his despicable advances. So please refrain from including the viscount in any future social events. Now, if you'll excuse me . . ."

Cyril stood also, tossing down his napkin. *"Now* where the deuce are you going?" he demanded.

Braden hesitated. "To my wife," he said at last.

Cyril's lips thinned. To his wife? It was broad daylight. "Why? Is she ill?"

Braden weighed his answer, then decided that it would not remain a secret for long—not with Alfred living at Sherburgh.

"She is in the drawing room with Alfred."

Cyril looked startled, then concerned. "With Alfred? Then she *is* ill!"

Braden shook his head, completely baffled. One moment Cyril wanted to banish Kassie from Sherburgh, the next moment he was worried over the state of her health. Perhaps he really believed she would be better off freed from this marriage. "No," Braden replied, denying both his uncle's statement and his own thoughts. "She is not ill . . . not really."

"What does that mean?"

Braden inhaled deeply, then released the breath. "It means that Kassie is still not sleeping well, continues to lose weight, and just yesterday fainted at the table." At Cyril's look of surprise and alarm Braden continued, "I believe that all three are due to the recurring nightmares she suffers."

Cyril looked as if he had been struck. "Nightmares? What nightmares?"

Braden glanced restlessly at the door. "It's a long story, Cyril, and I want to get back to Kassie."

"Then shorten it."

Braden met his uncle's ashen look. "All right. Ever since Kassie came to live at Sherburgh she has been suffering from some horrible dream that tortures her night after night. It is taking its toll on her health."

"You say these dreams started just after she came to Sherburgh?" Cyril asked.

Braden wasn't sure why, but he felt the sudden need to protect as much of Kassie's privacy as he could. He would reveal only what was necessary. "No, they started before that, but I'm not certain when," he hedged.

"And what exactly can Alfred do about these dreams?"

"I hope he can help Kassie to talk about them, to understand them, and eventually to eliminate them."

"Eventually?" Cyril broke off, raking his fingers through his hair, a muscle working in his jaw. "Are you trying to tell me that Alfred is going to be staying on at Sherburgh indefinitely for this nonsense?"

Braden started at the cold fury in Cyril's tone, the anger that raged on his face. "Yes, that's precisely what he will be doing."

Cyril slammed his fist upon the table, making the remaining dishes rattle. "And if word of this gets out, do you know how the *ton* will interpret it?" he roared. Red-faced, he didn't wait for an answer. "I'll tell you how they will interpret it! They will whisper to one another that your wife is mad. That besides being unsuitable in countless other ways, she is also unstable and daft. Has *that* ever occurred to you?"

Braden stared at Cyril, too shocked at first to absorb the meaning of his words. At last he shook his head, amazement and distaste registering in his eyes. "I will not dignify that with an answer, Cyril," he returned with deceptive calm. "Now if you will excuse me, I am going to see my wife."

Cyril watched Braden go, beyond words himself. Nightmares? How could he have lived in the same house with Braden and Kassandra all these months and have been unaware, first of their intimacy, and now of this? Nightmares. He shook his head, dazed. What were they about? What dark secrets did they contain? And what on earth was the doctor supposed to do about them? All he could do was probe and pry and hurt the family more than it had already been hurt. Cyril looked down at his shaking hands. Everything was coming apart; all his efforts were being thwarted. There had to be a way to stop this insanity. There simply had to be.

"You've told me all the details that you can recall of your nightmare," Dr. Howell said, leaning back in the carved mahogany wing chair and studying Kassie thoughtfully. "You've also said that the dream has been with you for years. Do you recall precisely how many years, Kassandra?"

Kassie twisted her hands in her lap, feeling the familiar chill set into her heart. How she hated—dreaded—talking about these dreams. And yet that was all she had spoken of for the past two hours. She was trembling, her head was throbbing, and she had the desperate urge to run from the room, to run from everything. But to do that would be to run from Braden as well. She closed her eyes, laying her head against the elaborate tapestry of the plush settee.

"Kassandra," Alfred said gently, placing a soothing hand upon her arm. "Please remember that I am here to help you. I understand this is difficult for you, but in order to *solve* the problem we must first *discuss* the problem."

Kassie opened her eyes and called upon an inner reserve that was fast deteriorating. "All right, doctor." She forced her mind back to the dreams, trying to remember a time when she *hadn't* suffered from them. She failed. "I'm sorry, doctor," she whispered, "but I just cannot answer your question. I've had the nightmare since I was a child."

He nodded. "We've accomplished a great deal this morning, my dear." At her bewildered look he smiled. "Any medical process takes time. We are beginning to isolate the illness. Once we have firmly located its source we can extract it, and then you can start to heal." He stood. "You are exhausted. And rightfully so. Let us go and partake of something more substantial than the scones and tea that your staff has kindly provided for us."

Kassie rose slowly, feeling utterly spent. "I don't know if I can do this," she whispered, half to herself.

"You can do it, Kassandra," Dr. Howell's voice replied. "Of that I have no doubt." He patted her shoulder reassuringly. "If not for yourself, then for Braden. He loves you very much."

Kassie's startled eyes flew to his. *He loves you very much.* How many times had she prayed for that to be true? And yet hearing the words spoken aloud by someone who knew Braden well made the possibility that much more real, made Kassie's core of determination return in full measure. She *would* get well; she *must.* She *had* to be whole, not only for herself, but for Braden.

"Thank you, Dr. Howell." Her beautiful smile was filled with gratitude. "Thank you for reminding me of what is important."

"Are we referring to Braden or to breakfast?" he asked, his kindly eyes twinkling.

Kassie gifted him with her musical laugh. "Both, sir. Both."

Braden was pacing the hallway when Kassie and Alfred emerged moments later. "Is everything all right?" His question was to Alfred, but his gaze was fixed on Kassie's face, searching for any signs of duress.

"Fine, Braden," the doctor assured him, "other than the fact that our stomachs are most displeased with our negligence."

Kassie disregarded her lingering mental exhaustion and gave Braden a radiant smile. "I'm fine," she answered softly, seeing his concern. "Really."

Braden saw past the smile to the strain and the pallor beneath, and he felt his gut twist with remorse. He had known this would be difficult for Kassie. What he hadn't known was how deeply her pain would affect him; how badly he wanted to take the burden from her narrow shoulders. Tenderly he rubbed his knuckles across her cheek. "I want you to eat something."

Kassie folded her arms across her chest, her smile impish. "What you *want* is to speak with Dr. Howell alone." A tiny spark of the old Kassie danced in her blue-green eyes. "Someday, Braden, I shall actually succeed in teaching you to say what you mean. I may have to undo one-and-thirty years of contradictory training, but someday I shall succeed." She turned to Dr. Howell, who was attempting to stifle a grin. "Thank you, doctor. I shall precede you into the dining room so that you and my transparent husband can discuss my progress in private."

Alfred laughed aloud.

Braden did not. Instead he silently gazed at Kassie's teasing smile, seized by an explosion of feeling so profound that it could no longer be diminished nor denied. It was a truth that his heart had always known but his mind had refuted, unable to give voice to the words. The words came to him now, despite a lifetime of caution and cynicism. *I love her,* he thought wonderingly, watching her small form disappear into the dining room. *I love her.* The realization, like all his experiences with Kassie, came not in romantic settings designed for just such revelations, but in a moment as unique as Kassie herself; in a moment when Kassie was Kassie.

Alfred did not miss the emotion on Braden's face, the completely besotted look. Wisely he refrained from commenting upon it. Rather, he said, "Kassandra and I are getting to know each other, Braden. Our initial talk went quite well."

Braden's head snapped around, and his concern returned. "What did you learn?" he demanded.

Alfred sighed, accustomed after so many years to Braden's impatience. "Just the details of her dream. Nothing more than you already know," he replied. "But Braden," he added hastily, seeing Braden's frustration in the clenching of his jaw, "your wife must learn to trust me, to regard me as a friend. Remember, you have known me all your life. Kassandra is first getting to know me. And allowing herself to rely upon me will not come easily to her. After a lifetime of having no one to lean on it is a miracle that she can depend upon you the way she does. Give her time. This nightmare is terribly painful to her, not only to discuss, but simply to recall. We are making progress, I promise you. You must have patience."

Braden nodded tersely. "I know, Alfred, I know. But I hate to see her suffer the way she is. And I don't know how to help her."

"You help her just by being there . . . just by giving her your love," the doctor replied softly. So saying, he strolled off toward the dining room. "Now I am off to be fed. Perhaps you and I will have an opportunity to ride together later. I hear that Kassandra has managed the impossible and properly domesticated Star. *That* is something I should like to see."

Braden stared after Alfred, only half hearing the last of his words, focusing on the first: *just by giving her your love*. Apparently Alfred had deduced Braden's feelings for Kassie even before he himself had.

"How did Dr. Howell's examination of Kassandra go?" Charles's quiet voice broke into Braden's startled realization. Turning to his friend, he felt a wave of compassion. He saw the lines of worry about Charles's mouth, knew very well that Charles had become intensely fond of Kassandra and was terribly worried about her condition.

"Alfred feels that he made good progress," Braden told him honestly. "They were together all morning. I believe that Kassie described the details of her dream. I know nothing more." He muttered an oath beneath his breath, his own veneer cracking. "Damn it, Charles, I feel so helpless!" He turned to his friend for support, letting down his guard, showing his fear and pain to the only man who was ever permitted to see it. "Ever since I met Kassie I've somehow been able to help her when she's been hurt. Until now. Now, when she needs me the most, I can do nothing." He rubbed his eyes wearily, missing the pained look that crossed Charles's face.

"You are Kassandra's world," the older man said soberly a mere heartbeat later. "I know she loves you. And whether she knows it or not, she needs you desperately. Just as, whether you know it or not, you are in love with her."

Braden's head shot up, his expression stunned. "Did *everyone* know of my feelings except me?" he asked in wonder.

Charles gave him an ironic smile. "Everyone but you . . . and Kassandra."

Their eyes met, Braden's dark with mixed emotion, Charles's warm with understanding. "You'll tell her," he said, his deep voice filled with reassurance. "When you're ready you'll tell her."

Braden nodded, too choked to speak. After a moment he

cleared his throat. "I think I'll take Star out for some exercise. Why don't you and Alfred join me later?"

"Fine. We'll catch up to you at the hurdles," Charles answered, understanding Braden's reaction, his quick change of subject. The feelings were too new and raw, the awareness too frightening to discuss. He needed time.

Braden's thoughts were much the same as Charles's. The knowledge of his love for Kassie stayed with him throughout the day, warming him and terrifying him all at once. It was ridiculous, actually. The feeling had been there all along; why did it unnerve him so to admit its presence?

He was unusually quiet during his ride with Charles and Alfred, excusing himself immediately thereafter to retire to his study, presumably to work. But the pile of correspondence on his desk remained unanswered; the business contracts on his desk were left untouched. Instead Braden spent much of the day staring out the window, watching the beauty of the late summer day. The trees were vibrantly green, the grounds immaculately manicured and alive with a rainbow of exquisite flowers. Three years ago, he mused, would he even have noticed nature's wonders? No. It was Kassie who had taught him the miracles that nature wrought; Kassie who had penetrated the hardened surface and the hollow exteriors of his life; Kassie who had reached down inside him and taught him what it meant to be loved. He shut his eyes. Now he needed to learn how to love in return. Perhaps she could teach him that as well.

Closing his desk with a firm click, Braden made his way purposefully toward the stairway. Kassie would be dressing for dinner. He needed to see her. Now.

He had his foot on the first step when he heard the commotion.

"Your Grace! Your Grace!" Perkins fairly flew through the hall, his weathered cheeks ruddy from the effort.

"What on earth is it, Perkins?" Braden had never seen his butler so near hysteria.

"It's the duchess's father!"

Braden felt everything inside him go cold. "Grey? What about him?"

"He is here . . . at Sherburgh," Perkins panted. "Insisting on seeing the duchess. The footmen, the gardeners, even the stable boys tried to stop him, but—"

"Where is he?"

"He tried to gain entry through the front door. I refused to allow it. I thought he had gone. But Dobson just told me that he saw him scale the great oak beside the house. Harding is there trying to restrain him, but—"

"My God." Braden was already in motion, taking the steps two at a time. The tree that Perkins was describing led to Kassie's bedchamber. Grey would have no way of knowing it, but assuming he was not too foxed to manage the climb, Robert would go directly from the towering oak to Kassie's balcony. And to Kassie.

Kassie stared at her reflection, seeing a very frightened, unsure young woman looking back. She was still unnerved from her session with Dr. Howell, and she knew that she had to muster the strength to face another talk tomorrow, and the next day and the next. She shuddered. Somewhere inside her was the answer. She only prayed that in finding it she did not destroy herself.

The sound of a heavy thud and a man's curse made her start and cry out in alarm. She spun about in time to see her father stagger onto his feet on her balcony. He peered down to the ground below him, muttering, "Damned valet," then stumbled into the room. His bloodshot eyes met Kassie's horrified ones, and he stopped, blinking, a stunned look crossing his face, as if he hadn't expected to find her there. Suddenly he gave a harsh laugh and went toward her.

"Well, this is certainly a rare stroke of luck. Imagine, my own little Kassandra . . . just the one I wanted t'see."

"Father," she whispered, beginning to tremble violently, "what are you doing here?"

"I came t'see you . . . my own little beauty."

"Father, please." She took an instinctive step backward. "Go. I have no money to give you."

He paused, narrowing his eyes. "What makes you think I came for money?" When she didn't answer he gave an ugly laugh. "I s'pose your husband told you about our little visit yesterday. I should've known you would tell him about my coming here." He stiffened. "And about those damned dreams," he muttered. He groaned suddenly, clutching his head as if to drive away some unknown demons. For a moment his words were totally lucid. "Can't you stop? Haven't you tortured me enough?"

"I don't know what you're talking about," Kassie cried out, moving further away. "How am I torturing you? It is *you* who are torturing me!" She needed to know. "Why did you tell Braden you knew nothing about my nightmares? Why?"

If Robert heard her question, he ignored it, lost again in his own broken thoughts. "Did you hear it?" he demanded. "Everything we said? Do you have t'remind me of it? I *know* it was my fault—all of it! But I never thought it would come t'this!"

He dropped his hands to his sides, staring at Kassie as if she were an apparition. "I begged you to leave him . . . begged you. But instead you left me. Why? Was it because of his title? Who the hell was he? Why did you leave me? I loved you so bloody much!" His eyes blazed with anger, with madness. "Damn you for leaving me, Elena! Damn you!" He lunged for Kassie. "Now you'll pay!"

Kassie's scream echoed simultaneously with the splintering sound of the bedchamber door being kicked open. Braden exploded into the room, grabbing Robert by the throat and flinging him against the wall. "You miserable son of a bitch!" Braden shouted, wild with rage, "I told you that if you ever came near my wife again, I would kill you!"

Robert staggered to his feet, rubbing his neck where Braden's hand had been. "Ah, the nobleman himself, here t'claim his prize. The question is, can you keep her? I couldn't."

Braden lunged for Robert again, propelling him out the open doors onto the balcony.

Robert seemed to come to life, driven by his own internal demons. He drew back his arm and swung, connecting his fist to Braden's stomach.

"Braden, please . . . stop, please!" Kassie was sobbing helplessly, moving forward and reaching out toward Braden, begging him time and again to stop.

Braden was beyond hearing anything save the deafening roar in his head. He was on his feet in an instant, charging at Robert and slamming him against the curved wall of the balcony.

Kassie watched in horror as her husband and her drunken father continued to battle, murder in their eyes. It was no contest. Smaller and slighter in stature, Robert was also severely lacking in coordination due to his intoxicated state. Kassie saw it coming before it happened. Her piercing scream accompanied Braden's final swing, which struck Robert squarely in the jaw, knocking him totally off balance. For an instant he teetered at the railing, and then with a frightened cry he toppled off the balcony, disappearing from view.

Braden rushed to the edge, peering down in time to see Robert being yanked from the thick shrubbery to his feet by a livid Harding one story below. More dazed than hurt, Grey did not resist as Harding dragged him along, away from the house and ultimately from Sherburgh.

Braden's blood was still pumping, the desire to murder Kassie's father so strong that he could barely contain it. His heart was pounding wildly, his fists clenched as he struggled for control. It was Kassie's frightened whimper that made him turn around, and what he saw made his heart contract with fear.

Kassie stood just behind him, her face white as a sheet, her breath coming in short, terrified pants, her eyes glazed with unnatural horror. Braden raced to her side, whispering her name, reaching out to hold her. But she remained as she was, staring yet unseeing, her lips moving wordlessly again and again, no sound emerging.

"Kassie! He's all right! See, he's unharmed!" Braden spoke rapidly, desperately to his wife, pointing at Robert's rapidly retreating figure. Still she remained as she was, trembling, unresponsive.

"Kassie!" Braden was frantic. He went to her, shook her, willing her to acknowledge him, to speak. But when she did he almost wished that she had not. For the one broken word she uttered was heartbreaking in its anguish, and its possible meaning left Braden ill.

"Mama . . ."

Chapter 25

❧❧❧

For the hundredth time that evening Braden eased open the door to Kassie's room and peeked in. It was hard to believe that the serenely relaxed angel enveloped by the multitude of bedcovers was the same hysterical young woman who had clung to him a few hours earlier. In contrast she slept, her breathing deep and even, her perfect features undisturbed. Beside her, looking as straight-backed and vigilant as a night watchman at his post, sat Margaret, ready to alert His Grace should the duchess awaken. In truth, it was highly unlikely that she would, since Alfred had assured them that the laudanum he had administered would keep Kassie dreamlessly asleep until dawn.

Silently Braden closed the door and stepped out into the hallway, only to collide with a tight-lipped Harding and a pacing Perkins. Calmly Braden assured the two men of Kassie's well-being, then headed for the stairway. No longer was he stunned by the obvious affection and loyalty his servants felt for Kassandra. She had won *his* heart; it seemed only fitting that she had captured the hearts of his impervious butler and austere valet as well.

Braden headed toward the dining room, where the gentlemen were taking their brandy. Three anxious faces looked up as he reentered the room.

Charles spoke first. "Is she all right?"

Braden nodded, easing into his chair. "She is resting comfortably."

Cyril frowned, toying with his half-filled glass. "I still don't understand what the devil is going on here!"

Braden sent him a withering look. Despite the seeming concern in Cyril's dark eyes, Braden couldn't help but remember their earlier argument, when Cyril had suggested that Kassie was mad. "I believe I explained everything to you quite clearly, Cyril." Braden's tone was positively frigid. "Grey gained access to Kassie's bedchamber, intending to do her harm. I got there just in time. I struck him. He went over the balcony. Kassie witnessed the whole struggle and was frighteningly affected by it. At first I thought it was because she believed her father to be dead. Then I realized that it wasn't her father at all. Because when she finally spoke, the word she said was 'Mama.'"

A look of combined disbelief and shock crossed Cyril's face. When he spoke his tone was disturbed. "But if it was her father falling, why would Kassandra call for her mother?"

Dr. Howell spoke for the first time. "From Braden's description of the incident, I don't believe Kassandra was *calling* for her mother," he said, his brows knit thoughtfully.

"Nor do I," Braden agreed quickly. "I believe she was actually *seeing* her mother." He shuddered, remembering the faraway, horror-stricken look in Kassie's eyes. At that moment she had been somewhere else, seeing something that existed only in her mind, in her memory. And it wasn't hard to figure out what that something was. "Kassie's mother died from a fall," he continued, determined to make his reasoning understood. "She fell from the cliffs surrounding their house—the same cliffs beside which Kassie cannot bring herself to walk." He looked from one man to the next. "I believe that Kassie witnessed her mother's suicide."

"My God," Charles breathed, his eyes wide with shock.

Braden went on as if Charles hadn't spoken. "Somewhere deep inside her, Kassie remembers what she saw that night. And so does her father. Because if my suspicions are correct, Robert Grey is the one who drove Elena to kill herself. And just as Kassie is a constant reminder of his wife, the nightmares are a constant reminder of her death."

"You believe these nightmares are a result of what

Kassandra saw?" Cyril managed, a muscle working in his jaw.

"I do," Braden answered. "It certainly fits with the endless drop she keeps describing in her dream, as well as her reaction to Grey's fall today."

"But she was no more than a baby," Charles whispered.

"Four years old, Charles." Braden's voice shook. "Old enough to absorb the horror of seeing her mother take her own life, and young enough to bury the memory where it could not be reached." Braden actually felt tears sting his eyes. "Kassie was alone, deserted by the one person who loved her unconditionally, with nothing but a heinous memory and a sense of total isolation."

"The details do make some sense," Alfred agreed quietly, his own mind racing rapidly ahead.

Cyril slammed to his feet. "This is preposterous!" he roared, dark eyes blazing. "Have the whole lot of you lost your minds? This young woman is under considerable stress, adapting to a life that is both new and foreign to her. Her father, a drunken animal, breaks into her home and accosts her, then gets into a physical battle with her husband and is tossed off the balcony to the ground below, where he could be injured or dead. Is that not enough to cause her to fall to pieces?"

"Another woman, perhaps. Kassie, no," Braden answered decisively.

Charles buried his face in his hands with a soft groan. "Oh, God . . . no," he whispered, half to himself.

Braden was startled by the fervor of Charles's words, but he was more furious with Cyril's total disbelief. "Why are you so adamantly opposed to my theory?" he demanded. "Is it because you'd prefer to think of Kassie as unworthy or insane rather than to view her as tormented?"

Cyril banged his fist on the table until the walls shook. "It's because your marriage has destroyed our lives!" he shouted. "Nothing has been the same since"—he hesitated, then spat out the words as if they were acid on his tongue—"your *wife* came to Sherburgh . . . and apparently, nothing ever will!"

"Damn you, Cyril," Braden exploded, instantly on his

feet, "if those are your feelings, I would suggest you get the hell—"

"Enough!" Surprisingly, it was Charles who interrupted the violent exchange, his voice booming like a cannon. "Hasn't Kassandra been through enough today? Would you like to awaken her with your futile, bitter argument as well?"

Braden froze where he was, then walked behind his chair, gripping the back until his knuckles turned white. "No. You're right, Charles." With an effort he brought himself under control. The look he gave his uncle was venomous. "Now is not the time for an altercation. Kassie needs our help."

"And she shall have it," Alfred put in. His speculative gaze swept over all three men, and he made the instant decision to reserve the remainder of his thoughts for Braden's ears alone. For if his theory was correct, there was a great deal more to the situation than had already been discussed. And a great deal more danger as well. He frowned, thinking of Robert Grey and the events of the afternoon. Much had been disclosed this day, yet much still remained buried, and only Kassandra could cast a revealing light upon the truth.

Braden headed for the door.

"Where are you going, Braden?" Charles called out, his eyes still suspiciously moist.

Braden turned. "I don't see the point in continuing this conversation any longer. I am going to my room to get some rest." *And to be close by, should Kassie need me,* he added to himself.

Charles read Braden's thoughts and nodded. "I will walk along. I would like a few words with you. Alone."

Braden shrugged. "Suit yourself." Ignoring Cyril completely, he turned to Dr. Howell. "We'll speak tomorrow?"

Alfred nodded. Tomorrow would be soon enough. Tonight he hoped Braden would get some sleep. Like Kassandra, Braden would need his strength for the days to come.

Charles followed Braden to the foot of the stairs. When he was assured they were alone he took his friend's arm. "You really believe what you just said about Kassandra witnessing"—he swallowed—"her mother's suicide?"

Braden fixed Charles with a level gaze. "I wouldn't have said it unless I did."

"Braden, do you intend to discuss this with Kassandra?" Charles looked positively green as he continued hastily. "Because I think it would be a big mistake. That poor child . . . if she did see her mother fall to her death, what can be accomplished by reminding her of it? It can only succeed in hurting her more, bringing back a memory that is best forgotten."

Braden was shaking his head. "I don't agree. The whole problem is that it has *not* been forgotten. Why else would Kassie keep having nightmares after all these years?"

"Couldn't it be something else? Something her father did?"

"No." Braden disregarded Charles's pleading look. "Oh, I'm sure Grey fits into the puzzle somehow, but not in some unrelated event. No, Charles, I am convinced that what I suspect is indeed what took place. And"—his voice softened—"even though I dread the thought of causing Kassie further pain, I must speak of it with her."

"But it will destroy her!" Charles burst out.

"I won't let it. I'll be there for her, Charles," Braden assured his agitated friend, "to absorb her pain, to hold her, to make her well. I will not *allow* this to destroy her. *That* I promise you." He turned to go upstairs. "My mind is made up," he said quietly. "Tomorrow I will take Kassie to the beach, the place where she feels the safest. And there, amid everything she most loves, we will talk." He glanced back at Charles's ashen face. "Don't worry, my friend. All will be as it should."

Charles watched Braden disappear onto the second floor landing. *All will be as it should.* Charles closed his eyes, reliving the pain and anguish he thought had long since been laid to rest. But it had returned to haunt him. All would *never* be as it should. And now his hand was being forced. Nausea welled up inside him. He knew what he had to do.

* * *

"Summer is truly at an end." Kassie stared out at the turbulent waters of the North Sea, feeling the chill that was in the air.

"Yes, love, it is." Braden stood behind her, wrapping his arms about her waist and resting his chin atop her silky head. "Autumn is announcing its arrival."

Kassie sighed, leaning back against her husband. "I wish we could stop time and keep moments like these forever."

Braden smiled. "I cannot promise you that we can stop time. But I can promise you that there will always be moments like these for us."

Kassie closed her eyes, willing it to be so, wanting to freeze this moment when the world and all its anguish seemed so far away; when there were only the two of them and nothing more. "I pray that you are right," she whispered.

"Do you doubt me?"

She sighed. "Braden, even *you* cannot control what fate has in store for us. Some vows are simply too difficult to keep."

"And of the vows I've made to you," he murmured in a husky voice, "have any been left unfulfilled?"

"No." Kassie's throat tightened.

"Then what makes you think I cannot make all your dreams come true?" he asked, pressing gentle kisses into her hair.

Kassie turned abruptly in to his arms, pressing her face against his broad chest. "I'm so afraid," she said in a tiny voice.

He stroked her back, rocking her gently against him. "I know you are, sweetheart." He took a deep breath, aware of how important his next words were. "I knew from the moment we met that you were one of the strongest people I'd ever known. I still think so. And one of the bravest as well. I know you are frightened. But I also know that you will not run from your fear. You'll face it . . . *we'll* face it . . . together."

She nodded, her face still pressed against him, her hands small, tight fists against his arms. It broke his heart.

"Kassie," he went on, praying for the strength to help her and the wisdom to know how, "you need to talk about what happened yesterday. I wanted to be the one you spoke to first, before Dr. Howell."

Again she nodded, saying nothing.

"How much do you remember about what happened?"

She lifted her head just enough to speak but remained within the security of Braden's embrace.

"I remember everything," she said in a weary voice. "My father's appearance in my room, the things he said, your fight, his fall. Everything."

Her words gave him pause. "The things he said?" he repeated slowly. "What things?"

Kassie shuddered. "He spoke of my dreams. He accused me of telling you about them just to torture him. I asked him *how* I was torturing him, but he didn't seem to hear me. He kept speaking of my mother . . . of why she had to leave him." She broke away from Braden with a soft sob. "It's the same thing over and over again. He blames himself for my mother's death. He always has. And it tortures him. I don't know why. . . ." she added.

"Yes, you do," Braden said tenderly, taking her by the shoulders and forcing her to meet his gaze.

"What do you mean?"

"Think, Kassie. Try to remember. I know it hurts. What else did he say?"

Kassie was shaking violently now. "I don't know. Nothing."

"Kassie!" He shook her gently.

"What do you want me to say?" she cried.

"I want you to tell me what he did to her," Braden pressed, refusing to back off. "What happened between your parents on the night your mother died?"

"He loved her!" Kassie sobbed, trying to free herself from Braden's grasp.

"In his twisted way, yes, he loved her. But something happened the night Elena fell. Something that made her run away. Something that only your father knows . . . your father and *you.*" He pulled her against him. "Yesterday,

271

when your father fell from the balcony, you screamed 'Mama!' What is it about your father that reminds you of the night your mother died? *Think,* Kassie, *think!*"

Through the overwhelming terror in her eyes there came a flash of something else. Was it remembrance? Braden plunged on, desperate to reach the goal that he sensed was just within reach. "What is it?" He gave her no quarter. "I see it in your eyes, Kassie. Those beautiful eyes that never lie to me. What is it you are remembering?"

"They were arguing." The words were so quiet, they were almost inaudible.

"Who was arguing? Your parents?"

"Yes." She closed her eyes, tears streaming down her cheeks. "They argued so much. I didn't understand most of it, and I didn't want to. But something my father said yesterday . . ."

"What did he say?"

"He asked me if I heard everything they said. The moment he said that a picture flashed through my mind. I had forgotten. . . ." She took a deep, shuddering breath, trying to control her sobs. "The night my mother died they had a dreadful fight. I was supposed to be asleep, but their loud voices awakened me. I remember sitting huddled on the stairway, listening to their angry words. When it was over my mother ran from the house, crying as if her heart would break."

"Did your father strike her?"

Kassie wrenched her arms away and wrapped them about herself. "Yes."

"Kassie, sweetheart, please . . . try to remember. What were they arguing about?"

"I was so young . . . so scared," she whispered.

"I know, *ma petite,* I know. But try. For me. Had your father been drinking?"

Kassie shook her head. "No. Father was sober. He was just so devastated that she would leave him—"

"Leave him?" Braden latched onto her words. "But she hadn't left him; she was still alive. Why would he think . . ." A sudden thought exploded into Braden's mind—one he should have thought of before. "Was your mother seeing another man? Is *that* what your father meant? Was he afraid she would leave him for someone else?"

Kassie gazed up at him with shocked, wet eyes, her face drenched with tears. *Damn you, Elena . . . damn you for leaving me! You're nothing but a slut . . . a slut, do you hear me? And I'll see you dead before I let another man have you . . . dead!* Kassie gasped, the words resounding in her head, replaying as if she were hearing them for the first time.

"Kassie, answer me!" Braden cupped her face, forcing her gaze to his. "Answer me!"

"Yes." She seemed to wilt before his very eyes, her knees buckling under her. "Yes . . . I remember." Braden caught her in his arms, taking her slight weight and all of her burden against him. She looked up at him, trauma and disbelief written on her white face. "Oh, my God . . . Braden . . ."

"Sh-h-h; it's all right now. Everything will be all right." He kissed her face, her cold hands, then lowered her to a sitting position in the sand, sinking down beside her and wrapping her tightly to his chest. There was more ground they had to cover. They had yet to discuss what had happened *after* the argument—the fall that Braden was certain Kassie had witnessed—the *true* cause of her nightmares. But he knew she had reached her breaking point. To continue now would be brutal. The rest would have to wait. "Nothing can hurt you anymore," he whispered, cradling her to him. "Nothing."

She was shaking violently, her teeth chattering uncontrollably as the initial door to her memory was unlocked, permitting the first imprisoned recollections to emerge. "Is *that* the guilt he's lived with?" she whispered. "Is *that* why he hates me so much? Because he knows I knew she was unfaithful? And I look so much like her . . . I thought that was a reminder of how much he missed her." She looked up at Braden, her lips trembling. "But it wasn't, was it? It was a reminder of the woman who had betrayed him! The woman who was in love with someone else . . ."

"She had reason, Kassie," Braden said gently. "Your father was hurting her . . . physically, mentally."

Kassie shuddered again. "I know."

"So she found someone else. Someone who could love her, take care of her. Certainly she was entitled to that."

"Who?" Kassie breathed suddenly. "Who was it?" She stood abruptly, walking away until she was sheltered by the shadows of the cliffs above them.

"I don't know, love." Braden followed her, wanting to absorb every drop of her pain. "Does it matter?"

"Yes, it matters." She turned to Braden, dashing the tears from her cheeks, a small flicker of hope in her eyes. "Don't you see, Braden? Whoever it is, he knew my mother well—probably better than anyone. And it is possible that he is still alive. And if he is, he can tell me about my mother. I remember so very little. Maybe he can give me some of the wonderful memories that I've had to live without!"

Braden stared at his wife, overwhelmed by the goodness of her soul. She had just relived one of the most shattering experiences of her life, and here she was, looking past the pain, finding the good that was born of it. It was beyond him.

"Sweetheart, I don't want you to get your hopes up."

"I won't," she responded simply. "But I have to try."

Braden nodded, reaching out for her. "If he's alive, we'll find him."

They both heard the rumbling at the same time. It began quietly from overhead, then intensified to a roar. Small stones began to fall at their feet.

"Braden!" Kassie screamed.

Braden reacted instantly. He lunged out of the way, grabbing hold of Kassie and rolling them to safety. Seconds later a huge boulder struck the sand in the exact spot where Braden had stood. Its impact made the ground tremble and brought small pellets of sand and stone careening to the ground beside it.

"Kassie, are you all right?" Braden gasped, still clutching his wife in his arms.

"Yes." She clung to him. "Yes. Braden, my God, you were almost killed!"

Braden didn't answer. He wasn't certain what made him look up at that exact second, searching the top of the cliff for the spot from which the boulder had fallen.

DREAM CASTLE

The man was straightening, hurrying from the cliff top. Had he been unfamiliar, Braden would never have been able to recognize him from this distance. But as it was, the breath lodged in Braden's throat as the undeniable realization struck home.

The man was Charles Graves.

Chapter 26

⌐⌐

Dinner was a silent, tense affair punctuated only by the occasional clinking sounds of the silverware and the hurried steps of the footmen as they hastened about serving roasted pheasant, stewed mushrooms, and asparagus in butter. The excellence of the meal went unnoticed. Each of the table's occupants was absorbed in his own thoughts, unwilling or unable to share them.

Kassie glanced up, trying yet again to read Braden's expression. He was moodily toying with his food and did not meet her gaze. Puzzled, she reflected on his odd behavior since their near accident on the beach.

After carefully checking Kassie for injury as well as assuring himself that she was unscathed by the day's revelations, Braden had helped her mount Little Lady, swung himself onto Star's back, and ridden home beside Kassie in strained silence. Immediately upon arriving at Sherburgh he had sought out Dr. Howell for confirmation of Kassie's physical well-being. The doctor had examined both her and Braden and verified that they were, thankfully, unharmed.

That was the last Kassie had seen of Braden until dinner.

Now he stared broodingly at his half-filled plate, as if he bore the weight of the world upon his shoulders, and Kassie had no idea why.

It was not only Braden's mood that disturbed her. Cyril was acting strangely as well, his dark, accusing stare turning in her direction several times during the course of the meal. Kassie was no fool. Abigail's appearance on the night of the ball had proven that Cyril hadn't accepted Kassie as Braden's duchess, nor would he ever do so. Sadly she had forced herself to accept that fact, continuing to show him the respect she felt he was entitled to as Braden's uncle. And until now Cyril had responded in kind, keeping his negative feelings well hidden, his disapproval of Kassie carefully buried beneath layers of cold cordiality and polite tolerance.

But today something had changed; there was a distinct alteration in his attitude. Anger and condemnation burned in his gaze, and Kassie shifted uncomfortably beneath his accusing scrutiny. He did not speak a word to her—nor to Braden, for that matter—but he exchanged an occasional pleasantry with Dr. Howell in between bites.

Charles was absent altogether. Earlier in the day, amid the rampant rumors of the duke's and duchess's dramatic episode, Charles had hurried in, tight-lipped with worry, to assess the situation personally. Then, convinced that Kassie and Braden were indeed unharmed, he'd disappeared as quickly as he'd come. Kassie felt the lack of his presence keenly, wishing with all her heart that he was beside her, his kindly blue eyes twinkling in her direction, his ready smile there to assure her that all would be well. At this particular moment she badly needed an ally.

She was about to scream with frustration when Braden roughly pushed back his chair and came to his feet. "I'm going to retire for the night," he said, his face, his tone expressionless. He nodded to the room in general, turned on his heel, and walked out.

Kassie stared after him in utter amazement. Not only was the time absurdly early for Braden to go to sleep, but he had never gone up to bed without asking her to accompany him. Even during the early weeks of their marriage when they had slept apart it had been thus. She was speechless.

"Kassandra," Alfred said gently, touching her arm, "you look rather peaked yourself. You've had quite a day, I suspect. I do believe that you should also turn in."

Kassie nodded, grateful to be spared further embarrassment. "Thank you, doctor. I will." Gracefully she rose, bidding everyone a good night and following her husband up the stairs.

Moments later she paused, her fingers on the door handle that separated her bedchamber from Braden's. She knew he was within; she could hear him moving about. Taking a deep breath, she opened the door and went in.

Braden turned, bare chested, a glass of port in his hand. "What is it, Kassandra?"

Kassie blinked, startled by his curt tone. "What is it?" she repeated.

For a moment concern softened Braden's taut jaw. "Are you experiencing any aftereffects from . . . anything that happened today?"

She shook her head. "No. Nothing like that. It's only that you left the dining room rather abruptly. I merely wanted to see if you were ill."

Braden gave a harsh laugh. "Ill? No, I don't believe that I am ill. At sea, perhaps; a fool, quite possibly . . . but, ill? No."

Automatically she went to him and placed her hand on his chest. "Braden . . ."

He withdrew as if her touch burned. "Kassie, please. I appreciate your concern; truly I do. But there is nothing you can do to help. This is something I must work out for myself . . . by myself. So please . . . just go to bed." He took a deep swallow of his drink and turned away.

Kassie recoiled as if she had been slapped. Love and pride warred with each other as she struggled to understand the reason for her husband's cold rebuff. There seemed only one plausible answer. Slowly she backed away, hurt etched on her flawless features. "If it is something I said or did . . . if it is shame based upon my father's disgraceful behavior, now or years ago, I am truly sorry," she whispered. "Good night, Braden."

Braden winced as the door shut behind Kassie's retreating figure. The knowledge that she blamed herself for his own thoroughly confused, bitter state of mind made pain and guilt slice through him like a knife. Reflexively he turned, taking several steps toward Kassie's room, then stopped abruptly. Regardless of his powerful feelings for his wife and the conflicting emotions she aroused in him, he couldn't go to her, couldn't share his torment with her . . . not now. Not until he had sorted things out in his mind.

Charles. Braden was torn between fury at his friend's possible betrayal and mortification at his own suspicions. After a lifetime of friendship and caring, why would Charles want to hurt him?

The question replayed itself over and over in Braden's mind. There was no motivation, nothing to be gained.

Except Kassie.

Braden couldn't shake the nagging memory of Charles's uncharacteristic behavior since Kassie had come to Sherburgh. He had developed an instant rapport with her, followed by an unusually close bond of friendship and, finally, an intense sense of protectiveness that bordered on the irrational. He had begged Braden to let the matter of Kassie's dreams rest. He had hated Robert Grey obsessively.

He had been at the top of the cliff when the boulder had fallen, nearly killing Braden.

Braden closed his eyes, trying to block out the loathsome thought. It didn't work. Neither did the port. Nothing would work—not until he confronted Charles and got some answers. Dizzy from the amount of alcohol he had consumed, Braden dropped down heavily upon his bed. Tomorrow. He would talk to Charles tomorrow.

As it turned out, Kassie found Charles first. After a sleepless night torturing herself about Braden's bizarre behavior she rose early and made a decision. Whatever her father was, whatever he had been, was no fault of hers. She could not shoulder blame for the events of the past. Nor could she apologize for her emotional reaction yesterday when she had remembered the details of her parents' argument on the night of her mother's death.

However, if Braden *was* upset about her past or about her reaction to its memory, there was no way she was going to involve him further in the quest to learn more about her mother's lover . . . and, consequently, about her mother. There was only one person she knew of that might have some answers. Her father. And with or without Braden's blessing, she would do what she must.

It was just after dawn that Kassie went looking for Charles, a slip of paper clutched purposefully in her hand. He was, as she had expected, at the stables, checking on the Thoroughbreds. She waited patiently outside Star's stall until he emerged.

"Good morning, Charles."

Charles looked surprised; his intense gaze quickly assessing her from head to toe. "Good morning, Kassandra," he said carefully, still studying her pale face closely. "Isn't it rather early for you to be up?" He waited.

Kassie shrugged. "I couldn't sleep."

"Are you well?" The question was instantaneous.

Kassie gave him a small but reassuring smile. "Yes, I'm fine. Totally unscathed. Thanks to Braden." In spite of everything, her eyes lit up when she spoke of her husband— something that was not lost on Charles. "If Braden hadn't pushed us both to safety . . ." She shuddered. "Anyway, he did, and we're both in perfect health, according to Dr. Howell."

Charles nodded. "Thank God." He took a deep breath. "So what can I do for you?"

"You can deliver a message to my father."

Charles looked as if he had been struck. "What?"

"You can deliver a message to my father," Kassie repeated. Knowing that more of an explanation was in order, she continued, "I cannot divulge all the details, Charles, but my father may have some information that is very important to me. If he does, I am willing to meet with him in order to get it."

"Does Braden know about this?" Charles demanded.

Kassie shook her head. "No. And I don't want him to know." She cut off Charles's next words with a wave of her hand. "Please, Charles. My mind is made up. I need to speak with my father. And I cannot risk riding out to the cottage to do so. Therefore, I am requesting that he meet me in a secluded spot at Sherburgh. If Braden knew, he would forbid it. So I am entrusting this message to you. All I'm asking is that you see to it that my father receives it. After that you may return to Sherburgh and have no further involvement. Please," she whispered, placing her hand on his arm. "If there was any other way, I would take it. But there isn't."

Charles looked down at the small hand on his arm, weighing his decision carefully. "Is it that important to you?"

Kassie nodded eagerly, sensing that he was wavering. "Yes. Terribly important to me. And with the exception of Braden, you're the only one I trust to do this for me. Please, Charles."

Charles gave a terse nod. "All right, Kassandra. I'll deliver the message for you. Under one condition. Should your father agree to a meeting at Sherburgh, you must not go alone." He shook his head firmly as Kassie opened her mouth to object. "I am not asking you to inform Braden of your plan. *I* shall accompany you to the designated spot, keeping enough of a distance away so that I will remain undetected. That way I can be assured of your safety." He paused, clearing his throat roughly. "I cannot allow you to endanger yourself."

Kassie's heart swelled with tenderness. "Very well, Charles. I accept your condition."

"Fine." He squinted up at the rising sun. "I'll leave for your father's cottage at once."

Impulsively Kassie flung her arms around Charles's neck. "Thank you," she whispered. "You are a wonderful friend."

Charles's features tightened. Slowly his arms came about Kassie, and he hugged her to him, his eyes bright with emotion. Then just as quickly he set her on her feet. Wordlessly he took the note from Kassie's outstretched palm, then gave her a strained smile. "I'd best be going," he said, his course determined. "I have a mission I must accomplish."

The moment he was alone in the carriage Charles unfolded the slip of paper and scanned its contents. Then he stared off into space, his stomach knotted with worry. It was just as he had feared. Kassandra was aware that there had been another man in Elena's life. And being so much like her mother, Kassie would not rest until she learned all she could. Of that Charles was certain.

Originally it had been a question of honor.

Now it was a threat of danger.

He had to deal with Robert Grey.

"Braden? May I see you for a few moments?"

Braden came to an abrupt halt just outside the library doors and turned impatiently to Dr. Howell. "Is it important, Alfred? There is someone that I must see this morning."

Alfred blinked. "I would say so. It concerns Kassandra. There are some things we need to discuss . . . alone. Pressing things."

Braden felt another pang of guilt. Here he was, so caught up in his turbulent thoughts about Charles that he had totally forgotten to tell Alfred of yesterday's revelations. He glanced at his timepiece. It was not yet seven; Charles would most likely be at the stables for some time yet. He nodded. "Of course, Alfred. I also have things to tell you."

Once they were alone behind the closed library doors Dr. Howell turned to Braden, wasting no time before he began. "I listened carefully to your retelling of the events that accompanied Robert Grey's visit to Sherburgh two days past. I do not believe that everything has yet come to light."

Braden clasped his hands behind his back, scowling down at the rug. "You're quite right, Alfred. In fact, I think it is important that you hear about the conversation Kassie and I had on the beach yesterday . . . before the unsettling incident that interrupted us." In full detail he proceeded to recount everything Kassie had remembered, the pieces that had fallen into place. "However," he concluded with a sigh, "I did not have the heart, after all she had been through, to tell her the rest—that I am convinced she witnessed her mother's death . . . a death that was not the accident Kassie believes it to be, but suicide."

"I don't believe it was suicide."

Braden looked startled. "Despite everything I've just told you? Despite Kassie's continuing nightmares? Despite the distance from the base of the cliffs to where Elena's body was discovered, you can still believe it was an accident?"

"No," Alfred corrected. "I believe it was murder."

Absolute silence permeated the room.

"Murder," Braden repeated slowly, his whole body beginning to shake.

"Yes, Braden, cold-blooded murder. Consider what caused Kassandra's reaction the day her father broke into her room—what actually happened to make her cry out her mother's name."

"She saw her father fall from the balcony outside her window," Braden managed, his insides cold.

"He didn't fall. He was pushed. In this case unintentionally, but that is irrelevant. Kassandra saw not only the fall itself, but the violence that preceded it. *That* is what triggered her recall." He paused, studying Braden's face, his unnatural calm. "Braden? Are you all right?"

"And the nightmares," Braden said aloud, not even hearing Alfred's question. "The beast that Kassie keeps seeing . . ."

". . . is the person who threw Elena Grey to her death," Alfred finished for him.

Braden's heart twisted in anguish. "And Kassie witnessed all this?"

"Yes, I believe so."

"Oh, my God." Braden leaned back against his desk, bowing his head as he struggled for control. "So that's what my poor wife has been living with for all these years."

"Living with, but trying desperately to forget." Alfred paused. "And Kassandra is not the only one who is desperate for her memories to stay buried."

Braden's head came up, his eyes dark with realization. "The murderer."

Alfred nodded. "It would explain many things. Why Robert Grey drinks himself into oblivion, why he is tortured with remorse and guilt, and why he refuses to relinquish all ties with his daughter. And now that you've told me that Elena Grey was involved with another man—well, that certainly would provide an unstable blackguard like Grey with motivation, would it not?"

Braden felt nausea well up inside him. "Yes. It would."

"Of course, we have no actual proof," Alfred said, frowning.

"I'll get some." Braden was already halfway out the door.

"Where are you going?" Alfred called after him.

"To see Grey. To find out once and for all what happened the night Kassie's mother died."

There was no time to wait for a carriage to be brought around. Besides, Braden decided as he fought to keep his escalating fear under control, he could travel faster on horseback. He ordered Star saddled and brought around front. Mere minutes later Braden took off at a gallop. Sensing his master's urgency, Star called upon all his skill and speed, flying through the woods leading to the secluded cottage that housed the answers Braden was determined to find.

Panting, Braden dismounted several hundred feet from the front door. Obviously Grey had company. A carriage stood before the house. Well, Braden would wait. He had no intention of alerting Grey to his arrival and taking the risk that the bastard would flee with his friends.

Silently, cautiously, Braden approached the neglected house, pausing in the thick growth of grass that hid him from view. He tensed suddenly, stunned to see the Sheffield family crest gleaming upon the carriage door. He had no time to investigate. Just then hurried footsteps sounded from within the house. Seconds later the door was flung open and a wild-eyed Charles Graves emerged. He looked frantically left and right and, never seeing Braden, hastened into the waiting carriage, which immediately sped away from the cottage.

Braden felt a deep sense of foreboding. With a heavy heart he climbed the steps and entered the cottage.

The house was deserted. Even Grey's manservant had apparently taken his leave.

After a moment Braden called out Robert's name. His own voice echoed eerily down the corridor. Then there was silence. Making his way down the hall, Braden glanced into room after room, only to find each one empty.

Until he reached the library.

There, on the dirty, stained carpet, amid a small pool of blood, lay Robert Grey.

Chapter 27

How was he going to tell Kassie?

That thought overrode all others in Braden's mind as he made his way back to Sherburgh. He was still in shock, sickened by the discovery of Grey's body, gripped by the horror of what Charles's presence there implied.

The assimilation of all the facts and where they led—that would come later. For now, Braden had to face telling his beautiful, vulnerable wife that her father—the only living link to her past and her only possible means for acquiring the information she so desperately sought—was dead.

He turned Star over to Dobson wordlessly and made his way toward the house.

"Good morning, Your Grace," Perkins greeted him.

Braden nodded. "I need a message to be delivered to the authorities at once, Perkins." He penned a hasty note and gave it to his butler. "Please see to it."

"Of course, Your Grace." If he was taken aback by Braden's curt tone or odd request, he gave no sign of it.

"Where is my wife, Perkins?"

"I believe she is out walking in the gardens." Perkins pointed in the direction Kassie had gone.

Braden hurried back out, striding through the exquisite gardens that lined the northern portion of his property. He wondered why he hadn't seen Kassie upon his arrival. She should have been visible from the front of the house.

Hearing a loud bark and a soft peal of laughter, Braden stopped in his tracks and glanced up. A burst of warmth soothed the chill that encased his heart. No wonder he hadn't seen her. She was flat upon the ground amid the kaleidoscope of flowers, rolling about with Percy and giggling at his antics.

An unheard-of mode of behavior for a duchess.

A typical display of exuberance by his Kassie.

A lump in his throat, Braden walked the remaining distance to her side. "Hello, *ma petite.*"

Kassie sat up at once, her eyes wide with surprise. "Oh, Braden—I didn't hear you."

Unwilling to end their frolicking, Percy began to bark loudly in protest.

"It's no wonder you didn't hear me," Braden teased gently, leaning over to brush dark strands of hair from her forehead. "Some of us"—he scratched Percy's ears—"have voices that would drown out a thousand booming cannons."

Percy barked his agreement.

Kassie was quiet, studying Braden's face. "Did you wish to see me?" she asked quizzically. After his upsetting behavior last night, she was unsure of what to expect. And yet, with her innate understanding of Braden, Kassie knew that he needed to speak with her. She waited.

Braden nodded, reaching for her hands and pulling her gently to her feet. "Kassie," he began, unknowingly caressing her fingers with his, "I know that there are things you don't understand . . . things we need to talk about. But unfortunately, they are going to have to wait." He looked into her eyes, willing her to be strong.

"Something has happened." She could feel it. She simply knew, needing only for Braden to corroborate the statement.

"Yes. Something has happened."

"What is it?" she asked, fear leaping into her eyes.

Braden drew a slow, unsteady breath. "It's your father, sweetheart."

"My father?" Her first thought was that Braden had discovered what Charles had done for her. But if that were the case, why wasn't her husband furious with her?

"Kassie, there is no easy way to tell you this." Braden's words dispelled her original thought entirely.

Inwardly she braced herself for what was to come. "Just tell me, Braden. What about my father?"

"He's dead, Kassie."

For a moment she stared at him as if he had lost his mind. Then her lips began to tremble. "Dead?"

Braden drew her to him, holding her in his arms as he told her only what she needed to know. "Apparently he'd been drinking. He fell and struck his head against the wooden desk in the library. The impact killed him."

Braden felt Kassie's hands knot into fists against his chest, clutching at the material of his shirt. "He's dead. . . . You're sure?" she got out in a broken whisper.

"Yes, love, I'm sure." He paused. "I saw him myself."

Kassie drew back and stared at him through wet, shocked eyes. "You were at the cottage?"

"Yes."

"Why?"

This was exactly what Braden had feared, what he had wanted to avoid. "We can discuss that another time, Kassie," he hedged, breaking eye contact with her.

"No." She stood up, brushing the tears from her eyes. She was beyond shock by now. The past days had brought so many shattering revelations, so many traumatic remembrances. And now this . . .

Her feelings about her father's death were mixed and too complex to analyze right now. But her instincts told her that Braden was keeping something from her. And she was determined to know what it was. "Not another time, Braden," she countered. "We can discuss it right now. Why were you at my father's cottage? Does it have anything to do with what we talked about on the beach yesterday?"

"Yes," he conceded, "but I don't think this is the time—"

"Let *me* be the judge of that."

She was giving him no choice. But maybe there would be no easy time to tell her. "Very well." He placed his hands on her narrow shoulders. "Dr. Howell doesn't believe that your mother's death was the result of an accidental fall." He carefully avoided any mention of suicide. "Alfred believes that she was pushed from those cliffs. And I agree. *That* is why I went to see your father."

Kassie blinked. "You think my father is the one—"

"It would all make sense then, wouldn't it?"

Kassie crumbled before Braden's eyes. Unbidden, a deluge of suppressed tears splashed down her cheeks. "But he loved her so," she sobbed, gripping Braden's forearms tightly. "Do you really believe he is"—she paused—"was," she forced herself to say, "capable of murder?"

Braden sighed, stroking Kassie's collarbone with his thumb. "Yes, sweetheart, I do." He looked into her horrified face and added, "I don't believe he *planned* to hurt her, but . . . if he found her with someone else . . . yes, I believe he was unstable enough to kill."

Kassie went white, then sank to her knees on the soft grass. "Braden, I think I'm going to be sick," she gasped.

He knelt beside her and held her head while she heaved helplessly between wrenching sobs. When at last her stomach was quiet and her tears spent, Braden rocked her tenderly in his arms, while Percy licked her damp cheeks lovingly.

At long last Braden stood, lifted Kassie to him, and headed back to the house. She lay silent and docile, her face pressed to his shoulder, her eyes closed.

Perkins looked positively green when they entered the hallway. His anxious gaze darted to Kassie's limp form, then back to Braden. "The constable is here to speak with you, Your Grace," he got out, his voice taut with worry.

Braden nodded. Quite possibly Perkins already knew. It didn't matter. It would not remain a secret for much longer. "Tell him I'll be with him shortly," he replied, heading for the stairs. "And send Dr. Howell up to the duchess's bedchamber immediately."

"Of course, Your Grace."

This time it seemed an eternity before Alfred's laudanum took effect. Braden stayed with Kassie until she slept, holding her while she alternately wept and clung to him, her body trembling with reaction. He ached for her pain, knowing all the while that there was nothing he could do to ease it—nothing save be there for her as she coped with the truth.

Although he lamented the loss of Kassie's last link to her

mother, Braden himself could not feel sorrow at Robert's death. At least now Kassie was safe from her father's madness, no longer threatened by the existence of a possible murderer.

Unless Charles . . .

Braden drew himself up short, refusing to speculate further. Gently he lay Kassie, now deeply asleep, on the bed and gestured for Margaret to stay with her. Margaret nodded fiercely, her customarily jovial face twisted with worry and sorrow.

Braden went down to the library, where Constable Benton was waiting. At Braden's entrance the constable rubbed his sweaty palms together, unnerved both by Braden's rank and by the cryptic, perturbing message the duke had sent him. It had been the second notification Benton had received of Robert Grey's demise. The first had been a scribbled, unsigned note left on his desk. Most unusual. And best left unmentioned until further investigation had been conducted. "Your Grace," the constable greeted Braden, watching the duke nervously from beneath dark, bushy brows.

"Constable. Thank you for coming so promptly." Braden crossed the room and poured two glasses of brandy, wondering where he was getting the strength to retain his calm veneer. He offered the drink to Benton, then began without further preliminaries. "Have you sent men to recover the body?"

"I have, Your Grace." Benton downed his brandy in one gulp. Normally he didn't drink while on duty. But dealing with violent death, especially among the ever-testy upper crust, was reason enough to indulge. "I do need you to give me any details you can."

"Of course." Braden heard himself relay the events leading up to his discovery of Grey's body; the time he arrived at the cottage, the silence that prevailed from within, the exact location where he had found the body.

Benton scribbled frantically on his pad. "You say it looked like Mr. Grey struck his head on the desk?"

"Yes. The duchess's father apparently had too much to drink, lost his balance, and fell."

Benton nodded sagely. He, like all the residents of the

town, knew of Robert Grey's frequent bouts of drunkenness, so the constable immediately understood the meaning behind the duke's discreet comment. "Did you see anyone else while you were there, Your Grace?" he asked instead.

Concentrating on his writing, Constable Benton never saw the tortured look that flashed across Braden's face, then disappeared instantly. "I saw no one, Constable." The answer was definitive, given without deliberation. "The cottage was deserted when I arrived."

Long after Benton had hurried off to file his report on what appeared to be a tragic accident, Braden wondered about the reasons for his own deception. Why hadn't he mentioned seeing Charles flee from the Grey cottage mere moments before he had discovered Robert's body? Was he protecting his friend out of loyalty, or was it some absolute knowledge inside Braden that Charles was incapable of committing such a heinous act? And if it was the latter, could he still trust his instincts where Charles was concerned, even after seeing him not only at the scene of Grey's death, but atop the cliff from which the boulder had fallen yesterday?

There was only one way to silence the warring voices inside Braden's head, and that was to confront Charles himself. And if Charles *was* guilty of murder, then *he* was going to be the one to discover it. Braden strode out of the house, determined to find Charles.

Charles found him instead.

Braden hadn't quite reached the stables when Charles called his name, rushing over to meet him. "The constable was here?" he blurted out. He looked totally ashen, creases of worry lining his face.

Braden's expression was dark with disbelief. "Yes, Charles. The constable was here. He came to Sherburgh to investigate a death. But then, you already knew that, didn't you?" Braden didn't wait for an answer but plunged on, unable to censor either his emotions or his words. They poured out at will. "Didn't you, Charles?" he pressed, his fists clenched at his sides as if to prepare for this ultimate betrayal.

Charles just stared at him. "Knew what? That the constable was here? Yes, I knew. *I'm* the one—"

Braden interrupted with a hollow laugh. "Yes, you are, aren't you?" He slammed his fists into the bunched muscles of his thighs, looking at Charles as if he were a stranger. "I was there, Charles. At the Grey cottage. I saw you. It was just before I found Robert Grey . . . dead." He waited, tormented, for a reaction.

"I didn't see you," Charles replied slowly, speculatively. "But then again, I wasn't thinking very clearly at that moment."

"No, I can imagine you weren't thinking at all," Braden fired back. "Actually, it looked like you were running away."

Now Braden got his reaction. Charles went still as death, shock, then anger, and finally pain flashing in his eyes. "What exactly are you accusing me of?" His quiet words were as cold as an Arctic wind.

Unconsciously Braden gripped Charles's shoulders. "Did you kill Robert Grey?"

Charles didn't flinch. "No."

"Then what were you doing at the cottage?" Braden demanded.

For a moment Charles hesitated. Finally he said, "I was doing an errand for your wife."

Braden gave a hollow, disbelieving laugh. "For Kassie? She wants nothing to do with her father." Even as the words left his mouth Braden knew they were inaccurate. After yesterday's revelations Kassie would indeed want to speak with Robert. "She would have asked me to contact him," he reasoned aloud.

"Would she?" Charles shot back. "Apparently you are wrong, Braden, because she asked me to deliver a message to Grey. And because she had nowhere else to turn, I agreed to help her. When I got to the cottage he was already dead."

"Then why were you fleeing the house?" Braden dug his fingers into the thick wool of Charles's jacket.

Charles's mouth dropped. "Good Lord, Braden, I had just found a dead body! What did you expect me to do? I rode into town to alert the authorities!"

At Charles's words a trace of uncertainty crossed Braden's granite features. *"You* notified the authorities?"

"How else would the constable have known to come to Sherburgh?"

"I sent a message to him after I returned home." Braden studied his friend closely, still tightly gripping his coat.

"I detested Robert Grey," Charles said, solemnly meeting Braden's scrutiny, "but I did not kill him."

Memory washed over Braden in a rush. "What about me, Charles? Did you try to kill me?"

All the color drained from Charles's face. "What?" he whispered.

Braden swallowed, unable to retreat. "Yesterday. When Kassie and I were on the beach. I was almost killed by a boulder, remember?"

"Yes, I know," Charles agreed, so quietly that Braden could barely hear him. "And you believe that I pushed that boulder?"

Braden shook Charles hard. "I saw you standing there, dammit! Just after the boulder fell!"

Charles threw off Braden's arms, stepping back with an anguished sound. "You saw me standing there," he repeated evenly. "So you concluded that it was I who tried to kill you." He continued to back away, his eyes suspiciously bright. "I raised you, Braden, since you were a boy. I know how deep your scars are, how impossible it is for you to trust. But I've always thought that I was the exception, the one person you could believe in." He shook his head, looking at Braden as if he were seeing him for the first time. "I know now that I was mistaken. So be it. If you choose to believe that I would—*could*—hurt you, then we have nothing more to say to each other." He stopped in his tracks. "I am going back to the house; I want to look in on Kassandra and assure myself that she is well. After that I will pack. I'll be gone from Sherburgh by daybreak."

Without another word he walked past Braden and toward the manor. He never looked back.

Slowly Kassie came awake feeling groggy, disoriented, and vaguely aware that something was amiss. She blinked, staring at the canopy above her bed, wondering why she was napping in the middle of the day.

Memory returned abruptly, causing her chest to constrict. Her father was dead. Gone was the man who had terrorized her, hated her, beaten her. But also gone was her last hope of discovering the identity of her mother's lover.

With a soft, anguished sound Kassie rolled onto her side and met the concerned gaze of the man who sat rigidly beside her bed.

"Charles?"

He came to his feet, still gripping the arms of the chair. "Yes, Kassandra." His eyes searched her anxiously. "Are you all right?"

She nodded slowly, a look of puzzlement settling over her face. "Why are you in my bedchamber?"

He frowned. "I apologize for intruding. I just needed to assure myself of your well-being." He turned toward the door.

Kassie pushed herself to a sitting position, brushing the rumpled dark curls off her cheeks. "Please don't go," she called softly. He stopped. "There is no need to apologize," she continued, giving him a tentative smile. "I'm grateful for your concern." She took a deep breath. "And I shall be fine. Truly. Thanks to friends such as you."

Rather than looking pleased, Charles looked bleak. He lowered himself back into the chair. "Kassandra," he began, staring at the carpet, "there are a few things you should know." He lifted his chin, met her gaze. "I am the one who discovered your father's body first. When I got to the cottage with your message he was . . . already gone."

To his amazement, Kassie leaned over and placed a gentle hand on his forearm. "Oh, Charles, I'm so sorry." Her beautiful features were soft with compassion. "How horrible that must have been for you."

Charles blinked. Was there no limit to this woman's precious gift of selflessness? His chest swelled with pride. Pride and love.

Without conscious thought Charles took Kassie's hand. "Now that I see that you are fine, I'll be fine as well." He forced a smile, then continued. "There is one more reason I came to see you, Kassandra. I wanted to say good-bye."

Kassie gave him a quizzical look. "Good-bye? Are you going on a trip?"

There was no point in putting off the inevitable. "No. I am leaving Sherburgh."

"Leaving Sherburgh?" Kassie gasped. "For good?" At his nod she asked, "Why?"

This was the part Charles had dreaded. Yet he knew it had to be said. Steeling himself, he replied, "Braden believes I killed your father."

"What?" Kassie shouted the word, nearly toppling off the bed.

"He saw me running from the cottage," Charles told her quietly. "It is only natural for him to assume—"

Kassie leapt off the bed, yanking her hand from Charles's grasp. "It is natural for him to assume nothing!" she shot back. "I will go to him at once, tell him about the message I gave you for my father. Then he will know—" She broke off at Charles's definitive shake of the head. "Why not?"

"I've already told him the truth. He doesn't believe me." He gave a sad sigh, standing up and keeping his back turned toward her. "Unfortunately, he is also convinced that I was responsible for pushing the boulder that nearly killed him yesterday."

"Dear God." Kassie felt the room spin, and she leaned against her bedpost for support. "How on earth could he believe that you of all people, who has loved him his whole life, would do such a thing?"

"I was there, Kassandra," he answered flatly. "I was walking on the cliffs, alone with my thoughts. I heard the rumble of the rocks, then your scream. I was frantic to make certain that you were unharmed—"

"You do not have to explain anything to me, Charles," Kassie interrupted firmly.

But he continued anyway. "When I saw you were safe I did not want to intrude upon your moment with your husband, so I took my leave. I suppose Braden looked up and saw me atop the cliffs and thought . . ." He broke off.

Kassie was silent as all the pieces began to fall into place.

Braden's strange mood since yesterday, the way he had rejected her last night, the emotional withdrawal she could feel. If Braden saw reason to doubt Charles, it would cause him to doubt her as well, for it would fragment the tenuous fibers that formed the very foundation of his trust. She wanted to weep for her husband's bewilderment . . . and his agony. At the same time she wanted to throttle him for allowing his damned cynicism and misgivings to cloud his mind to the truth—and, in the process, to cause his oldest and dearest friend to endure unnecessary and undeserved pain.

At Kassie's prolonged silence Charles turned around to face her, his jaw taut. "Do you, too, believe that I am guilty?"

Kassie went to him without hesitation and gave him a warm hug. "I believe you are one of the finest men in the world. You would never hurt *anybody,* least of all Braden." She stepped back, her gaze tender. "And what's more, Braden knows it, too. I don't care what he told you. He loves you, Charles. And in his heart he knows you are innocent." She laced her fingers together, wringing her hands in frustration. "Please don't leave Sherburgh," she implored Charles. "Give me a chance—give Braden a chance—to make things right. Please, Charles. Is your pride really worth more than Braden's love?"

For a moment Charles did not answer. He merely stared at the lovely young woman who embodied everything of value that remained in his life. She and Braden meant the world to him.

And she was his only link with the past.

"All right, Kassandra," he heard himself say. "I will stay on, but only if Braden agrees to it. If he should ask me to leave, I shall."

"He will not ask you to leave." Kassie's statement was positive. She looked relieved and determined all at once, her mind already racing ahead to the conversation she would soon be having with her foolish, misguided husband.

Braden ignored the knock on his door.

In truth, he barely heard it. Staring bleakly out the

window, he was lost amid the turmoil of doubts and the wrenching twists of guilt.

The door banged open, and Kassie burst in.

"I need to see you, Braden."

He turned, startled. She was still wearing the gown she had donned this morning, only now it was somewhat disheveled from her nap. Her face was drawn, and he went to her at once, concerned over her state of mind. "I didn't know you were awake," he said, brushing her cheek gently with the back of his hand. "Are you all right?" He lifted her chin with his forefinger, searching her face for signs of bereavement.

What he saw were signs of indignation.

"How could you?" she demanded, twin spots of color staining her cheeks.

Braden's brows went up. "How could I what?"

She didn't mince words. "Charles came to my room. He wanted to say good-bye."

Braden's hand dropped to his side, and he tensed. "That could be for the best."

"And *you* could be a damned fool." Ignoring Braden's stunned expression, she continued. "Charles is no more capable of murder than I am. And what's more, you know it."

A muscle worked frantically in Braden's jaw. "Leave it, Kassie. There are things *you* do not know."

"Such as what?" she shot back. "That Charles was on the cliffs yesterday when that boulder fell? Yes, Braden," she responded to his shocked, questioning look, "Charles told me the whole story. Which he would have told you, had you bothered to listen. But you didn't even wait to hear what he had to say, did you, husband? You were too eager to accuse him of attempted murder!" She took a deep breath, trying to bring herself under control. She was well aware that other than the night she had found Abigail in Braden's bed, this was the only time she had blatantly stood up to her husband. But she was determined to get through to him, for his sake, for Charles's sake. And for her own sake as well.

Disregarding the glacial coldness in Braden's eyes and the withdrawn rigidity of his stance, she pushed on, the trembling of her small chin the only evidence of her turmoil. "Braden," she said as she held his gaze, "are you so steeped in distrust that you can no longer recognize love and friendship in their truest form?"

"I'm not certain that either love or friendship exists." His tone was bitter, unyielding, but Kassie knew how badly he needed to be proven wrong.

She stepped closer to him. "They exist," she told him with tender conviction. "And they are reaffirmed every time I'm in your arms."

Braden made a tortured sound. "When you're in my arms I don't know what I feel—"

"I didn't ask what *you* feel," she interrupted softly. "I'm telling you what *I* feel. I love you." She gripped his powerful biceps. "So does Charles."

He continued to stare at her, unmoving. "I do not share your blind faith, Kassie," he said at last. "I've tried, but I cannot."

"You could if you would allow yourself to do so," she countered. She wanted to shake him, to force him to see the truth—that not only did she and Charles love him, but he loved them as well. But in her infinite wisdom Kassie knew that certain truths had to be discovered by oneself.

With the right guidance, of course.

A flash of emotion softened Braden's haunted look, then disappeared. "I have to sort this out by myself, Kassie."

She nodded sadly. "I know. But while you do, don't let Charles leave Sherburgh. Once you come to your senses you'll never forgive yourself." She stepped away from him—an unnecessary physical gesture, as she could already feel his emotional retreat severing the closeness they had once shared. For a moment she contemplated throwing herself back into his arms, begging him to love her. But she couldn't.

It was a question not of pride, but of pragmatism. She didn't want her husband out of guilt and obligation, only out of love.

Kassie blinked away the tears that wet her lashes. "If you need me, I am here," she said simply. Then, before she disgraced herself by helplessly succumbing to the racking sobs that threatened to erupt, she turned and left the bedchamber.

In the hallway she gave in, leaning against the wall and crying silent tears of pain and heartache. She felt empty inside, having lost more in one day than any person could endure.

"Your Grace, are you all right?" It was Harding, looking pale with worry. His kind face only succeeded in making her cry harder. "Your Grace?" Harding moved to her side.

"I'll take care of the duchess."

Kassie looked up in surprise as Cyril strode over and took her arm. "Come Kassandra," he said, in a voice more gentle than he had used in days. "I'll take you to your room."

She nodded, beginning to tremble. Apparently reaction was once again claiming her. And if Cyril's kindness was merely forced, and based on compassion at the loss of her father, she quite frankly didn't care. She accepted it gratefully.

He let her lean upon him and drench his shirt with her scalding tears while he guided her to her room. Once inside he continued to hold her, murmuring soothing words into her hair.

At last, utterly spent, Kassie drew back, wiping her cheeks with the backs of her hands. "Thank you," she said with quiet dignity.

He stared at her, his dark eyes enigmatic. "Will you be all right?"

"Yes. I just need some time."

Cyril glanced toward Braden's room, as if assessing the full reason for Kassie's tears. But all he said was "Very well. Should you need anything, I would be glad to provide it."

With another speculative look he was gone.

Chapter 28

~~~~

Robert Grey was laid to rest in a secluded spot beside Elena on the cottage grounds following a small, private service. As the vicar recited the last prayer Braden wrapped his hand tightly about Kassie's and held her in his arms while she cried.

But with the funeral behind them Braden withdrew, becoming distant and brooding, spending endless days pouring over business contracts and restless evenings racing Star wildly across the grounds of Sherburgh.

It was as if he wanted to exorcise the demons that plagued him, Kassie thought. This she understood, as her own days were bleak, her nights hell.

Outwardly nothing had changed since her father's death. Charles stayed on, though removed from the rest of the household; Cyril continued to offer sympathetic concern; and Braden displayed an outward show of support when their paths crossed. But it had been over a week since they had shared a bed . . . since he had made love to her. Kassie knew the chasm between them had never been greater, and she felt the loss keenly in her body and in her heart.

To compound her difficulties, she was devastated from the renewed outbreak of her nightmares. The frequency and intensity of the dream were worse than ever before, causing her to awaken in a cold sweat two or three times a night until she felt on the brink of a complete emotional collapse.

It was at this, her lowest point, that Kassie sought help. Ten lonely days, ten tortured nights were enough, she thought determinedly, climbing out of bed. It was just after sunrise, and Kassie dressed rapidly. She couldn't—wouldn't—succumb to self-pity forever. It was time to shape her own future.

The first floor was quiet, no surprise at this hour of the day. Kassie was unperturbed. "Perkins?" she called softly.

Instantly the butler was by her side.

"What can I do for you, Your Grace?"

She smiled. "You can see if Dr. Howell is up and about yet. I would really like to speak with him."

"At once, Your Grace."

Kassie wandered through Sherburgh's lovely green salon, waiting for Perkins's return. This room was one of her favorites, with lime velvet sofas, deep woven carpets, and a huge window that looked out onto the gardens. The splendor of a castle, the warmth of a cottage. It was perfect.

"You wanted to see me, Kassandra?"

Kassie turned to see Dr. Howell regarding her curiously. Neither the tension existing in the house nor Kassie's depressed state had gone unnoticed by him. Yet he patiently awaited her readiness to seek him out and discuss her feelings. Apparently the waiting had finally paid off.

"I hope Perkins did not awaken you." Nervously Kassie fingered the soft folds of her gown.

He shook his head, clasping his hands behind his back and glancing casually at the paintings that hung on the walls in order to put Kassie at ease. "No, my dear, not at all. I always arise early. I do my best thinking when my mind is fresh."

Kassie moistened her lips, plunging on without further preliminaries. "Dr. Howell, I believe that I have been neglecting my health and running away from my problems."

Alfred squinted, studying the brilliant watercolor before him with apparent fascination. "I imagine we are all guilty of both those things on numerous occasions," he replied. "However, it is only the cleverest of us who recognize when we are doing so."

Kassie smiled faintly. "You are very kind, doctor. And very wise as well. But in my case, recognizing the problem is but the tip of the iceberg. Solving it is another thing."

Alfred turned abruptly to face her. "Are we referring to your dreams or your marriage?"

"Both."

He nodded, gesturing for her to sit down. She sat at the edge of the sofa, and Alfred lowered himself into the wing chair beside her. "Braden is experiencing his own crisis right now, Kassandra." At her startled look he shook his head. "No, I am not privy to all the details. Nor, however, am I blind. And you must remember that I have known Braden for many years and recall his boyhood quite well. He is unused to unconditional love and selfless commitment, for he has never before experienced them. Until you."

Kassie stiffened. "Charles loves him."

At her words Alfred fell silent. Then he nodded carefully. "Yes, Charles loves him. But love and trust, though different emotions, are often inseparable." At Kassie's attempted protest Alfred held up his hand. "Whatever is between Braden and Charles must run its course, Kassandra. Have faith in your husband. And above all, love him."

"I do," she replied softly. "I always have. I always will."

He gave her a gentle smile. "If only the world were filled with Kassandras," he said softly.

She blinked back tears. "Then the world would be anguished and afraid."

"Have the nightmares not subsided at all?" He sounded surprised. Despite the unrest between Kassie and Braden, Alfred had felt sure that the dreams would fade.

"Meaning that with my father's death I should feel unafraid of the future and freed of the past?" Kassie gave voice to Dr. Howell's thoughts, her words tight with suppressed emotion. "Well, I don't." She covered her face with her hands. "The dreams have gotten worse, not better," she whispered. "And I don't know what to do."

Alfred cleared his throat. "Could the rift between you and Braden be causing you to sleep poorly?"

Kassie dropped her hands to her lap, sitting bolt upright. "Hardly, Dr. Howell. As you implied earlier, I am not a fool. These are not merely nights of poor sleep, these are vivid, violent recurrences of my nightmare."

"Violent?" He grasped onto her words. "Have you recalled another facet of the dream?"

The fight went out of her eyes. "No . . ." She struggled to pinpoint her thoughts. "The images themselves have not changed," she said slowly, considering the subtle changes in her dream over the past week. "Only now, rather than my seeing but a fleeting glimpse of the beast, he is more vivid than ever." She shivered, forcing herself to go on. "And I know that he means to kill me." Even as she spoke the words all the color drained from Kassie's face.

This was not what Alfred had expected to hear, and he frowned. It made no sense. If his theory was correct and Robert Grey was responsible for his wife's death, then Kassie should be experiencing a diminished rather than an intensified recurrence of her nightmare. Despite all the turmoil in her life, she should feel great relief that the threat of danger was no longer with her.

Unless the murderer was not Robert Grey.

The startling possibility inserted itself in Alfred's mind, rearing its ugly head. For a moment he contemplated speaking it aloud, then looked at Kassie's ashen face and abruptly changed his mind. It was strictly conjecture on his part, without any substantiation. He must think it through, explore the likelihood on his own, before he considered suggesting it to Kassandra.

Yet even as he dismissed the thought as improbable, a nagging doubt remained.

A few minutes later Kassie left the manor and headed for the stables. Her talk with Dr. Howell had yielded no further results, and her despondent mood prevailed, together with an unshakable inner chill. She needed the solace offered by her friends, the beloved Sherburgh Thoroughbreds and their compassionate trainer.

"Charles?" she called out, reaching the stable door. From within she could hear the restless stirrings of the horses as they recognized their mistress's voice. She went in. "Hello, my love," she greeted Little Lady, who nuzzled her hand affectionately. Kassie stroked her neck lovingly. "Perhaps when Dobson arrives I'll have him saddle you," she murmured. "A morning ride might do us both good."

The sound of a horse's hooves, followed by muffled voices, reached Kassie's ears. Curious, she gave Little Lady a final pat and left the stables. She nearly collided with Dobson, who was cooling down a predictably snorting Star.

Kassie barely saw the groom or the horse, nor did she hear Dobson's stammering apology as he led Star off. Her eyes were on her husband.

"Good morning, Braden," she said evenly.

Braden stared at her, his chest tightening painfully. After days of self-imposed isolation he was stunned by the impact Kassie's presence had on his raw emotions. And while he still felt exposed, vulnerable, he was aware that on some fundamental level he desperately needed his wife. Strangely moved, he drank in everything that Kassie represented: her innocence, her gentleness, her love.

"What are you doing about at this hour?" he asked carefully after a prolonged silence.

"The same thing that you are doing. I couldn't sleep."

Distress flashed across Braden's face. "I see." He looked at her closely for the first time in days—her pallor, the dark rings under her eyes, the too-slender lines of her body. And what he saw worried him. He frowned. "Are you all right?"

No, she wanted to scream. *I am not all right. I am so alone, so afraid. And I need my husband.* But "Yes, Braden" was all she said.

He didn't look convinced. "Have you seen Alfred?"

"What you mean is, has *Dr. Howell* seen *me.*" Kassie raised her chin, walking slowly to where Braden stood. "And the answer is yes, he has. We spoke just moments ago." She fought the urge to fling herself into Braden's arms, knowing that he would push her away. "You needn't worry about me, Braden. I am just fine. As you will recall, I am quite accustomed to taking care of myself."

A small smile flitted across his face, and he lifted his hand to trace a line down her pert nose to her mouth. "Yes, I recall," he murmured, rubbing her lower lip softly. "My independent, honest Kassie. Different from any other lady of my acquaintance."

The tenderness in his eyes was her undoing. It had been absent for too long, its reappearance a poignant memory of

303

all she had lost. "Not so different after all," Kassie whispered, all her defenses crumbling. "I miss you, Braden." Her voice broke. "I miss you so much."

"Kassie . . ." Her words pierced his heart, reminding him that she was the only one in the world who could reach that deep inside him. He cupped her beautiful, earnest face in his hands and lifted it to his.

Kassie's heart began a frantic hammering in her chest, and her eyes slid closed just as Braden's lips brushed hers once, twice, then claimed her mouth for a deep, drugging kiss of aching possession. Kassie stood on tiptoe, leaning into him, answering his kiss with her own and telling him without words that she wanted more. Just as she knew, without words, that he intended to give it to her.

Lifting her off the ground, Braden gathered Kassie to him and began to walk toward the house.

"Oh . . . pardon me."

Both Braden and Kassie jumped at the sound of Charles's voice. They had been so absorbed in each other that they hadn't heard his approach.

He shifted uncomfortably from one foot to the other, his face flushed. "I didn't mean to interrupt."

Kassie felt Braden tense, felt the magic shatter into a thousand empty fragments.

"You're losing your touch, Charles." Braden's tone was glacial. "Silent, undetected arrivals and departures are usually your forte."

Charles winced, and Kassie gasped, "Braden, stop it!"

Braden released her in one whisk of motion. "Consider it done." He ignored the stunned, hurt look on her face. "If the two of you will excuse me, I have work to do." He turned to Charles, his expression closed. "Star is being cooled down. Little Lady needs to be ridden. Noble Birth is favoring his right side. Any other information you can get from Dobson." Without a backward glance he stalked off.

"I'm sorry, Kassandra," Charles said quietly.

Kassie shook her head, still staring after Braden in amazement. "Don't be. It isn't your fault." She gave Charles a stricken look. "Why is he so filled with anger?"

Charles gave her arm a reassuring squeeze. "Braden's

emotions all appear to be very close to the surface right now. His anger is a good sign, one I haven't seen in over a week. At least it appears he is no longer apathetic toward me. I feared his indifference far more than his anger." Knowing blue eyes twinkled. "Nor does it seem that he is indifferent toward you, does it?"

Kassie flushed. "I suppose not." She watched Braden disappear from view. Shaken by their encounter, she mulled over the reality of her husband's unexpected show of rage and the joy of his equally unexpected show of passion. Diametrically opposed reactions—and additional complications in her already tangled life.

Charles was watching her thoughtfully. "Would you like to talk about it?" he asked astutely. "I am really quite a good listener."

Kassie hesitated. How wonderful it would be to unburden herself to Charles, to tell him everything—the memory of her mother's death, the reality of Elena's lover, the possibility of her father's guilt, and the horrible nightmare that seemed to hold the key to it all. But Charles had enough to bear, with his estrangement from Braden and his tenuous position at Sherburgh. No, now was not the time.

"Thank you anyway, my friend," Kassie said softly, touching Charles's hand. "Soon. But first I must attempt to deal with it on my own." She sighed. "For now, I believe I'll go to my room and rest. The thought of a ride no longer appeals to me."

Charles watched her go, an enigmatic look on his face. Eventually she would talk to him. It was only a matter of time. And once he was certain how much she actually knew, he would have a very difficult decision to make. One he had been dreading for an eternity.

Braden stormed into the house, slammed into the library, and poured himself a brandy. He was livid, and he wasn't exactly certain why. Was it his encounter with Kassie, or his encounter with Charles? All Braden knew was that his mind screamed with unassuaged bitterness; his body throbbed with unfulfilled need. And he felt an aching, wrenching void in his gut.

He tossed off his drink.

"Braden?" Dr. Howell poked his head into the library, concern written all over his face.

"Yes, Alfred." Braden's voice was laced with impatience. "What is it?"

Alfred came in and closed the door behind him, ignoring Braden's dark humor. "I need to see you. Now."

The urgency of Dr. Howell's tone penetrated Braden's ire. "Is it Kassie?" he asked anxiously.

"Yes." Alfred held up his hand as Braden tensed in alarm. "There is no cause for panic. Kassandra is well. But the conversation she and I had today disturbed me, and I feel it is my duty to discuss it with you without delay."

Kassie heard the rumble of male voices as she passed the library. She paid them no attention, walking up the stairway to the sanctuary of her bedchamber. Her lips still tingled from Braden's kiss, and all the feelings she had forced from her thoughts this past week sprang free. She had deluded herself into believing she could exist in Braden's house, yet be his wife in name alone. She could not. Nor could she return to being the innocent young girl of two months past. For she was a woman now, with a woman's needs and a woman's passions. And she needed her husband to make her whole.

Flinging herself upon her bed, Kassie succumbed to tears.

"Kassandra?"

Kassie jumped, staring wet-eyed at Cyril Sheffield. "Oh . . . Cyril." She brushed away her tears with the back of her hand, struggling for composure. "I didn't hear you come in."

He walked over to her bedside and drew her gently to her feet. "Can I help?"

It was too much. At the kindness in his tone the dam broke, and her tears exploded into wrenching sobs. Cyril put comforting arms around her, drawing her to him, stroking her hair lightly. Kassie pressed her face to the soft wool of his deep green morning coat, wishing she could bury herself in its warmth, keeping her pain at bay forever.

It was not to be.

When her sobs had subsided to occasional sniffles Kassie

drew back, embarrassed at her inexcusable behavior. It was the second time she had lost control in front of Braden's uncle. "Cyril, forgive me," she managed. "I don't know what came over me."

He kept his hands on her shoulders. "What has made you weep like this?" he probed, his eyes dark, piercing.

Kassie felt a warning twinge at his question, knowing instinctively that the implicit meaning was *who*, not *what*. "Nothing," she lied, seeing his jaw tighten. "This is just a very trying period for me. My father's death was very sudden."

Cyril did not answer but continued to stare at her. Her discomfort grew, for she could feel a suppressed anger beneath Cyril's soothing gestures.

Kassie pulled away. "Thank you for your concern, Cyril," she said coolly. "Now, if you don't mind, I'd like some time alone."

He pressed his lips together, and for a moment Kassie thought he meant to refuse her pointed request that he leave. Then he nodded. "As you wish." He gazed at her a moment longer, then turned and left the room.

It was midnight before Kassie slept.

After spending much of the day in her room she was mentally exhausted, but physically wide awake. Sleep was difficult and, when it finally came, fitful.

The nightmare unfurled like a dark blanket of shadows.

The scent of lilacs . . . her mother. Two voices . . . Elena's, frightened; the man's, angry, pleading . . . deranged. Herself . . . afraid . . . exposed . . . fleeing.

The trees were everywhere, yet they could not hide her. The shrill scream rang out, then echoed eerily throughout the night. The beast roared in response, raising its great head, looking about for its prey.

It found her.

She could not get away. He was gaining upon her, coming closer and closer, until there was nothing between them but the lingering scent of lilac and the abyss of death.

She screamed . . . Braden's name . . . but he could not hear her, for no sound emerged. She could feel the beast's breath upon her face, hear the rumblings of his rage, see his eyes glitter with madness.

She cowered, knowing he meant to kill her.

Green. Everywhere there was green. Before her. Beneath her. Why was there so much green? The ground. It was coming closer . . . closer . . . she was hurtling toward her death.

Braden . . . Braden . . . Braden . . .

"I'm here, sweetheart . . . I'm here." Braden shook Kassie again, more terrified than he had ever been in his life. For nearly five minutes she had been calling for him, hoarse, anguished cries. He had ordered Margaret away, demanding to be left alone with his wife, convinced that he was the only one who could help her. But for the first time, even he could not rouse her from her sleep. "Kassie!" She still wasn't hearing him. Bracing himself, he drew back his hand and slapped her hard, wincing at the thought of hurting her. "Kassie!"

She blinked, panting, the dazed look fading from her eyes as the effects of the nightmare subsided. Slowly she focused on her husband's clamped jaw and grim expression. "Braden?" He was shaking more violently than she. "Braden . . ." She reached up to caress his nape tenderly. "I'm all right," she soothed. "Truly I am."

Overcome by the fact that *she* was comforting *him*, Braden tugged Kassie into his arms, holding her fiercely. Weak with relief, he was now more than ever determined to unearth the nightmare's malignant core and to expunge it forever.

For a long while he said nothing, merely clasping Kassie tightly in his embrace. Then he attacked the ghosts head on.

"Was it the same?"

"Yes . . . no . . ." Kassie drew herself upright, sensing Braden's resolve and forcing herself to recount the still-fresh details. "It was clearer this time. All of it. I could hear their voices . . . two voices. Mama's and . . . *his*. The beast was furious; I could see it in his eyes. And I could see the trees, and the grass, and the ground far below. Everything was green. So much green." She covered her face with her hands.

"And the air was scented with lilacs. Braden, Mama always smelled of lilacs. . . ." Kassie's voice broke.

Braden felt a jolt of fear. It all fit with Alfred's theory that Kassie had witnessed Elena's murder—and that the murderer was still alive. The question was, would Kassie be able to accept this horrifying possibility? Further, could her remarkable internal strength, already severely taxed, rally enough to withstand the strain?

Gently Braden tugged Kassie's hands away from her face, interlacing her fingers with his. "Sweetheart, the nightmare is getting worse, not better."

She inhaled sharply. "Don't you think I know that?" she whispered. "I told Dr. Howell—"

"I know you did," he interrupted.

Kassie nodded. "He spoke to you," she stated. "I assumed he would."

Braden stood, pacing back and forth as he carefully considered his next words. But there was no putting off the inevitable. *"Ma petite,* we need to talk."

She tensed instantly. "What is it?" Her voice was high and frightened.

"The night of your parents' argument," he began quietly.

"You mean the night my mother died?" She was steeling herself; he could feel it.

He nodded. "I believe that something else happened that night, Kassie. Something even more horrible than the argument you overheard."

"I know," she choked out. "My mother fell to her death. Or rather, you believe my father pushed her."

Braden sat down beside her. "I agree that your mother was pushed. But your father might not have been the one who did it."

Kassie gasped. "What are you saying? You think someone *else* murdered my mother?"

"Quite possibly." Braden took her cold hand in his.

"Who?"

"I don't know."

"You . . . don't . . . know," Kassie repeated slowly. Then she gave an hysterical laugh. "Then how are we to find out,

Braden? Who can we ask? *Who does know?"* she shouted, coming to her knees.

"You do."

Silence hung in the air.

Kassie sank back onto the bed. "What?" Her voice was barely audible.

Braden forced himself to go on. "You were little more than a baby, Kassie, and probably very frightened by the argument you overheard. You followed your mother when she went out. Maybe she met someone, maybe she was followed . . . I don't know. But whoever was with her is probably responsible for her death."

Kassie wrapped her arms about herself, feeling the familiar chills begin. She closed her eyes. "This is all your theory?"

"No, not mine. Dr. Howell's. But I agree with it. And," he concluded in an agonized tone, "if he is correct, the murderer still lives . . . or your dreams would have subsided."

Kassie opened her eyes slowly, staring up at Braden as the impact of his words sank in. "You think the murderer is still alive?"

"Yes."

Something inside her seemed to snap.

"Then I shall find him." In a wild flurry of motion Kassie flew to the wardrobe and began yanking gowns out one after the other. "I shall find him," she repeated again and again, blind to her frenzy of activity.

"The hell you will." Braden stalked over, whirling her about and shaking her out of her hysterical, trancelike state. "Have you lost your senses?"

Suddenly an eerie, unnatural calm registered on Kassie's face.

She shrugged, her eyes vague. "Possibly. It doesn't matter, Braden. I have already lost everything else—my pride, my strength, my mind." She gave a hollow laugh. "So you needn't worry." She turned away.

Feeling Kassie's withdrawal, seeing her teeter on the brink of emotional collapse, Braden discovered the real meaning of stark terror—the terror of losing something vital to his very existence. Of losing Kassie.

Vehemently he dragged her into his arms. "Damn you, stop it. Don't talk like this. I can't bear it." He crushed her into him, willing the fight back into her eyes, the spirit back into her soul. "Dammit, Kassandra," he choked, "don't you dare leave me. I need you." He buried his face in her hair. "God help me, I love you."

She didn't respond, remaining limp and passive against him.

Braden refused to accept defeat. He gathered her closer still, desperate to make her believe his declaration and to have that belief make a difference. "Please, sweetheart. You were right. I *am* a damned fool. And I know it's taken me forever to say the words. But I'm saying them now, Kassie, I'm saying them now. I love you. I love you so much. Please, *ma petite"*—his voice broke—"tell me that it's not too late."

Braden felt her stir, then draw back to look up at him. Her eyes were damp, the faraway look gone, and she reached up to touch his cheek, her fingers growing wet with the tears he didn't remember shedding. She stroked his lips softly. "Say it again."

He didn't have to ask what she meant. "I love you," he repeated, joy and relief flooding through him in great waves. He kissed her fingertips tenderly. "I love you."

Kassie felt his words infuse her with strength, a strength she thought had long since dissipated. She pressed her face to his chest, listening to the sure beating of his heart . . . a heart that, at long last, belonged to her.

"You've rescued me once again, Braden Sheffield," she whispered. "And it's about time."

Chapter 29

❧

It's nearly dawn, sweetheart. You should sleep," Braden murmured into Kassie's hair. He leaned his head contentedly back against the bedchamber's deeply cushioned armchair and drew Kassie closer in his embrace. She had been that way for hours as together they had watched the night's inky blackness envelop the sky, then quietly give way to the first persistent rays of day.

At Braden's words she sighed and snuggled against her husband's warmth. Sleep? How could there be any room for sleep when Braden had finally given voice to the words that she had longed to hear forever? He loved her. Her dream had become a reality.

Kassie rubbed her cheek against the soft silk of Braden's robe, the frightening revelations of earlier that night held at bay.

"Well?" he repeated in a husky whisper. "Will you rest?"

"How long have you loved me?" she asked in hushed wonder, pointedly ignoring his nonsensical suggestion.

Braden grinned at the typically female question, asked in Kassie's uncluttered, straightforward manner. "Since before I should have . . . since you were little more than a child," he replied, knowing even as he answered that it was true. She had been written in his stars, a miracle that had entered his life long after he had ceased to believe that miracles existed. And even if everything else he believed in turned out to be a lie, Braden knew that what he shared with Kassie was real. "You are my heart . . . the very essence of my world," he told her softly, tightening his arms about her. "And I love you."

"I'm glad," she said with understated simplicity, pressing her lips to the exposed skin at the base of his throat, "because I fell in love with you the moment I first saw you. I've loved you ever since." She kissed his chin. "I'll always love you."

Emotion tightened Braden's chest at Kassie's honest declaration. For three years she had loved him . . . a love as unconditional as Kassie herself. And that love had never wavered, never faltered beneath self-doubt nor diminished beneath the hell of her life and the uncertainty that her love was returned. Braden felt humbled and proud—and fiercely determined to make everything up to her and to keep her safe at all costs.

"Kassie, I want to take you away," he said suddenly.

She looked up at him in surprise. "Why?"

He met her gaze solemnly. "Because if Dr. Howell's theory is correct and your mother's murderer is still alive, then it is only a matter of time before he becomes a danger to you . . . if he is not one already."

Kassie frowned. "Braden, are you implying that Charles—"

"I'm not implying anything," he interrupted. "I'm *saying* that I want to take you far from Sherburgh to a place where you won't represent a threat to whoever it is that is locked away in your memory." He nodded decisively at his own words. "We'll go to Paris. You've never been abroad, and I'm sure you would enjoy—"

"Braden, stop it!" Kassie jumped up, regarding him through stormy aqua eyes, hands firmly on her hips. "I'm not going anywhere."

Braden came to his feet in one fluid motion, his jaw tight with anger and frustration. "Did you understand what I just said?" he demanded. "Someone out there might be a killer. And if he suspects that you know who he is—"

"Then we'll just have to learn his identity first, won't we?"

He grabbed her shoulders, his fingers digging into her soft skin. "Dammit, Kassie, this is *not* a game!"

"I know that," she returned, raising her chin in stubborn defiance, "and I am *not* a child!"

"What the hell does *that* mean?"

"It means that it is time you stopped looking upon me as a little girl, Braden. I am a grown woman—not only in bed, but in fact." She pressed her fists firmly against the hard wall of his chest, willing him to hear her. "I am no longer the child of fifteen that you met on the beach. I am your wife, and I want a husband, not a guardian." She met his determined gaze with her own. "Stop trying to protect me."

He shook his head in amazement. "How can you ask me to stop trying to protect you when I've just told you that I love you?"

"It's *because* you love me that I ask you," she responded quietly. "You of all people know how strong I am. If I haven't crumbled by now, I never will. Please, Braden"—she gripped his forearms—"let me have a say in my own future. Please."

He stared down at her, warring emotions tearing him apart. He well understood what she was asking, what she required from him, and yet he loved her so deeply, needed her so damned much. He had only just realized how much. And having at last recognized the full extent of his feelings, how could he knowingly expose her to such great danger?

He saw the appeal on her face, and his resolve melted. "All right, Kassie," he heard himself say. At her relieved look he shook his head. "But only for a day or two. If after that time we are no closer to a solution, then with or without your agreement I am taking you away from here. Is that clear?"

Kassie's eyes glowed with love. "Perfectly clear, husband," she answered softly. "And thank you."

He tugged her to him wordlessly, praying that her thanks would not come with too high a price.

Kassie couldn't wait to tell Charles.

Immediately after breakfast she hurried off to find him. The stables were deserted, so she raced across the grounds, cupping her hands over her mouth and calling his name. The only answer she received was from Percy, who ran along by her side, his barks mingling with his mistress's calls and echoing back to them.

Kassie had just about given up and was heading back toward the house when she ran smack into the object of her search.

"Kassandra . . . I'm sorry, I didn't see you." Charles looked preoccupied and tense.

"I've been looking everywhere for you!" She clutched his arms, radiant with pleasure.

"What is it? What's happened?" Charles lost much of his faraway look, his blue eyes fixed on Kassie's jubilant face.

Laughter bubbled up inside her. "He loves me!" she cried, throwing her arms around Charles's neck. "Braden told me he loves me!"

Charles found himself hugging her back, her explosive joy contagious. "Kassandra, that is wonderful," he said with warmth and sincerity. "Truly wonderful."

Kassie released him and dropped lightly to her feet. "Where have you been?" she demanded. "I've been searching forever!"

Charles's expression closed. "I was out walking. I had much I needed to mull over."

Kassie studied him thoughtfully. "Braden wants to take me away," she blurted out. "Now. To Paris."

Charles's eyes narrowed. "Why?"

"He feels that I am in danger." She paused. "My dreams have worsened. Last night . . . it was horrible." She shuddered.

Charles's mind was racing. "I don't see the connection between your nightmares and Braden's decision to whisk you off to Paris," he said, managing to keep the fear out of his voice.

Kassie didn't have to think. She made her decision. Charles deserved the truth. "It is Dr. Howell's belief that I witnessed my mother's death." She paused, gauging Charles's reaction. She could tell by his silence that her revelation came as no surprise. "You knew."

"Yes, Kassandra, I knew." Charles sounded tired, drained.

"Did you also know that he does not think Mama's fall was accidental?"

Charles swallowed, his eyes growing damp. He said nothing.

"Both Braden and Dr. Howell are convinced it was murder."

Charles's head snapped back as if he had been struck. *"Murder?"* he cried out, white-faced and shaking. "Murder," he repeated in a hoarse whisper, as if to negate the word with its utterance.

Kassie was grateful she had never doubted Charles's innocence. His reaction more than proved her right. "Yes, murder." She licked her lips, providing the heinous details in a wooden voice that didn't belong to her. "Further, while they originally believed my father to be guilty, the question exists as to why I am still tormented by nightmares if the cause of them is dead. Hence, the possibility exists that the real murderer is still alive . . . and close by."

Charles looked dazed, his gaze unfocused. He shook his head once, twice, trying to bring himself under control and failing. Everything inside him was unraveling; his strength, his wits, his sanity. "Elena," he whispered almost inaudibly. "Elena, no . . ."

Kassie started. It was not only Charles's use of her mother's given name, but his agonized tone. Almost as if . . . "Charles, did you know my mother?" Her heart began to thump in her chest.

He stared right through her, his vague expression giving no indication that he had even heard her question. "You should go away with your husband, Kassandra," he answered instead in a voice that was shaken, distant. "It would be for the best."

Kassie felt a lump in her throat. If Charles was trying to frighten her, he was succeeding. But she shook her head emphatically. "I can't run away, Charles. I need to come to terms with my past, to understand it. It is the only way I can ever find peace."

"Even if what you discover causes you pain?" His hands were clenched at his sides.

"Yes," she whispered. "Even then."

Charles closed his eyes. "Go back to the house, Kassandra," he said at last. "And listen to Braden, for he loves you very much."

"But Charles," she began, then stopped. She had so many questions, for whatever secret was locked inside Charles, Kassie suspected that it concerned her mother, if not her mother's death. But she couldn't risk pushing him when he was not ready to discuss it, for then she might never learn what she so desperately needed to know. Of one thing she still felt certain: No matter what mystery Charles carried, he was not a murderer. And difficult as it would be, she would have to be patient.

"All right, Charles," she conceded softly. "I shall give you the time you are wordlessly requesting, because you are my friend. But I will be back later today. And then you will tell me what I need to know."

Charles heard her walk away, his eyes still tightly closed. Her perception was so acute it was almost uncanny. She knew there was something . . . just as he knew the time had come.

And just as he knew that Elena would want it this way.

Harding was whistling cheerfully when Kassie entered Braden's bedchamber. She stopped in surprise. Her husband's valet was not usually so noisy.

"Good morning, Harding," she greeted him. "Have you seen Braden?"

At the sound of Kassie's voice Harding's whistling ceased, and he broke into a broad grin. "Good morning, Your Grace. And no, I haven't seen the duke."

Kassie gave him an odd look. It seemed that *not* knowing Braden's whereabouts was giving Harding great pleasure. "I see," she responded. "Well, would you mind telling me the last time you *did* see him? I need to talk to him."

Harding's grin widened. "I'm afraid I haven't spoken with His Grace since last night, although I did see him for a moment or two quite early this morning when he came in to change clothes." His gleeful gaze fell on the untouched bed. "But he was eager to begin his day. In high spirits, actually." He beamed his approval. "I'm certain, however, that he is equally eager to speak with you."

Kassie didn't know whether to burst out laughing or sink through the floor in embarrassment. Apparently Harding had deduced that she and Braden spent the night together. And judging from his reaction, the idea appealed to him very much.

"Thank you, Harding," she managed, ducking out of the room, pink-cheeked. She hadn't the heart to tell him that her night with her husband had been entirely chaste. It would shatter the poor valet's illusions.

"Hello, lovey!" Margaret sailed by Kassie on her way to her mistress's bedchamber. "I'm going to select your gown for dinner tonight." She gave Kassie a knowing wink. "I planned to do it hours ago, but I didn't want to disturb you." Her happy voice trailed off behind her.

In a houseful of well-meaning servants, nothing was sacred.

Kassie descended the stairs, a smile tugging at her lips. Mere moments ago she had been besieged by tension, haunted by unanswered questions. Now she felt a warm glow touch her heart. The servants at Sherburgh were more like family to her than mere employees. And their tender caring was what made Sherburgh a home.

"Your Grace!" An ever-efficient Perkins hurried over to her. "I have a message for you."

Kassie wondered if the news of her reunion with Braden had reached Perkins's diligent ears yet. Seeing the twinkle in his eyes, Kassie had her answer. "A message?" she asked, trying not to blush.

"From the duke. He has asked that you meet him at the stream on the far side of the estate." Perkins paused, his brows knit. "I believe his words were 'at our picnic spot.' Does that make sense?"

Kassie felt her mouth curve upwards. "Yes, Perkins. Perfect sense."

He nodded. "Good. Little Lady has been saddled and brought around front for you."

Kassie flashed her dimples at him. "Thank you, Perkins. I'll go at once."

She rode as quickly as her cumbersome gown permitted, now very much at home in Little Lady's saddle. When she reached the clearing by the stream she stopped, grinning at the sight that met her eyes.

On the grass was spread out a blanket, complete with a basket of food, wine . . . and Braden.

At the sound of Kassie's approach Braden sat up lazily, squinting at his wife. "Welcome, my beautiful duchess," he greeted her, coming smoothly to his feet and walking over to Little Lady's side. "It occurred to me this morning that you and I began a picnic that has yet to reach its natural conclusion. A picnic that commenced delightfully at this very spot some weeks ago." He reached up and lifted Kassie from the saddle, lowering her slowly to the ground.

"I haven't forgotten," she said breathlessly, holding on to his arms.

"Nor have I," he replied huskily, his voice deep, suggestive. "I haven't forgotten . . . anything."

Kassie felt his words seep into her pores, drenching her in melting liquid heat. Her pulse began to race, and she gazed up at him, undisguised longing in her blue-green eyes.

Perhaps the servants would not be disappointed after all, she thought with giddy anticipation. Perhaps today would mark the end of the week's long, celibate nights.

Braden watched Kassie's breath quicken, her lips part softly in silent invitation. With burning eyes he caressed her exquisite features, running his fingers lightly up and down her arms beneath the sleeves of her gown until he could feel the little bumps of pleasure tremble on her bare skin.

"Soon," he promised in a low-pitched, intimate tone, "but not yet. First, my impatient wife, we shall have our meal."

"Meal?" she murmured dreamily.

"Um-hum." He rubbed his thumb over her lower lip. "Our meal. Food."

"I'm not hungry."

His lips twitched at her blunt protest. "You will be." He dropped his hands to his sides.

Trying not to smile over the obvious disappointment on Kassie's face, Braden led her to the blanket that beckoned them. "Sit."

She complied, stretching her legs out before her and leaning back on her hands. "All right, Your Grace." She brushed her hair back over her shoulders, where it cascaded down her back like a shining black waterfall. She gave him an impish grin. "Now what?"

He drank in her flawless beauty, wanting nothing more than to tug off her clothing and bury his lips, his body, in her welcoming softness. "Now I serve you." He dropped down beside her and began to remove food from the basket: bread, cheese, fresh strawberries, and a bottle of port.

"I provided a far more extensive banquet at *my* picnic," she pointed out with dancing eyes.

"I have allocated very little time for the eating portion of our day." His hot gaze raked her explicitly, filled with sensual promise and a prelude of the pleasure yet to come.

Kassie felt her breasts swell, tighten painfully.

As if he knew how his carefully chosen words were affecting her, Braden's eyes dropped to the bodice of her gown, restlessly watching as her nipples hardened in anticipation.

"Braden . . ." She uttered his name in a breathy whisper.

Wordlessly Braden broke off a small chunk of cheese and brought it to her lips. "Bite," he commanded softly.

"Are there no utensils?" she murmured, her breath warm against his fingers.

"None."

"A pity." She took a bite of the cheese, chewing it delicately, then licked the crumbs from her lips.

"Duchesses are required to eat only from the hands of their dukes . . . when on picnics," he said hoarsely, his gaze fixed on the motions of her mouth. "Allow me." He leaned over and nibbled gently at her lips, letting his tongue take over her task. Kassie's eyes slid closed, and her head dropped back. She was aware of nothing but the feeling of Braden's mouth on hers. "Better?" he asked in a passion-rough voice, sitting back on his heels.

"Much."

He raised the bottle of port. "Would you care for some wine?"

"Are there glasses?"

"Not a one." He leaned forward and pressed the open bottle to her lips. "Crystal is also prohibited from use by duchesses."

"When on picnics," she clarified, settling her mouth on the open bottle.

"When on picnics," he agreed softly. "Now drink."

The wine flowed onto her lips and slid down her throat in a cool, soothing stream. Small droplets of port, having escaped the confines of her mouth, trickled onto her chin, and instantly Braden caught them with his tongue, absorbing the sweet taste of the wine and the sweeter taste of Kassie.

Kassie's breath was coming in quick pants. "And dessert?" she managed. "As I recall . . . dessert is . . . the first course . . . when . . . on . . . a . . . picnic." She shivered as Braden's mouth closed possessively over hers.

"Yes . . . dessert." He pressed her backwards onto the blanket, covering her with himself. "I believe dessert is where we left off scant months ago, is it not?"

He didn't wait for her answer. Tossing the bottle aside, he gave in to his true hunger, the desperate craving that had gnawed inside him from the first moment his wife had dismounted. He buried his lips in hers, filling her mouth with his tongue, his breath; tangling his hands in her luxuriant hair and abandoning himself to the voice that cried out for Kassie, the urgent need that was beyond bearing.

"Kassandra . . ." He kissed her cheeks, her neck, her throat, drawing the fragile skin into his mouth, wanting to consume the very essence of her. He brushed his open mouth across the soft curves of her breasts, which were exposed over the low-cut bodice of her gown. With shaking hands he tugged down the sleeves until Kassie's naked shoulders were revealed. These he worshiped, as well, caressing them with his hands, bathing them with his tongue. And all the while he reveled in her response, her soft cries of pleasure, the sensuous twists of her body beneath him as she begged for more.

The sound of her pleas, the uninhibited offering of herself—neither was lost to the eyes and ears of the man who stood concealed by a wall of trees, his eyes ablaze. He raised a near-empty bottle to his lips, gulping down the burning liquid, then stared at the couple so intimately entangled on the lawn, fury and madness twisting his handsome face.

She was mine . . . mine, he thought. *Untouched and innocent, needing all that I could offer. And now . . .* He shuddered, his fists clenching and unclenching at his sides. *Now she is just like her mother was. A deceitful, manipulative slut. Promising the world with her damned beauty and her trusting sighs; in truth, nothing more than a lying, scheming bitch. Just like Elena. Elena . . .* His gut knotted, and he refocused, seeing only Kassandra . . . in Braden's arms, writhing and moaning in the grass like a common whore.

He bit his lip until he tasted blood, then washed it away with another deep swallow. *Things could have been so different, Kassandra, so different. But you've sealed your fate . . . chosen another . . . another . . .*

You'll pay. You'll both pay.

Turning away, he staggered back into the trees and disappeared.

Unaware that they'd been observed, Kassie and Braden knew only each other. Braden slid one arm beneath Kassie's back and lifted her, rapidly unfastening the row of tiny buttons at her back. She helped him with her gown, wriggling out of it and kicking it away from them. Braden would have smiled at her eagerness if he weren't so frantic himself. Urgently he pulled off the rest of her clothes, struggling at the same time with his own.

When at last they lay naked and unashamedly hungry for each other, Braden drew her into his arms, melding her body's softness to the rigidly hardened contours of his.

"I love you," he breathed into her hair, filled with all the wonder of discovery, the joy of giving voice to feelings long denied. "Kassie, I love you so much."

Awash with sensation, Kassie pressed her open mouth to the warm skin of Braden's chest, teasing the crisp, dark hair with her tongue. How she had needed to hear those words, and now that she had, how she needed her husband's body to convey them. "Show me," she whispered. "Show me that you love me."

The fervent longing in her voice was all it took. Aroused beyond bearing, Braden rolled Kassie to her back, sliding his knee between her legs and reaching down to assure himself of her readiness.

She was more than ready for him.

Their gazes locked in that moment, and the love he saw shining in her eyes told him all he needed to know.

"Braden," she breathed, reaching up for him, opening herself for their joining.

He said her name, whispered it as a love word, and pressed himself slowly forward, entering her with tender reverence. He felt ripples of pleasure surge through him as her body stretched to accept him, and he closed his eyes, easing forward, waiting until he had totally filled her, until he heard her melting sigh of pleasure, before he began to move.

And then the world began to tremble as they let their bodies speak for their hearts.

Again and again Braden thrust into her warm wetness, wrapping his arms about her fiercely, lifting her to meet each deliberate thrust. He heard her soft cries, felt her body tighten around his, beneath his, and all at once nothing mattered but Kassie's pleasure. He urged her legs higher around him, leaving her open to the deep, deep penetration of his body as it stroked on hers, in hers.

Kassie was lost amid a swirling vortex of sensation that dragged her down into its sultry core. She had wanted Braden in the past, but never like this. Never with an intensity that burned her from the inside out; never so that she thought she might die if he were to stop, so that the mere touch of his hands, his mouth, caused her body to throb with a longing so acute it was like pain. Never so that the waiting was beyond bearing.

"Braden," she pleaded, past logic or sanity. "I need you . . . I . . ."

". . . love you," he finished for her, watching her flushed, rapturous expression as she strained for fulfillment.

". . . love you," she echoed, arching up to meet him.

They reached the towering peak together. Kassie cried out as the shuddering spasms claimed her, and Braden matched her rhythm, pouring into her in great, pulsing bursts of heat.

Unwilling to separate, they remained as they were, Braden's lips buried in the fragrant cloud of Kassie's hair, his body still deep inside hers.

"I don't want to hurt you," he murmured at last, attempting to raise up on his elbows.

But Kassie would have none of it. "Don't go," she protested, wrapping her limbs more tightly around him. She kissed his damp shoulder. "Please . . . stay with me."

He stared down into her enchanted face, love welling up inside him. "I want you to have my child," he said with sudden intensity. "I want a little girl with hair the color of midnight and eyes like pieces of the sea." He brushed her lips softly with his, tasting her joyous tears. "I want her to have not only her mother's breathtaking beauty, but her fierce courage, her extraordinary spirit, and her rare, unspoiled innocence. Then, someday, when she meets a very lonely, very jaded man, she, too, can teach him how to love." He gazed down at her soberly. "And when she does, he will make her forget all the pain of the past by treasuring her for the rest of their lives."

Kassie blinked away her tears. "I love you, Braden," she whispered.

"And I love you, my magnificent wife. Now and always."

With his words Braden pledged his heart to the enchanting, selfless angel in his arms, knowing fully and finally that she was his life's richest blessing. And though Kassie had told him time and again that it was he who had rescued her from a living hell, Braden knew the truth.

It was Kassie who had rescued him.

Chapter 30

❧

The afternoon sun had grown warm, forcing its rays insistently through the encumbering clouds when Kassie and Braden finally and reluctantly began to think about returning to the house. The entire morning and much of the afternoon had been spent in total sensual abandon, alternately splashing in the stream, feeding each other bits of bread and cheese, and mostly making slow, lingering love. Each moment was pure joy unto itself, almost as if by wrapping a cocoon of pleasure about them they could keep the intruding forces of the world at bay.

But the real world could not be shut out forever.

Kassie chewed her lower lip anxiously as Braden buttoned the back of her gown. "Charles is keeping something from us," she blurted out at last. Although she couldn't see Braden's expression she could feel him tense, feel his hands pause in their task.

"Meaning?" Braden asked the question carefully, knowing full well that Kassie was fiercely loyal to Charles.

Kassie turned to face him. "I don't believe Charles had anything to do with my mother's death," she began defensively. When Braden didn't answer but only continued to wait impassively for her to continue, she sighed. "Braden, I'm so confused."

"Tell me." All traces of nonchalance gone, Braden's words were a command.

Quietly and without pause Kassie told Braden of her earlier conversation with Charles. "I'm certain he knew my mother," she concluded.

Braden nodded. It all fit. "I'm sure he did know Elena."

There was something in her husband's voice that set off warning bells in Kassie's head. She squinted thoughtfully up at him. "You know something that you haven't told me."

Braden smiled faintly, amazed as always at his wife's keen perception. Gently, protectively, he tugged her to him, offering her the security of his arms. "Charles is the person who discovered your mother's body on the beach," he replied softly, feeling Kassie's start of surprise. "I only just found out some weeks ago," he responded to her unspoken question. "And at the time there was no point in telling you. But I've always wondered what Charles was doing at the base of the cliffs that night. It seemed a bizarre coincidence."

Ingesting that new piece of information, Kassie took a deep breath and verbalized the thought that had nagged at her all day. "Do you think Charles might have been the man who was involved with my mother?"

Braden had wondered the same thing. "I honestly don't know, sweetheart."

Kassie pulled free of Braden's embrace. "Oh, why can't I remember?" she choked out, anger and frustration welling up inside her.

"You will."

"When?" she demanded in a tortured voice. "When will I remember?" She didn't wait for Braden's reply, having come to a rash but necessary decision. "Braden, I want to go to the cliffs . . . to the spot from which I supposedly saw my mother fall." Her expression was determined, only the slight quivering of her lips hinting at her unvoiced fear.

Braden started. "Why?" he demanded. He remembered a beautiful, frightened fifteen-year-old girl telling him that she never walked the paths along the cliffs. He had long since guessed the reason why.

Kassie met Braden's gaze resolutely. "It is time for us to stop evading the obvious, Braden. If I am to remember what happened that night, I must return to where it occurred. Perhaps then my memory will be jarred."

Braden was shaking his head vehemently. "No."

"Yes."

He recognized the stubborn lift of her chin, the firm glint in her eyes, but this time he was unyielding, his every instinct alerted to the possible dire consequences of Kassie's intentions. "I won't have you subjected to that kind of anguish. Some things are better left untouched."

"Tell me, husband," Kassie asked shrewdly, "are you afraid for my safety . . . or my sanity?"

Braden's answer was equally straightforward. "Both."

Kassie remained silent for a moment, then began to refill the basket. "We should return to the house."

Braden frowned, distinctly unhappy with his wife's response. He knew her too well to believe that she had been so easily convinced. Her quick acceptance of his decision made him extremely uneasy. "Kassie," he began, "I want you to promise me—"

"I understood you perfectly, Braden," she interrupted, gathering up the blanket. "There is no need for further discussion."

He felt a small measure of relief. "Fine. As long as you understand why it is I worry about you."

At that she turned and smiled. "I do. How could I not?" She dimpled. "It is because you love me. You've told me so countless times today."

"I have, haven't I?" His grin was slow, melting. "So see that you remember it."

"I shall," she answered softly.

Braden rode back to Sherburgh alongside his wife, convinced that she understood him and deeply grateful that she would obey.

Kassie had no intention of obeying.

She retreated to her bedchamber, lost in the process of formulating a plan. She was determined to solve this mystery, whatever the cost.

"Kassandra?"

Charles's voice brought her up short. She hadn't even seen him where he stood in the darkened corner of her room.

"Yes, Charles, it is I." She watched him walk toward her, feeling no fear, only relief.

He stared down at her, a tortured look on his face. "Would you care to leave the door ajar?" he asked, a touch of bitterness in his voice. "I would like this talk to be private, but I will understand if you are afraid to be alone with a potential murderer."

Kassie did not flinch but left the door as it was, fully closed. "There is no need for me to open the door, Charles," she answered softly, studying his tired, lined face. "I never once thought you were guilty or capable of murder."

Some of the harsh lines around his mouth softened. "Thank you for that," he said simply.

Kassie shrugged. "There is no need to thank me for speaking the truth. I would much rather you showed your appreciation by doing the same."

Charles sighed. "And so I shall."

"You knew my mother." Kassie wasted no time in beginning.

Charles nodded. "Yes, Kassandra, I knew your mother . . . I knew her quite well."

"Were you lovers?" Kassie asked with customary directness.

Charles looked stunned. "Lovers?" He laughed, shaking his head in bewildered amusement. "Sometimes it amazes me how much like Elena you are. She was just as outspoken, often scandalously so. No, Kassandra, your mother and I were not lovers." He paused for a fraction of an instant. "Elena was my sister."

Kassie sank down on the bed. "Your sister?" she repeated, shocked.

Charles rubbed his hands together, fighting the familiar pain that talking about Elena brought. "Yes, my sister. Well, actually my half-sister. Although neither Elena nor I ever made that distinction . . . at least not between ourselves." He walked toward the window and stared out with unseeing eyes. "But the rest of the world is not as kind, Kassandra, as you yourself have found out. Bloodlines count heavily in the world of the *ton,* and it was no different with Elena's father . . . *our* father." His tone held no bitterness, only resignation.

Kassie searched her mind frantically, trying to remember what she could of her grandfather, an esteemed member of the *ton*, titled and wealthy. She had seen him but several times, as he had all but denounced his daughter when she had married beneath her station. All Kassie could recall was a grim-faced, white-haired man whose rare visits to the cottage always left her mother unsettled and in tears.

"Your grandfather was a stubborn, pompous man whose reputation meant more to him than anything else . . . including his family," Charles continued, as if reading Kassie's mind. "My mother was one of a large parade of women in his life and in his bed. She was a chambermaid at his estate, barely sixteen, too young to differentiate love from lust. When she discovered she was carrying a child she assumed Edward would be as thrilled as she." He made a choked sound. "She was wrong. He was livid. And when I turned out to be a boy, a potential heir to his wealth, he was enraged. He denied being my father and threatened my mother with bodily harm if she should ever dare accuse him publicly. She was terrified, not for her own safety, but for mine. I was but a few months old when she bundled me up and took me far away, where neither Edward nor his influence could reach me. She told the next family who employed her that she was a widow, and they accepted her story without question. But she never really recovered from the shock of Edward's rejection." A muscle worked in Charles's jaw. "My mother died eight years later. She never saw your grandfather again, and after her death no one but myself knew the secret of my paternity. Until Elena." He smiled fondly, remembering. "Elena was more than ten years my junior, and I knew nothing of her birth. One day my curious little sister, now a woman grown, discovered some old notes to Edward scribbled in my mother's hand and deduced the truth. She made some discreet inquiries and found out I was a groom at Sherburgh. She came to see me"—his eyes filled with tears—"not to denounce me, but to claim me as her brother. I argued, but your mother was a very persistent young woman. At last I agreed to let her acknowledge me privately, but never publicly. The repercussions from your grandfather would be too severe. So she agreed that our infrequent meetings *had* to be held in secret, and *never* at Edward's estate or at Sherburgh. By this time Elena had met your father and fallen desperately in love with him. The match was forbidden by Edward, which, of course, made it twice as appealing to my rebellious Elena." Charles gritted his teeth. "For the first time I actually agreed with Elena's father. For despite his reputed good looks and charm, I never trusted Robert Grey; pure instinct, since we had never officially met. What I heard of his excessive gambling and the occasional confusion I read in my sister's eyes screamed their warning to me. But being headstrong like yourself, Elena would not listen to reason. Despite my objections, she married your father.

"At first they were wildly happy; so happy I was almost convinced I had been wrong. And then a few months later, everything changed. He became vehemently jealous, irrationally possessive, putting obsessive limitations on Elena's freedom. She rebelled, fought him . . . until you were born. Then she was terrified that during one of his crazed tirades he would take his anger out on you. She had nowhere else to turn, so she complied docilely with his wishes, never going to parties, never speaking with other men."

Charles inhaled sharply, then let out his breath on a shudder. "And Robert had one other obsession. He was ridden with hatred for the nobility, convinced that it was he who deserved their rank, their power, their wealth. He boasted everywhere of his nobly born wife who had given up everything to marry a man more deserving. I made Elena swear never to disclose my existence, for there was no telling what he would do if he knew she had a bastard brother who was the son of a lowly chambermaid. It was ironic. Your grandfather had just died, and we actually believed we were free of the past. Now it seemed that the present was even more ominous. There was no escape, although God knows we tried. Countless times I begged Elena to let me take the two of you away, but her fear of your father was just too great.

"And then she met someone." Charles's voice had grown soft, and Kassie stood shakily, straining to hear his words. "This man gave her a reason to live again, to love again. The sparkle was at last back in my sister's eyes, and I couldn't bring myself to denounce the very thing that had put it there."

"A man," Kassie repeated, coming to stand behind Charles. "What man, Charles? Who was it?"

Charles wiped tears from his cheeks. "I don't know, Kassandra. Elena always met him covertly, and she never divulged his name. All she said was that it was better that I not know, that enough pain had been caused by crossing forbidden lines."

Kassie's brows rose. "Forbidden lines? Was he married to another?"

Charles shook his head. "I don't think so."

"Then why didn't my mother leave my father and stay with the man she loved?" she persisted.

Sadly Charles replied, "Because she *was* married to another. And she was afraid of how a possible scandal would affect you. She was always so protective of her precious, beautiful daughter," he said with a gentle smile.

Kassie swallowed past the lump in her throat. "What happened on the night my mother died?" she made herself ask.

Charles's smile faded. "I was worried about her. She'd been different the last few weeks—quiet, strained. I begged her to tell me what was wrong, but she wouldn't. I assumed your father was abusing her again." A tremor went through him. "His rampages had been more frequent and had become physical as well as verbal. I wanted to kill him." His hands closed into fists at his side. "I *should* have killed him. But I didn't." He turned to face Kassie, his features contorted with pain. "I knew Elena sought refuge walking along the cliffs. She always said that it gave her a sense of peace she could find nowhere else. The night she died I felt jumpy and uneasy all evening long. I couldn't dispel the feeling that something horrible was going to happen. Finally I went out to the cliffs to see if I could find her, to assure myself of her well-being." He let out an anguished sound. "But it was too late. She was already gone . . . lying there on the ground . . . pale and broken and . . ." He covered his face with his hands, unable to continue.

Her own cheeks wet with tears, Kassie went to Charles and gently tugged his hands from his face. "You're my uncle," she whispered. "Why didn't you tell me?"

Charles stared down at the perfect replica of his sister, this exceptional young woman who was Elena's child. "How could I?" he choked out. "I was so afraid for you. After Elena's death there was no one to protect you from that monster who called himself your father." For the first time Kassie knew the depth of Charles's hatred for Robert Grey, heard it in his voice. "I kept a silent vigil over you, checking on you as often and as discreetly as I could. Especially after the day Braden and I brought your father home from York . . . drunk." He spat out the word. "At that time Braden made my role much easier by asking me to keep an eye on you. That gave me an excuse to do openly what I had been doing secretly all along." He shook his head, anguish etched onto every plane of his handsome face. "Don't you think I longed to tell you who I was? To share my love for Elena with you? But what would have been the result? If Grey had found out . . . I don't know what he might have done to you. Although," he added bitterly, "he did it anyway, didn't he? He hurt you . . . and I could do nothing before it was too late. Just as it was too late for Elena." Charles caught Kassie's hands in his. "Forgive me, Kassandra," he said in a voice that tore at Kassie's heart. "I let you down . . . I let you *both* down." He dropped his head, utterly defeated.

Kassie wrapped her arms about his waist. "You've never let me down, Charles," she told him in a fierce whisper. "Nor did you let Mama down. She loved you. Just as I love you . . . loved you long before I knew you were my uncle. But now that I do know, I feel doubly blessed to have you not only as my friend, but as my family."

Charles hugged her tightly to him. "Elena would be so proud of you, Kassandra," he managed softly, "so very proud." He stroked her hair gently. "As am I. You are every bit as beautiful as your mother was, both inside and out. You are also the most loyal and loving wife that I could ever want for Braden."

At his words Kassie looked up and met her uncle's tender gaze. "You love Braden very much, don't you, Charles?"

"He is the son I never had."

"Let him know that." She stepped back, gripping Charles's forearms tightly. "That was the advice you gave me not long ago," she added with a watery smile. "And it worked. Talk to him, Charles. Tell him everything you told me. Give him a chance. Because as a very wise and wonderful man once told me, 'I know you love him. Now go home and show Braden.'"

Charles studied Kassie for one silent moment, then leaned forward and kissed her gently on the forehead. "Very well, Kassandra. I will." He squeezed her hands. "Thank you for coming into my life," he said simply, then he was gone.

Kassie's legs felt weak, and she lowered herself to the bed, fighting the delayed reaction that was beginning to set in. Charles was her uncle. She had to cling to that fact, for it was the only good to come of this madness.

But the mystery remained, terrifyingly close. Kassie began to tremble violently, some inner voice warning her that she was nearing her answers, approaching the truth. For the first time she forced herself to accept the fact that the beast in her dream had to be her mother's unknown lover.

Unknown to everyone but Kassie.

Her mind made up, Kassie wrote a hasty note for Braden, propped it on her bed, and left the room.

Past the unseen man who watched her go.

Braden was smiling as he headed toward his room to change for the evening meal. Now that he had declared his love for Kassie, his body and his heart were finally at peace.

Which left only his mind to follow.

Braden's smile faded, and he paused outside Kassie's closed door, his hand poised to knock. She could be asleep, he thought, hesitating, since neither of them had slept last night. He would just check on her, he decided. Lowering his hand, he pressed the door handle and entered the semidarkened room.

It took him less than a minute to realize she wasn't there. And while the discovery made him distinctly uneasy, he didn't panic. Until he saw the note.

Reaching the bed in three strides, Braden snatched the note from the pillow, taking it to the open door to read by the hall's light.

Dear Braden, it read, *I'll be back shortly. In the interim, please talk to Charles. He has much to tell you. I'm asking you to do this, if not for yourself, then for me. I love you very much. Kassie.*

With a muttered oath Braden crumpled the note in his hand. What was Kassie up to, and where did Charles fit in? Braden was just about to toss the note to the ground when Kassie's words reappeared in his mind's eye: *I'm asking you to do this, if not for yourself, then for me.* Slowly Braden opened his hand, staring at the wrinkled piece of paper. *All right, Kassie,* he told her silently, *I'll do it. For you.*

"Charles. I need to see you."

Braden stood at the stable door, watching as Charles absently stroked Little Lady's neck. At the sound of Braden's voice he turned, his eyes red and swollen.

Without thinking Braden went to him, taking his arm. "Charles, my God, what is it? What's wrong?" In over thirty years Braden had never seen Charles look so haggard and beaten.

Charles stared down at Braden's hand clutching his arm. "Have you spoken with Kassandra yet tonight?" he asked in a raw voice.

"Not directly. She left me a note asking me to talk with you." Braden dropped his hand to his side.

Charles nodded. "I see." He pressed his fingers to his throbbing temples. "Then we have much to discuss."

Braden could feel his heart begin to pound. "About Kassie?"

"Yes, about Kassandra . . . and about Elena, her mother."

Braden braced himself for the worst. He was prepared for many things, but not for the heartbreaking story that unfolded as Charles, with all the quiet dignity he possessed, proceeded to reveal everything to Braden that he had to Kassie.

Braden said not a word throughout, but by the time Charles had finished, Braden's own eyes burned with unshed tears. "You never told me . . . any of this," he got out.

Charles made a choked sound. "You believe me?"

There were no words to say, so Braden said but one. "Yes."

Charles went to him silently, and the two men embraced.

"I'm sorry I doubted you," Braden managed.

"And I'm sorry I kept this from you," Charles replied when he could speak. "But when Elena was alive I promised her my silence. When she died I was so very frightened for Kassandra. I wanted there to be no possibility that Grey could learn who I was—the lowly bastard sibling of his nobly bred wife—and to take out his rage on their beautiful, innocent daughter, simply because her relation to me represented a potential scandal. Also, with Grey's propensity for violence, I was determined to keep an eye on Kassandra . . . and I needed to remain unnoticed and anonymous in order to do so. She was all I had left of Elena; I couldn't risk losing her, too. So I told no one . . . not even you." Charles swallowed. "Then, seeing Cyril's reaction to Kassandra . . . the idea of a Sheffield bride without a title . . . I was convinced I had made the right decision. She had endured so much, I could not subject her to anything more. Cyril was already condemning her for her pseudo-aristocratic birth." He gave a harsh laugh. "Compared to the vast Sheffield empire, Kassandra could boast only a minor title on her mother's side, and nothing on her father's. A mere pittance amongst the *ton*. Imagine their reaction if they'd learned that I was her uncle—a lowly groom." Charles shook his head. "No. I would protect Kassandra any way I had to . . . with my life, if need be."

Charles's words triggered a sharp, intrusive thought in Braden's mind, painfully jolting him from his joyous reunion with his old friend.

"Where is Kassie?"

Charles looked surprised. "I assumed she was in her room, awaiting the outcome of our talk."

Braden frowned. "No . . . her room is where I discovered the note. She was nowhere to be found." He swallowed, suddenly terribly unnerved. "Charles, Kassie is desperate to resolve the mystery of her nightmares. You don't think she would go to the cliffs by herself . . ." The question hung in the air.

Charles paled, then forced himself to relax. "Let's remain calm, Braden. Whatever Kassandra's intent, she couldn't have gone far." He stroked the velvet forehead of the graceful mare beside him. "She obviously went by foot. Little Lady is still here. There is no other mount that Kassandra would try to manage on her own."

As soon as the words had left his mouth Charles froze, his alarmed gaze locking with Braden's, panic streaking through them both simultaneously.

It took seconds before their worst fears were confirmed.

Star was missing.

Kassie's hands felt like blocks of ice when she dismounted. With the coming dusk the wind had grown brisk and now whistled through the craggy peaks of the cliffs. Far below, Kassie could hear the sound of the waves as they struck the beach, taking layers of sand in their wake.

The cold intensified.

Star whinnied his concern as Kassie tied him securely to a sturdy tree. She shook her head in reply, having no intention of endangering her beloved horse by allowing him to come too close to the cliff's edge. "Thank you for getting me here so quickly, my spirited friend," she murmured. "If all goes well, I shall go home cured."

So saying, she turned and walked boldly along the path that led through the jutting rocks. The wind sharpened with each heartbeat, and Kassie wrapped her arms about herself, her teeth chattering uncontrollably.

She reached the edge.

For a timeless time she stood staring down at the deserted

shore far below, her dread growing stronger by the second. Had her mother felt this nameless, faceless terror as she stood there all those years ago? Or did Elena's fear have both a name and a face?

A flash of memory, dark and forbidding, darted through Kassie's mind and was gone. She shook her head, willing it to return, but her brain, intent on protecting itself, stubbornly refused to comply.

The dusk grew thicker, the night sounds more pronounced. There were eyes all around her, watching . . . waiting . . .

It was more than Kassie could bear. Trembling violently, she backed away from the edge, from the fear of the past, from the pain . . . and came up against the solid wall of a man's body.

She whirled about, weak with relief, certain that her husband had come after her. "Braden . . ." She broke off in surprise. "Cyril?"

Cyril Sheffield stared down at her, his face masked by the shadows of dusk.

"What are you doing here?" she whispered. "How did you know . . ."

"I was concerned about you," he replied in a wooden tone. "So when I saw you ride off to the cliffs, I followed. I do that whenever I see you go off by yourself." He reached out and drew her to him. "You shouldn't be out here alone, Kassandra. It isn't safe."

Kassie nodded against his shirt, unable to free herself of her internal chill. "You're right, Cyril, and I appreciate your concern. Let's go back to the house." She attempted to pull away.

Cyril held her to him. "Concern?" he repeated softly. "I would hardly describe my feelings for you as *concern*, Kassandra."

Kassie tugged against his restraining arms. "Please let go of me, Cyril, you're frightening me."

"Nor is fear what I desire," he continued, as if she hadn't spoken. He lifted a handful of her hair, bringing it to his face. "Have I told you how lovely your hair is? How it shines

337

when the sun strikes it? How exquisite it looks spread upon a blanket . . . even if it is being sampled by another man?"

Kassie's eyes had grown wide with alarm. "I don't know what you are talking about." She snatched her lock of hair away from him. "But I want you to let go of me this instant."

She felt the change in the stiffening of his body. *"You* want?" he demanded. "I know exactly what *you* want, Kassandra. I saw it quite clearly this afternoon by the stream. Unfortunately, Braden was never meant to give it to you."

The realization that Cyril had witnessed their lovemaking infuriated Kassie. "How dare you?" she spat out, heedless of the danger.

"How dare I?" he roared. "I dare because it is I, and not Braden, who is entitled to your practiced little body. I, Kassandra." He dug his hands into her arms, lifting her off the ground until she was staring into his blazing, deranged face, his eyes glazed with madness. "I offered for it, I was willing to pay seventy thousand pounds for it, and it belongs to me. *To me,* you traitorous little slut. *To me!"* He shook her so hard that her teeth rattled.

"Oh, my God," Kassie gasped, remembrance washing over her like a tidal wave. "You were the man I overheard with my father . . . the man who wanted to buy me—"

"The man to whom you rightfully belong!" he shouted. "But I should have expected deceit, betrayal. You're just like her, aren't you? Not only your beauty, but your vicious, conniving heart." His insane laughter blended with the wind. "I should know better by now, shouldn't I? I could have given you everything, Elena, *everything* you desired— wealth, a title, and a man who adored you. Instead of that pathetic drunk you married . . ."

His ravings continued, but their sound grew faint, for his last words had struck a hellish chord inside Kassie. She closed her eyes as her head began to buzz with sound. It was another voice intruding into her delirium, a voice from far away. *Why would you stay with that pathetic drunk you married, Elena? All for a child? Leave him . . . come back to me. I can give you the world . . . you know I can. We're so good together . . . and I love you, I adore you. Damn you,*

don't turn away from me . . . damn you . . . Elena . . .
Elena . . .

Kassie heard herself scream, and the echoing sound from
the past merged with her primal cry of terror. She opened
her eyes, focusing wildly upon Cyril's dark green coat . . .
the same coat he had worn yesterday when he had com-
forted her. Green. So much green. Just like in her nightmare.

Kassie let out another piercing shriek.

Cyril. It had been Cyril. He was the one who had
murdered her mother.

The pieces fell rapidly, heinously into place. Kassie had
been but four years old, frightened by her parents' argument, intent on preventing her beloved mother from going
away. She had followed Elena to the cliffs, where she had
heard the strange man's anger, heard her mother's anguished sobs . . . and hidden, listened, and watched.

It replayed itself in slow motion before her eyes: the
violent fight, the harsh words, Elena slapping Cyril across
the face. And then his rage, his maniacal fury as he had
seized her and thrust her over the cliff's edge . . .

And Elena's scream . . . her horrible, fading scream as
she had fallen to her death.

Cyril had watched her fall, a satanic smile on his face. He
had turned away . . . and looked straight toward Kassie
where she crouched, cowering, in the clump of trees.

Without pause she had fled, racing for home as fast as she
could. . . .

She had been running ever since.

Slowly she refocused on her surroundings, everything
inside her frozen, numb.

Cyril was staring at her with predatory intensity.

"It was you," she whispered, beyond reason or caring.
"You . . . you killed my mother."

"Your mother was a whore, Kassandra." Cyril's voice was
steel and fire. "As are you. And your father was a fool and a
weakling. He never knew I was the same man Elena had
loved. He promised you to me, but he betrayed me . . . and
he died for it. I warned him time and again. But his greed
and his liquor made him pitiful and useless. It took but one
push to end his miserable life."

Kassie stared blankly, gaping in noncomprehension.

"And Elena . . . my Elena . . . she also betrayed me," Cyril continued in a chilling monotone, "so she died for it as well. And now you . . ."

The implication was lost on Kassandra until she felt him dragging her back to the edge of the cliff. Then her instinct for self-preservation took over.

"No!" she cried, freeing her hand and pounding on his chest. "No, I won't let you . . . no—"

"Kassie!"

Braden's agonized shout exploded through the air. He dismounted before Little Lady stilled, tearing toward where Cyril had paused, still clutching Kassie to him.

"Stop right there, Braden, or your wife will be dashed on the rocks," Cyril warned.

Braden strove for control, seeing that his uncle was quite mad. "Let her go, Cyril. It's me you want, not Kassie. I'm the one who took her from you. I'm the one you detest. If you want to kill someone, kill me."

Cyril gave a harsh laugh. "How noble of you, Braden. But ineffective, I'm afraid. Because it's too late. Kassandra has already betrayed me, and she must pay . . . pay with her life."

He turned back toward the cliff's edge. And in that brief second Braden dived at him, knocking him backwards and to the ground.

"Braden!" Kassie screamed as she fell free, but not far enough, from Cyril. With a feral growl Cyril lunged at her, murder in his heart. But Braden got there first.

"Stay down, Kassie," he ordered, shielding her from his uncle's crazed hands. Completely berserk, Cyril attacked Braden, ripping him off of Kassie and dragging him to the jagged brink. Kassie lay paralyzed with gripping, all-encompassing fear.

"You should be dead!" Cyril panted, his hatred giving him unnatural strength. "That boulder I hurled should have killed you. But this time there will be no escape, Braden. None." With a frenzied shove he heaved Braden over.

Frantically Braden grabbed hold of the jutting rock and clung, his legs dangling uselessly in space, small pebbles of stone breaking off and toppling into the bottomless abyss below.

With an ugly laugh Cyril leaned over to break Braden's precarious hold on life.

The realization that Braden was in danger broke through Kassie's immobilized state.

Leaping to her feet, she seized the largest rock she could find and, without pause, crashed it down upon Cyril's head.

She held her breath as Cyril looked slowly up at her, his expression glazed. And then he fell, plunging forward over the side of the cliff. Kassie squeezed her eyes shut, unable to close out Cyril's piercing shriek as he fell to his death. The sound merged with the shattering memory of Elena's screams, roaring through Kassie's head in unendurable explosions of agony. She clamped her hands over her ears, crying out with pain, cringing down on the craggy cliff.

As if from a great distance she could hear a rider approach, and seconds later running footsteps sounded. Still in a trance, Kassie opened her eyes in time to see Charles lean forward and lock hands with Braden, hoisting her husband to safety.

It was only when she felt Braden's arms go around her, heard the sound of his voice, that reality descended and the dam inside her broke.

"He killed her, Braden. He killed Mama," she wept piteously, her body burrowed into Braden's.

"I know, love, I know." Braden's heart twisted with grief. "But it's over now."

Kassie continued as if Braden hadn't spoken, her face buried against his chest. "How could a man who made Mama so happy be such a monster?" she choked, gripping Braden's shirtfront. "How? He tried to buy me . . . and when I married you, he stalked me . . . convinced himself I was Mama . . . then hated me because I wasn't." She took a shuddering breath. "He was going to murder me, Braden . . . *and* you. He already murdered my mother, my father . . ." Abruptly she stopped. "I killed him," she whispered brokenly. "I killed him, and I'm not even sorry."

"He was insane, Kassie." Braden lifted her tear-streaked face and cupped it in his palms, forcing her to emerge from the hell of her past. "But now he's gone. He can never hurt you again." He kissed her damp cheeks. "It's over, sweetheart . . . over."

Braden said the words again and again, refusing to allow Kassie to retreat back into her paralyzed shell.

Kassie clung to her husband's vow, concentrated on his beloved face, felt Charles's strong hand on her shoulder. "Over," she repeated, finally allowing herself to believe.

"Yes, *ma petite,* all over." Braden enfolded her in his shaking arms, saying a silent prayer, knowing how close they had come to losing each other. "God, how I love you," he breathed, healing Kassie with his words.

"I love you, too," Kassie echoed, looking from her heroic husband to her newfound uncle. Slowly she came back to them, accepting the peace of knowing that the past had at last been laid to rest. "I love you both very much."

Braden stood, keeping Kassie clasped tightly to him. "Let's go home, my courageous wife," he murmured.

Kassie never looked back. Secure in Braden's embrace, she nodded. "Yes, husband," she answered softly. "Let's go home."

And on the very spot where it had first begun, the nightmare ended.

And the dream came true.

Epilogue

H appy?" Replete in the aftermath of their lovemaking, Braden nuzzled Kassie's neck, tasting the fine sheen of her perspiration, now rapidly drying in the summer sun. A warm breeze blew across the grounds of Sherburgh, calm and filled with the same peace that pervaded Braden's heart.

Kassie gave a sigh of utter contentment. "M-m-m, yes," she breathed, opening her sated blue-green eyes . . . the fathomless eyes that never ceased to touch Braden's soul. "Very happy." Stretching contentedly upon their oft-used blanket, she gave her husband an impish grin. "I have grown to enjoy our picnic ritual more and more as the months have passed."

Braden chuckled at her pleased expression. "You have *grown* more and more as the months have passed," he teased, running a possessive hand over the rounded swell of her bare abdomen. He felt the responding kick with wonder and renewed pride, still amazed by the miracle that Kassie was carrying their child. "I do believe our picnics are going to have to come to an end soon," he said with a worried frown. "At least until after my daughter is born."

At that, Kassie raised up on her elbows, her delicate brows arched. "Your daughter?" she grinned. "You sound so arrogantly convinced that our child will be a girl! And here I thought that every gentleman wanted sons to carry on the family name."

Braden's eyes twinkled. "Well, then, I suppose I must be unlike any other gentlemen of your acquaintance, wouldn't you say?"

343

Kassie laughed and slid her arms around his neck. "Definitely," she agreed, tugging him down for a kiss.

Another sharp kick broke them apart, and Braden shook his head, chuckling. "I believe our child is telling me that enough is enough." He rubbed Kassie's flushed cheek with his knuckles. "Besides, we should be getting back, sweetheart. It will soon be dark."

Kassie gave an exaggerated sigh. "I suppose we must. Although I don't know who will miss us," she complained. "Margaret spends half the day sewing newborn clothes and the other half instructing Dr. Howell in the proper method of delivering a child. Perkins is forever fighting with Harding over who will be the first to hold the baby, and Charles has made three trips to Tattersall's this month to purchase the appropriate first horse for the child. However," she added, her lips curving upward, "I do believe Charles has another reason for going to London so often. He's dropped a few hints." She leaned forward conspiratorially. "I think our Charles has met a lady." At Braden's surprised look she nodded emphatically. "My instincts are rarely wrong, Braden. And I'd be surprised if our child doesn't turn out to have not only a great-uncle, but a great-aunt, as well." She dimpled. "Oh, Braden, wouldn't that be wonderful?" She flung herself into her husband's arms. "I'm so happy," she whispered, "and I want everyone I love to be happy, too."

Braden hugged her back, burying his face in his wife's hair. Happy didn't begin to describe what he was feeling, what he had felt since Kassie. She'd given new meaning to his life, filled his world with her goodness, her joy, her love. She'd given him everything he needed, infused in him all that had been missing in his life. And for the first time Braden was whole.

"Thank you," he murmured huskily.

Kassie drew back and gave him a questioning look. "For what?"

"For everything," he told her, love shining in his eyes. "You've given me all I could ever wish for . . . you've given me you."

Kassie pressed her forehead to his, her eyes damp. "Then

we're even, my love," she whispered back. "For you've given me just what I wished for as well."

"And what is that?" he asked softly, his breath warm against her lips.

Kassie gave him the look of a woman who knows she is loved, gratefully relinquishing the memory of the frightened young girl who was no more. "Don't you remember?" she reminded him gently, happiness glowing in her eyes. "Four years ago I asked you to wait for me to grow up." She kissed him. "And just as I wished for, you did."

Dear Readers:

I truly hope you've enjoyed your time spent at Kassie's dream castle. Relaying Kassie's and Braden's story was an exhilarating, absorbing, and, as always, indescribably joyful experience for me. If you feel even the slightest bit reluctant to say good-bye to the residents of Sherburgh, I've accomplished all I set out to do.

I have just completed my first newsletter, which combines tidbits on me, news about the writing of *Dream Castle* and my prior Pocket historical, *My Heart's Desire,* and a sneak preview of Dane and Jacqui, my latest hero and heroine, who seem to be exploding onto the pages of my next Pocket historical!

If you drop me a note and a legal-sized, self-addressed, stamped envelope, I'd be delighted to send you an autographed bookmark and a copy of my newsletter. You can write to me at:

P.O. Box 5104
Parsippany, NJ 07054-6104

I can't wait to hear from you!

All the best,

Andrea Kane

Andrea Kane